MW01133782

Savage

Iain Rob Wright

SalGad Publishing Group
Worcestershire, UK

Copyright © 2014 by Iain Rob Wright.

All rights reserved. No part of this publication may be reproduced, distributed or transmitted in any form or by any means, including photocopying, recording, or other electronic or mechanical methods, without the prior written permission of the publisher, except in the case of brief quotations embodied in critical reviews and certain other noncommercial uses permitted by copyright law. For permission requests, write to the publisher, addressed "Attention: Permissions Coordinator," at the address below.

SalGad Publishing Group
Redditch, Worcestershire/UK
www.iainrobwright.com

Publisher's Note: This is a work of fiction. Names, characters, places, and incidents are a product of the author's imagination. Locales and public names are sometimes used for atmospheric purposes. Any resemblance to actual people, living or dead, or to businesses, companies, events, institutions, or locales is completely coincidental.

Book Layout & Design ©2014 - BookDesignTemplates.com

Ordering Information:
Quantity sales. Special discounts are available on quantity purchases by corporations, associations, and others. For details, contact the "Special Sales Department" at the address above.

Savage/ Iain Rob Wright. -- 1st ed.
ISBN: 978-1497392434

BOOKS BY IAIN ROB WRIGHT

Animal Kingdom

2389

Holes in the Ground (with J.A.Konrath)

Sam

ASBO

The Final Winter

The Housemates

Sea Sick

Ravage

Savage

The Picture Frame

Wings of Sorrow

The Gates

Tar

Soft Target

Hot Zone

End Play

For my wife, Sally

for all that she goes through.

"He who refuses to learn deserves extinction."

–Rabbi Hillel

GARFIELD

FUNGUS SPROUTED UNDERFOOT. It covered everything lately. With each lumbering step that the dead took they shed flesh, which melded with the earth and gave life to all manner of strange flora. Even in death things grew.

But the world had not died yet, not really: it had just changed – tilted in such a way that the lowly fungus was better sustained for life than the once mighty human race. Perhaps we were never cut out for ruling the earth in the first place. Maybe it was always intended for the mushrooms and the insects. They're the only things thriving.

Garfield was one of the last humans left alive and, as he crested a muddy hill, his steel toecap boots sank into a muddy puddle left behind by a recent drizzle. Winter was still winter in England and the heavens still enjoyed a good downpour. One thing the dead could not change was the weather.

"There's a garage over there," Kirk informed Garfield, a fellow member of the foraging party. The younger man pointed his gloved hand off to the east, at an old petrol station with shattered windows.

Garfield nodded. "Checked it out last week with Lemon and Squirrel. Empty."

Kirk grunted and stomped off to continue his search.

Garfield shook some of the wet mud from his boots and glanced around from the top of the hill. He thought about all that had been lost, as he gazed across the barren landscape, which had once hosted horn-blaring lines of gridlocked traffic and rushing ambulances. Nothing moved anymore, though: the cars on the highway were relics, rusted bumper to rusted bumper, long abandoned and forever unable to get where they were going. It was like a twisted oil painting of what life used to be like – all murky greys and decaying browns. Garfield missed all of the vibrant colours that no longer existed: the bright reds and greens of Christmas decorations or the gleaming yellow of a sleek sports car. Now there was only rusted metal and faded cloth.

The nearby petrol station held little use, the fuel in its pumps useful only for starting fires (and there were many simpler ways to do that). Food and drink were valuable, not oil and petroleum, and Garfield knew that the modest forecourt contained none of the former. Very few places did any more. We're going to have to trek further. There's nothing left around here anymore. We've picked it all clean.

The area around basecamp was relatively safe. It was a rural area and mostly deserted. There were, of course, packs of the dead wandering around from time to time – that was true anywhere – but their presence could be spotted early and avoided easily. Even now, half a mile away, Garfield could see a shambles of perhaps a half-dozen dead in the distance. The rotting men and women were bumping and clawing against a chest-high wooden fence meant to keep horses contained – now it contained them. Garfield knew their clumsiness would keep them there forever – eternally penned in by an obstacle that would have been easily surmountable had they still been alive.

The sprinters would have leapt that fence easily, Garfield thought.

Since the last of the sprinters (infected people, flooded with rage and the desire to kill) had died out and become slow, rotting zombies, it had been much easier to survive. Garfield and the group of foragers had now only to contend with a foe that was clumsy and stupid – still very dangerous, but predictable also. There had even been rare words spoken around camp lately of hope – fantasies that things might one day go back to normal. Garfield was not so childish to believe such notions. There was no coming back from what the world had become. It was irreversible. The best any of us can hope for is to survive. The time of feeding ducks in the park with ice cream in hand has slithered from our grasp forever. There are no more children's parties, no more fireworks, no school holidays or trips to Disney. It's gone. All of it.

A sharp yell from behind Garfield made him spin around on his toe-caps. Immediately he yanked a long screwdriver from a pocket inside his black woollen overcoat and held it out ready – ready to pierce skull and brain. So used to fighting was Garfield that the slightest bump or thud could prompt him to uncoil like a spring. And now it's time to uncoil once again.

At the bottom of the hill, one of the foragers had slipped in an oil puddle leaked from the chassis of an articulated lorry. Beneath the vehicle's rusted axels crawled a rotting corpse. The dead man held a firm grip on the forager's ankle and was clambering towards him through the oil slick.

Garfield reached the bottom of the hill in a flash; with a speed he'd never possessed in his previously sedentary life as mechanic. He leapt towards the struggling forager and wasted not a single second in driving his long screwdriver into the side of the dead man's skull, piercing the temple with a loud crack!

Like the sound my old ma used to make taking apart a crab.

The corpse stopped its attack. The screwdriver stuck out of its head like a lever. The frightened forager lay frozen beneath the corpse, panting and moaning for help. Garfield kicked the dead body away and helped the forager to his feet. His name was Marty, a nineteen year old lad who had survived the early days of the infection by locking himself inside the pet shop in which he worked and living off the animal feed – then eventually the animals themselves. He often spoke with a smile on his face about how good chinchilla meat was compared to chipmunk. Despite the grizzly admission, Marty was a good lad, friendly and helpful.

"Thanks, Garfield," Marty gushed. "I thought I was a goner."

Garfield smiled. "You're welcome." Then he pulled a claw hammer from a hidden compartment up his sleeve and smashed it into the top of Marty's skull. The other foragers backed away, staring at Garfield like he was a murderous lunatic. Perhaps he was. Is anybody sane anymore?

Garfield wiped the bloody hammer on his black woollen overcoat, adding to the darker patches already staining the fabric, and then replaced it up his sleeve. He shrugged his shoulders at the other foragers and pointed to Marty's body. "I did him a kindness."

The other foragers glanced down at Marty's ankle and saw the wound there, clear as day: a bright red gash in the shape of a human mouth. The corpse beneath the lorry had doomed Marty the moment its mouldy teeth had broken skin. Garfield had done nothing but put an animal out of its misery.

The other foragers sighed, but they nodded also. Each understood the way of things. A bitten man was a dead man. Nobody wanted to become a zombie.

"Come on," said Garfield. "Let's get back to camp. We're going to have to plan a new route for next time. There's nothing left around here anymore." Probably nothing left anywhere.

The men shuffled their feet, picked up their backpacks, and got moving. Garfield had just turned away when a banging inside the articulated lorry's container alerted him. The foragers turned back around, various makeshift weapons instantly at the ready. They were well trained for battle.

Garfield pulled a small hand axe from his belt and joined them.

The banging continued, weak but obvious.

"It's just one of them," said Kirk. "We should just leave."

Garfield knew it was stupid, but his mind kept turning to the half-dozen men and women forever trapped inside the horse paddock half a mile away. The thought of a creature, which had once been human, trapped inside a rusty container for all eternity, brought him a peculiar sadness. "Open the doors," he grunted. "There might be supplies inside. If there's a dead man, it means nobody has checked it out recently. We can't afford to ignore what supplies we might find."

The foragers sighed. As experienced as they all were with handling the dead, nobody ever took it for granted. They had just lost a man to a bite, and they knew it could happen again to any of them in an instant. A dead man's jaws closed fast, and taking unnecessary risks made the possibility of being bitten far greater. Garfield stood firm in his decision, though.

Kirk crept around to the back of the container and took a firm grip on the release handle. The other foragers readied their weapons and waited.

Garfield stood in front of the container's doors with his axe ready. "Soon as the doors are open," he told them. "Keep back. If it's anything we can't handle, make back for camp immediately. If I'm still intact I'll come with you."

Kirk nodded, then shoved the steel lever down and pried open the locking bar. He yanked open the left-side door.

Creeeeeak!

Garfield stared into the black rectangle of darkness. The banging inside the container had stopped, replaced by a delicate shuffling. He grabbed a hold of the right-side door, which was still closed, and began edging it open. Soon both doors were hanging wide and the black rectangle of darkness grew in size.

The shuffling continued.

Garfield glanced at the foragers. All of them stood ready, primed to attack, but so far there was nothing to alert them other than the shuffling noise. At least it sounds like there's only one dead man inside. But it only takes one to end you.

Garfield placed a gloved hand onto the lip of the open container and heaved himself up onto one knee with one leg still hanging down, ready to carry him backwards at the first sign of danger. Once it was clear that nothing was going to lunge at him, Garfield gained some confidence and pulled himself fully up inside the container. Into the darkness I fade. May my light lead me through.

It was a quote Garfield often told himself. He'd first seen it almost a year ago, written in blood on pavement outside a mosque. Often he wondered who had written it and what had become of them – and whether or not the blood had been their own or someone else's. *I'll never learn the answer.*

As Garfield entered the shadows of the container, his eyes began to adjust and the blackness turned to grey. The container was almost bare, save for a few loading pallets stacked towards the back. The contents towered up towards the ceiling and blocked any view of what lay behind them. Something moved ahead of him, a brief shift of the dusty air. Garfield took a slow step forward. The thud of his heavy boots on steel echoed around him.

The shuffling resumed.

It knows I'm here.

Garfield took another step, his axe out in front of him ready to split open a skull. His eyes gazed up...down....up...down....

Can never tell where they're going to come at you. Just as many chomp on your ankles as those that face you head on.

One more step was all it took for Garfield to spot the squirming body on the floor. His eyes had now fully adjusted to the dim light and he could see clearly. The discovery was pretty much what he'd expected. The dead man wriggled between two pallets stacked high with toilet paper rolls. A grubby brown blanket covered him and two steel crutches lay on the floor nearby. *A blanket? Crutches? Guy must have been injured; came in here to die in peace.*

Garfield raised his axe, ready to bring it down on the man's exposed head. It was hard to tell in the dim light, but the zombie may have had a rusty crop of ginger hair matching the colour of Garfield's own. That was a strange thing. Most of the dead had nothing left on their heads but dirty grey clumps laced with maggots. Being trapped in here must have kept him in better shape than being out in the open. *Maybe he died recently.*

Garfield placed his boot on the dead man's chest and squeezed the shaft of his axe. "I never asked for this," he whispered, "and I'm sure you didn't either."

Garfield swung his axe.

The zombie reached up a hand. "Please."

"Shit!" Garfield managed to divert his swing at the last moment. The axe buried itself in a roll of toilet paper and ensnared itself in the plastic wrapping that secured the rolls to the pallet. "Jesus Christ! You're alive."

The man was weak, skinny, and in obvious pain, yet he was undoubtedly alive; though the stink of him was as bad as any dead man. Garfield could see sweat on his forehead and upper lip.

"You're bitten."

The man managed to shake his head. "No. No..."

Garfield snorted. "You're not bitten? You sure about that, because you don't look too perky."

"I...I'm sure."

Garfield felt he was being lied to; and that made him angry. He flicked aside the man's blanket with his steel toecap and was vindicated by the blood that caked his t-shirt. "Not bitten, huh? Looks to me like something took a good chunk out of you."

"Bullet."

Garfield raised an eyebrow. "Somebody shot you?"

Guns were outlawed in the United Kingdom and now that the world had ended they were even harder to come by. Garfield had not seen a firearm since the Army's initial failed response to the infection. Their automatic rifles and machines guns had quickly run dry and the brief appearance of firearms had ended. Bullets did very little to stop the dead when you don't know to go for the head. It was a lesson most of the world had learned too late.

Bullets can still put a nice dent in a living man, though.

The injured man moved a feeble hand to his t-shirt and pulled it up over his thin stomach. Sure enough, there was a perfectly round hole where something – quite possibly a bullet – had entered his torso at the side. It was hard to say for sure if the man had been shot, but at the very least it was clear that he had not been bitten.

He may as well have been, though.

"There are no doctors," Garfield said. "Probably best that I put you out of your misery."

"N-no. I can make it."

"I don't think you can."

The injured man waved a hand. "I've been badly injured before. I can make it. I just...I just need some help."

Garfield let out a long breath. The best thing to do was to end the man's suffering right here. A dying man was nothing but a burden – to himself and anybody who tried to help him.

"Please..."

Garfield pulled his axe free of the pallet's plastic lashings and lifted it onto his shoulder. The man looked up at him pleadingly, but his eyes were rheumy and weak. Death was closing in on him fast. Best to just end it now.

Garfield made a decision. He turned and walked away, exiting the container and re-grouping with the foragers outside.

"What did you find?" Kirk asked him.

"Couple pallets of toilet paper. Would make good kindling for our fires, as well as having more obvious uses. It's a luxury, but it's all we have. Get it out and load it up on the sledges."

Kirk nodded. The toilet paper was better than nothing. They all enjoyed returning back to camp to the cheers and back-pats that accompanied a full sled, and hated the sullen faces that greeted them whenever they came back empty handed. The toilet paper would probably suffice in lieu of anything else.

"Was there a dead man inside?" Kirk asked. "The shuffling?"

Garfield cleared his throat. "Oh...yeah, there's an injured man inside. If he's still alive by the time we leave then I guess we should take him with us."

"Was he bitten?"

Garfield shook his head. "No, but he may as well have been. The poor sod's been shot. Slim hope he'll even make it back to the pier with us."

Kirk seemed surprised. "But...who has guns? Do you think there's another group out here someplace?"

"I don't know," said Garfield, "but I would much rather avoid them if there is. They have guns and we don't."

POPPY

ARFIELD AND THE others had been gone ages. Poppy knew
they'd be okay – they went out all the time – but she could never
help but worry. For the last hour she'd been sitting, shivering on
the rooftop of the Sea Grill restaurant with her adult's cardigan wrapped
around her shoulders, anxiously watching the horizon for Garfield's return. During that time, she had absentmindedly tied her white-blonde
hair into two long plaits. I wonder if Garfield will like them.

The Great Southern Pier was all there was for miles. The seaside
village that surrounded it was just a few bed-and-breakfast hotels and
places to eat, with the odd pub interspersed – boozers her daddy used
to call them. Poppy had never been inside a pub, but she knew it was a
place that only adults were allowed in. Now nobody went in the pubs;
they were all empty.

The pier was the biggest in England after having been rebuilt following a big fire – at least that's what Garfield had told her. He said the
pier had only just opened when people got sick. That's why everything
was so new and unused. There was even an oven in the Sea Grill restaurant that was still wrapped in plastic and had never been plugged in.
What a waste of money.

The people who'd built the pier had planned on bringing lots of visitors and making the village so rich that it would grow into a town and
have more shops and nice houses. None of that ever happened, though,
and now the great big pier looked silly next to the tiny village. And all
of the people live here instead of in the houses.

Behind Poppy, the rest of the camp went about their usual business.
The pier had lots of shops and restaurants on it and a big building

shaped like a tent at the far end. The tent was full of games and rides that no longer worked because there was no electricity. It made Poppy sad whenever she looked at them. They would have been so much fun.

Everybody was safe at the pier because it sat on big metal stilts above the sand and could only be accessed from a big long deck barred at one end by a fat metal gate. Sometimes dead people would come up to the gate and try to get inside, but it never worked. The gate was too big and strong. The dead people would eventually go away if everybody on the pier kept quiet enough. And if they didn't go away, Garfield would go out and hit them. That always made her sad; to see the dead people hit. They looked so lonely at the gate, like all they wanted in the world was to be inside with the living people. But if we let them in they'll try and hurt us.

At least there were no zombies around at the moment. When Garfield and the others left yesterday, all the dead people in the village had followed after them until they'd disappeared into the distance, at the point where the main road took them out of sight. Poppy had a feeling that Garfield probably hit the dead people when they were away from the village. He always tried to avoid hurting them near the pier – he said their smelly bodies would make people sick. One time at the pier, Poppy had gotten a poorly throat and it was terrible. She'd wanted so much to be better, but the pain and aching went on forever. There was no more medicine like her mummy used to give her to make the hurt go away quicker. Lots of things are gone. I miss my bed with the pink pony sheets and my fluffy dressing gown. I miss my parents, too.

Poppy's mummy was gone now and so was her daddy. The only person she had to look after her was Garfield – and he was never there. No sooner would he return to the pier then he was off again. She understood why he had to go. He would always say to her, "I never chose this," but she would still miss him when he was gone. Sometimes when he returned, he would bring food, or toys, or comic books for her. That almost made it worth not having him around, but not really.

She liked having him near, even if he was grumpy all the time. Grumpy Garfield I call him, but really I think he's brave.

Poppy shuffled around 180-degrees until she was facing away from the village and towards the sea beyond the pier. Some of the group sat at the edges of the deck, holding fishing rods out over the railings. There was a fishing tackle shop on the pier and almost every person in the group had a rod or two. Poppy liked some of the fish they caught, but there were so many different kinds that she never knew what she would get one day to the next. Sometimes they caught big fat fish with white meat that tasted good, but other times they would catch thin, ugly fish with red meat that tasted yucky. Her favourite food back home – back when she had a mummy and daddy – had been macaroni and cheese, with a glass of fizzy apple juice. She hadn't tasted cheese in such a long time and all she ever drank was water. It made her sad to think about.

So she thought of something else.

She thought about getting older and becoming an adult. She could go foraging with Garfield and Kirk then (although she didn't really like Kirk. He was always making fun of her). She wasn't allowed to leave the pier because she was still just a kid, but from up on the rooftops of the various buildings she could see for miles around. She could see the hills and the roads, and an old railway that cut through them both. There was a whole world out there waiting to be explored – one she could barely even remember. She just wished she'd taken the time to appreciate the things she used to have, because now they were all gone forever.

She used to moan and complain about having to get up for school, but now she would give anything to be surrounded by other children her own age. She would love to sit and listen to old Mr Stead prattle on about the Ancient Romans and how they changed the world with their roads and sewers. There was so much she could have learned back then, but now her entire world was on this pier at the edge of the sea. I hate it.

Being stuck in one place made her feel panicky, like she couldn't breathe. One day, when she was older, she would leave the pier and find all of the things she'd forgotten. She'd learn about all the things the world used to care about. Then, one day, she would teach it to kids the same way Mr Stead had once taught it to her. I'm going to teach them about how the Romans built the aqueducts and had lots of baths.

"You up on that roof again, lass? You're going to break your bleedin' neck one o' these days, huh."

Poppy looked down to see Alistair standing on the deck below. He had his hands on his hips and his fat belly was hanging over his belt the way it always did. Everyone else in the group was skinny, except for Alistair.

"What do you want?" Poppy asked him.

"What do I want? Nothing, lass, but it's about time you started helping out around here instead of farting around on the rooftops all the time, huh."

"I'm just a kid."

"No such thing anymore. You're either useful or you're not. No mummy and daddies to look after kiddies these days. You have to be useful, whether you're nine years old or ninety."

Poppy rolled her eyes. She'd never liked Alistair, not since she'd first met him. He was always nagging at her. "Garfield says I'm just a kid and I shouldn't grow up too soon. I asked to go foraging with him, but he said no."

Alistair sniffed a wad of snot back through his nose. His dirty brown hair fluttered in the breeze. "He should've let you go with him, if you ask me. Better than having you hanging around doing nothing like a chimp with a hairdryer, huh. The time for child's play died along with everything else. You need to start making yourself useful."

"I will..." said Poppy.

Alistair grinned and nodded.

"When Garfield tells me to."

Alistair pointed his chubby finger up at her. "Now you look here, Poppy. Garfield ain't here, and when he ain't here you do as you're told by your elders. I was at this pier long before Garfield, so don't you believe I take orders from him. You need to start pulling your weight, girl, or else you'll be gone. Got no time for freeloaders."

"You can talk! If it wasn't for all the food that Garfield brings back, you wouldn't be able to stay so fat."

Alistair went bright red. "You just wait until you come down from there. You'll have my hand across the back of your legs."

"Touch me and Garfield will beat you up."

Alistair snorted. "We'll see about that, young lady."

"Yes, we will," said Poppy with a sudden grin on her face. There was movement on the horizon at last. "Because he's on his way back right now." At last.

In the distance, Garfield and the foragers were coming down the main road. They dragged their wooden sleds behind them, carrying the things they'd found. Any luck and they would have some food. Even better and they might have found some books or toys.

Give me something to do around here, please!

As Poppy squinted into the distance, she noticed something unexpected. One of the forager's sleds held no food or toys at all; it carried a man. Somebody was injured.

Oh no. I hope we can help them. I hate it when people die.

Poppy glanced down at the pier, to tell Alistair what she could see, but the fat man had already gone, so she hung down from the edge of the roof and dropped down to the wooden deck below. Her ankles stung as she hit the ground, but the pain soon left once she started running. She headed for the gate, wanting to be the first to greet Garfield when he returned.

But when she got there, she heard rattling and moaning. There were dead men at their door.

ANNA

ANNA HEARD THE moans followed by the rattling of the pier's main gate. It was not unusual to find dead men on the pier's walkway, but it was something that always needed dealing with. If enough of the dead gathered together then they might manage to bring the gate down beneath their sheer weight. Anna had seen what the collective strength of the dead could do several times over the last year. *They're like a force of nature when they group together.*

Anna was tucked up in her sleeping bag, re-reading a paperback, when she saw members of the pier race by the window of the gift shop in which she lived. It wasn't a reason for great concern, but she put on her jacket and followed after them, wanting to see what the fuss was. She joined up with them at the gate where a dead man and woman were thudding against the iron bars. A light rain had begun falling and a wind whistled in from the sea. Seagulls circled in the air, as they always did around the dead.

"Why aren't we staying out the way?" Anna frowned. When dead people arrived at the gate, the common thing to do was to lay low and wait for them to lope away. More often than not, they did so within the hour.

"We can't afford to leave them at the gate," Alistair informed her. "Garfield and the others are coming in. We have to clear the way."

Anna studied the two zombies on the other side of the wrought iron bars and felt confused. The female was little more than a skeleton, with a waistline she probably would have killed for in life. *Hell, I would kill for it.* Her entire stomach had rotted away and the crusted remains of her lungs had fused to her spine. The man beside the dead woman was a boxer, still donning his ring shorts and gloves. Once upon a time it may have been comical to see the sportsman in full gear, but the people at the pier were all used to the oddities of the dead and long past paying any notice. Previously the gate had been host to a dead policeman, several old-aged-pensioners, a Chinese chef in full kitchen whites, and once they even had a ghoulish clown trying to get in at them. There was no humour to be found in the dead. The boxer was just another corpse with a story untold.

"There's only two of them," said Anna, bemused. "Garfield can handle two zombies easily enough."

"He has somebody injured with him," Alistair said.

"How do you know that?"

"Because I saw him," said little Poppy who was standing in the gap between the Sea Grill restaurant and the pier's block of toilets. She looked lost in her oversized cardigan.

Anna took the child to one side. "Was it Garfield who was hurt?"

Poppy shook her head. Two long blonde plaits swung back and forth behind her and Anna suddenly resented her own lank brown locks. "No, it was somebody else," said the girl. "I couldn't see who."

Did they find a survivor out there, or did one of the foragers get hurt?

"Okay," Anna said. "Let's do this quickly and by the book." Everyone got to work quickly, all of them knowing the drill after having performed it so many times before. It was just another daily chore – no different than ironing used to be, or washing the car. Alistair went up to the gate, donning a thick pair of neoprene fishing gloves. He worked the key in the padlock and began to loosen the chain that bound the gate's half-sections together. The two dead people snapped and grabbed at his hands, but Alistair was quick enough and calm enough to avoid them.

Anna picked up a large sledgehammer, which the group always kept propped up beside the gate, and hefted it over her shoulder. Fellow campmates, old man Bob and Jimmy, took up two great fishing nets and fanned them open. Jimmy used to be a forager, but twisted his knee by jumping down from the second level of a supermarket to escape a group of zombies. Now he had to remain at camp, but always sought to make himself useful. Old man Bob was...old. Chris and Samantha were also present, but stood back so that they would not get in the other men's way.

Alistair yanked the chain and opened the gate wide.

The dead people stumbled down the deck, arms outstretched and decaying jaws snapping. Bob and Jimmy threw the nets down over their heads, trapping them in place as they fought clumsily to free themselves. Anna brought the sledgehammer down on the boxer's skull first, caving in his head like an overripe melon. Some juices exploded from the skull, but it was mostly just dry, flaky flesh, long ago rotten, that remained.

The boxer fell to the floor and stopped moving. Anna raised the sledgehammer once again, and this time brought it down on the dead woman's head. Her skull split open the same way the boxer's had. Now both of them lay on the deck benignly, their threat extinguished, their skulls obliterated. Anna looked down at the boxer and sighed. Out for the count.

Without comment, Chris and Samantha grabbed the two dead bodies and dragged them down the pier towards the strip of walled pavement that separated the beach from the road. There they left the bodies in a pile, ready to be taken away by Garfield's next foraging party. Before the sun turns them into viral breeding grounds, Anna thought with a grimace.

Chris went and stood by the gate, ready to close it once everyone was inside. The shy man was wearing his favourite red wellies. They made him stand out like a children's entertainer, which was a stark contrast to his personality. Anna wondered if the wellies meant something to the man, but she never asked. Samantha stood beside him, the only survivor at the pier that still had the fashion sense to wear a skirt and heels on occasion. Thankfully, today she was wearing black jeans and Ugg boots. She still wore enough jewellery and bracelets to weigh-down a horse, though. Despite her love of nice things, the twenty-year old was headstrong and brave and reminded Anna a lot of herself. *She just gets on with it.*

Two hundred yards distant, Garfield and the foragers were getting nearer. They dragged their sleds behind them and managed a brief wave as they saw the gates of the pier laying open to greet them. Anna put the sledgehammer back down against the wall of the toilet block and was just in time to catch Poppy by the arm as the girl made to run off. "Where do you think you're going, princess?"

Poppy skidded on her heels and moped at Anna. "I want to go see Garfield. He's only down the road."

"So it will only take him a few minutes to get here, won't it? You can wait like everybody else."

Poppy huffed. "You have to let me out sometime. I'm not a prisoner."

Anna smiled. "No, you're not. But you're alive, and you have this place to thank for it. You shouldn't be in such a hurry to leave."

Poppy sulked. Anna ignored her. The girl liked to act hard-done by. *That was how she managed to wind Garfield around her little finger all the time. I'm not such a pushover, though.*

"The zombies are all gone," Poppy argued. "These two were the first we've seen in ages. They've all gone off someplace to die."

If only that were true, thought Anna. "They're still everywhere, Poppy. The only reason we're safe here is because it's far away from anywhere else. If you go running around out there you'll attract attention, and it could land us all in a lot of trouble. You need to grow a little more before you earn the responsibility to leave the pier."

Poppy folded her arms in a grump, but she knew better than to argue. The girl stood silently while they waited for Garfield to return. *All she needs is some consistency. A few rules never hurt a child.*

The foragers rounded a burnt-out Mini Cooper sitting in the middle of the road just beyond the pier, and then started up the decked walkway. Three other foragers accompanied Garfield, but that concerned Anna – because he'd left with four.

"Where's Marty?" she asked Garfield as he came up the walkway with Kirk, Lemon, and Squirrel.

Garfield's expression was grim – but then it most often was. He avoided making eye contact with Anna, which was a bad sign. "Marty got bit."

No more explanation was needed. Everyone knew that if you got bitten on a forage, you didn't come back. Knowing Garfield, they probably buried poor Marty where he fell and moved on without a word. It was just the way of things – nobody's fault.

Poppy broke free of Anna's grasp and rushed down the deck to meet Garfield halfway down the walkway. Anna sighed. The girl had defied her, but only by a little. Probably okay to let it go.

"I was worried about you," Poppy gushed, wrapping her arms tightly around Garfield's waist.

"You're always worried about me, Popcorn. But don't I always come back?"

"You do."

"Who's he?" Anna pointed to the stranger on the sledge. The man had copper-coloured hair just like Garfield's, and was soaked in blood. The other sleds were loaded with what looked like toilet paper. *They'll be no shortage of something to wipe our arses with, but food would have been better.*

Garfield glanced down at the injured man and then shrugged his shoulders. "Found the guy close to death in a container. Don't hold much hope of him making it through the next couple hours, to be honest. Poor sod was shot."

Anna folded her arms. "Shot?" There were very few guns about, which made anybody who had them inordinately dangerous.

"I was hoping you'd have a go at fixing him up, Anna. You'd have a better chance than anyone else."

Anna kept her arms folded tight. "I was a vet, not a doctor."

"Still makes you the best hope this guy's got."

Whether she liked it or not, it was true. She sighed. "Bring him into the diner."

The pier's American-style diner was one of the largest spaces and was used as a communal area, as well as the place where they stored all the rainwater they collected and supplies that the foragers found. Rene was in charge of allocation, and right now Anna needed boiled water. Stat!

When Rene saw the injured man, his eyes went wide and he quickly came over to help. The man did not speak, but his body language made it clear he was ready for immediate orders. Anna nodded at him and smiled. Rene had been her trusted friend since the beginning and the only person she could rely on.

"Rene, I need boiled water and the sharpest knife you can find. I also need a latex glove filled with one part salt and five parts water – and bring me all the hand sanitizer from the kitchen. Anna knew they had all of those things, because she'd gathered them herself. The things she lacked, however, included proper surgical equipment, pain-killers, and medicine of any kind (she had once tried to grow penicillin from some stale bread, but it was long gone now). There were no hos-pitals in the area and those further afield were hot zones of infection. The dead were everywhere inside hospitals and getting medicine would cost more lives than it saved. She and Rene had once entered a local Doctor's clinic, hoping to find bandages and antibiotics. What they found was a waiting room full of dead people. That was the last time they ever searched for medicine.

Garfield carried the injured man over to one of the diner's large square tables and dumped him down on it. Anna took her jacket off and told him to leave, along with anybody else not named 'Rene'. The less people crowding me the better. Poppy would probably pop a blood vessel, anyway, if Garfield didn't go and catch up with her right this instant. Glad I don't have the responsibility of looking after that girl. She's a handful at the best of times.

Anna went and got her kit bag from underneath the cashier desk. It contained a needle and thread (actually a reel of 6lb thin-diameter fishing line), as well as some glue and bandages. So far the kitbag had been needed only for scrapes and bruises, but it had been prepared in case of something worse. Most serious injuries were from being bitten, and there was no point wasting time or supplies on someone with a bite.

But this man was shot.

By whom?

Since being carried along the pier and into the diner, the injured man had stirred only slightly. He mostly just moaned and muttered with his eyes closed. Whether from the fever of infection or the delirium of blood loss was unclear. Probably both.

Anna handed a long sewing needle to Rene and told him to boil it in the saltwater he had on the go. There was no gas or electricity anymore, but the diner had a small stockpile of disposable lighters, cooking oils, and petrol that the group used exclusively for starting fires and cooking. Anna knew that she could also use some of those chemicals to disinfect the injured man's wounds, but they were all very caustic. She had better methods.

Anna pulled out some sharpened scissors from her kit bag and cut away a strip from the patient's t-shirt. Blood was everywhere, mostly crusted and caked. That was a bad sign; it suggested the man had been bleeding out for some time. He may have already lost too much.

The bullet wound peered up at Anna like a malevolent black eye. She rolled the man onto his side and saw that the round had not exited through his back. Most likely it was still inside him. "Rene, she shouted. I need you to sterilize some tongs and a tea spoon."

Rene did not reply, but she knew he would have heard her and that he would comply. Rene heard very well, but he spoke very little. His words were precious to him.

She had met the Nigerian with another group of survivors back when the infection first hit. At the time, she'd been a vet at an amusement park zoo. Rene's group eventually joined up with the survivors already living at the park, and for a while they had co-existed. Suspicions were high, however, and egos prevailed. The fact that Rene had been part of a group of prison inmates did not help the tension. Eventually the group dissolved and the safety of the amusement park had been ruined. Rene was one of the good guys, one of the people who'd stood by Anna when things had turned ugly. He was also the only one left alive from that original group which Anna had left the park with. She often missed the people who hadn't made it. Especially Mike.

When Anna and Rene fled the amusement park in a beat-up truck, there had been two others with them: Mike, a man she had almost loved; and Eve, a feisty young girl who'd fallen apart after her friend, Nick, died. The first few months on the road had been tough on them all, and by the time they made it to the south coast where they hoped to find a boat, only Rene and Anna remained. They would probably have died, too, if they hadn't eventually fallen across the Great Southern Pier. That mutual journey of survival had bonded them as family. She trusted him completely.

Several minutes later, Rene approached with the items Anna had requested. He handed her a latex glove full of saline and various kitchen implements, which had been sterilized, as well as her sewing needle. The patient moaned again, louder. He was either becoming more lucid, or the pain was increasing. Either was a good sign. Pain meant a person was alive. Lucidity meant a person was alive. Every moan was the man fighting to hold onto his life.

"Hello, my name is Anna. I'm going to try and help you. Can you tell me how long ago you were shot?"

The man mumbled but made no sense.

Anna sighed. She took the latex glove and pierced the bottom with a sharp knife that Rene had brought her. A trickle of saline leaked out of the slit and Anna angled it above the man's injury. She squeezed the glove and began to irrigate the wound with the thin jet of liquid coming through the slit, clearing away the old blood and stemming any fresh. Once the wound was clear, she grabbed a bottle of hand sanitizer. "This might burn," she told the patient, who just moaned at her weakly.

Anna removed the pump handle from the sanitizer and upended it, allowing a thick tide of alcohol to pour onto the open wound. The patient hissed. His eyes fluttered.

"Stay with me," Anna said firmly. "The pain is good. The pain is me helping you."

"Y...yes."

"Good, good. I'm glad that you understand me. I am just cleaning your wound. You don't want to get an infection."

"N...no."

Anna made sure she covered the entire wound with the sanitizer. The liquid quickly effervesced but enough coated the wound to burn away any bacteria. At least she hoped so. A shitload of iodine would have been better. Without being asked, Rene handed Anna the tongs and teaspoon. She swallowed a lump in her throat. Once, she'd been a vet, but there was very little cause to trust her abilities after them being so long dormant. Plus, I've never had to remove a bullet from a man's stomach before.

Anna shoved the sterilized tongs into the wound and pried the edges open. The patient screamed. Rene immediately held the man by the shoulders. Anna made sure the tongs were steady and then took a firm grip of the teaspoon. Holding her breath she dug the spoon deep into the wound. She knew she was causing agony and likely doing even more damage, but if she didn't get the bullet fragment out, the patient would have no chance at all. Infection would take him within the night if the bleeding didn't kill him first.

As she dug about in the wound, the black shard of blood-caked metal exposed itself. It was buried deep within the tissue, like a stone trodden into wet mud a hundred times over. Anna worked the edge of the spoon around its edges, trying to get a purchase on it. The patient struggled against Rene's restraining hands, but Rene leant close to him and began to hum. Anna didn't recognise the tune, but it was delicate and soothing. After a few moments the patient began to struggle less. Rene had learned First Aid in prison, she knew, but his soothing way with people was not down to any training.

Anna dug the spoon beneath one side of the bullet fragment and felt it shift within its fleshy womb. The patient gritted his teeth as she began to scrape the fragment upwards, away from the wound. Luckily the bullet had not buried itself in bone or passed through any organs. Likely, the man had been shot at a distance, the velocity of the bullet all but spent. Someone still wanted him dead, though.

Anna released a pent-up breath as she slid the bullet fragment clear. A small shard still remained in the wound, but fortunately it came away much easier than the larger fragment had. From what Anna could see, the wound was clear and no arteries had been nicked. It was time to close the patient up. She took her sterilized needle and tried to thread it with shaking hands. Jesus, Anna. You've done this a thousand times. Calm down.

She took some deep breaths and counted to ten. When she tried to thread the needle again, her hands were steady as stone. She got the fishing line attached to the needle and used her sharpened scissors to cut away the excess. Then she got to work, plunging the needle into the swollen red flesh surrounding the wound. The patient let out a pained squeal, but Rene's humming soon calmed him down again.

She dragged the fishing line through the edge of the wound and sutured it to the other side, then dove back the other way. Back and forth with the needle she went, poking through flesh and threading, then poking through flesh again on the opposite side: zig-zag, zig-zag.

Slowly the wound drew closed, puckering up like a cod's mouth. With the final stitch Anna pulled tightly and closed the wound up as neatly as she could. She tied off the end of the thread and cut above the knot. She doused the wound with more sanitizer. It's done. I did it.

The last thing she did was to squeeze a thin line of superglue along the split ridge of the wound, adding a seal against invading bacteria. Hopefully its application wouldn't do more harm than good.

She stepped away from the patient and stumbled over to one of the diner's chairs. Her feet were unsteady and her stomach was roiling. She could hardly believe how nervous she'd been doing something that had once been her profession. Never had to stitch up a man before, though. "Can you bandage him up for me, please, Rene?" she asked.

Rene nodded and unfurled a bandage from the kitbag.

Garfield entered the diner with Alistair right behind him. Both men often caused Anna stress and she wasn't particularly pleased to see either of them in the state she was in. Garfield was a constant worrier, with little to no humour, and Alistair had too much humour, but it was only he who found himself funny.

"Is he going to die?" asked Garfield.

"Probably."

Alistair shook his head. His flabby jowls wobbled as he did so. "Don't understand why Garfield even brought him back. Food would have been better. Better a box full of Kit Kats than another mouth to feed."

"I almost didn't bring him back," said Garfield, "but what kind of a man would I have been then?"

"A smart one."

Anna sighed and closed her eyes. When she opened them again, both men stood looking at her. "Garfield was right to bring the man back," she told them both. "There's not enough of us left to start leaving each other to die. We have an obligation to help each other. More heads the better."

"More tummies to feed more like," said Alistair.

"We have the sea," said Anna. "At the very least we have that. We won't go hungry." You least of all, she thought as she eyed Alistair's ample gut.

Garfield cleared his throat. "Did you find anything out about the man? He had these with him."

Anna looked down at what Garfield was carrying. "Are those...crutches?"

"They were lying next to where I found him. I don't know if they're his or not."

"I don't know either," said Anna. "He hasn't spoken."

"Hopefully he'll get a chance to soon. I'd like to know who shot him and whether or not they're heading our way."

Alistair bristled. "I'd like to know that, too. There's a lot we could get done with some guns."

Rene chose this as one of the rare occasions he spoke up. His Nigerian accent was thick, despite having left his homeland a decade-and-a-half ago. "There is nothing to be achieved by guns," he said, "except fear and suffering to those still living. Guns are ineffective against the dead. Guns are loud and bring attention. Their very nature is to threaten and kill other men and women. Of all the things lost to us, guns are not something for which I mourn."

Alistair grinned, wide and jowly. "I'll be damned; it speaks. Haven't heard you spout your nonsense for a long while, Rene. This time you're quite right, though. Guns are indeed for threatening and killing people – they would give us the power to intimidate, the power to protect ourselves, the power to-"

"Take from others," said Anna. "Civilisation didn't do too well with that approach first time around, so let's try something a little more original than killing people for their cereal."

Alistair huffed. The way the man looked at her sometimes, made her mad. It was if he was always thinking, silly woman. "I think civilisation did pretty damn well last time," he said. "Every advance in human history came off the back of war. We all know that there are other groups out there, scattered about – we've seen some of them, traded with others. I would rather us have the guns than them."

It was true that on occasion Garfield came across a wasteland survivor or two. Sometimes he brought them back, such as in Kirk's case, but other times the strangers were dangerous and had to be frightened away. Guns could potentially have a use, but she wasn't sure it was a path worth taking. One group having guns just led to another group getting bigger guns. It was a race nobody won in the end. "We're fine," said Anna. "I trust that we can get by on our charm and wits alone. I've seen enough bloodshed without making our own contribution."

Garfield stared down at the floor as he spoke. The man rarely held eye contact. "I'm sorry, Anna, but I agree with Alistair."

Anna raised an eyebrow. "That surprises me. It's not often that you two see eye to eye."

"On this we do. Whether we like guns or not...they matter. He who has them has power over those who don't. I just don't want to be in a position where we have a gun to our heads and aren't able to respond."

Anna chewed at one of her nails before saying, "Well, regardless of whatever each of us thinks, we have no guns and no inclination of where to find them, so why are we even discussing this?"

"Actually," said Garfield. "I think I might know where we can find some. Will you hear me out?"

Anna sighed. Garfield would do whatever he wanted to – he was bull-headed that way – so why he felt the need to seek her council, she didn't know. It seemed to be more out of manners than anything else.

"I need to take the foraging group further," he explained. "There's nothing left around here anymore. We've scavenged it all."

Anna laced her fingers together across her lap. I knew it would come to this eventually. We've had it too easy for too long.

Things had been safe and productive for the last several months at the pier. The village and surrounding countryside had been bountiful and easy to explore. They had raided supermarkets, petrol stations, even farms. Along with the plentiful fish they caught, they had more than enough supplies to keep them going for a while. Alistair even still had the luxury of being fat. But Anna knew they would eventually strip the carcass clean and have to search for pastures new. "Okay, that's your call," she told Garfield, "but I'm getting that there's more you want to say."

Garfield nodded. "There's an Army base on Salisbury Plain. There might be troops there. If not then we might have access to a lot of abandoned weaponry."

"I like the sound of that," said Alistair.

Anna huffed. "We all know the Army fell to pieces. There are no troops left. As for weapons, well, I'd imagine they were looted a long time ago. But, as I said, it's your call, Garfield. You're our man in the field. I'm just the mother hen at home." Which is another way of saying I'm middle-aged and useless.

Garfield looked over at the injured man on the table and sighed. "Guess I'm just making sure you're okay for me to set off for a while. Salisbury Plains is a good distance and who knows what the journey will be like. It would take a three-hour drive even if the roads were clear. The way things are it's more likely to take us three days there and the same amount back."

Anna nodded. She knew what Garfield wanted, even if he was prodding limply around the vagina concerning it. "You want me to look after Poppy. Just come out and say it."

Garfield stared at his boots. The man rarely made eye contact, but there was a flicker of expression across his face that showed his heart still beat with emotion. "I'm all she's got," he muttered. "If I don't make it back, or even if I'm just gone a while, she'll be hurting."

"And when she's hurting," said Alistair, "that little pup gets wild."

Garfield shot Alistair a chastising look, but ended up nodding and agreeing with the statement. "Yes, she does. She doesn't like being confined. You know I found her trapped in a dirty house with her two dead parents locked in the bedroom. Imagine what it was like for her, having to remain quiet for weeks so that they wouldn't crash through the door and get her. When I found her, she was starved and mute. It's taken me a year to bring her back from that dark place, but I can't do it on my own anymore. I need help – especially while I'm away." The man looked close to tears.

Jesus Christ. And here was me thinking soap operas were dead. "I know what the girl has been through," said Anna. She rubbed at her forehead and cringed when she realised her hands were caked in her patient's blood. She didn't like what Garfield was asking of her. She wasn't good with kids – having never had any of her own beyond an ill-fated miscarriage – and the last time she'd cared about another she'd lost him. It had been a point of hers ever since to keep her emotional distance. Looking after an unruly child was not part of her five-year plan. In fact the only words written on her five-year plan were: LOOK AFTER YOURSELF.

"Please, Anna. You're the only person I trust."

Alistair pulled a face. "Charming."

The statement of trust surprised Anna. To her understanding, nobody really trusted anybody at the pier. They all worked together for mutual benefit and played at friendship, but really they were only together by circumstance. "Well," she eventually said, "if you're saying that you need to venture out for the good of the group, then I guess I have no choice. As for finding weapons, I'm not particularly interested. I would rather you find something more useful than a bloody tank. Like Doritos. Why do you never bring back Doritos?"

Garfield smiled, visibly relieved by her agreeing to look after his girl. "I'll see what else I can find along the way," he said. "Doritos will be first on my list."

"Just get going sooner rather than later," she said. "Sooner you're back the sooner life can go back to normal." What is normal anymore? I don't even know.

"I'll go first thing in the morning," Garfield said. "I just need to eat and get some sleep first. I'll take some of the fuel we have stored up and try to get a couple of vehicles working. There's a Range Rover parked at the old church on the edge of the village that I think I can get started. I'll be taking the full team to make the most of whatever we find. Cat and the other foragers should be back this evening, so I'll brief them all then."

"I don't like the sound of that," said Alistair. "You'll leave us short-handed."

"For what? There's not much to be done around here other than fish."

"Garfield is right," said Anna. "If he's going further afield, it makes sense to maximise how much he can bring back. It's not like he can make such a trip every day. Besides, he's likely to be in more danger than we are. He might need the backup."

Alistair shrugged irritably. "Fine. Just don't get everyone killed out there, Garfield." He turned and walked away. "I'm going to get something to eat."

"There's a surprise," said Garfield.

Anna looked at him. "Alistair has a point, you know? You best come back in one piece, along with everybody else."

"I'll do my best, that's all I ever do. I never asked for this."

"None of us did. You just take care out there."

"I shall. Thanks, Anna." With that, Garfield left the diner, his overly-dramatic coat flapping as he walked. I swear he thinks he's Batman in that thing.

Anna turned back to her patient, and to Rene. Her friend was wide-eyed and wanting her attention. "What is it?" she asked him.

Rene nodded towards the patient.

Anna approached the table and heard a sound: a soft mumbling. She knelt down and placed her head close to the injured man's lips, listened.

"Roman," he was mumbling deliriously. "Roman, Roman, Roman."

FRANK

"**R**OMAN HAS RETURNED," Frank informed his adopted son.

Samuel Raymeady laced his slender fingers together across his long metal desk. Everything aboard the HMS Kirkland was made of metal, and the only colour was grey. Sometimes Frank longed for a bit of wood or plastic. The den he used to keep at his home in Gloucester was full of warm oak and supple leather. He missed it.

"Did he do what I asked of him?"

Frank sighed, straightened up at the shoulders, and gave an answer his adopted son never liked to hear. "No."

Samuel lent forward, sharp elbows propped on the aluminium surface of his desk. His dark eyes seemed to swirl for a moment before he spoke. "No?"

"He was unable to get a confirmed kill. He wounded the target, but..."

"Wounded the target? How?"

"Roman shot him with the pistol you gave him." The Kirkland's armoury was meagrely equipped with a dozen handguns and a small cache of ammunition. Whilst Samuel's company, Black Remedy, had possessed a contract to build and maintain several new British Naval frigates, along with it's onboard weapons systems, it did not have permission to provide small arms. The modest collection of handguns had been provided by Black Remedy's security arm, so that the ship could at least be minimally protected whilst it was being built. Samuel kept a tight lock on all of the handguns, but two of them currently hung on the wall behind his desk, and Frank knew his son also kept one in a drawer in his desk. "The target took a 9mm round in the guts," Frank explained. "He was badly wounded."

"Then he may well be dead."

"More than likely."

"So why couldn't Roman verify it for certain? The man he was chasing is a cripple, after all."

Frank sighed. "There were a lot of dead in the area. Roman claims to have become separated from the target and was only able to fire off a single shot before retreating. The target got away, but was badly injured."

Samuel smashed his fist down on the table, shaking the paper and pens on its surface. "I ordered that cripple dead. He tried to murder us all, father, or need I remind you?"

Frank stood in silence for a moment. His adopted son's rage was a closely guarded secret that only a few people ever became aware of – usually to their detriment. It was best to give Samuel a second or two to calm down before answering him. "You do not need to remind me, Samuel. It was me who told you about the engine room bomb in the first place."

"A bomb which would have taken down this entire ship, along with hundreds of innocent lives that I have personally saved. I won't have my good work undermined, father. Do you understand me? Those who work against me must be dealt with else I appear weak. The respect the members of this fleet have for my authority is the only thing keeping order. It isn't enough that I have the biggest ship. I must also have the biggest shadow."

"I am sure Roman did his best, Samuel. He has never failed you before."

"Nor have I ever given him a task worthwhile before. Fetch Roman. I would have words."

Frank nodded. He left the captain's chambers and sent a runner to go and collect Roman. The man could usually be found out on deck, brooding alone, but he had a tendency to make himself elusive when it suited him. It was close to forty minutes later when Roman finally appeared and the irritation of having been summoned was clearly etched on his muddy face. Does the man ever crack a smile?

Roman told no one his real name and had instead earned the notorious moniker for the fact that he wielded an antique short sword in his right hand and a makeshift metal spear from the fleshy stump where his left should be. The man had shoulder-length, dirty-blonde hair and kept no friends. He had his uses, though, which Samuel never failed to utilise when needed. Roman did not fear the dead as most men did. He was willing to go ashore for the most frivolous of tasks and battled the dead head-on. Frank had seen the same kind of suicidal behaviour in the Gulf War. They called it a deathwish, and it was the domain of men with nothing to lose. Facing mortal danger was the only thing that made some people feel alive. This time, though, Roman had been given a gravely important task and failed.

Frank nodded to the man. "Roman."

"Frank."

"The captain would like to see you."

"Does he, now?" Roman shoved past Frank and went through into the captain's chambers. Frank followed him closely, and anxiously. This may get heated.

Samuel's chambers were custom built. The Kirkland was based on the British Navy's Type 23 Duke Class frigates, but was a third longer and six times as modern. It was the first of several that were to be built to replace the Type 23, but the end of the world had ensured that the Kirkland was one of a kind.

The captain's chambers consisted of a utilitarian, red-carpeted office intended to impose itself upon underlings, and a plush suite and bathroom in an adjoining room designed to give the ship's CO maximum comfort. Samuel very rarely made use of the room's king-size bed, though. Some of the ship's officers also had private berths, but most of the ship's personnel slept in a series of bunkrooms.

Samuel remained seated as Roman strode into the room like a tribal warrior; all covered in mud and blood and armed with sharp steel. Frank narrowed his eyes. *Long as he keeps that sword at his belt and his spear pointed at the floor, there won't be a problem.*

Roman concerned Frank greatly. There was something dangerous about the man, an air of wild fury that bubbled beneath his surface constantly – not unlike Samuel in that respect. Frank found the younger man difficult to read. Roman never gave anything away.

Samuel nodded. "Hello, Roman."

"Hello, Samuel."

Most of the men aboard the Kirkland referred to Samuel as sir or captain; but not Roman. He never called any man by their rank. It was an unsafe attitude to maintain aboard another man's ship. Samuel bristled at the slight, but acted as if he hadn't noticed. "Roman, I have been informed you failed your task. Disappointing."

"If you mean I didn't kill a man you wanted dead, I can't say for sure. He might be dead; he might not be."

"And if he lives, then you have failed me."

Roman said nothing. He stood unflinchingly and made no movement other than blinking. The spear attached to his arm was completely still. His sword remained at his belt. Samuel stared right back, equally as implacable.

Frank studied Samuel's face and remembered the unassuming little boy he'd once been so long ago; a world apart from the powerful magnate he became as a young man and the fearless leader he was today. Thousands of men owed their lives to Samuel and his actions during the early days of the outbreak. His megalithic corporation, Black Remedy, had been building frigates for the Royal Navy at the time of the infection. Samuel had commandeered the vessel nearest completion and used it take people away from the land. The HMS Kirkland had been used to rescue a great many lives. Including Roman's. Samuel could have left him to die at sea in that old dinghy we found him floating in.

What was the name of the man who was with him...was it Henry? No, it was something else.

Samuel blinked and swatted away a lock of jet-black hair, which had fallen across his brow. "Do you enjoy being here, Roman?"

Roman said nothing.

"Let me rephrase that. Do you prefer being here to not being here?"

Roman cleared his throat. "Life is easier aboard a ship than on land among the dead."

"I'll take that answer to mean you prefer being here. I do wish you wouldn't talk in riddles. Now, as you've said, being aboard my ship is much better than being on land – nobody would dispute that – but, as such, being on my ship comes at a premium. Your premium is that I expect you to get things done. When you fail, your place aboard my ship falls into question."

"So eject me."

Samuel laughed at that. "Does anything ruffle your feathers, Roman? Did losing that hand bother you? Or did you strap a spear in its place before the bleeding even stopped?"

"The spear came later, after the dead made having one so useful."

Samuel laughed again. From the corner of the room, Frank relaxed a little. Samuel seemed to admire Roman's dry wit and unflinching manner. Perhaps it was because Roman was the only man aboard the Kirkland who didn't treat Samuel like the Messiah. Frank imagined that people could become pretty tiresome when their only interest was pleasing you. Samuel had suffered sycophancy his entire life – from being the coddled child in his needful mother's arms to the CEO of the world's most powerful commercial entity. For Samuel Raymeady's entire life, people had bent over backwards to please him. But not Roman. I remember a time when I was so bold. When did I get so old?

"Maybe your use is not at an end just yet," Samuel said. "I'm just making a friendly statement of the facts, that is all. All men aboard my ship must have value. You only have one hand, so you cannot do much aboard the Kirkland, but one thing you do very well is going ashore to face the dead. That is what your use is to me, as other men have uses in other areas. That is the way of things. Those without value must leave to be a burden elsewhere. I would prefer that you remain here, Roman. I would prefer that you remain useful."

Roman blinked. "If I could have killed the cripple, I would have, but I am one man, not an army. I could not fight all the dead even if I wanted to."

"Perhaps one day you will lead an army," said Samuel. "That would be my hope."

"An army needs an enemy. I see none."

"What do you call the dead?"

"Dead."

Samuel laughed again. He rubbed at his eyes and stood up. "Perhaps we should agree to disagree about that. I thank you for listening to my concerns. Might I ask where you last saw the cripple? Where were you when you shot the man?"

"I was near the coast. I saw signs for Dartmouth and Paignton. He was holed up inside a petrol station. I tracked him from the smoke coming from a fire he started. When he saw me coming, he smashed out the windows and attracted the dead with the noise. It was the only thing that saved him."

Frank muttered. "It appears the man feared you more than he feared the dead, Roman."

"Don't blame him. I was there to kill him."

"But you failed," said Frank. "Perhaps next time he will fear you less."

"Not if he's smart."

Samuel clasped his long hands in front of him. "Frank, tell the Bridge to make for the coast. We'll look for any signs of the cripple and send a landing party to search the area where he was last seen. I know it may seem unnecessary, but I hate uncertainty. I would rather know one way or the other if the man lives."

"And if he is still alive?" asked Frank.

Samuel grinned. "Then Roman will be given a chance to redeem himself."

Roman said nothing. Frank sighed.

ROMAN

ROMAN MARCHED THROUGH the Kirkland's narrow passageways with a face of thunder. Various crewmen and civilians stepped aside to let him pass, but he made no acknowledgment of them. He just kept his eyes forward and walked wherever he wanted – God help any man who got in his way while he was in such a mood.

Up ahead, the bulkhead hatch was open, allowing access to the aft deck. The aft deck's intended purpose was as a helicopter-landing pad, but without a Lynx helicopter it had been designated as the ship's main common area. Even now, exposed to the cold biting winds of January, a third of the ship's personnel mingled outside on the deck beneath the drizzling rain. Most men liked to play cards of an evening while the few women aboard sat on their knees. Not as many women had survived the plague as men, so their company was a luxury.

Roman glanced around, searching for someone, but was hailed by one of the ship's officers before he could locate them. The man who approached him was a weasely petty officer named Dunn. No one aboard the ship was true military, but Samuel had instigated Navy rank and given out uniforms in order to help him command the fleet – it gave some men an inflated view of themselves. Petty officer Dunn was tall and blonde, but had the facial features of a rat. Roman found the man irritating – as he found all men irritating.

"Roman, good to see you returned to us," he said. Roman said nothing. He eyeballed the man scornfully. Dunn shifted awkwardly, cleared his throat and continued. "The captain has instructed us to dispense justice. One of the civilians has been found stealing liquor. We found a supply of contraband beneath his bunk after somebody informed on him. Your input would be welcome."

"Who informed on him?"

Dunn frowned. "Does it matter?"

"Wise to know which men like to tell tales, so that I can better hide my own misdeeds."

Dunn laughed nervously. "Yes, erm, very witty. We have been instructed to put the man to death. We were just discussing the method. If you were to take part it would-"

"You're going to put a man to death for stealing?"

"Well...yes. The captain told us that a thief has less honour than a murderer, for at least a murderer has the courage to face the victim of his crimes, instead of slinking around behind their backs."

"Not always," said Roman. "Samuel does like his speeches, doesn't he? Perhaps he expects to be quoted someday."

"The captain instructed that the man be shown no leniency."

Roman looked across at the baying mob at the rear of the ship and narrowed his eyes. "I agree. But lack of leniency does not mean that the sentence should be harsh to begin with. Let me see this man. I'll deal with the bloody matter myself."

Dunn shrugged. "It is not your place. Your input would be most welcome, but only an officer of the fleet may-"

Roman shoved the man aside. "Tell someone who gives a shit." He approached two crewmen at the rear of the ship. The barrel-chested pair were holding the guilty man down on his knees. The prisoner was dirty and unshaven. His bloodshot eyes betrayed his fondness for alcohol.

Roman pointed his spear arm at the two crewmen. "Stand him up." The crewmen allowed the civilian to stand. "What's your name, civilian?"

The man sighed and shook his head, beaten and defeated. "Wade Cannon, sir."

"That's quite a name."

"American, sir. I was a tourist when…"

"When the dead started walking around like the world was a horror movie?"

The man nodded, his droopy eyes solemn.

Roman asked another question, an important question. "Why do you drink?"

The thief shrugged.

"I'll ask you again and I suggest you answer." Roman slid his antique sword from the scabbard at his belt. The sword had belonged with a suit of armour at an old castle he had come upon during the first days of infection. It was as sharp as any modern blade and ten times as threatening. "And don't bullshit me."

"I miss my family," the man spluttered. "My wife was with me at the start…but she didn't make it. My two sons were still back in Skokie staying with their uncle during the holidays."

Roman lowered his sword so that it pointed at the ground. "You don't know what became of them?"

The thief shook his head. There were tears on his cheeks.

Roman sighed. "So you drink? Even when the alcohol is not yours to swallow?"

The American shrugged. The man was beyond caring. There was no joy or hope left inside him to drive him onwards – no reason for living. Roman understood.

The man needed to be given a reason.

Roman nodded to the crewmen. "Hold him back against the rail. Spread his arms out."

The American struggled, but his defiance was half-hearted.

"Looks like somebody's taking a trip overboard," said Dunn with a grin on his rattish face, but the man was wrong. Nobody is dying today, Roman decided. Especially not for that prick, Dunn's, amusement.

Roman pressed up close to the American and looked him hard in the eyes. "I think you'll find that pain and personal loss is preferable to death.

It will help you to focus on something tangible – a pain you can feel. Losing part of yourself can be cleansing. I know from personal experience."

The man looked confused.

Roman swung his sword and lopped off the American's left hand. It tumbled backwards into the sea. The man screamed, blood jetting from his wrist. Roman prodded his chest with his spear arm and shoved him back against the railing, cutting short his screams. The man's eyes were wide as Roman spoke to him.

"Now your loss is plain for all to see. You are not the man you were anymore...so be someone else. Find your pride instead of a bottle, and focus on the pain I have given you. It will remind you that you're alive. One day, if you choose to seek me out, you may try to exact your revenge. Focus on that, the future, not the past." Roman stepped away from the man and let him resume his howling. He sheathed his sword, turned to Dunn, and said, "Get his arm patched up and then leave him alone. He's paid the cost for his actions and should be treated the same as anybody else." The petty officer was white as a sheet, but he nodded vigorously as Roman left him to his duties. He wanted blood. I gave it to him.

At the inner edge of the aft-deck, near the giant shutter doors that led to the ship's vast equipment house, was the man Roman had been hoping to see. The man was rough and slender, wrapped in an oversized jumper, but there was no mistaking his identity. When Roman was sure nobody else was watching, he gave the man a great big smile. "There you are, Harry. I've been looking for you."

Harry smiled. Wrinkles creased at the corners of his eyes. "The mighty Roman has returned to us."

"A name given to me, not asked for."

"Maybe you should tell people your real name, then. They would have no need of silly nicknames."

"I tell my name to friends – and you're the only one."

"I'm honoured." Harry nodded over to where the one-handed American was being carried across the deck to receive medical attention. "A bit of a bloody business you were involved in, there. You do enjoy your drama."

"They were going to kill him. I did him a favour."

"Doubt he sees it that way."

"He will, if he has any sense. If not, he's free to take a swipe at me and I'll take his other hand."

"Come on," said Harry, shaking his head and smirking. "Let's take in some air and chat for a while. And talk normally, instead of giving me that whole warrior routine you give everybody else. You sound like a right prat. I almost miss the way you used to talk when I met you, blud."

Roman huffed and nodded. "Just my way of having a bit of a laugh, innit? Got to entertain myself somehow, geezer."

Harry smiled. "That's better. You almost sound a like a real person again. Sometimes I think you imagine yourself a lord with that sword at your hip. I preferred you as a gangster. Steph would be laughing her arse off if she could hear you sometimes."

Roman nodded. "You ever wonder if she made it?"

Harry sighed and shrugged. "I doubt it. I know she was working in a bar in Manchester when things went bad. Manchester wasn't good."

"Well, we can hope she's out there someplace, I guess."

Harry nodded. "She was a tough chick. If anyone could make it, it's her. She used to keep us two in line."

Roman chuckled, but inside he pushed aside memories of his past. The man he'd been before the infection had a complicated past. The new world was miserable and dangerous, but it was simpler at the very least and it gave everybody a fresh start.

The two of them strolled over to the portside promenade deck where they leant over the gunwale and stared out at the frigid sea of the English Channel. Harry took in a deep lungful of air. "Beautiful, isn't it? Did I ever tell you I used to own a little boat years back? I had it docked in Southampton."

Roman nodded. Harry had been a successful businessman once, but had lost it all to booze long before the world had ended for everybody else. Harry had been a broken, grief-stricken soul years before everyone else became one. "Tell me about her," Roman asked his friend. It was good to talk about old times with a friend, although he preferred to hear the stories from others than speak of his own dirty past.

Harry stared into space and smiled. "It was a 60-footer princess yacht, the name Blue Saloon painted on her bow. Huh, I guess even then I loved the booze a little too much. It was never empty of a crate or two of wine." Roman nodded. Harry had been an alcoholic when they'd met, but had cleaned himself up soon after. He'd been clean and sober for almost the entire time they'd been friends, but Roman knew that alcohol had taken a lot from his friend. The death of his wife and son in a car accident had pushed him to the brink of madness and booze had been the only understanding friend he could find. He drank to forget the things he lost, but all he did was lose whatever few things he had left.

But even the apocalypse hadn't tipped Harry off the wagon. He turned his nose up at any drop of plonk placed in front of him. He was a stronger man than most, by far. But sometimes Roman sensed a brief glimmer of weakness in Harry's eyes lately, like he was getting tired.

"I had some of the best times of my life on that boat," Harry chuckled, "even if I was on the firewater at the time. My son used to love dangling a fishing line into the water, trying to catch crabs near the seawall. He never caught anything, bless him, but he always enjoyed it. It was the hope of catching something that kept him there, I think. My son was always optimistic; he always saw the best outcome for everything. He took after his mother in that way. I was the opposite. I wished you could have met him."

Roman patted his friend on the back. "Me too." He knew that even now, years later, the wounds were still raw. Harry's memories of his wife and child were like flayed skin that never healed. "At least you didn't lose your son to this shithole existence," Roman said. It was the only upside he could think of. "Most men did."

Harry ran his hand along the gunwale and nodded. "I know. If anything I'm lucky that I didn't have to watch him get torn apart by the dead." Harry sniffed in another deep breath of sea air and changed the subject. "You think they will ever truly rest again, the dead? You've been out there on land. What do you think?"

Roman stared out at the cold grey sea and thought about it. "I don't know," he said honestly. "The dead are falling apart at the seams, but most of them still walk. I think they'll keep going until there's nothing left of them but dust and bone. Even then they might not stop."

"Maybe they'll stop when there's nothing left of us," said Harry.

"Maybe you're right, although it's a bloody miserable thought. You haven't got any cheerier with age, have you?"

The two of them laughed and Roman stared out at the boats and ships floating beside the Kirkland. All of the men and women on the ragtag group of vessels were safe and well-fed for the time being, but he often wondered what their end game was, their plans for the future. Were all these people, families and strangers, content to float around the seas for the rest of their lives? Would humanity ever regain the earth? Samuel spoke of an army. Was that what they needed? An army to reclaim what they had lost?

He thought about the day he and Harry had fled their carpentry workshop in Wolverhampton, hoping to escape the infection. They made it all the way to the south coast without finding anything resembling safety. They stole a dinghy from the back of a trailer and threw themselves into the sea from a dockside in Kent. They had floated aimlessly for days before Samuel's fleet picked them up. Back then,

Damien had been grateful to the sea for keeping the two of them safe, but now he had begun to hate it for its vast nothingness.

"We're heading inland," he told Harry. "You'll get to see for yourself what the dead are like."

"Inland? Why?"

"To search for the cripple."

"I thought you killed him. Isn't that why you went ashore, to make him dead?"

Roman nodded. He didn't tell Harry how Samuel was obsessed with making sure the man on crutches was dead. If he was honest, he didn't understand what the big deal was. Of course, the cripple needed punishing for trying to blow up the Kirkland, but being wounded and on land was as certain a death sentence you could give a man. The issue had been dealt with. Roman had dealt with it. So why did Samuel give me a tonne of shit for it?

Harry rubbed at his eyes. He was starting to look very old. His short brown hair was turning greyer by the day. For some reason, the news that they were going ashore saddened him, which was the opposite reaction Damien expected. Usually the members of the fleet were excited at the briefest glimpse of the land they'd long abandoned. It was like coming home.

"How are the headaches?" Roman asked is friend.

Harry shrugged. "They come and go. At the moment I am waiting for them to go. But no worries; there's nothing can be done. What happened with the cripple? I thought escaping you was impossible, or so the people around here like to whisper when you're not listening. You're quite the living legend."

Roman sighed. "I shouldn't be. I failed my mission. The dead got in my way. The cripple was wounded well enough, though. That's the difference between the living and the dead. The living run away when you shoot at them."

Harry seemed to wince for a moment, but then his face became an expressionless mask. "How did it feel? Trying to kill another human being?"

Roman looked down at the 9mm tucked into his belt beside his sword. Samuel had given it to him, but he had taken it only reluctantly. There was something dishonourable about a gun. It made killing too easy. He plucked the weapon free and examined its brushed steel contours and machine-cut grooves. Then he tossed it into the sea. "It's not something I wish to do again," he said earnestly.

Harry nodded knowingly. "Killing a man is different to slicing up an already-dead man."

Roman had not enjoyed the feeling of firing at the cripple. He had done many bad things, but murder was not something he relished. "The cripple would have killed us all if he'd gotten his way. He deserved to die."

"But you don't want to go searching for him again, do you?"

"It's an unnecessary risk and one I don't understand. Even if the cripple lives, he can't hurt us on land. He's doomed out there on his own with a gunshot wound. I don't know what Samuel is so concerned about."

"Others call him captain, or sir."

"The same fools call me Roman."

"If only they knew your real name, Damien."

"Damien was the man I used to be. Only you knew that man."

Harry smiled knowingly. "Only I know the man you still are. You may have sharpened an antique sword you found in a museum and attached a rusty spear to your stump, but I still remember the lost youth you were when I met you. You've come a long way. You should be proud. You gave up drugs and violence for courage and honour, but that doesn't mean you have to go running into danger everywhere you find it. You should take an easier job like mine. We were both tradesman; I could get you work in the ship's tool room."

Damien looked out over the sea, at the two hundred boats and ships. Soon they would all be sailing north to meet with the coast, and he would once again be going ashore to contend with the dead. And perhaps the living. They are no better. What Harry was suggesting was a nice thought, but it was beyond Damien's reach. A man with one hand and a hundred battle scars did not simply lay down his sword and start making replacement engine parts. That was only the surface of it, though. The deeper truth was that Damien felt more at ease ashore amongst the dead than on the claustrophobic ship amongst the living.

Harry placed a hand on his shoulder. "People aren't as bad as you think, you know?"

"The people aboard this ship are. They've become like the zombies out there. No one thinks for themselves, they just follow orders."

"Perhaps. But some of them might surprise you."

"They haven't yet."

"Give it time." Harry squeezed Damien's shoulder.

"Time is the only thing I have left," said Damien. He turned away from Harry, shrugging his hand away, but then reconsidered and turned back around. "And an old friend, of course. I still have that."

"More than most have, nowadays," said Harry.

"Then I must be blessed."

"Or cursed. It means you still have something to lose."

Damien sighed and glanced back out at the sea. *Never you, Harry. I must never lose you.*

HUGO

"ZUT ALORS!" HUGO sidestepped to avoid tripping over the woollen sheep that stared innocently up at him from the cabin floor. He picked it up and stuffed it into the gap between the dusty television and the cabinet on which it stood. "Daphne, Sophie, will you please pick up your things? You'll send me overboard one of these days."

His two young daughters were sitting on the yacht's cosy sofa, playing with a set of cards atop the oak-veneer dining table. The eight of spades had fluttered overboard some time ago, but all the other cards were still present.

"Désolé, papa," they said in unison with the voices of innocent choirgirls. They were growing up – eight and nine – but they were still just children.

"Please, my loves, speak English. We are surrounded by them, so you will do better to talk as they do. In fact, we may be the last French speakers alive, as much as it pains me to think about, so don't waste effort with a language no longer used."

"But we are French, papa."

"Nobody is anything anymore. We're all just...people. And most people speak English, so we shall also."

"D'accord," said Daphne, making her younger sister giggle.

Hugo laughed, too, but he gave his eldest daughter a stern look of disapproval. "No more, okay?"

"Okay, papa."

Hugo smiled and left the cabin to go out on the deck. Dozens of other boats surrounded him on the sea, both big and small. The largest ship was the frigate in the centre of the fleet, where the kind man, Samuel, gave his orders. The smallest boats were mere single-mast sailboats that struggled to stay afloat when the winds were bad. Hugo had witnessed more than a few go under during the nastier storms. The English are not the sailors they think themselves to be.

Despite his longing for home – a modest cottage on the outskirts of Brest – Hugo was grateful for the safety of the fleet. What Captain Samuel had done, bringing so many sailors together and providing refuge to the weak and weary, was a kindness beyond most men. Whilst the world had been crumbling, most men thought only of their own survival, but not Samuel Raymeady. True to the humanitarian he'd been as the head of the monolithic Black Remedy Corporation, Samuel had turned his resources to rescuing those lost and frightened. The fleet, now a thousand bodies strong, sailed as a testament to the man. The world had ended, but Samuel Raymeady had kept the human race alive. And for that, all men should love him. As I do. My daughters live because of him.

When France had fallen to the biting jaws of the dead, Hugo had made immediately for the marina where his small yacht was berthed. The carnage and bloodshed he witnessed during the short journey had horrified him enough that he would gladly never set foot on land again. He had gawped in horror at his countrymen tearing into one another, children and men alike. He had spectated impotently as a coach full of pensioners caught alight in the ensuing riots. The old men and women burned alive inside, with nobody doing a thing to help them. It had not been the dead who had done that. We were the real monsters when things fell.

The marina had been teeming when Hugo arrived, and desperate people were begging to board the various boats departing. Many forwent begging in place of outright stealing. Hugo himself had needed to wrestle with a fat man who sought to take his keys and steal the éternuer from him. Hugo had won that battle when he drove his keys into the man's left eye, leaving him screaming on the jetty and half-blind. Hugo's daughters had not spoken to their father for days after that. I barely blame them.

But he succeeded in sailing them free of their homeland and into the English Channel. There, he and several other seafarers had chanced upon the HMS Kirkland. A dozen boats – fishing trawlers mostly – already surrounded the frigate but a messenger had been quick to inform each newly arriving party that they were free to join the growing fleet and that all supplies would be shared out equally. Regular landing parties early on, raiding both French and English coastlines, had been successful in liberating great caches of food, whilst the fishermen of the fleet caught bountiful loads of fish. Life was still greatly lacking, but it seemed that life was becoming a little less about survival and a little more about rebuilding. It was the best any man could hope for in the savage new world. I do sometimes miss being on land, though. Can we live out here forever?

A sudden yip! from behind him made Hugo turn around. Houdini – named so because of his talent for getting in and out of the strangest places as a pup – was sitting on the coachroof above the yacht's main cabin. The tan and white Papillon often chose to spend his time outside, watching the hustle and bustle of the surrounding boats and fishermen. Even in the rain the dog preferred to remain outside, although in the high winds Hugo would carry Houdini inside the cabin. Such a small dog could easily be swept away.

Hugo reached up and patted the dog on its head. "What are you up to, mon ami?"

Yip!

"Just watching the world go by, huh? You and me both. Boys together, no? We must spend our time thinking so that we are best able to protect our delicate young ladies."

The little dog hopped down from the roof and came to Hugo's side, wagging its tail like a maniac. The six-year old dog was a good companion for the girls, but it was heart-breaking to see the animal without a field in sight on which to run and chase a ball.

Hugo patted the dog again. "One day things will be different. You might be a very old dog by then, but I promise you that you will once again get to run amongst the pigeons."

Yip!

Out across the Channel, the Kirkland cast a vast shadow against the twilight background. Its thick cannons and spindly radars jutted out at sharp angles and made the mighty vessel's silhouette seem like it belonged to some exotic beast. Hugo wondered what the captain was doing right now.

Hugo had met Samuel Raymeady only once, early on, when the captain had assembled a man from each ship of the fleet and introduced himself, although it was unnecessary. Everybody knew who Samuel Raymeady was. The richest man in the world. Who'd have thought a businessman would be responsible for saving so many lives. I used to think the man was greedy with all his money and power, but how wrong I was. He is a saint.

At the time, the men and women who had come aboard the Kirkland were broken and battered, some of them dying from wounds and infection. Samuel had assured them all that they were now all safe. The world had plummeted into the abyss, but they had survived extinction. They would survive upon the sea, regain their strength, and retake the earth one day. He promised them salvation, and from the fire in his voice and the passion on his face, Hugo believed every word of the man. Samuel Raymeady was their saviour.

As Hugo thought about how grateful he was, his mind inevitably turned to his losses. His wife, Patricia, had not survived the infection. She had come home from work sick one day and gone straight to bed. Hugo had nursed her as best he could and left his job as an accountant to pick up the girls from school. It had seemed no different to the flu, that night. The next morning Hugo had awoken to find his wife in the en suite. She was raving and mad. When she tried to claw and bite at him, he had smothered her in a blanket and lay on top of her. When Daphne and Sophie called to him, he shouted back that school was cancelled and that they could go watch television. Hugo restrained his wife for almost three hours, pleading with her calm down, but she was like a wild animal beneath the sheet.

Then she had fallen into a coma. Nothing he did could wake her. He sprinted into the kitchen and grabbed the phone, but when he called emergency services, the line was busy. That was when his precious daughters came and told him that all of the cartoons were cancelled and that the news had come on every channel. Hugo had watched the reports for twenty minutes, barely blinking and barely breathing. He had taken his daughters and ran. That day seemed so long ago. I wonder whatever came of my darling, Patricia. I hope she is in peace.

As Hugo stared out at the Kirkland's long silhouette, he noticed that it seemed to be wheeling around and pointing back towards the English coast. Other boats were turning around as well.

"Are we on the move, Houdini? Are the fishermen displeased with this spot or is there bigger intrigue afoot?"

The fleet often travelled, yet sparingly. Fuel was at a premium and not all of the boats had sails. Hugo placed a hand over his brow and tried to see past the glare of the setting sun. He spotted the signal off the Kirkland's starboard bow. A small Coast Guard ship that remained ever close to the frigate had hoisted a flag upon its tall radio tower. The flag was green and it meant 'follow'. The Kirkland moved slowly and there would still be time to rest, but Hugo disliked falling too far towards the rear of the fleet. The Kirkland was the centre of law and order. The closer Hugo was to it, the safer he felt – the safer he felt about his daughters.

Hugo patted Houdini on the head one last time. "Time to go inside, mon ami. We're on the move."

When Hugo started the yacht's 43HP diesel engine, his daughters joined him in the pilot's cabin. Both of them looked apprehensive. "Where are we going, papa?"

"Wherever the good captain takes us, my beauties. Do not worry. The kind man, Samuel, would never do us wrong."

Yip!

"You see?" Hugo laughed and set off after the HMS Kirkland. "Houdini agrees."

POPPY

"**S**O WHAT DID you bring me?" Poppy asked excitedly. She and Garfield were sitting inside the ice cream shop where they lived. Behind the long refrigerated counter was Poppy's space, with her toys, games, and old mattress, while Garfield slept on the shop's tiled floor in a simple sleeping bag. Right now, both of them sat on stools beside a bench that ran the length of the wall.

Garfield almost smiled at her; he never managed a full one, but Poppy had begun to read the subtle signs of whether or not he was happy. Right now, Garfield was happy. "I may have a thing or two I found on my travels," he said, delving into the rucksack he had with him. "Let me have a quick look." Poppy placed her hands on her knees and waited anxiously. The first thing Garfield pulled out was a pair of toothbrushes, still in their packaging. "How about this?" he asked. "You need to look after your teeth, Popcorn."

Poppy frowned and shook her head.

The next thing Garfield pulled from his bag was a stapler. "Can never have enough office supplies," he said.

Poppy growled.

"Okay, okay. Let me have one last look and see if I have anything inside my bag." He fumbled around inside for a long time, tutting occasionally and raising his eyebrows thoughtfully.

Poppy could contain her excitement no longer. "You're killing me," she spluttered.

"Got it!" Garfield pulled out a colourful stack of glossy paper and held it in front of her face. He gave another of his brief almost-smiles to go with it.

Poppy glanced down at the magazines and frowned. There were pictures of women on the front covers, along with makeup and perfume adds. "What are these?" she asked.

Garfield flicked the top one open, revealing an article about weight loss. "They're women's magazines. They have all kinds of articles. They were really popular, before...well, you know."

Poppy took the magazines and leafed through them. There were lots of articles full of words, and pictures of food, lipstick, mobile phones and other boring stuff."

"You don't like them." Garfield said. His eyelids drooped like a sad puppy's.

Poppy shrugged. "I...yeah, they're great. I just didn't expect them."

Garfield sighed and looked away. He always looked away when he felt bad. Poppy was the only person he ever kept eye contact with for more than a few seconds. Poppy's mummy always said it was rude not to hold eye contact, but Poppy thought it was because Garfield was shy, not rude.

"I just wanted to get you something you can use," he muttered. "You're growing up so fast and...and I don't really know what you'll be going through. Your body will change, for one thing."

Poppy blushed.

Garfield blushed too. "Sorry, it's just...I..."

Poppy reached out and touched his wrist. "I know. You want me to read about woman's things."

"Sorry you don't like the magazines."

"I would just rather have you around to teach me things, than read about them in a bunch of old books. We haven't spent time together in ages."

"I have to go out, Poppy. I have to feed us."

"I know you do. But I'm growing up, you said it. You got me these magazines because I'm growing up, so let me come with you."

Garfield shook his head immediately. "We've spoken about this. It's too dangerous out there. The dead..."

"I want to come with you, Garfield. I hate it around here. We were fine on the road before we found this place."

"We almost died a dozen times and you barely spoke a word you were so traumatised."

"I'm older now."

"Less than a year."

"But-"

"Enough!" Poppy was startled. Garfield never raised his voice to her. "I won't take you out there, Poppy. It's too dangerous. I won't let you get hurt. I can't..."

Garfield never showed how he felt, but right then it looked as if he were about to cry. Poppy suddenly felt very guilty. She nodded slowly and looked down at the floor. "I-I'm sorry. I didn't mean to make you mad."

Garfield huffed. "I'm not mad, you silly girl. I'm scared. It's my job to keep you safe, but you're growing so fast that I can barely keep up. I'm worried I won't be able to look after you soon. The others will have to help me."

"I don't need looking after," said Poppy. "I just need you, but you keep going away. You keep leaving me and sometimes I wonder if you're ever going to come back."

Garfield looked at her, keeping eye contact the whole time he spoke, even though she knew he would have found it hard. "I'll never leave you, Popcorn. I'm always thinking of you and I will always come back. Everything I do, I do because I have no choice. I do it to keep you safe. I made you a promise, didn't I? When I cooked you bacon in that old hotel outside Oxford and we played eye-spy all night, laughing. When we set out the next morning, you told me you wanted to live at the hotel because you liked it there. I told you that it wasn't the hotel you liked, it was the fun we had had the night before. I said that we could have fun wherever we went but that we must keep moving. When you said you were scared, I promised to keep you safe. Remember?"

Poppy nodded and smiled. She looked back at their time on the road fondly – it hadn't all been bad, not after they got used got it. They had never been apart back then, and towards the end, before they had found the pier, they were always giggling. It never mattered that they were always in danger and that terrible things surrounded them every day, they would always cheer each other up. Now, neither of them ever often smiled. Garfield was always foraging and she was always alone.

There were tears in her eyes as she spoke, she knew. She had to stop crying all the time. "I love you, Garfield. I miss you when you're gone."

Garfield's eyes went wide as she said the word 'love'. She had never said the word to him before, had not said it at all since her parents died. She did love him, though. He was all she had. The only person she could rely on and her only friend. He had looked after her for more than three months on the road and she would be dead if not for him. He took me away from that horrible place where my mummy and daddy were monsters. He brought me here where it's safe. Even if the pier is boring, it is safe.

For a moment, Garfield looked as though he was going to say the word back to her, but instead he just said, "I miss you, too. Now go get ready for bed. I have to leave early in the morning. One game of eye spy and then we sleep."

Poppy nodded. She slid off her stool and walked away silently. Tears tried to spill from her eyes, but she fought them away. She didn't want Garfield to go. He was always leaving her and she started to wonder if he really did care the way he said he did. Why didn't he say it back? She climbed onto her mattress and closed her eyes to sleep. She didn't want to play eye spy.

Why didn't he say 'I love you' back?

GARFIELD

ARFIELD PACKED THE last of the smoked mackerel into his backpack and placed it next to his bottled water. It would not be enough to sustain him permanently, but he intended to find supplies on the road. The infection had ravaged the country so fast that most supermarkets and petrol stations were still well stocked. There had not been enough time, or enough survivors, that looting had ever taken a firm hold. The world had died on its feet before people's minds ever had a chance to turn to long-term survival.

The chef's knife in Garfield's belt was accompanied by a claw hammer, a screwdriver, corkscrew, and a metal pipe all hidden about his person. It was foolish to rely on a single weapon. Garfield had seen good men perish who had.

The other foragers – they could be called his men, although he would never say so himself – were all ready and waiting. They stood with heavy backpacks and had armed themselves with various weapons. The plan was to make haste to the church on the edge of town and get a couple of vehicles working. There were ten foragers plus Garfield. Lemon was their master of unlocking, a shy, stumpy man, who stuttered when he was stressed. There wasn't a door he couldn't get through or a car he couldn't hotwire. His bag of tricks contained everything from wire cutters to hacksaws. Kirk was second-in-command and the group's resident badass – if a little too cocky for Garfield's liking. Cat was the only female member of the group, and tougher than all of the men. She travelled with David, her lover. Squirrel and Danny were the pier's screw-ups, lazy and stupid, but agreeable and humorous. Last came Luke, Tom, Gavin, and Lenny – a group of sensible middle-aged men that made up the reliable backbone of the foraging party. Each of them insisted on wearing a bunch of red football shirts they had found in a sports shop. They believed the bright colours made it easier to see each other in the field. Perhaps they were right. Our little band of brothers, Garfield thought. Closest I've ever had to friends.

The group would need to get the largest vehicles it could find and pray that the batteries still had a spark, and that the petrol in the tanks had not evaporated. The foragers would be leaving behind their sleds, so whatever vehicle they found would also act as the carriage for whatever supplies they managed to scrounge. Guns and ammo, hopefully.

The morning tide was out and there was nothing but moist sand and seaweed beneath the front section of the pier. It had started to rain and the smell of salt was thick in the air. Garfield would be glad to be rid of that familiar smell for a few days. He missed the old smells of car exhaust and greasy spoon cafes, but those things were no more. They had been replaced by the stink of death.

Anna headed towards Garfield, holding something in her hands. When she got close enough, she offered the item to him. "For the road," she explained.

Garfield took the can opener from her and smiled. "Good thinking. I'm so used to bringing canned food back that I forgot I'm going to need one for the journey."

"No point finding a tonne of food if you can't get at it. Sometimes it's good to carry something other than a whole bunch of weapons. How many do you have on you right now in that magnificent coat of yours?"

Garfield shrugged. "Weapons? I'm not sure. Seven, maybe...no, eight."

Anna laughed. "Well, I hope that you won't need any of them. You be safe out there. There's no way of telling what you'll find."

Garfield knew well enough what he would find in the towns and cities. "I expect to find the dead."

"For starters," said Anna. "But I worry more about any people left alive. Take it from me, the living are just as dangerous as the dead."

Garfield nodded – he knew that well enough already. Several times on the road he had caught hungry-eyed men spying Poppy from a distance, hoping to take her. A handful of them had tried, but Garfield had dispatched each one without mercy. He would not allow Poppy to be used and spoiled like a can of beans. Her innocence was more precious than anything else left in the world, and Garfield would kill a hundred men to protect it. Finding the pier and the relative safety of the group living there had been a true blessing. Poppy had been safe from the leering gaze of feral men ever since. But she's fighting me all the time to go back out on the road. She doesn't remember how bad it was. She looks at the past through rose-coloured spectacles. Not that I blame her after all she's been through.

Garfield bent over and placed the can opener inside the shin pocket of his cargo pants then straightened back up. "I plan to stick to the countryside as much as possible. With a bit of luck I'll be able to bypass any trouble. There's no need to worry." Anna looked at him oddly for a moment, as if she wanted to say something. "What is it?" he asked her.

"It's…it's just something the injured man you brought back said."

"Oh, yeah. How's he doing?"

"He's been pretty stable over night, but just after I patched him up he said something strange."

"What did he say?"

"He said…" Anna stopped and chuckled to herself. "You're going to laugh at me, but he kept saying the word 'Roman' over and over again. It went on for nearly an hour before he fell unconscious.'"

Garfield smirked, but not because he thought it was particularly funny. "Don't people say all sorts of things in that kind of condition? Couldn't the pain have made him delirious?"

"Yes, it could have. In fact, that was probably the reason. Gave me a bad feeling, though. Whoever shot him is still out there. Be careful, okay?"

Garfield had thought about the group that might be out there with guns. If they were a threat, he would much rather encounter them away from the pier where it would not endanger the others.

"I'll be safe, I promise. You look after Poppy for me, okay? She's... growing up. It might help her to spend some time with a woman for once, rather than hanging around rooftops waiting for me all the time. Where is she, anyway?"

"She's coming, don't worry. She told me she needed to get something and that you weren't to leave until she saw you."

Garfield rolled his eyes. "As if I would. Silly girl."

Like a genie summoned, the talk of Poppy brought her racing around the corner of the Sea Grill restaurant and over to the open walkway leading up to the gate. Her white-blonde plaits trailed in the air behind her like tentacles from a squid.

"Hey, Popcorn. I was just about to leave. You almost missed me."

Poppy scowled. "You would never leave without saying goodbye. I would kick your butt as soon as you was back."

Garfield fought a smile. *She's not kidding.* "You're right. I wouldn't dare cross you, Popcorn." Poppy giggled. She jumped the two feet between them and gave him a great big hug around his waist. "Careful," he warned her. "You'll cut yourself on my knife."

Poppy broke off from the hug and looked up at him. She was still such a tiny girl, but had grown nearly a foot in the time he'd known her. Eventually she'd start to become a woman. He dreaded to think how he would keep her safe then. *She's already a handful at nine. Last night she said she loved me. Should I have said it back?* Saying 'I love you' to a child that wasn't his own felt wrong somehow. *In the old world, the relationship he had with Poppy would have been scrutinised, but the truth was that he felt for her the same way as any father would. He could never replace her real parents, but she was his to love and protect, and he would do the very best job he was able. So why didn't I say the word back to her?*

"I did you a drawing," Poppy said, handing over a curled sheet of sketch paper. Three months ago, Garfield had found an art set in one of the abandoned shops on the sea front, along with a few reams of paper. He'd given it to Poppy as a gift. With so little to do around the pier, the girl had become quite the accomplished artist.

"What is it?" he asked her.

"Well, if you looked at it you would know, dummy."

Garfield studied the sketch and saw that it was a finely detailed drawing of a pond. There was a large overhanging fern tree, shaded in multiple browns and greens, and a slick sheet of moss across the water. In the foreground was a family of what looked like moorhens – their beaks red with a pointed tip of bright yellow crayon. "This is great," he said, truly meaning it. "When did you get so good?"

Poppy blushed. "It's the pond by my house – my old house. My mum used to take me out to feed the birds. I think about it whenever I'm sad. I thought you could look at the picture whenever you get sad."

Garfield felt a lump in his throat but swallowed it. He pulled Poppy close and kissed the top of her head. "Thank you." I should say the word now. I should tell her that I love her. "Poppy, I lo-"

"Ready to go?" asked Alistair, marching towards them with a grimace on his face. "I still think this is a bad idea, you know? If it was just you and a few others leaving, Garfield, then perhaps it would be okay, but you're taking half the camp with you."

Garfield sighed. Alistair could let nothing go without an argument. "We've already discussed this, Al. You'll be fine. The more supplies I can carry back with me the better."

"I just think it's selfish."

"Selfish? How?"

Anna interrupted. "It's decided now, so let's not bicker."

Alistair folded his chubby arms across his fat chest and looked comically irate, like a red-faced cartoon villain. "I suppose it is decided," he muttered. "Doesn't mean I have to like it, though. Just make sure you bring back something useful," he said to Garfield. "We're running low on salt, for one thing. We need it to cure the fish we catch."

"Grab some multi-vitamin pills, too, if you get chance," Anna told him. "People are starting to get sickly. All we eat is fish and beans. There's stuff our bodies aren't getting."

Garfield nodded. "Salt...vitamins...got it." He turned around and did a quick head count of the foragers. Alistair was right: he was taking more than half the camp with him – eight, nine, ten, plus me. Everyone was present and ready to go. Garfield was the only one holding things up. Poppy's picture went into the breast pocket of his heavy woollen overcoat.

Anna folded her arms and sighed. She was usually a stern and un-emotional women, but she seemed unusually apprehensive. It would be the most dangerous forage Garfield had embarked on, so he supposed a few nerves were understandable. "Looks like it's time to go," she said. "You take care out there, okay?"

"Yeah," said Poppy. "You promised me you would always come back, so don't die."

Garfield huffed. Women did like to worry. "It's nothing I haven't seen before," he assured them. "I'll be fine. Before you know it, I'll be back with a truckload of supplies."

"And hopefully some guns," said Alistair.

Garfield nodded. "That's the plan."

Poppy was beginning to sniffle. There were tears brimming at the bottom of her eyes, but she was chewing on one of her blonde plaits to keep from crying – she often did that lately. Garfield forced a smile onto his face. Happy expressions weren't something he wore well, but he knew the girl needed a gesture from him right now. Like telling her that I love her. She spat her hair out. Her bottom lip quivered. "I-I don't like it when you leave."

Garfield bent down so that they were eye to eye. "I don't either, Popcorn. While I'm gone, you need to listen to Anna, okay? She's going to keep an eye on you for me. Part of being a grown-up is being able to listen to other people, okay? Will you listen to Anna for me?"

Poppy nodded. Anna patted her on the shoulder. "We'll be fine."

"Good." Garfield straightened up and cleared his throat. "And stay off those bloody rooftops. You're gunna have a fall one day."

Poppy grinned. "Never. Climbing is one of the only fun things to do around here."

"Just be careful, then."

"Garf," Kirk shouted from over by the gate. "We're wasting light, man. Let's get our arses in gear."

Garfield nodded. He gave Poppy one last smile and then turned around. He could hear the girl begin to sob behind him, but he didn't turn back to look at her. The sight of her crying wasn't something he wanted to take on the journey. It hurt badly enough just knowing that he was the reason for her tears, without having to see the pain etched on her innocent face and remembering it every time he closed his eyes. Rescuing her that the day was the best and worst thing I ever did.

When Garfield had found Poppy inside the big house beside the pond, he had been looking only for food. He was getting so desperate that the notion of beating other survivors and taking their food was beginning to seem less and less like a crime. He had not spoken to another human being in weeks and was beginning to forget the sound of his own voice. His hygiene and manners had become meaningless. The only thing that mattered was surviving, no matter what. He was becoming like an animal.

But then he had found a little girl close to death and everything had changed. Focusing on her needs and keeping her safe brought back his humanity in one fell swoop and refocused him on what it meant to be alive. The temptation to kill and steal from others went away, replaced by love and affection. Poppy reminded him that there were still help-less, innocent people in the world and that they needed looking after. She had stopped him from becoming a beast. He owed her his humanity. But I don't know what I'm doing with her anymore. She wants so much from me, but I have nothing to give. I never asked for this.

And neither did she. I should have told her that I loved her.

Garfield headed over to the gate and got going with the group, heading towards the church. He forced himself not to look back until the pier was far behind him.

POPPY

HE DIDN'T LOOK back once. Doesn't he care about me?

Poppy sat atop the souvenir store where Anna lived, and stared off into the distance. She'd watched Garfield and the foragers right up until they'd become black dots on the horizon. Now they weren't even dots anymore, they were gone.

Why didn't he look back? Isn't he going to miss me?

The tears in Poppy's eyes had finally dried up, but first they'd spilled down her cheeks for close to an hour. Her cheeks were sore now and the cold was making her shiver. The rain was falling harder, but she fought against the discomfort for a while longer. She didn't want to get down from the roof until she knew Garfield was completely out of sight and not coming back.

Anna had called to her a few times in the last hour, warning her about catching a chill, but Poppy just ignored her. The woman would just want to talk – adults always wanted to talk – but the last thing Poppy wanted right now was chitchat. I just want Garfield back, and talking won't make that happen.

Once upon a time, Poppy had thought her parents were like God. They were never wrong and always had the answers to her questions. They seemed to know all the secrets of the world and were never scared of anything. Poppy was certain they'd live forever.

But then they had died.

Watching her mummy and daddy get sick and turn into monsters had shattered everything Poppy thought about the world. Her parents weren't Gods anymore. They had become weak and smelly. Slowly, their skin turned grey and their eyes bulged. Eventually they had barricaded themselves inside their bedroom and told Poppy to wait outside for help. They said she must never try and come inside the bedroom, no matter what. Poppy had waited so long to be rescued that she thought she would spend the rest of her life in that dark, smelly house. The electricity went first. Then her food disappeared and the water flowed weaker and weaker from the taps. Poppy wondered if that meant she would die soon. Once, in desperation, she shouted out to her parents and begged them help her, but all she'd been met with was a scary growling that sounded more like two wild animals than her mummy and daddy.

In the end Poppy had started to grow poorly. She had lain down on the living room floor and listened to the silence. So far away in her dreams had she been, that when Garfield entered her home, she didn't even notice. When she opened her eyes the big ginger-haired man was standing over her, staring down at her face curiously. He might have been there to hurt her, she knew that deep down, but somehow she didn't care. For a long time the only thing that had bothered her was the raging hunger in her belly, but even that had gone away after a while. All she felt in the end was tired and numb and sad. She wouldn't have minded dying. But Garfield saved me.

He had taken her away that night, fed her, re-clothed her, and talked to her; but she said not a single word back to him. He didn't seem to mind – in fact he seemed to like her silence. He was a quiet person himself.

She didn't speak for weeks.

Eventually, one night while they were camping inside an old garden centre surrounded by the dead, Poppy had managed to utter one single word to Garfield. She had said: "thanks."

That time seemed so long ago now. Much had happened between then and now. She'd grown more than she thought she was supposed to in a single year; toughened up so much that her parents would probably not even recognise her anymore. She hoped they would be proud. I miss them.

Poppy could stare at the horizon no more. Looking into the distance at the last place she'd seen Garfield was making her too sad. She swivelled around on her bum and stared in the opposite direction, out towards the sea. The grey-green water kept them alive, Anna often said, and even though everyone was sick and tired of eating fish, they never failed to cast their rods out every single morning and night. They rarely failed to catch something or other. Anna said the fish were having lots more babies than they used to because there was less people eating them. I remember when there used to be lots of human babies. I wonder what happened to them all. Are they all gone, or are some of them safe? I hope so. I would like to hold a baby someday.

Maybe one day when I grow up I will hold my own.

Poppy often stared out at the sea, hoping to spot a dolphin or a whale. Garfield told her those animals didn't live in the English Channel, because the sea was too cold, but Anna disagreed and said that they could never tell anything for sure anymore. Once the dead had not walked, but now they did. Perhaps, one day, great big whales would belly flop in the waters beyond the pier and make a new home for themselves. Poppy wanted to make sure that she didn't miss it if it happened. Maybe I could ride away on one.

She noticed movement on the horizon. It could have been her mind playing tricks on her, though. She wanted so badly to see a whale that she might have tricked herself into believing she'd just seen one.

Sunlight bounced off the surface of the water. There was movement there for sure. Poppy edged off her bottom and shifted onto her knees. She leant forward and squinted, trying to see past the glaring morning sun and the streaks of falling rain.

What is that? Am I about to finally see a whale?

No, that's not a whale. It's...something else.

It took almost ten minutes before Poppy could work out what she could see growing on the horizon. Once she finally realised, her eyes stretched wide and her mouth dropped open in shock. "No flippin' way!" she almost shouted.

Poppy leapt off the roof and went to get the others. She wore an excited grin on her face and almost wet herself. They're not going to believe this, she thought. Never in a bazillion years.

FRANK

FRANK ENTERED THE captain's chamber and stood before his son's desk. Samuel was reclined back in his leather chair, staring hard at the ceiling. He would often do that when there were no immediate matters at hand; just sit and think until there was. "We've spotted survivors off the Devonshire coast," Frank told his adopted son. "Small village with a pier, just past Dartmouth."

Samuel sat forward and leant across his desk. He raised one of his dark eyebrows. "Oh? How do we know there are survivors?"

"We've spotted people fishing from the railings."

"Fishing? My, how very relaxed. They must be well set-up at this pier. Any sign of the cripple amongst them?"

"No. What are your orders?"

Samuel smiled as if his orders should be obvious. "I won't have that terrorist roaming free. Send a sortie ashore to meet with these survivors. If they are the only camp in the area then there's a good chance the cripple may have chanced upon them. We need to question them."

"Question them?"

Samuel smiled wider, showing long white teeth. "Yes, just words. No needed for anything stronger...yet. Send Roman. Maybe this time he'll do something useful."

Frank's mood worsened at the talk of Roman. "I worry about that one. He doesn't respect you."

"Oh, he respects me enough, father. His very presence is proof of that. He had no need to join us here, and even less to stay. There was nothing to stop him from staying in his dinghy and waitingß for the next chance of rescue."

"There would not have been any chance of another rescue."

"Exactly. I saved that man's life. He owes me."

"He has a friend aboard, the man who was with him when we rescued him. I think the only reason he stays with us is because it keeps his friend safe. He's been trying to keep the relationship secret, but petty officer Dunn informed me about it earlier today. The man's name is Harry."

"That just proves my point," said Samuel. "I keep Roman's only friend safe. Thus he has every reason to obey me."

"But he shows you no respect."

"Respect is for the weak, you know that. If I had shown respect to my peers I would never have made Black Remedy the greatest company on Earth. To truly thrive, a man must stand alone and tower above all lesser men. Roman will be a leader one day, if he doesn't screw up his potential. I can make use of a born leader, but if he disappoints, then I'm sure there will be more humble uses for a man like him."

"But if he doesn't respect you, how can you trust him?"

Samuel folded his arms across his chest. "If you had shown respect for my dead father, you may have resisted sleeping with my mother."

Frank spluttered. Falling for Samuel's mother while he had been the family's bodyguard had been a poor show of integrity, but when Samuel's father died in a freak accident, Frank had been there to comfort her. They had grown unavoidably close. Her premature death had taken a piece of him. He'd loved no woman since. His sole devotion had been raising the son she had left behind. I just hope she'd be happy with the job I've done.

Samuel grinned. "It's okay, Frank. Don't blush. You know I forgive you. When mother died you were there for me. I will never forget that."

Samuel's mother had been an alcoholic. Her death had been tragic and left the boy without a parent. Frank had gladly taken the responsibility. "I've always wanted the best for you, Samuel. That's why Roman bothers me so much."

"I trust Roman more than the whimpering fools who come before me on bent knee. I need men of action, not subservience. Believe me, father, I have a way of seeing into a man's heart, and Roman's is as black as my own. He seeks redemption. I intend to give him opportunity."

Frank sighed. Reading into his adopted son's intentions was a folly he'd ceased pursuing long ago. As much as Samuel spoke in riddles, it could never be said that he did not understand the men around him. He knew every weakness, flaw, and vulnerability of every man he ever crossed, often within minutes of meeting him. That was just one of the many reasons Samuel had nigh on controlled the economic world via his megalithic Black Remedy Corporation – a company started by Samuel's father and American business partner, Vincent Black. Both were long dead.

And now Samuel commands probably the largest group of survivors left on the planet. He was made for leadership and power, but now, instead of a company, he owns a burgeoning nation on the sea. It's a lot of influence for such a young man.

"Father, you are over-thinking. I can always tell because another of the hairs on your head goes grey. You are aging quicker than I would like. I'm rather fond of having you around, so please don't grow too old on me."

Frank nodded. He felt older than he would have liked, that much was true. The end of the world had been a weary ordeal, and even from the safety of the Kirkland he'd witnessed more bloodshed than he ever thought possible. He himself had partaken in the initial culling of the infected brought on-board. God forgive me.

Taking in groups of survivors had been a perilous task and many came to the Kirkland with bites and scratches. Frank had hurried them away hastily under the guise of medical attention, but had shot them in the head at the rear of the ship before dumping them overboard. The other survivors knew it was happening, but they said nothing. Survival of the fittest and selfish denial were the only traits that mattered anymore – in fact they were probably the only traits that had ever mattered. They were just less well hidden now that society had crumbled.

"If the survivors have no knowledge of the cripple, if they seek to join us, what then?"

Samuel shrugged his bony shoulders and blinked his dark eyes slowly. "Do they have a boat?"

"No."

"Then we take those useful to us and urge the rest to remain at their camp."

"Isn't that a tad...cruel? If they have a doctor or a strong leader, shouldn't they stay together as a camp? Leaving the weak behind and taking away their strength is the same as-"

"Killing them?" asked Samuel. His gaze bubbled with a fury that was always close to the surface, hiding just behind his smile. "There is no place left for ideals, father. Taking aboard the weak and useless, feeding them and housing them while others more deserving starve and die, that would be the true crime. There is no place for the meek. Their days of inheriting the world are over. My world will be a world of the strong and proud. Humanity will rise again in glorious fashion, I promise you that."

Frank cleared his throat. "Your world?"

Samuel's face drained of anger and he let out a chuckle. For a fleeting moment he looked just like the young boy Frank had raised in the countryside of Gloucestershire. That boy had possessed the energy of a hundred normal children and the intelligence of two hundred. By the time Samuel was sixteen years of age, he had read more books than most librarians read in their lifetimes.

Samuel cleared his throat. "That was a trifle arrogant of me, perhaps, but this new world needs a leader – someone to bring the tired and suffering together and show them their new path. If someone more befitting for the task exists, I would welcome him with open arms. Until then, I will do what I can for my people. I am a leader, father. I was born a leader and that's what these people expect me to be. Without me they are lost."

Frank nodded, but inside he was thinking, Are you a leader or a dictator? Would you truly relinquish power if it were in the interest of the fleet?

Samuel's expression darkened and Frank wondered if he knew what he was thinking. "Go and fetch Roman," he ordered. "Send him ashore again. If the cripple is there, I want him brought back to me. Alive or dead; it makes no difference. I merely seek to piss upon his face before tossing his bones into the ocean."

Frank sighed. Some say a leader is judged by the way he treats his captives. I don't think Winston Churchill spoke much of pissing on his enemies. He turned away and left with a sigh, wishing he didn't love the young man as much as he did. The boy had grown up in his care. All that Samuel was came from the lessons Frank had taught him. There was a lot of good in his son, Frank knew it (just look at the number of lives Samuel had saved and brought inside the protection of the fleet), but there was a deep darkness, too, something Frank dared not think about most nights. It's always been there. Even as a boy. Frank loved Samuel and would try to steer him right. That's what fathers did. Samuel Raymeady was born to be a great man and a great man he would be. The arrogance of youth was no reason to condemn him. He'd done well so far. Everything would work out for the best. Is it love that makes me trust him? Or is it fear?

One thing Frank knew for sure: with all the death and destruction in the world, there was nothing Samuel could do to make things any worse.

ANNA

ANNA WAS IN the diner, applying a fresh dressing to her patient's wound. The flesh was pale rather than red, which was good; there seemed little sign of infection. At first she'd held little hope of the man surviving, but slowly her opinion was beginning to change. He had made it through the night, the morning, and now the afternoon. His breathing was steady and his eyelids flickered as he dreamed.

"He may yet live," said Rene. "A fighter."

Anna fastened the last of the fresh bandages and stepped away. "Fighters are the only people left."

Rene nodded. He offered Anna a glass of water. "You have cut your hair, Anna. I like it."

Anna took the glass and smiled. She had cut her scruffy brown hair to shoulder-length a few days ago. Up until now, nobody had noticed. "Thank you," she said. How are we doing for supplies?"

"Plenty of rain lately. We have lots of water...and fish – always so much fish."

Anna chuckled. "Yep, no lack of Omega-3 in our diets. Hopefully, Garfield will bring us back something to get our taste buds dancing again."

"You think he will return to us?"

"You think he won't?"

Rene looked sad. He always looked sad – like a scorned puppy-dog. "I think we have all forgotten the danger that stalks the earth. We have become too comfortable on this pier: fresh fish, water, safety. We forget the journey we all took to get here."

Anna thought back to the people who had not made the journey: Nick, Grace, Dave, Shawcross, Jan, Mike...oh, how she missed Mike.

Her next thoughts were of the creatures that had ripped her past companions apart. She could easily recall the screeching wails of the infected and the soft moans of the dead. Sometimes those sounds filled the silence whenever she sat alone. It would force her to grab a paperback and read just to keep her mind focused on things other than death. Losing so many people had made her hard and cold – even more than she had already been. Before the infection, the death of her unborn child haunted her daily. Now the death of her unborn child was just one of a hundred deaths she mourned. It had left her heart unable to beat with anything other than mistrust and scorn. The infected and the dead had removed her capacity for anything approaching joy.

Fortunately the infected – who ran and leapt like ferocious tigers – had all but died out. Only a living person with a bite became infected, but once they died they would soon rise again and continue their murderous quest as zombies. The dead were slow and stupid – they could be avoided in small numbers and were only a danger in great crowds. Fortunately, there were very few around the village and the pier. Anna surmised that the local residents had owned boats and fled to sea when the first wave of infections began.

When they found the pier, Anna, Rene, and the half-dozen other survivors they'd met on the south coast, including Alistair, had cleared the village of as many dead as they dared, before breaking into the pier and securing the gate behind them. The pier's location, built almost a half-mile out to sea on huge metal struts, had kept them safe for almost a year. The gate was the only way in and out and the narrow walkway made it easy to corral the dead and deal with them in small groups. Perhaps Rene is right, Anna thought. Maybe we have become complacent.

Anna sipped from the water and placed the cup down on a nearby table. She glanced again at her resting patient. From the soft moans and the random sniffs coming from him, she was hopeful that he might wake soon. He would be in a lot of pain, no doubt, but he might just heal if he was lucky. And then we'll learn his story.

Just then, Poppy came racing through the doors of the diner.

Anna put her hands up. "Slow down, you're going to break your neck. Who put so much sand in your knickers?"

The girl was panting, so much so that she couldn't get her words out. "Out...on the...sea. B-boats. Ships."

Anna's eyes went wide. "There are ships? Are they abandoned or are people on them?"

Poppy doubled over, hands on her thighs, still trying to catch her breath. "I don't know. I-I...think so."

Anna pulled Poppy up straight and dragged her along as she headed outside onto the deck. Alistair and the other survivors were huddled at the end of the pier, pointing and leaning over the rail. Beyond them was a huge fleet of ships and boats taking up the sea for miles.

"Can you believe it?" said Alistair. His chubby face was bright red and gleaming with excitement. "It's got to be the Navy. We're rescued at last."

Anna frowned. Rescued? Rescued from what? They were already safe. How could they be any safer, unless there was some island someplace with no dead whatsoever? If this was the Navy, then why did so many of the boats look like leisure cruisers and yachts? The fleet did not look like any navy she knew of; in fact there was only one boat that even looked at all like military – a large grey frigate taking up the centre. Maybe it's escorting these other boats to safety. Perhaps it is the Navy after all.

Despite her hopes, Anna didn't buy it.

They waited nigh on an hour for the fleet of mismatched ships, boats, and yachts to come closer. Anna could make out numerous men and women on the various crafts. Many of the sailors waved a friendly hand or blared their horns. Poppy waved back at them all, jumping up and down excitedly.

Anna placed her arm on the girl's back to calm her. "Let's just wait and see what they want, Poppy. We can't trust anybody until we know a little more about them."

"But look at all the people. There are women, too. They look friendly. They're waving. HELLO! YES, HELLO, PLEASED TO MEET YOU."

Alistair turned and scowled at the girl. "They can't hear you, stupid. They're too far away."

"You're the one who's stupid," Poppy mumbled so that Alistair did not hear. Anna tried not to chuckle. Alistair had no idea how to deal with the little girl and grew increasingly flummoxed by her with each passing day.

The vast fleet came to a stop. Only a single boat – a small white yacht – broke away and headed for the shore. A greeting party, Anna thought. Her anxiety dissolved slightly at the show of diplomatic convention. She hoped the small group coming ashore would extend the hand of friendship and offer trade, but the truth was that there would be no way of knowing until the strangers were already at the pier. *I really wish Garfield and the others hadn't left. There're only a handful of us left. If something bad happens...*

Anna took a deep breath and cricked her neck to the side. She never played the victim and was irritated just for thinking like one. She parted the group of her fellow survivors and moved up to the railing. The group would be looking to her to take charge of the situation. *Time to put my mother hen suit on.*

Patiently, she waited for the small white yacht to reach the end of the pier. It was a small boat and slow. When it finally arrived, Anna was shocked by what she saw. Standing at the bow of the yacht was a grim-looking man with a missing hand. Where his left fist should be was a jagged metal spear. Sheathed inside a scabbard on his belt was what looked like a medieval short sword or a Roman gladius. With his long blonde hair and muddy face, the man looked like a character from a comic book. His age seemed to be just north of thirty, but it was hard to tell for sure. Nowadays, even twenty-year-olds could have grey hair and wrinkles.

Two other men accompanied the man with the sword. An older man with long grey hair stood at the wheel inside the boat's small pilothouse, while a third man, large and brooding, stood at the back of the yacht.

"Hello, there," the swordsman said.

"Hi," said Anna abruptly. The onus was not on her to state her business, so she opted to remain quiet for the time being. Thankfully, Alistair and the others took her lead and did the same.

"We are fellow survivors," the swordsman continued. He spoke strangely, like he was acting out some part in a play. "Some twelve hundred in total. We wish you no harm, only to discuss a short matter. May we disembark?"

"No," said Anna. "Not until you state your business."

"Very well. I'm looking for a man. A man that tried to sink our flagship." He turned around and pointed to the large frigate in the distance. "The HMS Kirkland. Do you see it?"

"I see it," said Anna. The big ship was like a bristly grey sea monster. Radars and towers rose up from it like spines and bristles, while its long pointed bow was like the sharp beak of a condor. "Why did this man try to sink it?"

"Because he's a bloody nutter, luv," said the large man at the back of the yacht. "Have you seen him or not?"

Anna shrugged. "Seen who?"

A look of irritation came over the swordsman's face. When he spoke again, the nature of his speech had changed. He sounded less like a Shakespearian actor and more like a thug. "Don't piss about, darling," he snarled. "Just answer the question."

"Or else what?" As soon as Anna said it, she glanced out at the vast fleet of ships. She wondered if she should tone down her obstinacy and be a little more polite. She knew little of these three men or the people aboard the boats. Distrust is one thing, she thought. But I shouldn't go looking or a fight.

Alistair was spluttering, but he managed to speak up before Anna had another chance. "What did this man look like?" he asked.

The swordsman cleared his throat. "Skinny geezer, hair the colour of a two-pence piece. A bullet wound in his guts."

Anna's eyes went wide. *We have the guy, all right. He's lying unconscious in our diner right now. Oh, Hell's bloody bells.*

"We have the man you're looking for," Alistair said immediately. He shrugged at Anna. "Sorry, but I don't think we should get ourselves in the middle of this. We don't owe that man anything. We patched him up and kept him alive. What else can we do?"

"*I* patched him up," Anna corrected. "And he's been unconscious this whole time. Shouldn't we wait to hear what he has to say before we hand him over to a bunch of pirates?"

Alistair shook his head. "It's not our business. You see all those ships out there, right? This could be our ticket out of here."

"When did getting out of here become so goddamn important? We're safe here. We look after each other. I don't think we should be in such a hurry to leave. As much as I mistrust you, Alistair, I trust those men even less."

Alistair frowned, but then seemed to think for a moment. It became clear he wasn't changing his mind. "We can decide what to do after we give these men what they want."

Why should we? Why do we owe them our immediate trust? Just because their group is bigger than ours? While Anna had no reason to protect the wounded man in their diner, something inside of her was loathe to hand him over. There was something brutish about the way the huge fleet had swarmed up on the pier out of nowhere and brought its demands. She'd never liked bullies in the old world, and she liked them even less now.

The swordsmen hit the edge of the yacht with his spear, making a clang and getting their attention. "Hurry up and hand the man over," he yelled up at them. "I don't have all day"

"Why should we do what you want?" Anna asked him.

"Because if you won't hand him over then I'll come up there and take him myself."

"You can try, but I wouldn't recommend it." Jesus, Anna. Stop picking a fight.

"What are you doing?" Alistair whispered to her irritably. The man's jowly chin was jiggling with frustration. "Let's just hand the man over before something bad happens."

"What's happening?" asked Poppy. "Are these men bad?"

"They're not bad," Alistair told her. "We're just helping them with something."

Anna whispered back to Alistair in the same irritated tone he had used on her. "Why should we? Because this guy is ordering us to? We don't take orders from him."

The swordsmen stood restlessly on the bow of his yacht and let out a long, contemplative sigh. He closed his eyes for a moment and seemed to be thinking. His light-blond hair was blowing in the breeze. After a while, he pointed his spear at them. "This is going in a bad direction. I said I'm not here to hurt anyone, but I'm beginning to change my mind. You know that frigate we were talking about, the HMS Kirkland? Let me tell you a little bit about her. She's a Type 27 'Duke'-class frigate, originally constructed for use by the Royal Navy. 193 metres in length, she has a displacement of 6,000 tonnes. Most interestingly of all, though, are the two 30MM guns on each side, starboard and portside. The starboard gun is currently pointing right in our direction. If I give a signal, or if anything happens to me, this place will be ripped apart in seconds by so many rounds of API incendiary fire that you will think that Hell itself is raining down on you." The swordsman raised an eyebrow as if to implore them. "I suggest you people let me up there and take me to the man you're hiding. My only interest is taking the man back to the Kirkland to stand trial for his crimes."

"Alleged crimes," Anna corrected him. "How do I know he even did anything?" Alistair scowled at her and shook his head disapprovingly.

Anna gave up. Even her own people were against her and perhaps they were right. Did she really want to start making enemies? "Okay," she shouted over the rail. "You can come up. We'll get a rope."

"Thank you," said the swordsman, already tying a mooring rope around one of the pier's thick struts. "You lot aren't as dumb as I thought."

Anna ignored the insult and stepped back from the railing. She felt wrong about what they were doing. She didn't want to give up an unconscious man without knowing for sure what the situation was. Regardless of whether Alistair was a coward or just being pragmatic, she was irritated that he was at odds with her. She'd survived alongside the man for close to a year; she would have liked him to have her back.

Alistair took a rope from old man Bob and secured it to the railing before tossing it over. Down below, the three strangers secured it to the moorings of their yacht, and then started to shimmy up the rope, one at a time. The swordsman went first, climbing awkwardly with one hand. When he hopped over the railing, his heavy boots planted down on the deck with a resounding thud!

"Pleasure to meet you," Anna said with sharp politeness. "What's your name?"

"Call me whatever makes you happy."

"You are speaking to Roman," said the older man with long grey hair, hopping the railing. Anna's breath caught in her throat. Roman! Roman, Roman, Roman.

"Good to meet you," said Roman, extending his right hand. "I'm sorry for the acrimony. That was not my intention." His speech had returned back to the chivalrous tones of some deluded knight.

Begrudgingly, Anna shook the man's hand. It felt rough and scarred. "My name is Anna. This is Alistair, Jim, Chris, Samantha, and Bob."

"And I'm Poppy," said Poppy, hiding behind Anna nervously.

Roman looked at the girl and smiled. "Well, it's nice to see such a little miss. Not many around nowadays. I am very pleased to meet you."

"Me too," said the large man who came over the railing last. He grinned at Poppy with crooked teeth. "Such a young girl."

Poppy shook hands with all three of the new men before giggling coyly at their apparent leader. "What happened to your hand?"

Roman didn't seem offended by the question. In fact, he smiled warmly. "I lost it a long time ago in an accident, long before the bad men started walking around. They say two hands are better than one, but I tell them that one hand is still better than none."

Anna placed a hand on Poppy's shoulder and manoeuvred the girl behind her. It wouldn't do to have her becoming too enamoured with the strangers.

The two men accompanying Roman were complete opposites. One man was fat, sweaty, and unwashed, with random zits covering a balding pate; the other was thin and older with a full head of grey hair falling all the way to his shoulders. His beard was clean and fluffy and gave him a wizened and friendly appearance. He introduced his name as 'Fox.' Instantly, Anna began to think of him as Grey Fox. The larger man introduced himself as 'Birch.'

"Take me to the man you're holding," Roman demanded. Anna shook her head in dismay and did nothing. Alistair took the three strangers and led them away.

Old man Bob, the resident elderly person of the pier at the ripe old age of sixty-four and a retired bus driver, stayed behind with Anna and Poppy whilst the other members of the group broke away to follow after the three guests. He was staring at Anna with his rheumy, grey eyes. "You all right, duck?" he asked her in his usual Yorkshire way.

Anna sighed. "I don't know. I think I'm being stupid."

"Why's that?"

"I have a problem handing over that injured man."

"They said he was a terrorist or something – a bad egg."

"If he's a bad egg," said Poppy. "We should give him up. The new people will be angry with us otherwise."

"Exactly," said Anna. "I shouldn't have a problem with this, but it just feels wrong somehow. I don't trust anyone anymore. I've been burned too many times before."

Bob smiled. Several of his teeth were missing and his dentures had gone bad with no fluid to sterilise them. "Not a bad way to be nowadays, duck. I think all of us survived by having a touch of the cynic about us. Doesn't pay to be too trusting, but hopefully, if we play ball with these new fellas, we might be able to tag along with all those boats. They seem to have their act together."

Anna stared out at the fleet. The numerous boats sat beneath the grey sky and bobbed up and down like writhing insects. She wasn't sure they were any better off out on the sea. It seemed unnatural to live away from land. "Would you enjoy being cooped up on a boat all the time?" she asked Bob.

The old man shrugged. "I think enjoyment went down the swanny along with everything else. Just being safe and sound is good enough for me. Unless you know a bookies that's still open."

"We're safe here," said Poppy. "But it's boring."

Bob smiled at the girl and tussled her hair. "We are very safe, little lass, but we'd be even safer out on the sea. Zombies don't have a cat in hell's chance of getting at us there, unless they learn how to doggy paddle."

Poppy's face screwed up in conflict. "I don't know which I want most. I like it here, but I want to go new places."

Anna cuddled her. "We'll all have a chat with the new men and sort something out." New men. Why does that thought fill me with dread? We haven't seen anyone in months and now a thousand-odd people turn up right on our doorstep. I didn't even know there was that many still left alive.

Anna had met so many desperate, struggling people in the first chaotic months when the infection hit that it had sullied her opinion of the human race forever. When law and order evaporated, those left alive had stole, fought, bullied, and even murdered for their own gain.

Women had wandered the streets raped and bloody. After leaving the amusement park with Rene, Anna had watched entire cities topple as much to desperation as to the dead. She was eternally grateful that she had become part of the little community at the pier. It was the only place she knew where people hadn't resorted to stabbing and killing each other over bottles of water. We're a family – a dysfunctional, messed-up family, but a family all the same. Maybe I'm wrong not to trust them more.

Muffled shouting erupted from the diner.

Alistair had taken the visitors into the diner several minutes ago, but now they were shouting. Anna felt herself grow pale. I knew this was going to go bad. She took Poppy by the hand and hurried towards the diner. Bob limped along behind them, trying to keep up. Once Anna reached the American-style eatery, she wasted no time stepping inside.

Roman had his spear against Alistair's throat and had shoved him backwards over one of the tables. His two companions were standing rigidly either side of him, their hands curled into fists.

"What the hell are you doing?" Anna demanded.

The man released Alistair and spun around. Alistair slumped to the floor, his blustery face as red as a blood-soaked rose. "Where is he?" Roman demanded, raising his spear so that it pointed right at Anna's face.

Anna frowned in confusion. She glanced across at the table where her patient had earlier been lying. There was no sign of him now, save for some blood spots and a scrap of dirty bandage.

"Where is he?" Roman demanded again.

"I don't know," said Anna. "He...he was here."

"Well, he ain't here now, luv."

"No shit."

Alistair straightened up off the floor, his legs wobbling. "H-he must have gotten up and escaped."

"Escaped?" said Anna. "He wasn't our prisoner. If he wanted to leave then good luck to him."

Roman snarled at her. He held the tip of his spear right up against her chest and spat a word at her. "Bitch!"

Anna bristled. "What did you just call me?"

"Calm down there, chuck," old man Bob pleaded. "No need for talk like that."

Anna's lip turned into a snarl. "You better get that thing out of my face before I break it off and whip you with it."

Roman glared at her for what seemed like minutes, but in fact must have been only seconds. Eventually he lowered his spear and grinned at her. There was no humour in the expression, though. "I don't know what game you muppets are trying to play, but there's a very powerful man sailing just a mile away from here, and if he doesn't get what he wants then bad things are going to start happening, you get me? I never came here to have a barny with you, I honestly didn't, but I'm following the orders of a geezer that don't give a shit either way."

"That's what the Nazis used to say," said Bob. "Just following orders."

Roman nodded. "And, like me, they had a gaffer with a nasty temper. I'm going to give you people a chance to save your arses. I'm going to camp here 'til morning. You have until then to produce the man I'm looking for. Otherwise I'm going to have to go back with bad news, and the captain won't like that. Tell you the truth, I don't even like the prick very much, but I do appreciate that he has the power to shag things right up for you lot. So be smart. Use your fucking loafs."

Roman marched out of the diner with Fox and Birch close behind him. Anna took in a deep breath and held it while Alistair gritted his teeth, bright red and seething. It was then that Anna noticed that the 'cripple' wasn't the only one who was missing. Where did Rene go?

POPPY

THE ADULTS WERE tense. They were all frowning and fidgeting. Anna kept chewing her nails and Alistair kept huffing and puffing. It was all because of the new men; the one with the silly name and his two friends. He don't look like a Roman to me. After the argument, the three men from the boat had said that they were not leaving. They were going to stay at the camp until the man with the poorly belly showed up again. Anna said the injured man had run away, but the Roman said that Anna was playing games. Then Anna told him to leave and when he refused she had got angry. Eventually, Poppy had decided to leave the adults to themselves. She was tired of all the shouting

She passed the time inside the games pavilion. It was a building shaped like a big tent at the very end of the pier and was full of arcade machines and indoor funfair rides. Poppy wished the machines still worked, but she knew none of them ever would again. They had died along with everything else. Funfair rides were just like the Roman coliseums now: dusty and broken. Does anything last forever?

Poppy sat down on a pretend motorbike fixed in front of a big television screen and imagined she was tearing down a road someplace, the sun shining down on her and mountains up ahead. She imagined she was heading away from the sea, away from the salty air that made her lips sore and her nose red. There were so many places out in the world and she wanted to visit them all. She wanted to ride a motorbike for real and parachute off a cliff. I want to leave this pier. I wish Garfield would take me.

With a sigh, she slipped her leg off the motorbike and hopped back down to the floor. As she landed, she thought she saw movement – a shadow flickering past a group of penny pusher machines in the middle of the pavilion.

"Hello? Is somebody there?" Maybe it's Rene. He was missing earlier when everybody was arguing. "Hello?" she repeated. "Is anybody there?"

There was no answer.

She must have been seeing things. The pier could be so lonely sometimes that her mind would wander all over the place. She would often get spooked when she was all on her own. It's stupid. Grown-ups never get scared.

She strolled over to the basketball machine. It was one of the few games that could still be played. The ball return didn't work without electricity, but you could reach over and grab the basketballs directly from the pit inside. The act of throwing a ball into a net was as fun as ever; it broke the monotony for a while. Sometimes Garfield would come and play with her, or they would remove one of the balls and play catch or football somewhere else. The basketballs weren't proper ones, so they didn't bounce very well, but they were easy to throw and kick.

Poppy arched back and let off a shot. The ball hit the backboard and teased around the basket. Eventually it tilted and fell through the metal rung. Poppy had gotten pretty good at making baskets.

"Good shot," said a voice behind her.

She spun around, her heart drumming against her ribs. It was one of the new men; the big fat one who said his name was Birch.

"You scared me," she said.

The man grinned. He was ugly with lots of spots and a bald head. "Sorry, sweetheart. I was just checking out where you people live. It's quite a place. Lots of space and things to do."

Poppy shook her head. "It's boring."

The man looked surprised. "Really? Where would you rather be?"

Poppy shrugged. She picked up another basketball and threw it. It went straight through the hoop this time with a satisfying swish. "Anywhere," she said. "I'm just tired of being stuck here."

The man came closer. "Maybe you could come with me. We go sailing everywhere out there on the sea. The things we see.... Every day is someplace new."

Poppy tried to imagine. "Really? You go exploring?"

"We do. Different countries, different islands. It's beautiful...and so much fun." He stared into space dreamily and grinned. The man didn't seem so scary anymore.

"Maybe Anna and Garfield will come," said Poppy.

"Whoever you want." He reached for her, but just as he did, someone shouted out from over by the pavilion's entrance.

It was Anna's voice. "Poppy? Are you in here?"

Poppy ran to her, darting between the various games in her way. "I'm here," she said. "I was just playing basketball and speaking with Mr Birch."

Anna put her arms around Poppy and peered into the pavilion. "Mr Birch? What is he doing here with you?"

Birch appeared from around the side of a change machine. "I was just checking out your digs and I stumbled upon the girl. She's very sweet."

Poppy nodded to confirm the story. Anna seemed angry but she didn't understand why.

Anna folded her arms. "Perhaps you should stay where we tell you to, Mr Birch. It's rude to make yourself at home on somebody else's property."

Birch grinned. A pimple on his chin seemed to stretch wider and burst. "Oh, I didn't realise this was your property. I assumed you were just squatting here. You'll have to tell me more about how your family built the pier. I'm sure it's fascinating."

Anna glared. "You know what I mean. We claimed this place. It's ours. Whoever used to own it is long dead."

"You assume."

"I know so, and if not then they are very welcome to come along and join us. Perhaps you should show a little more politeness, Mr Birch."

"As should you. A guest should be made to feel welcome." He glanced at Poppy and then back at Anna. "You should offer whatever comforts you can provide."

"Does that stand for uninvited guests as well?"

Birch bellowed, his fat belly rumbling with laughter as he strolled towards Anna. He shoved his way past her and headed back out to the deck, but before he left he said, "Even more so, my sweets. Even more so."

Anna grabbed Poppy by her shoulders and knelt down to face her. "You stay away from that man, you hear me?"

Poppy scrunched up her face. "He was saying we could go with him. They go everywhere on the sea. They go exploring."

Anna shook her and it hurt. "Poppy, listen to me. Do not go near that man. In fact, I am telling you to stay with me until the new men leave. You told Garfield you would listen to me, so do you promise?"

Poppy rolled her eyes.

"Do. You. Promise?"

Poppy huffed. "Fine. Yes, I promise."

"Good. Now come on. We should get something to eat before bed."

Poppy went along reluctantly.

They ended up having fish. No surprise there. Poppy wondered if the people on the boats ate nothing but fish. I bet they don't. I bet they find all sorts of good stuff on their travels. I bet they have sweets... and chocolate!

After dinner, everybody retired for the evening. It was winter and the nights got cold, so nobody wanted to hang around outside. Anna slept inside the gift shop and told Poppy that she had to do the same until Garfield came back, so she went and fetched a blanket from a pile on one the shelves and made herself a bed below a display of blow-up whales and sharks. The animals had all deflated a long time ago and now just looked like puddles of blue and grey plastic. The only light inside the shop was from a fat wax candle. There were lots of candles stored around the pier – one of the knickknack shops had sold them in all shapes and sizes – but the group decided only to start using them when the nights began to arrive early. Hopefully there would be enough to last a long time. I hate the dark. I'm such a baby.

Through the gift shop's window, Poppy could see out across the sea. Some of the boats were all lit up, with real lights – electric lights. She wondered how that was possible. Did they use petrol? Or did they have batteries? It almost seemed like magic now, so long had it been since she'd seen anything with power. I wonder if they have toys and games, like I used to have at home. I wonder if they watch cartoons and listen to music, like that silly woman who wore a telephone on her head and sang all those catchy tunes...I can't remember her name anymore. I wonder if people will ever get to be silly like that again, instead of serious all the time.

Thinking made Poppy sad, so she took one last look at the lights across the sea and closed her eyes. Maybe tomorrow we can talk about joining the men on the boats. We could all leave here.

Sleep didn't come easily that night. She listened to Anna's snoring for what seemed like hours while she lay awake wondering where Garfield was and what he would bring back upon his return. I heard him talking about guns. I don't want him to bring guns. Guns are dangerous. Why can't they bring back something nice, like a puppy, or a bicycle, or a bow and arrow...or a guitar...or...a...

Poppy must have been half-asleep when the hand on her arm caused her to flinch and sit upright. She peered around in the darkness, wondering what had just happened, wondering if she had merely woken from a nasty dream. I don't think I was having a nightmare...

But then Birch whispered in her ear. "Come with me, sweets. I want to show you something."

"Mr Birch?" she whispered.

"Sshhh," he said. "Just come with me."

Poppy was confused that the man would wake her in the middle of the night. Maybe he wanted to give her a gift, or talk to her more about living on the sea. Maybe he has sweets!

Poppy knew she shouldn't go with the man – Anna would be really mad – but if she was quiet, she could be back in bed without Anna ever knowing. I'll just be quick and see what Mr Birch wants, then come right back.

Carefully, Poppy crawled out from beneath her blanket and shivered as the cold air got at her. Birch wrapped his arm around her shoulders and she felt a little warmer. His hand was hot and sweaty against her skin. She wanted to look around for her cardigan but he never gave her time. "Come on," he whispered, "and keep quiet." he added. "The secret is just for you, so we can't wake anybody else, okay?" Poppy nodded. They stepped outside onto the moonlit deck and she asked where they were going. "Just to the end of the pier," he told her. "I want to get some sea air."

The end of the pier was where the games pavilion was located. It was far away, a five-minute walk. "Okay," she said, confused. "What do you want to show me when we get there?"

"You'll see."

"I hate surprises."

"You'll like this one."

Mr Birch led Poppy along the pier. They walked in silence, yet there was a subtle smile on the man's face, as if he wanted to laugh but dared not. Poppy sometimes wore that same expression when she was playing hide and seek and trying not to be discovered – the urge to laugh would always take over her and Garfield would find her in an instant.

"Here we go," said Birch, moving over to the railing at the end of the pier and waiting for her to join him.

"Can I see what you want to show me now, please?"

"Not yet, it's still a surprise."

"Oh, pleeease?" Poppy hopped up and down.

Birch shushed her. "Quiet! You don't want the others to hear us. It'll ruin our fun."

Poppy frowned. "I don't see what fun we're having yet."

Birch grinned at her. His teeth were a little crooked and the moonlight shone off them in all directions. He stepped up against her and started to rub her shoulders. It felt nice, but weird. She barely knew this man and he was touching her. Not even Garfield ever touched her like this. "What are you doing?"

"Just being a friend. Doesn't that feel good?"

"Sort of. It feels weird."

Birch rubbed deeper, his thumbs and fingers probing over her neck, shoulders, and chest. "People used to make each other feel good all the time back before things got so hard. It only feels weird because nobody ever taught you about making another person feel good. Do you want to learn?"

Poppy chewed at her lip. She suddenly felt very alone with this man, yet he wanted to teach her things – and treat her like an adult. "I guess so," she eventually said.

Birch smiled and leaned closer. He planted a soft kiss on her cheek and Poppy could smell the sweat on him. "Good girl," he whispered. "Now, you rub me."

Poppy reached forward. Her hands were trembling. When her fingertips were only inches away from his neck, Birch grabbed her wrists. "No," he said. "That's not where you rub a man." He kept a firm hold on her wrist and began to move her hand downwards, towards his...

Poppy pulled away.

Birch twisted her arm and made her cry out. He grabbed her chin with his other hand and snarled right in her face. "Now you be quiet, you little cunt, or I'll throw you over the railing and watch you drown. I'll say you was messing around and fell in. Adults never trust children so they'll believe me. Behave, little girl, or else."

Poppy whimpered. "Please," she begged.

Birch ignored her and shoved her hand up against his crotch. She cringed as she felt something hard and warm beneath his trousers. "There you go," he said, shuddering. "Now you're learning."

"Step the hell away from her."

Birch released Poppy's hand and spun around. Poppy fell to the deck and and started wailing. She looked up through her tears and saw a man emerging from the shadows. It was Alistair. Am I going to be in trouble? Alistair is always telling me to behave and I've been really bad. Really really bad. I've let Anna down. I promised to stay with her.

Birch straightened and smiled merrily. "Hello, there. Not just me who has trouble sleeping then, I see? How are you doing tonight, friend?"

Alistair's eyes narrowed into slits. "I'm doing just fine. I told you to step away from the girl."

"Of course. I was just having a chat with her."

"Like hell you were. Poppy, sweetheart, come over to me." Poppy leapt up off the floor and raced over to Alistair. She felt safer as he shoved her behind him, but even so, she couldn't help but tremble and sob. I don't understand what's happening.

Birch put his hands out in front of him and clasped them together like he was saying a prayer. "I think there's some sort of misunderstanding here, friend."

"He made me touch his thing," said Poppy between sobs.

Alistair patted Poppy on her head but kept his eyes on Birch. "Seems like things are pretty clear to me."

"This is ridiculous." Birch went to walk back down the deck, but Alistair blocked him. The two men stood and stared at each other. Both of their big bellies wobbled.

"Get out of my way." Birch snarled.

Alistair shook his head with disgust. It was the same face he pulled whenever they had crab for dinner. Alistair hated crab. He made a snorting sound, too, like the rhinos at the zoo. "Who the hell are you people?" he demanded. "Pirates and Paedophiles? I guess the world's a playground, huh?" He turned his head and spat on the deck. "I have more respect for the dead."

Poppy grimaced. Alistair didn't usually spit; her mummy told her it was a dirty habit.

Birch's eyes narrowed and he licked his lips. "Watch yourself, friend. You don't want this fight, believe me." He went to move past Alistair again, but Alistair blocked him same as before. Birch snarled and went to say something, but didn't get a chance.

Alistair punched him right in the face. Poppy was shocked and frightened, but also a little glad. He should hit him again. Birch stumbled backwards, but didn't go down. He spat blood and swore loudly. Then he rushed at Alistair with his fists in the air. Alistair ran to meet him head-on, like a charging bull, and the two men collided. Birch rolled back on his heels, off-balance, and Alistair hit him in the face again.

This time Birch went down and his nose began to bleed. "You're a dead man," he snarled from on his back.

Alistair laughed. "You're the fat knacker sat on his arse, not me."

Birch leapt up and came at Alistair again. This time Alistair kicked the man in the shin. Birch flinched and bent over to grab his poorly leg, which allowed Alistair to drive his knee up into his face and send him flying backwards. Poppy winced at the cracking sound.

Birch hit the deck again. Blood covered his face and looked like an oil slick under the moonlight. Poppy scurried away and cowered behind the pier's rusty pretzel stand. She wanted the violence to be over, but couldn't help but watch. Alistair was winning, but the fighting was still making her tummy sick. I don't like it.

Birch clambered unsteadily to his feet again. His snarling, blood-soaked face made him look like a monster. Poppy watched him pull something shiny from his belt, and when she saw that it was a knife she almost threw-up in fear.

"You don't want to take it to that level," Alistair growled, but he suddenly seemed less sure of himself. Poppy's heart beat fast. Boom boom

boom. If Alistair got hurt, would the bad man get her again? I don't want to touch his thing.

Birch came forward with the knife. The metal caught the moonlight as he waved it back and forth. Alistair stood his ground. Then Birch pounced, much quicker than a man his size should have been able to. He thrust out with the knife and managed to slash Alistair, who was barely able to sidestep in time to avoid the knife entering his ribs. Blood poured from a newly opened gash on his left forearm.

Poppy placed a hand over her mouth.

Birch swiped the knife again, but this time he missed completely. Alistair grabbed at the man and tried to wrestle the weapon away. Poppy stood frozen while the two men shoved and twisted against one another, each of them battling to gain control over the knife.

Just as it seemed like Alistair was getting the upper hand, Birch head-butted him right on top of the nose. Blood exploded from his face and sent him staggering backwards.

Birch leapt forward, knife plunging through the air.

Poppy screamed out as loud as she could.

The noise distracted Birch for a split second and Alistair was able to react in time to block the knife attack and lock in a bear hug. The wrestling match continued.

Poppy could watch no more. She had to get help. She had to get Anna or...someone. Before she knew it, she was racing back down the pier, screaming and shouting for someone to come. She would have called for Garfield, but he was not there. I told him not to leave.

Poppy thanked God when she went hurtling into Anna. "What is it?" she asked her. "What the bloody hell are you doing out here in the middle of the night? Garfield is going to be so upset that you disobeyed me."

"It's Alistair," Poppy spluttered. "He needs your help."

"Alistair, why, what?"

Poppy grabbed Anna by the arm and pulled her. "Just come, quick." She raced back towards the end of the pier, taking Anna with her. Anna demanded explanations, but there was no time. Alistair was in danger.

They reached the end of the pier and the two men were still fighting. Alistair now bled from a wound on his chest as well as the one on his forearm. Birch still held the knife and was swinging it through the air wildly.

"What the hell?" said Anna.

Alistair spotted her and shouted out. "Anna, you need to get the others. He was trying to hurt Poppy. We need to make the new men leave."

Anna looked down at Poppy and frowned in confusion.

Poppy looked at her and tried not to cry as she spoke. "He tried to make me touch his thing."

Anna seemed to glow bright red in an instant and a scary look came over her face. She trembled for a moment, clenching and unclenching her fists. Then she ran straight at Birch. The man turned to face her, but he was too late to stop her from kicking him right in the balls. Poppy didn't have balls but she winced all the same. Ouch!

Birch said a bad word as the breath exploded out of him all at once. He swung his knife at Anna's face, but Alistair tackled him just as the blade was about to part her cheek. The two men tumbled to the ground and resumed their fighting, rolling around like duelling cats, biting and scratching and punching. Blood spattered everywhere.

Alistair was on top.

And then Birch.

Then Alistair again.

Then Birch got the upper hand. He had the knife and was on top of Alistair again.

Anna kicked Birch in the back just as he was about to plunge the knife into Alistair's chest. She kicked him so hard that he bucked forward and dropped the weapon completely. The blade skittered across the deck and came to a stop over by the railing. Alistair punched Birch in the face three times and the man finally stopped struggling. He slumped forward and fell asleep.

The fighting was over.

Anna dragged Birch away from Alistair who remained on his back, panting. Poppy stayed by the pretzel cart, trying to catch her breath but finding that her lungs had turned to sand.

There was nothing but silence for a long time. Only the sound of people breathing.

Eventually Alistair let out a moan from on his back. Blood stained the front of his shirt, but belonged to Birch as much as it did him. Poppy went and knelt beside him, before giving him a great big hug. "Are you okay?"

"I'm fine, lass. Another fine mess you've got me into, huh." Poppy laughed. She had always hated the way Alistair moaned at her and told her off, but she was glad of it now. If he were gone she would miss him. He went to get up off the deck but collapsed back down again and moaned again. "I'm too fat for this nonsense," he muttered.

Poppy giggled. "You are a bit fat."

Alistair rolled his eyes. "Bloody charming! I save you and that's the thanks I get, huh."

Poppy kissed him on the cheek. "Thank you."

Alistair gave her a serious look. "Are you okay, sweetheart?"

Poppy nodded but felt like she needed to cry. She tried to be brave and didn't.

"I'm sorry I didn't find you sooner, girl," said Alistair. "If not for the fact I'm so paranoid, I may not have found you at all. I knew those men were trouble after the way they behaved in the diner. I was up and about, making sure they weren't up to no good. Worst I expected was theft, but not...this."

"I didn't do anything," Birch said between laboured breaths. He'd woken up again, but was still flat on the deck. "You people just screwed up big time. You'll pay for this."

Anna booted the man in the face and sent him back to sleep. Poppy winced. "He was hurting me," she told Alistair, "but you stopped him before he did anything really bad. Why did he want me to do those things?"

Alistair sighed. "One day you'll understand, but it's not something a young girl should worry about. Stay a child for as long as you can, because it don't get any easier with age."

"I thought you said I had to grow up and start being useful."

"And when did you ever listen to me?"

"I'm listening to you now."

"Well, I was wrong. You grow up when you're good and ready." He kissed her on the forehead.

"Everything's okay now," Anna told her. "Nobody is going to hurt you."

Footsteps on the deck made them all look up. It was Roman and the older man called Fox. Roman had his sword drawn and was glaring at them all. "You just made a big mistake," he said.

DAMIEN

DAMIEN COULDN'T BELIEVE what he was seeing. Birch was bloody and beaten, lying half-conscious like Sonny Liston with the woman standing over him like Ali. Birch had come ashore in peace, an envoy for the fleet, and these idiots had beaten him half to death. The woman, Anna, who Damien had met with earlier, was standing over Birch with a defiant look on her face, while her fat companion was bleeding on the ground nearby with the little girl in plaits kneeling beside him. What the hell did I just miss?

Birch was no friend of Damien's, he barely knew the man, but his treatment was inexcusable. This tiny group of survivors at the pier seemed intent on defiance at every turn. They were protecting the cripple he was after, and now they had done this. Were the fools planning to turn their attacks on Damien next? Would he be forced to cut them down and return to the Kirkland soaked in their blood? He hoped not, but he was willing to do what was necessary. "You just made a big mistake," he said, staring down at Birch.

Surprisingly, it was not the fat man or the woman who came forward with an explanation, but the young girl, Poppy. "He started it," she said, pointing her finger at Birch. "He took me out here all alone and was trying to get me to touch his thing. Alistair was just stopping him."

Damien's mouth fell open. "Wha...?

"It's okay, Poppy," said Alistair, dragging himself up off the floor and patting her on the arm. "There's nothing to be afraid of anymore."

Damien narrowed his eyes. Had Birch really been attempting something unthinkable? The man was lying on his back covered in his own blood, but when Damien spotted the man's own knife lying on over by the railing, he began to have concerns. "Birch, can you get up? I need to know what happened."

Birch moaned and rolled onto his side. "Give me a second." Everybody stood by in silence while he struggled up to his knees and then eventually onto his feet. The man's nose was bloody and bent. His lower lip was swollen.

"What the hell happened here, Birch?" Damien demanded.

Birch spat a mouthful of blood, and when he spoke his words were wet and spluttery. "They attathed me for no reathen."

Alistair disagreed immediately. His plump face was a picture of hostility. "You tried to assault a child!"

"Lieths."

"Quiet," said Damien. He stood there impassively, trying to make sense of the situation. *Who do I believe? My own man, surely? But what if he's guilty?* In the end Damien decided to get the truth from the horse's mouth. He turned to the young girl, Poppy, and asked her what had happened. *If she lies, I'll know. She's just a kid.*

The girl looked pale and frightened, but when she answered her words were clear and confident. "He wanted me to touch his thing. He grabbed my arm and told me he would throw me off the deck if I tried to struggle."

Alistair snorted angrily.

Birch denied the accusations.

Damien rubbed at his forehead with the back of his forearm. "Please tell me they have the wrong end of the stick here, Birch."

"Yeah," Fox chimed in. "Because if it's true, you're the one who should take a trip over the railing, Birch. Only a monster would hurt a child."

Damien gave Fox a chastising look. The last thing he needed was one of his men condemning the other. "Is it true, Birch? What the girl says?"

Birch cleared his throat and managed to speak clearly. "No, of course not. I was out here, taking in the night, when the girl came running around the corner like a bat out of hell. We was chatting for a while, but then the next thing I know, this fat shit is taking a swing at me."

Alistair snarled. "You've got a few rolls there yourself, mate. Least I can get myself a woman, instead of going after kids, huh."

"Quiet," said Damien.

"Who are you to quiet us?" said Anna.

"All I know is that you've assaulted one of the men sent here in friendship. Not to mention that you're harbouring a terrorist of the fleet. I'm in a fine goddamn position to make demands. In fact, I think it would be bloody cushty if you people stopped playing silly beggars and gave me what I came for. You're starting to get right on my tits."

Alistair spat. "We ain't giving you nothing."

Damien sliced his sword downwards in an arc and slit a furrow into the fat man's blubbery gut. His shirt tore away and blood appeared. "Give me what I ask for," said Damien, "or I'll take it in strips of bacon." Poppy cried out as Alistair fell backwards onto his elephantine backside. "It's okay," Damien assured her. "He's not hurt. I was just giving him a warning." It was true enough that the blow had been intended only to split a few layers of skin. There was more to gain from a threat than a murder.

The little blonde girl looked up at him with fire burning in her eyes. "You're a bad man."

"They're all bad," said Alistair from the floor, clutching his belly with his bloodstained fingers. "Nothing but bullies."

Damien frowned. While he didn't consider himself a good man exactly, he didn't consider himself a bully either. I'm not trying to hurt these people; don't they see that? Why are they acting like I'm the enemy? The fat guy looks like he wants to kill me, and the woman looks like she'll want to piss on my remains.

Damien bristled. He was unsure how to proceed. He didn't know whether their accusations against Birch were true or not, but he knew that they at least believed them to be. Damien was an unwanted guest who had brought trouble to their doorstep. They weren't about to compromise with a man they saw as defending a rapist. Even an alleged rapist.

Damien lowered his sword. "Look, I don't know what happened here. All I can say is that my sole intention is to locate the man I came here for. I don't want to cause you people any more trouble than I have to, but I'm not leaving here until I have him."

Anna folded her arms across her chest. "He's not here. You already know that."

"I know that's what you say."

"They're a pack of liars," spat Birch. "They have him hidden somewhere."

"You're the liar," said Poppy in a voice as forceful as any adult. Girl needs a good hiding.

"I'm not leaving," said Damien. "I can't."

Anna laughed at him spitefully. "Well, then we're shit out of luck, because you say you're not leaving, but I promise you that you are. Either you go nicely or we'll send you back to your precious mothership in bait buckets."

Damien sighed. "You're not being smart. I'll fight you all if I have to."

"And I'll back you up," said Fox.

"Try and stop me," snarled Birch.

Alistair laughed. "You think you can cut us all down? I dare you to try."

Damien raised his sword and let out a long sigh. "Don't make me do this. Just hand over the man I came for." I really don't want to have to do this.

"We don't have him," said Anna.

"I don't believe you." Don't make me do this. You're pushing me.

Anna shrugged. "Then you'd be best off leaving."

Damien glared at the woman. Her stony gaze showed no signs of wavering. Her brown eyes were like orbs of conviction. "I can't leave," he said coolly. "Not without the man I came for."

"For the last time, he's not here."

She's not going to budge. She has balls as big as I do. Damien gripped his sword tightly, preparing to use it. But violence isn't going to solve anything. That's not why I'm here. From the corner of his eye, Damien saw Birch move. He was edging along the deck towards the railing. Damn it, Birch. Don't do it.

"He's going for his knife," shouted Poppy. "Stop him."

Alistair charged at Birch, but Birch was quicker. He couldn't get a decent grip on the handle in time, but was able to smash the grip into the fat man's nose, dropping him to the deck.

"Stop," shouted Damien. "Birch, stand down. This is not helping."

Birch turned on Damien and snarled. "Fuck you, Roman. This prick broke my nose."

"Stand down!"

Birch ignored him and marched over to Alistair. The man was clutching his face and bleeding heavily from a broken nose. "Now we're even, you fat fuck," snarled Birch. "But maybe I need to teach you a lesson on top."

Damien shoved Birch aside just as he was about to deliver a kicking to the downed man. "Will you cool it, you bloody muppet!"

"Calm down, Birch," said Fox. "You're acting like a bleedin' psychopath?"

"He is a psychopath," said Alistair, spitting blood onto the deck as he propped himself up on his elbow. "He's a kiddie fiddler, too."

Birch exploded with rage. "You're a dead man."

Damien tried to restrain Birch, but the larger man threw a punch and struck him on the jaw. Damien's vision exploded with stars and he stumbled sideways.

Birch charged at Alistair and booted him in the ribs. Alistair cried out in agony. Anna dove at Birch and clung to his back, clawing at his face. Birch thrust his head backwards and caught her under the chin. She dropped to the floor like a sack of spuds.

Birch resumed his attack on Alistair, standing over the man and snarling like a wolverine. He raised his knife in the air, blade pointed downwards. "Say goodnight, you fat piece of shit."

Alistair grinned wide. Blood stained his teeth red. "Kiddie fiddler."

Birch roared and plunged his knife downwards.

Damien had shaken the stars from his vision but had not recovered quickly enough to stop Birch. As it turned out, it was Poppy who managed to stop him from killing Alistair.

A split-second before Birch drove his knife into Alistair's gut, the young girl barrelled into him from the side. He stumbled onto one knee, cursing, but was quickly upright again. He glared at Poppy and snarled. "You little bitch!"

He slashed his knife at her face.

She screamed.

Damien leapt. Drove his spear into Birch's ribs. Yanked it free. Stabbed again.

Birch wheezed and dropped down onto his knees. Then he started bleeding...badly. He glared at Damien and went to speak, but only blood spilled from his mouth. He fell face down on the deck and stopped breathing, looking like a washed-up seal.

Poppy staggered backwards, a small sliver of blood on her cheek where the tip of Birch's knife had kissed her. I saved her just in time.

Fox was shaking his head and pacing. "This is a complete mess. Jesus. What the hell, Roman? You killed Birch"

Damien swallowed back a mouthful of bile. "I had no choice."

"No, you didn't," Anna said quickly. "Birch tried to hurt a child and you stopped him. You had no choice."

You people gave me no choice. Damien stared down at Birch's body and let out a snarl. "I came here to collect a criminal. If you people hadn't messed me around then this would never have happened. I wish you'd just fucking lied about having him here in the first place."

"He's not here," Anna said. "He was, I admit it, but he disappeared. I don't know where he is. I'm telling you the truth."

"I'm here," said a voice, which caused them all to turn their heads as one. Damien's eyes narrowed. There you are indeed.

The cripple was striding down the pier on his double crutches like some strange insect. A slender black man walked beside him with a look of noble concern upon his face. The remaining members of the pier approached, too, several paces behind. Suddenly Damien and Fox were outnumbered ten to two. I really shouldn't have killed Birch.

"Here I am," said the man who Damien had shot just a few days ago. "I hope you're not disappointed to see me alive. I owe my life to the kind people of this pier. They patched me up and kept me safe until I had some of my strength back. I must have a guardian angel for them to have found me in the state you left me in."

"I must own the blame for having hid him," said the black man in a soft African accent. "We have been beneath the pier," he added. "On the sands."

The cripple hobbled forward on his crutches. "You wanted me, Roman, so here I am. But why don't you tell these people what this is really about before you take me away."

"This is about you rigging a bomb in the Kirkland's engine room. Over three-hundred people would have died if you'd set the bloody thing off – not to mention the danger it would have posed to the rest of the fleet."

The cripple grunted and edged closer on his crutches. In the moonlight of the pier, his copper hair looked silver, as if the night itself were an alchemist. His ripped t-shirt was heavily bloodstained, but it was obvious his wound was healing. He wouldn't have been on his feet if it were not. "You're absolutely right," he said. "I did try to bomb the Kirkland, but not to kill innocent people. There's just one man I mean to kill."

Damien pointed his sword out to sea, over towards where he imagined the Kirkland to be positioned in the darkness. "The captain. Samuel."

"Yes, Samuel Raymeady, former CEO of Black Remedy Corporation. Former billionaire and all-around badass dude. I hear Time magazine were about to do a cover on him just before everyone went all Night of the Living Dead. A shame, really."

Anna's eyes went wide. "Samuel Raymeady? You mean the richest man in the world is in charge of all the boats out there?"

"Makes sense," said Alistair. "The richest man in the world probably had a better chance of surviving than anybody else bloody well did, huh."

Damien growled. "It makes no difference who the captain is or used to be. He's the reason all those people out there are alive right now – him and the money he put to good use when it mattered. He's a hero and you tried to kill him, along with a bunch of innocent people."

"So it's true?" Anna asked the cripple. "You did try to blow up the ship?"

"I did, yes, although I failed quite epically. I have no idea how they discovered my plan."

"Then I can't protect you," she said. "You're guilty."

Damien lowered his weapon and turned to Fox. "Thank Christ for that. We can finally get the hell out of here. Fox, go and grab him. I want to get off this pier before anything else goes wrong."

"What about Birch? Should we bring him back with us?"

Damien shook his head. "I'm sure our friends here will do the honour of tossing him in the sea. Best place for him."

"But he was one of us. We should-"

"He was a bloody moron, and the reason this situation went so far south. Long as we get the cripple back, that's all that matters. Samuel won't care about the rest."

The cripple tutted. "I do wish you'd stop calling me that. My name is Tim, not 'cripple'. I'll go with you willingly," he said, struggling with his crutches. "But just let me share a little secret before you take me off to be executed."

Damien took a step forward and raised his sword. "You've got nothing I want to hear. I've already killed one man tonight. Don't make me finish what I started with you several days ago."

"I think you should hear him out," said the African man.

"Do you know something, Rene?" Anna asked. "Is that why you hid him?"

"Yes, he tells an interesting tale."

Anna nodded. "Then I want to hear what he has to say."

Damien shook his head and grunted. "I'm not interested in stories. If you don't come with me now, you're going to get these people killed."

"Then you should let him speak quickly," said Anna. "The night has been long enough already. What are a few more minutes going to hurt?"

Damien shrugged. "Fine. Speak. Then you're coming with me."

The cripple propped himself up tall on his crutches so that everyone could see him clearly. When he spoke he spoke slowly, as if he did not want a single word to be misheard. "The man in charge of that Royal Navy frigate is Samuel Raymeady, former CEO of the UK-American conglomerate, Black Remedy Corporation. As its majority shareholder, he gained control of the organisation after the death of his biological father and mother, their American partner, Vincent Black, and all of that man's heirs as well – their collective demise is a coincidence, I assure you. Since taking over the company, Samuel Raymeady has had one intention – controlling the world, and then destroying it. With all his wealth, power, and numerous philanthropic facades, he made the world love him, which allowed him to succeed with his life's work. That work is clear for all to see. He brought it all down on us. He caused the apocalypse, just to prove he could. I imagine it's the ultimate power trip for a man that has already risen as far as any man can go. With unlimited wealth, power, and respect, what else is there but to become a god?"

Everyone stood in shocked silence. Damien shook his head in disbelief. These people are buying it. I've never heard such a load of bollocks in my life.

The cripple pointed to Damien. "This man here was the man who shot me, and he claims that Samuel Raymeady saved all of those people out there on the sea, but that's not the truth. The truth is that Samuel Raymeady killed all but a few of us. The virus that took everything, the ungodly bio-weapon that wiped out 99% of the world's population, was his sole creation. He made it, he released it, and he is responsible. Samuel Raymeady is the Devil, and from the ashes of the world he hopes to become a god. Those boats out there are his nation, and with them he hopes to build an empire. An empire of the damned."

Damien gripped his sword tightly and waved his spear arm through the air in a furious slash. "The world has ended, you muppet. We've lost doctors, scientists, Olympic athletes, inventors, and yet despite all that, we're still stuck with deluded maniacs trying to blow people up because of misplaced blame. It's ironic, that even now the world has been crushed to dust, there are still madmen combing over the rubble and trying to find a crusade to kill people for."

The cripple wobbled on his crutches and suddenly seemed to weaken. His wound was obviously still taking a heavy toll on him. "Perhaps I am a little nutty – I certainly wonder about my state of mind after all I've seen – but I promise you that I didn't imagine Samuel Raymeady breaking my back when he was an eight year old boy. Not that anyone ever believed he was guilty – angel-faced little monster that he was. There were, of course, a few other true believers that joined my cause over time. Monopoly commissioners ignored at every turn, victims of Samuel's aggressive corporate expansion tactics, competitors who stood in his way and were crushed, and even a group of priests who believed him to be the antichrist. We all tried to expose Samuel's true intentions, but each of us was dismissed as hacks or paranoid fantasists. Samuel was too well loved and beyond reproach. Any deep digging into his affairs would be blocked at every turn. He controlled everything."

Anna put her hands up and rubbed her face. "Whoa, whoa, whoa. This is frying my head. Are you saying that Samuel Raymeady, the world's biggest philanthropist, tried to exterminate mankind?"

"And broke your back?" Alistair added.

Anna cleared her throat. "Yeah, and that."

Tim nodded. "Pushed me from the balcony of his home – but that's a jaunty little caper to be told some other time. That was when I first met Samuel Raymeady. I've been keeping tabs on him ever since: hacking his computers, researching his financial activities, generally spying on him in whichever ways I could. I managed to gain a little traction on the Internet, and even got a few column inches in the paper, but Samuel wielded too much power – most of the press were in his pocket along with most politicians. It was impossible to stop what he was planning. I was helpless to do anything as he loaded a cruise liner full of deadly virus and sent it sailing for mainland Europe with a crew of doomed souls. I tried to leak his plans, and so did my colleagues, but the newspapers, the authorities, Samuel's competitors, didn't want to hear it. They dismissed me as a crank. Bet they wished they'd listened to me when the infection finally hit. That cruise liner was Samuel's Trojan horse and the whole world was his Troy."

Anna frowned. "Are you talking about the cruise liner that sank in the Med over a year ago? How could it have released a virus in Europe if it sunk?"

"Rescue workers contracted the virus from the wreckage and took it with them inland. It was all over then."

Damien stabbed the point of his sword against the deck with a thud! "What an absolute crock. This is all just a load of nonsense you read in an airport thriller novel." He turned to the members of the pier. "This lunatic isn't worth your lives. Hand him over."

"If I'm such lunatic, then why did I have help rigging the bomb on the Kirkland?" He grinned at Damien mockingly. "That's why your glorious dictator wants me dead so badly. He knows someone else aboard the Kirkland is working against him, but he also knows that I will never give up the name of my co-conspirator. But my death will serve to send a clear message to my partner not to try anything again. It would also stop me telling my story to the people on his precious ship. Last thing he wants is a mutiny. Don't you think it's strange that he sent you ashore to kill me several days ago, Roman? Why not bring me in to answer for my crimes? I'm only a poor cripple after all."

"I'm bringing you in now," said Damien.

"Only because Samuel doesn't want the people on this pier to see his mercilessness. They may yet be of use to him; there's no point scaring them unduly." He looked down at Birch, face down on the deck. "Although, I think you might have ballsed that up already, though. Nice going, hero."

Damien was out of words. Was the reason Samuel was so adamant that Tim be killed that he did not wish the man to share his wild conspiracy theories? Was he so afraid of this man's insane ramblings? Who would believe such a far-fetched tale anyway? And what about the man's co-conspirator? "Tell me who your partner is," Damien demanded, "or so help me I'll cut you down right now and your new buddies will have to sweep you off the deck."

Tim looked amused by what he was about to say, like a Barrister ready to present a killer piece of evidence in some grand courtroom. "Of course, I'll tell you," he said. "It's somebody you know, Roman — a good friend of yours, in fact. As I understand it, he's the only friend you have. Which, might I just say, is pretty sad."

No.... Damien swallowed. "Harry?"

"Yes," Tim said. There was a belittling smirk on his bony, unshaven face. "Harry and I were working together. When he heard my story, he was more than willing to help. He's a good man, but you already know that, right? He pretty much brought you up, or so he told me? So, Roman, tell me, do you still want to take me back to the Kirkland? What if Samuel breaks me? What will become of your only friend then?"

"You lie!"

"Speak to him, Roman – or should I call you Damien."

He knows my name. Only Harry knows my name. Damien felt feint. If Samuel found out that Harry was conspiring he would kill him. Is it even the truth? Or just the cripple's veiled threat? If I take him aboard, will he insinuate that Harry is a terrorist? Is that his play here? Is he using Harry as leverage?

Could Harry be a terrorist?

No way. I know Harry. He would never hurt anybody. He helped me when nobody else would. We survived the apocalypse together.... He would never keep something like this from me.... No, he would have told me. Damien stumbled backwards towards the railing. He suddenly felt very weak. "Come on, Fox," he said, sheathing his sword. "We're leaving. These muppets deserve whatever they get."

"You want to leave without him?" asked Fox, nodding towards the cripple. The man was such a worrier, and Damien had no time for it right now.

"Yes, without him."

"But he said he'd come voluntarily."

Damien shrugged and swung a leg over the railing. "Ask him to come then."

Fox turned around and faced the cripple. "Will you come with us?"

Tim chuckled. "I changed my mind. I'd quite like to stay here if my hosts will have me."

"You're very welcome," said Anna.

"But you gave your word," said Fox, flummoxed.

"I'm a terrorist, remember? I have no honour. My word counts for shit."

Damien snorted. "There's your answer, Fox. I'm not about to start a fight that's ten to two against us. If you want to stay behind and scrap, then go for it, but I'm going back to the Kirkland. Samuel can deal with this shit later." The rope down to the yacht was still attached and Damien started to descend it, but the woman, Anna, stopped him. For a moment he expected to be attacked.

"It doesn't have to be like this," she said. "We should trade, share information. There's too few of us left to be enemies. You killed your own man to protect us."

"To protect a child."

"Exactly. You did what was right."

"You talk to me about doing right, but are you willing to hand over that man? A man who admits he is a terrorist."

Anna glanced at the cripple and then back at Damien. "Do you believe what he says?"

Damien went to say 'no', but found himself stuttering. "I-I...don't know. It's crazy."

Anna nodded. "You need to talk to your friend, Harry, don't you?"

"Yes," said Damien. He couldn't deny that speaking to Harry was the only thing on his mind right then.

"Well, until you do," said Anna. "Until you have no doubt that this man is guilty of trying to commit cold-blooded murder for no good reason, then I cannot in good conscience hand him over. If your captain is responsible for...well, everything, then-"

"Then I can't help you," said Damien, and he was telling the truth. Samuel would send more men to the pier as soon as he found out the cripple was there. The fact that Damien was coming back empty handed would make Samuel furious. He'll kill them all. He'll send a dozen men ashore with guns from the armoury.

Damien had once witnessed Samuel fire the ship's cannons at a petroleum tanker that would not share its fuel with the fleet. The hit had torn the ship almost in two. The mere danger of the fuel tanks going up in a huge fireball had been enough to make those still living surrender. They worked as kitchen staff on the Kirkland now. Samuel had been willing to destroy the tanker rather than be denied use of it.

Damien gave Anna one last piece of advice. "You should move on from here."

"This is our home."

"Then enjoy it while you can." Damien shimmied back down to the yacht and waited while Fox came to join him. The older man was surprisingly limber and made it down the rope much quicker than Damien had – although he did have use of both hands.

Damien unhitched the mooring rope and Fox started the motor and shoved the boat into reverse. They puttered away from the pier and were heading back towards the frigate in less than a minute, passing by various boats idling at the edge of the fleet. On the horizon, a tinge of orange had appeared, heralding the arrival of the morning sun. *I need sleep. I can't process any of this until my head is straight.*

Fox banged his fist down on the centre of the steering wheel. "The captain is going to shit a brick when we return empty handed, Roman. We were told to recover the cripple at all costs and we're just walking away."

"I know."

"He won't like that you killed Birch either. He was part of the Kirkland's roster. We didn't even bring his body with us. He has friends aboard the ship."

"I know."

"And when Samuel hears about your friend, Harry, being involved in everything he's going to string the fella up by his ears."

No! Damien drove his spear through Fox's back, slumping the old man over the steering wheel. Blood poured from his open mouth and splattered the windshield. *Fuck fuck fuck. What did I just do? That's the second man I've killed in the last hour. I am so screwed. I am so screwed.*

Damien froze. He stared down at the blood dripping from his spear. Murder was taken very seriously in the fleet and he'd just committed the act for the second time – and this time in cold blood. There would be no mercy for Damien if Samuel found out about Fox. His sentence would be harsh. *All of Samuel's sentences are harsh. That's why I can't let him find out about Harry. Not until I know the truth.*

Glancing around for spectators, Damien carefully folded the old man over his shoulder and carried him to the edge of the yacht. *I'm* sorry, Fox. You seemed like an okay guy. He slid the body over the railing and let it sink into the sea. Fox's body was light and floated on the surface of the water. Damien held his breath while he waited for it to descend beneath the wave. The boats and ships all around him were shrouded in the darkness of early dawn. Any of them could have been watching him.

There could be a dozen witnesses. Or none. I just need to stay calm.

Eventually Fox's limp body slipped beneath the sea and Damien took control of the yacht's motor. He continued on towards the frigate. He had no idea what the hell he was going to do, but the first thing was to talk to Harry. My dear old friend has a lot of explaining to do, and if the answers are all wrong, I might just have to kill him, too.

HUGO

HUGO CROUCHED DOWN behind the railings of his yacht. He held Houdini in his arms and prayed the little dog did not bark. *If he makes a sound, the man will see us.*

Having once been a heavy smoker, Hugo had woken at dawn craving nicotine. With cigarettes all but non-existent – not to mention his specific brand of Gitanes – the best he could do was go outside to breathe some fresh air. That was when he had seen the other boat.

It was not uncommon to see other people out on their boats so early in the morning – many of the fleet's fishermen would rise well before the sun to haul in their catches – but what Hugo had witnessed was most definitely not a common occurrence. *I think I just witnessed a murder. Bon sang!*

Hugo had been rubbing the sleep from his eyes when he'd noticed a small yacht puttering away from the shore. He'd heard rumours that there were many people living on the nearby pier, and that a greeting party had sailed out from the Kirkland to meet with them. There was yet to be any word on whether or not the new people were friendly, and every time Hugo asked one of the other boats what was happening, they would tell him that the greeting party from the Kirkland had yet to return. Hugo had assumed that the yacht coming towards him was that team finally coming home.

The yacht had stopped suddenly and sputtered to a standstill. Shadows moved within its small pilothouse. Hugo had stared intently, trying to make out the details. Eventually, a grey silhouette came into focus; a man, carrying something over his shoulder. Hugo hadn't realised it was a body until the man dumped it over the side and let it sink beneath the waves. It was then that Hugo leapt down and hid. Houdini had been sleeping outside as usual and had come up to Hugo for a friendly sniff. Hugo fussed the dog and patted his belly in an attempt to keep him quiet. Praise the lord it had worked. Before long the other yacht revved its engine and resumed its journey, heading towards the Kirkland until it was out of sight. Hugo stayed hidden for several more minutes before finally straightening up with a click of his knees. I pray they did not see me. I have daughters to protect.

Houdini let out a shrill bark, almost as if he'd been waiting for the chance to do so. Hugo patted him on the head. "Clever boy. You and me make a good team, mon ami."

Hugo swallowed. What should I do? Do I even know what I just saw? He chewed the inside of his cheek and tried to think things through. If he had just witnessed a murder then he needed to do something. There were no policemen anymore, or even newspapers to run a story, but there was still law and order in the fleet. I should tell Mr Raymeady. He is our centre of law and order now. He will do what is right.

But nobody got to see Mr Raymeady easily. The man never left the Kirkland and civilians were not allowed on the frigate without good reason. But you have a good reason, Hugo. You need to report a murder.

Yet, what information do I have? I saw a silhouette of a man, nothing more. I didn't even see a murder take place. What I actually saw was a body being dumped. No more, no less.

Then it'll do no harm bringing it to Mr Raymeady's attention. He is the captain of the fleet. He needs to know everything that goes on.

Hugo walked across the short aft deck of his yacht and entered the main cabin. His daughters still slept beneath the covers of the converted sofa bed. The yacht was single berth and the one bedroom belonged to Hugo. Being a father was hard even before the dead walked. Somehow, even in this new world, it's still the actions of men that scare me most.

Hugo sat down on the floor with Houdini on his lap and waited for the day to arrive. Once it did, he would head for the Kirkland at once.

GARFIELD

GARFIELD BLINKED AS the sunlight filled his eyes. The windows surrounding the drained swimming pool were long and tall and let the morning through in full force. It was January, so the fact that the sun was well risen meant mid-morning was upon them.

It was too dangerous to travel by night. The dead could creep up on you in the dark. Garfield and the other foragers had taken advantage of the lie-in – even now they were curled up beneath their sleeping bags and blankets, snoring – but it was time to get going. Can't sleep forever. A man sleeps long enough he gets to not wanting to wake up at all.

Garfield gathered his things together and placed them back inside the old Army Bergan he'd brought with him. He'd found the bulky satchel at a Salvation Army store several months ago and would always wear it when heading out for more than a day. Before he zipped the bag up, he slid out a couple of knives and strapped them to each of his thighs. He was already armed with a hand axe and a screwdriver, but wanted to have a few more weapons handy. They were about to enter unknown territory. It was best to be prepared.

The dead were already beginning to grow in number as the foragers trekked further from the pier. The fringes of Torquay had swarmed with them – especially a little place called Brixham.

Brixham was a seaside town with a life-sized replica of the Golden Hind sitting in its harbour. Garfield had only taken them there as a way of circumventing the larger towns, which started with Torquay, but things turned out badly. The foragers had gotten cornered inside a little newsagent and had needed to hack their way clear of a dozen dead men. They almost hadn't made it – Lemon tripped and stumbled right into a dead boy's arms at one point, and only just managed to dodge its snapping jaws – but luckily they'd left a vehicle idling nearby and were able to get the hell out of there before the dead closed in on them.

The Range Rover at the church had been a no go. Despite its fine condition, it just wouldn't start. Eventually the foragers chanced upon a Nissan minibus built to hold seven. It started more or less straight away, once they discovered the keys still inside. It was surreal to hear an engine start after so long, but once they were safely on the road, Garfield almost felt like he was back in his old life – commuting to his job at a tyre fitter's garage with sleep in his eyes and whiskey on his breath. Not sure I miss it all that much. I certainly don't miss the hangovers.

Garfield had led a lonely existence before the world fell. Besides his elderly mother, he'd had no one he cared about – and no one who cared about him. He visited the pub with his co-workers from time to time, but never held any of them dear. He'd been single for nigh on two years, ever since a particularly bad break-up with a girl named Jenny. The feisty brunette had dumped him for his lack of ambition, but the truth of it was that she wanted a man with more money. When she later took another lover, Garfield was not surprised to hear that the man was rich. Garfield's self-worth had never been lower.

But once the world ended, his old failings ceased to matter. All around him people died, every second a new person torn to shreds. But Garfield survived. The Army shattered and the police were torn apart in the street. But Garfield survived. The Prime Minister himself had died and the American President had gone missing. But Garfield survived. He was stronger than them all. He was a survivor. Suddenly he was worthy. Pretty soon people were relying on him, counting on him to protect them. Garfield had become someone who mattered. He relished the feeling of being needed, and when he'd rescued Poppy, he even felt heroic. But that feeling soon changed into something less welcome – responsibility. The young girl's survival was his number one priority. He'd assumed ownership of her when he plucked her away from her undead parents. Whether she lived or died was on him, and that had been more power than he'd been looking for. Eventually his responsibility turned to affection and perhaps something even more. Providing Poppy with what she needed had become his all-consuming focus, but it was difficult. He had to keep leaving her, for one thing. The group needed food and supplies; Poppy needed food and supplies. And right now they needed guns, too. If Poppy was going to grow up safe and protected, Garfield needed to make sure that they were never at the mercy of a bigger, badder group of survivors.

Kirk was heading towards him. He was one of the newest members of the foragers and one of the youngest also, yet he had been voted in as second-in-command to Garfield. The group had done that mainly to make the guy feel included. He was often insecure about the fact he had not been at the pier as long as everybody else. It made the kid eager to prove himself, and a little reckless. He was carrying a bottle of water and offered some to Garfield. "Breakfast?"

Garfield waved a hand. "Keep it. I have my own."

Kirk shrugged. "So what's the plan? I say we start making directly north. Yesterday proved that we're going to run into trouble regardless of where we go."

Garfield sighed. "I agree. We'll stick to the countryside, though."

Kirk took a swig of water and then said, "Why not use the motorways?"

"Because the motorways are full of zombies." Most people had been in their cars fleeing when the infection began its work. Nobody had known where he or she was heading; they'd all just been overtaken by the urge to run. Eventually the traffic gridlocked and the infection caught up with them. The motorways choked up with slaughter for hundreds and hundreds of miles. Garfield had seen it with his own eyes. He never wanted to go back to the motorways.

"Everywhere is full of zombies," said Kirk. "At least on the motorway we can just drive through 'em."

Garfield hoisted his Bergan up onto his shoulder and sighed. "You can't just run through a crowd of bodies, not to mention all of the wrecks on the road. Best chance we got is to head through farmland; the fewer obstacles in our path the better. Every time we get held up our chance of not making it home increases."

Kirk sniffed. "Whatever you say, boss. I'll get everyone ready to leave and set off in ten."

"Five," said Garfield. "We need to get a move on."

Kirk nodded. "Five minutes, then." He walked away.

Garfield didn't have a great deal of affection for Kirk. Up until three months ago, he'd been surviving on the road, ever since the dead first rose. He understood the walking dead better than anybody and for that reason, Kirk was perhaps better suited to lead than Garfield was – a notion clearly not lost on Kirk – but Garfield had been at the pier for almost a year and had always led the foraging parties. The group trusted him. And while he exercised caution wherever possible, Kirk seemed to prefer running into situations headfirst. That was all well and good when it had just been him alone on the road, but when other people's lives were at risk caution was the way to go. Can't deny the man is useful, though. No man takes on the dead like he does.

"Garf, everybody is ready," Kirk shouted impatiently from over by the changing room entrance. Garfield did a quick spot check of his weapons and then headed off to join them. Everyone looked well rested, which was good because Garfield planned on moving nonstop until nightfall. By the time they camped again, all of them would be tired.

Cat nodded to him as he approached. "I just stuck my head out the door. It seems all clear."

Garfield nodded. "Good. Let's get going then."

Outside the leisure centre sat the Nissan minivan. It was currently empty. They'd taken their supplies inside overnight in case of looters. Encountering other survivors was rare, but it happened from time to time. They were more often hostile than friendly. Not much different from the way the world used to be in that sense.

One of the foragers, Lemon – so-called because of an unexplained tattoo of the yellow fruit on his forearm – nudged Garfield and pointed with his chin. Garfield glanced across the road and saw what he was referring to. A dead man stumbled towards them. It wasn't moaning like most did, because of a carving knife sticking out the front of his throat. Someone had obviously tried to take the man's head off, but gave up when the knife got stuck.

Cat cursed. "He wasn't here a minute ago. Sneaky git!"

"He's s-s-seen us," Lemon said. "We'll have to deal with him."

Garfield cleared his throat and glanced at Kirk. "You want to do the honours?"

Kirk grinned. "Nothing I'd enjoy more, boss." He swaggered up to the zombie in the road and waited calmly in front of him. The dead man reached out with grasping hands, but Kirk threw himself into a delicate cartwheel and ended up behind his attacker. The other foragers cheered. Kirk kicked the zombie in the rump, sending him flopping forward onto his belly. The other foragers laughed.

Garfield sighed. Here we go.

Kirk waited for the dead man to get up off the ground, before leaping up and kicking him in the side of the head. He topped the move off by spinning around and backheeling the zombie in the chest and cracking some ribs with an audible clack. None of blows were effective – the only way to take down a zombie was to injure the brain – but Kirk seemed to find a type of sport in battering down his enemies before dispatching them skilfully.

"Just get on with it," shouted Lemon, laughing heartily. "Or marry the guy and b-b-bugger off."

Kirk looked back at his colleagues and chuckled. He gave them a quick bow as if to conclude his performance. A claw hammer appeared from his belt and he smashed it into the dead man's forehead. It dropped the zombie immediately, but the body still twitched on the floor. Kirk gave the skull one last blow from his hammer and it was done. The dead man's head crumbled like it was made of papier mache.

"You done?" asked Garfield.

Kirk came back over to them. "No, he is, though."

Cat rolled her eyes. "Men and their testosterone."

"Okay, let's load up," said Garfield. "We're wasting light."

The foragers set about loading up the minivan. They opened up the hatchback and shoved their supplies into the boot. Then they squeezed themselves into the front and middle seats like sardines. Cat sat on David's lap – the two of them had become husband and wife of sorts – but everyone else made do with what little space they could find, eleven people inside a vehicle designed for seven. It was lucky everyone was so skinny and malnourished, or else the vehicle's chassis might have fallen out beneath them. We need a second vehicle.

Garfield sat up front with Kirk, who was the man at the wheel. Ideally there would have been a map between them, but the day of the smartphone and satnav had made paper plotting redundant. There were no maps to be found.

"You sure you don't want to try the motorway?" Kirk asked him. "I think it would be best."

"No," Garfield said again. "Let's just get on the same page, shall we? We're taking the scenic route."

Kirk started the engine and put his hands on the steering wheel. "You're the boss."

"So they tell me."

The minivan gave a whinnying grunt and crept forward. Kirk navigated down the main roads for a few miles, dodging burnt-out wrecks and small assemblies of the dead. Many of the houses they passed were black and charred, some merely ruins and foundations. For the first few months of infection, fires had consumed most of the country. At least the destruction the inferno had wrought had taken as many dead men as it had the living. It was almost like Mother Nature had been trying to even the odds. Not that it helped. The dead outnumber us a thousand to one.

Eventually the minivan came upon a cow gate bordering a field. There they stopped while Lemon hopped out and smashed the padlock with one of his many tools. Once the gate was open, Kirk put the van into first gear and drove onto the grass. Once he picked up a bit of speed, he moved into second and kept it there. The field was sodden and uneven from recent rain, and everyone cried out in misery as Kirk's driving threw them about inside the confined space.

"Sorry, everyone," said Kirk. "Not much I can do. Garf wants us to take the farmland and this is the farmland."

Garfield narrowed his eyes at Kirk, but the younger man just smiled amiably. "Just slow it down," he said, "and we'll be fine."

Kirk chuckled and dropped their speed by a few miles. The bumpiness was instantly less pronounced. They were able to drive on for almost ten minutes without complaint. As they travelled uphill, the ground became less sodden and Kirk was able to shift into third and fourth. We're making good time, thought Garfield.

"Farmhouse coming up ahead," Kirk said. "Want to check it out?"

Garfield spied the small cottage at the edge of the field and thought about it for a moment, weighing up the pros and cons. The plan was not to fill up on supplies before they got to where they were going, but it wouldn't hurt to check out the odd little place here and there. Some farmhouses had the occasional shotgun stashed away in their pantries. It was worth checking out. "We'll take a look," he said. "Three man team; you, me, and Lemon; quick sweep for any food and supplies."

"Okay dokey," said Kirk, turning the wheel slightly to take them directly towards the cottage.

The building was old grey brick with a red slate roof and a small porch over the front door. It looked entirely benign and as safe a place as existed nowadays, but each of the foragers knew that looks could be deceiving. The dead did not distinguish between nice places and bad.

You could just as easily find a horde of them at a quaint farmhouse than you could at a rundown shopping mall or hospital.

Still, it's a cute little farmhouse. I bet Poppy would like it here. All this space to run around and explore. The girl is always wanting to explore – she's like a little blonde squirrel. Maybe someday she'll get to live in a place like this. Or someplace beside a pond like the house she grew up in.

Kirk pulled the van to a stop outside the cottage and applied the handbrake. They all sat and waited for a minute, making sure that nothing came out of the nearby outhouses and sheds. Once the coast was clear, Garfield opened his door and stepped out onto the gravel, the stones crunching beneath his boots. Kirk stepped out, too, from the driver's side, and slammed his door loudly. Garfield winced. "Do you want to bring the dead down on us? Try and be a little less obvious."

Kirk huffed. "Sorry, boss. Wouldn't it be best to attract them, though? Least that way we can see 'em coming."

"I'd rather them not come at all."

"Fair enough. Lem, you ready?"

Lemon was coming out of the sliding door at the side of the van. He hopped down onto the gravel and nearly stumbled. His skin was pale. "I think I'm g-g-gunna throw up."

Kirk laughed and punched him on the arm. "Man up, Lem."

"It's just because you're not used to being in a vehicle," said Cat stepping out behind him and rubbing him on the back. "Your tummy will settle down soon, hun."

Lemon took a deep breath and nodded. "I'm okay. Shall I check out the front door?"

Garfield nodded.

Lemon sorted through his tools in the back of the minivan and then proceeded cautiously towards the cottage's front porch. He held a steel pole in his hands that was bent and sharpened at one end, not unlike a crowbar. Lemon often referred to the tool as his 'skeleton key'. At four foot long, it was almost as tall as he was.

"Get her opened up, Lem," Kirk shouted.

"But be careful," Garfield added.

Lemon shoved his skeleton key into the door's wedge and yanked. The lock broke easily and the old oak door swung open in its frame.

The smell came at them immediately. It was not as ripe as the smells of their early foraging days when the dead had still been fresh and moist. It was the odour of long time decay and animal droppings. It was a smell every forager was used to. It meant there was death inside.

Lemon gripped his skeleton key at the bottom of the shaft like a baseball bat. He looked to Garfield for orders. "S-s-should we back out? Smells like this place could be a r-r-risk."

Garfield was about to agree when Kirk let out a snigger. "Where's the fun in life without a little risk?" He shoved past Lemon and headed inside the cottage, disappearing into the dank, dark hallway.

Garfield shook his head and grunted. He couldn't leave Kirk to sweep the house alone. Foragers always backed each other up – even impetuous fools like Kirk. "Wait here," he told Lemon. "Keep a watch with the others and be ready."

Lemon nodded and stepped back from the porch. Garfield went inside.

The reception hallway was narrow and cluttered. An old-fashioned bureau sat off to one side, a framed family photo perched on top of it. The family in the picture looked hard and serious – tough farming stock that had probably owned the farm for generations. Garfield wondered what had happened to them, and if they were still inside the house. I'm sure I'm going to find out.

Garfield crept down the hallway and entered a kitchen on his left. The large room was chilly and had a musty, faintly sweet odour. The smell was not coming from the dead, though. It was coming from a bin in the corner. Flies swarmed around the lid, breeding and living in whatever filth had been left to decompose inside. Garfield pulled his shirt up over his nose and tried not to breath more than he had to.

The only thing of interest in the kitchen was a large carving fork on the centre island, which Garfield wrapped in an old tea towel and secured to his left triceps with a couple of elastic bands from a drawer. It could come in useful. The weapon he was currently carrying was a claw hammer, not unlike the one that Kirk favoured. Blunt force trauma was much more effective against zombies than stabbing. Plus the hammer always came back for a second and third blow, whereas knives sometimes got stuck in bone.

There was a thud from somewhere else in the house. Garfield headed cautiously back out into the hallway. He was pretty sure the noise had come from up ahead, so he followed the hallway to its conclusion and gently slid through the door at the end and entered the room beyond.

The smell overwhelmed. The sickly sweet odour of the recently dead had given way to the earthy, spicy smell of the long rotten. When Garfield moved further into the old-fashioned parlour he saw the reason it smelled so badly. Dear God.

Kirk was standing still, shaking his head and blinking slowly, uncharacteristically forlorn. "Just when you think you're used to it all," he said glumly, "then you find something like this."

Garfield studied the three swinging bodies and wondered if they belonged to the family in the photo. His guess was that they did. An old man and woman wriggled from thick nooses around their necks strung over an oak beam crossing the centre of the ceiling. They'd obviously been infected and had hanged themselves in hope of not coming back. The caked shit down their inner thighs showed they'd been alive when they'd taken the noose. Not everyone understood that it did no good to commit suicide when infected. If you were bitten, you came back.

The dead old man and woman reached out for Kirk, trying to grab a hold of him with their gnarled fingers, but he was too focused on the third hanging body to pay them any attention. Garfield turned his attention to the swinging child and immediately thought of Poppy. While he'd been able to rescue one little girl, there were innumerable children who'd been doomed to fates such as this.

The little girl was about Poppy's age. She had long brown hair all the way to her waist, but much of it had slid away from her scalp and was hanging loosely down her bony shoulders or on the floor beneath her dangling feet. She, too, reached out her hands for Kirk, trying to draw him closer, trying to taste him with her snapping jaws.

After a while, Kirk turned away to leave. "You do the honours," he said to Garfield, then went back out into the hallway."

Garfield swallowed back his sadness and dealt with the family as quickly as he could. He wanted to get out of there. He didn't like the way the dead family looked at him so hungrily and he couldn't bear the stink that filled the room. Three clean strikes from his hammer and it was over. Garfield dropped the tool on the floor afterwards. He did not want to keep it.

Back outside, he was surprised to find not ten other men waiting, but eleven. There was a stranger amongst them. The newcomer had been shoved down onto his knees by Cat and wore muddy jeans and a brown leather jacket. The smile on his face was handsome.

"We found this guy skulking about the sheds," said Cat. Like her name suggested, the proud look on her face made her look like a feline who had caught a mouse. "He surrendered quickly enough."

"How's it going?" said the stranger.

"Who the hell are you?" asked Garfield, taken aback. "And where did you come from?"

The stranger grinned widely. "Why, you can call me Sally if you're a mate. Call me what you want if you're not." The man had an Australian accent.

Lemon chuckled. "Sally's a bird's name."

"A name is what you make it, cobber. My name might be Sally, but I'm no less a man than you, I can promise yer."

"Where did you come from?" Garfield asked again.

Remaining on his knees, the man pointed. "From inside that yonder shed. Bloody freezing it was, but safe enough."

"Why didn't you go inside the house?"

"Not my place to go breaking into people's houses and using their dunnies. I live off the land; not trespassing."

"You do know everybody is dead, right?" said Kirk incredulously. "You can go wherever you like."

"Yer, I do know that, fella. Still doesn't make me king of the world, now, does it?"

Garfield glanced around at the nearby fields and the main road about a hundred metres away beyond a row of high hedges. He rubbed at the stubble on his chin as he took in the sight of the man. The Australian was amiable enough, but that in itself was sending up alarm bells. For someone to be so cheery after surviving out here alone was unnatural. The dead family inside the cottage added to Garfield's unease. "Are you alone, Sally?" he asked.

The Australian nodded. "I am. Bit of a lone wolf, you might say. Never stay in the same place too long."

"Why is that?"

"Because them dead buggers tend to come and eat everyone after a while."

"So you were with a group?" asked Kirk.

"For a time, yer. Was holed-up in a bar where I used to work. Place in Bristol called Tuckers, ever been?"

Everybody shook their heads.

Sally blew air into his cheeks and let it out. "Ah, well, shame that. I take it you fellas must have a camp around here someplace. There's too many of you to last long on the road. Plus it looks like most of you have had a bath in the last year, which is more than I have."

"We have a camp," said Lemon.

Garfield put a hand up to stop him from saying any more. It would not do to give away the location of the pier to a stranger. "We have a camp," Garfield said, "but it's not around here. We're heading up north for supplies. What were you doing here?"

"Just staying alive. I stick to farms and the countryside because there's less o' them dead buggers about. You can find the odd veggie growing wild in some places, too. I just wish I could find me a field full of tinnys."

Lemon looked confused. "Tinnys?"

"Larger, mate."

"Oh."

Kirk looked at Garfield and rubbed at his nose to cover his mouth. He whispered, "What do you want to do with him? I say we leave him here and keep on."

Garfield's first thought was to agree. He didn't have a good feeling about the Australian; but it didn't feel right to just leave him out on his own either. "What are your plans, Sally?"

"Well, I'd quite like to stand up, if that's okay? The gravel is killing my knees." Garfield nodded to Cat who helped Sally to his feet. "Strewth, that's better," he said. "Now, as for my plans..." He shrugged. "I told you, just staying alive. I don't think much beyond that most days."

"You can join up with us if you want," said Garfield, regretting it as soon as he said it.

"For real?"

Kirk didn't miss a step and followed Garfield's lead for a change. He was less cocky since coming out of the farmhouse. "As long as you tow the line and don't give us no reason to dump you, cobber."

"I would be most grateful to join you good men."

Cat cleared her throat.

"Oh, pardon my manners. I would be most grateful to join you good men and Sheilas."

"That's lovely," said David, "but I would just like to point out that it was hard enough with eleven of us in the minivan. Now you want to add another body? I don't mind Cat on my lap, but that's my limit."

"He has a good point," said Squirrel, who folded his arms and became grumpy. "I can't take any more elbows and knees in my ribs inside that bloody coffin."

Sally had a big grin on his face. "I think I might have just the thing for you fellas."

Garfield was wary. "What?"

"Check behind that shed over there."

Garfield looked across at the old rickety shed and wondered what the Australian was talking about. It was full of old, rotten hay. "You best not be planning anything stupid," he said.

Sally chuckled. "Just go check it out. I promise yer'll like it."

Garfield slid a chef's knife from the band on his left thigh and crept towards the shed. He walked with a little extra bend in his knees, ready to spring at the first sign of an ambush, but he made it to the shed without any cause for alarm. He stepped around the side carefully, stopping every couple of feet and listening for any movement behind the shed. Zombies were easy to hear, shuffling around and clicking as their joints wore down, but the living could still lie in wait silently. The Australian said he was alone, but that didn't mean he was.

Garfield took the corner of the shed and stepped out into the open with his knife held high. He was surprised by what he saw, but also very pleased.

"You found it yet, cobber?" Sally shouted from the front of the cottage.

Garfield stared at the old horsebox trailer and nodded. It was wide enough to hold a single stallion. Or four men and a good load of supplies. "Yes, I've found it," he shouted back to the others. "It's just what we need."

But the price for the horsebox was taking along a stranger named Sally. Whether or not that would turn out for the best remained to be seen.

ANNA

NNA RUBBED THE tiredness from her eyes and yawned. The events that had transpired at dawn were now like a day-dream, just two hours later. Despite what Roman suspected, the members of the pier had not dumped Birch's body into the sea. The sea was theirs and they would not spoil it with the dead flesh of a rapist. Chris and Jimmy had carried Birch through the gate and dumped him next to the boxer and the skinny woman they had killed not two days before. He can rot with them.

Now everyone stood huddled in the diner. Despite their fleeting victory over the three strangers from the fleet, each of them now wore a look of deep concern on their faces. There were a thousand members of the fleet currently floating on their doorstep. If they'd just made an enemy, they had made a big one.

Tim eased himself down onto a chair in the diner and let his crutches collapse to the floor. Blood oozed beneath his bandages but there was little Anna could do about it. She would just have to keep the wound clean and hope for the best.

He glanced around the room. "It's very good to meet you all. Sorry it's not in better circumstances."

"Save it," said Anna. "I stuck up for you, but only because I liked those men less than I like you."

Tim nodded. "Understandable. I've brought trouble to your door-step and for that you must hate me, but everything I told you was true. The reason we're all in this situation, the reason we had our lives ripped from us, is Samuel Raymeady. That man is the Devil."

Alistair grunted. "So you said, but his side claim you're a terrorist. Who are we to believe? How is it you ended up with a bullet in you? Garfield said he found you inside a storage container."

"He did. That's where I went to die after Roman shot me."

"Why did he shoot you?" Poppy asked. She had a stern look on her face. "Did you do something bad?"

"When the infection first hit," Tim explained. "I knew Samuel's plan was to commandeer a navy frigate his company was building and start collecting people. I made sure I was amongst the first group of survivors brought on board. The arrogant swine didn't even recognise me."

"You knew him as a child?" Anna confirmed.

"Yes. He was...sickly...as a child, the only son of an extremely wealthy family. I was sent to see him as part of an investigation into any external causes at the home that could have been causing his ill health. The family had tried everything, but nothing got Samuel out of his bed. At the time, I was a sort of an environmental scientist. I tried several experiments to find a cause for Samuel's condition, but nothing gave any answers. Needless to say, things turned out badly for me in the end. I went into that Gloucestershire manor house whole and came out with a broken back. It was six years before I could even stumble around like an insect on these crutches. Once I managed to leave my wheelchair, though, I devoted my life to bringing that evil boy to justice. But that evil boy grew into an evil man and I remained a cripple." He sighed and shook his head. "I thought that by getting aboard the Kirkland I could at least finally put a stop to the man before he ruined what little left there was of the world. I failed to do that as well."

Alistair folded his arms. "You tried to blow the ship up?"

Tim shifted in his seat and winced in pain. Sweat beaded on his brow. "I admit there would have been casualties, but in the long run lives would have been saved. I've witnessed Samuel bulldoze through anybody who dares stand in his way his entire life. By stopping him I was hoping to save all of the victims he is yet to meet. The men and woman aboard the Kirkland are already lost. They worship their captain. They think he saved their lives. If only they knew the truth."

Rene came and brought them all a glass of water each. Tim sipped his gratefully, as did everyone else. No one had realised how thirsty they were. Rene stopped when he was in the middle of the group and rubbed his hands together thoughtfully.

"What is it?" Anna asked him.

Rene sighed. "This man, Tim, speaks of terrible things. He says that the man, Samuel Raymeady, is a tyrant and a monster."

"He is," Tim confirmed. "He's like Hitler crossed with Godzilla."

"Then my concern is that our actions may anger him and that we have made an enemy of a monster – of a Godzilla. I fear that Samuel Raymeady may bulldoze us next."

Anna sipped at her water and nodded wearily. In the heat of the moment she had gone with her gut and done what she thought was right, but now that the events were laid out more clearly it seemed like they had all made a big mistake. We still did what was right, though.

"What should we expect to happen?" Anna asked Tim.

Tim didn't seem hopeful as he spoke. "I think they will come again, but this time with more men and weapons. They have a few guns aboard – pistols mostly – but they're more likely to snap an arm than fire a gun."

"They shot you," said Alistair.

"They did. Once my gunpowder plot was discovered – although I still can't work out how Samuel found out – I managed to flee the ship before anybody caught me. I headed inland and disembarked at Dartmouth. From there I followed some train tracks, hoping it would lead me north. Roman, although his real name is Damien Banks, managed to track me, probably from the fires I lit to keep warm – stupid of me, really, but it was either that or freeze. I was holed up in an old petrol station when he came. I broke the windows and screamed and shouted, tried to raise hell. Luckily the dead were near and heard me. They swarmed, and as Roman was out in the open, they all went for him first.

I hobbled from the petrol station, hoping to go in the opposite direction while my enemy was distracted. Roman took a shot at me and hit the target. Before I passed out, I managed to climb inside an open storage container and close the door. All I was hoping for was to die in peace, but then your man found me. A miracle really. We should make a movie about it. Where is he, anyway? Always nice to meet a fellow ginger."

"Garfield went on a supply run with the others," said Anna. "They'll be gone for a few days."

"He goes out a lot," said Poppy grumpily. "He gets us all our food."

"Well, I hope he returns soon," said Tim. "The more of you here the better. Hopefully Samuel will leave you be once I give myself up."

Anna raised an eyebrow. "You're going to give yourself up?"

"I've put you people in enough danger already. Samuel won't stop until he has me. I don't plan on running forever. I don't have the spine for it, or the legs."

"Then why did you resist in the first place?" said Alistair. "We could have given you up and there'd be no danger."

"Of course there would be. Samuel is a danger everywhere he goes. The reason he wants me dead is because I know the truth. And now so do you people. My burden is shifted. I can die in peace. I've been trying to get someone to believe me about Samuel for years, and now that I have I'm giving up. A cripple has no place in the wastelands. I've told you all what I know, but quite frankly I'm happy for Samuel to just do what he wants with me and be done with it."

Rene was shaking his head. "Your burden is now ours. You have doomed us all. Samuel will become our enemy as he was yours."

Anna raised her hand. Rene could be a tad dramatic at times. "Not if we give Tim up and say we don't believe him. We'll explain that after what their man, Birch, did to Poppy, we were angry, but that we think Tim is a lunatic and don't want anything to do with him."

Tim folded his arms and winced as his wound creased. "I think that would be smart. Samuel wants followers, not enemies. The battlefield on which to fight him is not head-on. The fact that you people know the truth is enough to light the fires. It means the entire world does not belong to Samuel Raymeady, even if he thinks it does. You people need to give me up and keep your heads down. Survive and grow and don't let Samuel turn the world into his own private dictatorship."

Alistair folded his arms. "As long as Samuel doesn't just destroy us all and be done with it."

Poppy whimpered. Anna placed a hand on her shoulder. The girl shouldn't really be listening to any of this, but nor was it fair to keep her outside after what had happened to her.

"Samuel won't do that," said Tim. "He's too smart. He's wearing the hat of benevolent leader. Killing innocent people isn't in his interests. Roman will be back, I promise you, and when he comes, you people need to play nice and hand me over. They'll string me up on the Kirkland and make an example of me, but you'll be okay. I'll die a coward and a traitor, but I'm cool with that. Meeting you people and telling you what I know is redemption enough for me. Everything will work out fine. Trust me."

Anna nodded. It all sounded like a good idea.

DAMIEN

DAMIEN HAD MANAGED to re-board the Kirkland without anybody important seeing him. He'd climbed the rigging, which ran down the starboard side and allowed people to moor their yachts and climb up. Only a single guard patrolled the gunwale and he had seemed half asleep when Damien headed past him. Hopefully Samuel would not even know he'd returned. The longer Damien could put off meeting with him, the better. The first person he wanted to talk to was Harry. I don't even know where to begin. Which question do I ask first?

Before he sought out his friend, though. He had retired to his private berth to get some sleep. After the events on the pier Damien was out on his feet and just wanted to sleep. He washed the blood from his spear in the stainless steel sink and stared into the cracked mirror. His stump was bleeding, too, which added to the mess. It was all he could do just to get out of his clothes before collapsing on his bed and passing out.

He slept through the entire morning and part of the afternoon, dreaming the whole time, but remembering nothing once he awoke. It was probably for the best considering what nightmares he might have been having. As soon as he rubbed the sleep from his eyes, Damien thought about seeing Harry.

Harry didn't have a private berth on the Kirkland – he stayed in the bunkhouses with a majority of the other civilians – which was why it was a surprise when Damien opened his hatch and found him waiting there against the wall of the passageway.

"I thought you'd never wake up," he said with a smile on his face.

Damien snatched at Harry's shirt and yanked him inside the berth. "Does anyone else know I'm back?"

Harry shook his head. "I doubt it. I was the only one out on deck waiting for you."

Damien thought about the events of last night and suddenly became overwrought with rage. "Why were you waiting for me? Wanted to know the latest about your partner in crime, Tim?"

Harry didn't seem surprised. He sat down on the bed and sighed. "Tim told you, then? I wondered if he might. To be honest, I assumed he was dead after you shot him. How did he survive?"

"Some people on the pier patched him up. Anyway, what the hell, Harry? Tim said..." He lowered his voice. "He said that you were involved in trying to blow up the sodding ship."

Harry sighed. When he looked at Damien he was tired and weary. There were wrinkles on his forehead that seemed to have come overnight and his skin was grey. For a second all was forgotten. "Your headaches are getting bad again, aren't they?"

"Yes."

"Bad, bad?"

"Bad as before. Worse, actually."

Damien sat down on the bed beside his friend and said nothing. There was nothing to say. Harry had developed a brain tumour three years ago that had grown rapidly. The pressure on his brain had caused excruciating headaches, made him blind in one eye, and half-crazy. At its worst, Harry used to space out and start mumbling religious nonsense; talking about an endless snow storm and Angels coming to reap the Earth. He would point at Damien and tell him that everyone was supposed to be dead, that they were all buried in ice and snow. It had got pretty frightening towards the end and the prognosis was that it wouldn't get any better in Harry's final months. There was nothing to be done, the doctors said.

But Damien hadn't accepted that. Harry had taken him on as a teen-ager, took him away from the crime-ridden council estates, and trained him up to be a master carpenter. Learning a trade and finally having a father figure had changed Damien's life completely. He had once sold drugs and dealt violence to those who crossed him, but had gradually become a hardworking man who wanted to put his past behind him and do good things. It was Harry's kindness that had changed the course of Damien's life for the better. He owed the man everything. So when the doctors had said Harry was going to die, Damien had refused to allow it. He took to the Internet and researched every clinic, health trial, and treatment he could find. Eventually he had come across an experimental drug trial in South Africa. The only problem was that it had been expensive. Damien had needed to sacrifice everything he had to gather the money to pay. But he had done so, and it had worked. Harry got better. The cancer went away...almost. Harry had been due to fly out for the final round of treatment, to eradicate the last few cancer cells remaining. But then the world had ended, along with any notion of healthcare. Both he and Harry worried that the cancer would return from the few cells remaining, but tried to put it out of their minds; there was nothing they could do but hope.

Then, several weeks ago, the headaches started again. Neither of them had wanted to admit what that meant.

"I'm sorry," said Damien.

Harry nodded. "Me too."

"Is that why you tried to set off the bomb? Are you losing it again?"

"No! Tell you the truth I had nothing to do with the bomb Tim tried to set off. It was me who helped get him off the ship before they found him, though. I got him in a lifeboat during the night and sent him away."

"Why, Harry? How did you even get involved with this guy?"

"By seeing what is right in front of me. Samuel Raymeady is evil."

Damien snorted. "Wow, you and this Tim really have it in for the captain, don't you?"

"Are you really so blind? Samuel is a dictator in the making. He's building his little empire, rescuing stragglers and earning their love, but the harsh reality is that the captain of this ship is the man who ended the world in the first place. Samuel Raymeady destroyed everything."

"So that he could rise up as the leader of the new world, right? I'm not buying it."

Harry blinked. "Have you ever noticed how many people go missing around here? There was a guy named Dennis, worked in the mess hall, remember him?"

Damien vaguely remembered a man with glasses and a crooked nose. "I think so. What about him?"

"When did you see him last?"

"I don't know."

"Exactly. Dennis let slip that he intended taking a boat with a couple of his friends and heading down to Spain where it would be warmer. They wanted to find someplace quiet and try to live on the land again. Dennis disappeared the night before he was due to leave and everyone assumed he'd finally set off.

"Maybe he did."

"Except I knew the friends he was leaving with and none of them had seen him. I can promise you that Samuel made Dennis disappear. He won't have any dissenters or want-aways in his fleet."

"You have no proof."

Harry went to say something but stopped himself.

"What?" Damien asked. "What were you about to say?"

"I...I saw Samuel on the aft deck one day and....and I saw what he was. He's the devil, Damien. I'm telling you."

Damien leapt up from the bed and marched the room. He placed his hand on his head and swore at the ceiling. "Damn it, Harry. It's just the brain tumour. You're having funny turns again. You're talking bollocks."

"They're not funny turns. I see things that others can't. There's a layer beneath the surface that most people don't know about, but just you wait. You'll see what Samuel Raymeady truly is. He's not our saviour. The only thing he cares about is collecting his kingdom."

"That bomb would have killed hundreds of people, Harry. How can you judge Samuel when you were party to something like that?"

Harry stood up from the bed and faced Damien. He winced for a second as if getting up had hurt his head, but when he recovered he gave his friend a hard stare. "I told you I knew nothing about that. My own plans were to be more surgical. I only wanted to take out Samuel."

He's going to get us both killed with this nonsense.

Damien looked down at his spear. He was already guilty of murder. Once Samuel found out about Birch and Fox, Damien would be a dead man himself. But if he took Harry's life and revealed him as the second traitor, perhaps all would be forgiven? Harry was dying of a brain tumour, anyway, what harm would there be in ending his suffering?

The weight of Damien's spear suddenly made his arm ache. He tried to raise it but couldn't. *What the hell am I thinking?* He couldn't hurt his friend, no matter what the reason. Harry had looked out for him when nobody else had. Harry had made him a man, been a father to him. There was no way he could turn his back on the only person he'd ever loved and respected. Especially not for a dickhead like Samuel Raymeady. "If Samuel finds out that you're planning against him..."

Harry shrugged. "Way my head feels, I'll be dead soon anyway."

The thought made Damien's stomach roll. Whatever happened, he was going to lose his only friend – either to cancer or execution. The world had just become even shitter than it used to be. Damien was soon to be alone. Harry was the moral centre that had given him his path through life. He didn't know what would become of him once Harry was gone. *Will I go back to being the useless thug I was when he found me? Maybe a thug is all I am deep down.*

Harry came and placed a hand on Damien's shoulder. "I'm getting old, Damien. My time is nearly done, but there are still people out there who have futures left. Not if Samuel Raymeady gets his way, though. You need to stop him."

"Stop him from what? You'll get me killed for saying things like this."

"Dying is better than living beneath the throne of a despot."

"You sound crazy."

"Perhaps I am; but I'm not wrong."

"If Samuel finds out, I can't help you."

"I know. Don't worry about what happens to me, Damien. You just keep yourself safe."

"Some chance of that. I've come back onboard without doing my job for a second time."

"What do you mean?"

"I mean your buddy, Tim, is still alive. He's out there on that pier now, and when Samuel finds out he's probably going to kill everyone there."

Harry looked sick to his stomach. "How many?"

Damien shrugged. "A handful. There's a kid with them."

Harry rubbed at his forehead with the heel of his fist. For a moment it looked like he might collapse. "You can't let him hurt a bunch of innocent people, Damien. Don't you see that this proves what I'm saying? Only a monster would be so intent on causing death. You've seen his temper before. What right does he have to attack those people at the pier?"

"Maybe you should have thought about that before you helped Tim escape. He's the real reason those people are in danger. You still haven't told me how you two ever got involved with one another."

Harry sat back down on the bed. He cleared his throat and rubbed at his temples for a moment before speaking. "One night, my headaches were pretty bad, so I went outside to get some air. I found Tim on the promenade deck, hanging over the edge and looking down at the sea."

"He was going to jump?"

Harry nodded. "I asked him what was wrong and he just said "I couldn't stop it." "Stop what?" I asked. He looked at me and said that he "couldn't prevent the end of the world." My reaction was to laugh. Nobody could have stopped the end of the world, so why was this guy beating himself up about it? I told him not to blame himself; what could he possibly have done? That's when he told me, "I could have killed the man responsible.""

"He told you that man was Samuel Raymeady?"

Harry shook his head. "Not at first, but I convinced him to get down from the edge and have a drink with me."

Damien raised any eyebrow. "You don't drink."

"I did that night. I fell off the wagon so that Tim could share his story with me over a couple bottles of beer. I told him I was ten years sober but that I was making an exception to be his friend. I could tell it meant a lot to him to have someone to talk to for an evening, but it was still several days before he told me his story. When he did he told me how he'd been following Samuel Raymeady since the man was a boy. Tim told me about all the things he'd witnessed and researched over the last two decades – all of the money Black Remedy funnelled into secret medical research projects and the heavy funding they gave universities working on epidemiology – but he was too late to stop any of it. Samuel Raymeady wiped out the world without anybody ever suspecting him – anybody except for Tim and handful of kooks he called friends. Tim knew everything, but nobody important would listen. When the virus was finally released, it was too late for anyone to do anything. There was no hope.

"The final stage of Samuel's plan hinged on rescuing people with a Royal Navy ship. Three years ago, Black Remedy managed to tie up a contract for four new destroyers to be built. That was when the plan went into motion. Samuel needed a flagship for his new nation and Black remedy were given the excuse to build it. Captain Raymeady would be the saviour of mankind, the new messiah."

Damien stared at his friend in disbelief. "This is all the word of a madman. His mind is as crippled as his back. How are you so gullible?"

"I believe him," Harry said firmly. "And in the end, I hope that you do, too. Just open your eyes, Damien. Don't let Samuel hurt the people on that pier. They're innocent."

Damien sighed. "If Samuel is as maniacal as you say, then you know I have no way of stopping him from doing whatever he wants."

"I think you underestimate your own potential, Damien. I saw it the day I plucked you away from your life as a drug dealer. You're a leader. You have courage; and people follow courage."

Damien couldn't think of anything further from the truth. "I'm no leader, nor do I ever want to be one. I have one hand and a bad attitude. I'm the last person people would follow."

"Some leaders don't have to lead men and women, they can lead by example. Do the right thing, Damien, and people will follow the path you leave them."

Damien had heard enough. Harry was beginning to sound more and more delusional. The days ahead were not going to be kind. Last time, Harry's brain tumour had sent him into an almost constant state of mania. Damien had almost lost his only friend back then, but he had managed to get a second chance. This time there would be no reprieve.

"I have to go," Damien said. "It's time I faced the music. If Samuel grows horns, I promise I'll kill him."

FRANK

"**I** WAS WONDERING WHEN you'd grace us with your appearance," said Frank when he saw Roman coming down the passageway. He'd received reports from petty officer Dunn shortly before dawn that Roman was back onboard, but it had taken until now for him to present himself. There was much that could be read into that.

"Is Samuel in?" Roman asked with a hint of sarcasm in his voice. He knew very well that Samuel rarely left his chambers.

"Samuel is always free to see you, Roman. Step inside."

They entered the captain's chambers and found Samuel behind his desk as usual. Frank stood close by, hoping that Roman would bring his adopted son good news for once.

Samuel got right to the point. "Is he dead?"

Roman shrugged. "Who?"

Samuel's eyes narrowed and his lower lip trembled. "The cripple, the man who tried to blow me up. Is he dead? Was he at the pier?"

The man who tried to blow us all up, Frank thought. I must remind Samuel that a leader says 'we' not 'I'.

"He was at the pier, yes," said Roman. "The people there patched up his wounds and gave him a place to rest. He was up and about when I found him."

"But you dealt with him, I take it?"

"No. He's still at the pier. The people there didn't play ball."

Samuel's face creased. For a moment it looked like he might leap over his desk and throttle Roman. Frank sighed with relief when

Samuel chose to remain calm. "So...the cripple is alive because of the people on this pier?"

Roman seemed to struggle for a moment. His eyes flittered back and forth and his mouth opened and closed, searching for words. "I...I wouldn't necessarily blame them. Tim told them a bunch of wild stories. He manipulated them into protecting him, but they didn't know any better."

Sam's expression darkened. "Tim? You use the man's name. Did he manipulate you with his stories? Pray tell, what did he say? Was it about me? Some grand conspiracy, I'd imagine. I have heard it all before. But the people on the pier, they believe these stories about me?"

Frank watched Roman struggle again for words. He's trying to protect the people on the pier. Why?

"The stories were nonsense," Roman said. "I paid no notice, but he had longer to convince the people on the pier."

"Why did you not take Tim by force?" Samuel asked with venom. "You had two men with you. Two men who, might I add, did not return with you last night. Would you care to shed light on their location?"

Roman swallowed and shifted uncomfortably. He was not his usual stoic self. There was fear in him today, but Frank doubted it was for himself. Roman was a man who cared little for self-preservation. That was why Samuel had found him so useful. A man without fear is a rare weapon. But there's fear in him today. He's trying to hide something.

"Where are Fox and Birch?" Samuel asked.

"Dead," said Roman.

Frank spluttered. "Dead? How?"

Samuel raised his hand for silence. "I'll handle this, Frank." He turned his charcoal eyes back to Roman. "Why are they dead? And who killed them?"

Roman cleared his throat. "I-I killed Birch. He was out of control. Fox tried to calm him down, but got a knife in the chest for his efforts. I did everything I could to restrain Birch but he was wild. He caused everything that happened. I had to kill him just to stop him from dishonouring the fleet more than he already had."

Sam leapt up from his chair and sent pens skittering across the surface of his desk. His usually pale skin went bright red in an instant. Frank took a step backwards. "You killed Birch? You killed a member of the fleet?"

"Yes. He gave me no choice." Roman's reckless disregard had returned to him and he looked ready for a fight. "As for the reason why, perhaps you should have warned me that Birch was a goddamn sex offender. They had a child at the pier and Birch tried to abduct her in the night. It was a right bleedin' shambles."

"Is that the truth?" asked Frank, taken aback and feeling quite sick to his stomach. "That is...unfortunate." The men and women of this fleet devolve by the day. Samuel's already had to deal with a dozen rapes, thefts, and beatings, and more and more happen each day. Sometimes I think people left their humanity back on land.

Roman glanced at Frank. "Yeah, no shit. When the people on the pier caught Birch, they were damn near ready to lynch all three of us. Rather than beg forgiveness, the moron tried to stab the little girl right in front of everybody. I had no choice but to put him down. Fox ended up being collateral damage when he tried to help me take Birch down. In the end I had to get out of there while I could. Things went bad, but the people on the pier were just defending themselves. It was Birch's fault that things went so wrong. The cripple's stories ended up holding so much weight because Birch played the role of the bad guy so effectively."

Frank had a feeling that wasn't the entire truth – he's hiding something – but Samuel didn't challenge what had been said to him. In fact, he seemed to have calmed down completely. Some of the crimson seeped away from his cheeks and he stood up straight and loose, instead of hunched forward and confrontational. He placed his fingertips together in front of his face and let out a sigh. "If what you say is true, then I am at fault for not knowing my men better. These people on the pier, are they good people?"

Roman answered without pause, "Yes. From what I saw they were all good people. They stick together and they look after one another. One of them must be pretty handy, because the cripple was patched up and walking again after I left him half-dead."

"But they protected him when you asked to take him into custody? This terrible man who tried to take hundreds of innocent lives? "

Roman nodded.

"And in doing so," Samuel continued. "Two members of the fleet were murdered and the mighty Roman was sent back to me with his tail between his legs."

Roman shifted on the spot. "Yes, but-"

"Then the people on the pier are my enemies, and they must be dealt with accordingly." Samuel turned to Frank. "Frank, tell the gunnery sergeant to fire on the pier."

Frank spluttered. "Sorry, Samuel? You want us to fire on them?"

"You heard me. Fire on them. If what Roman says is true, then they're harbouring a terrorist. That makes them as guilty as he is."

"Wait a second," Roman said. "You don't need to do this. I'll meet with them again, explain the consequences if they don't hand Tim over."

Samuel grimaced at the sound of the man's name being spoken once more. Frank winced too because he knew the reaction it would illicit. Samuel glared at Roman. "I would be very careful how you conduct yourself, Roman. You have failed me again, and if it is not the fault of these other survivors, then it is yours. Should I fire on them, or should I fire on you?"

"Me," Roman said without pause. "Punish me, not a bunch of innocent men and women. They're just trying to survive."

"Well, they're doing a pretty bad job of it, because I'm about to destroy them. Frank, I won't ask you again. Give the order, and take this man out of my sight before my mood worsens further."

Frank wavered. He knew his son was quick to temper, but there seemed to be zero doubt in Samuel's command. He wanted the pier destroyed. "I...Samuel, I think-"

Samuel gave him a look so harsh that it almost made Frank want to weep. It was a look no man wanted to receive from his son – adopted or otherwise. "Do not even think about arguing, Frank. I am the captain of this ship and I have given my command. Now see it done."

Frank nodded.

Roman was standing in front of Sam's desk and staring in disbelief, but Frank could see that his initial shock was rapidly giving way to anger. Frank grabbed Roman and took him away before he did anything stupid. Outside, in the corridor, he had to restrain the younger man from rushing back inside and confronting Samuel. "Let go of me," he shouted. "He can't do this. It's wrong."

"It's war," Frank told him resignedly. It wasn't the first act of wanton aggression he'd witnessed in his lifetime. His younger days in the army had been filled with a callous disregard for human life. I just hoped Samuel would be better than that.

Roman looked at Frank like he was an idiot. "War? What war?"

"The war of survival. In a harsh world, harsh methods are needed. If people doubt Samuel's temerity, there'll be chaos. Trust me, I served enough years as a soldier to understand that. I saw weak-willed captains shot in the back by their own men a dozen times over. In times of peace, mercy rules, but in times of war, mercy weakens."

Roman was shaking his head. He didn't buy it. "So a bunch of innocent people have to die, just so Samuel can be seen to have a big pair of balls? This is wrong. I'm going to stop it."

"Like you stopped Birch and Fox?"

Roman paused in the midst of his anger and stared at Frank. "What did you say?"

Frank folded his arms and huffed. "I don't buy the lynch mob story. Birch might have been a thug, but he could handle himself. Fox was as amiable as they come. I can see the people on the pier attacking Birch, but I don't see Fox getting involved the way you tell it. I think there's more to it than you're letting on."

"You're talking bollocks."

"Perhaps, but I've spent enough time around Samuel to learn how to read people well enough. If I can see through your lies, then I guarantee he will, too. If I was you, Roman, I would lie low and let the situation sort itself out."

"I can't just let him fire on those people. They're innocent. I have to stop it."

"You can't and you won't. You don't give the orders around here, Samuel does, and the men aboard this boat love him. You act against him and you'll be killed. You can't do anything to help those people, so just focus on the next group we find that might be worth saving."

Roman shook his head, but the defiance had not yet left him. He held onto it like a loved one. "You give that order to fire, Frank, and you're as guilty as Samuel. I hope that dead little girl fucking haunts you in your dreams." Roman shook his head one last time and then walked away, shoving aside a startled engineer who had the misfortune to be standing in his way.

Frank shook his head and sighed. *Why is everybody so eager to rule from their pulpits? My son is doing his very best, but survival of the human race is no easy task. It's a war for our very existence and harsh decisions must be made. Only great men can make the tough decisions. Samuel is a great man and people resent him for it, but they do not see that he is still a young man. He needs guidance...whether he asks for it or not.*

Roman is right. I cannot be party to this. Samuel will thank me in the end.

Frank sighed, took a deep breath, and then went to give the firing orders to the Kirkland's gunnery sergeant. When he got there, he made sure to tell the man to 'miss'.

HUGO

HUGO'S STOMACH WAS in knots. He'd been waiting on the aft deck of the Kirkland in the rain for almost three hours now, waiting for someone to take him to see the captain. The entire time, his daughters had been alone, back on the yacht with only Houdini to look after them. It was the first time he'd left them in almost a year, but the frigate was not a place for young girls and he preferred not to bring them along. It turned out to be a good judgement call.

Hugo was disgusted by what he saw aboard the Kirkland. The civilians were dirty and unwashed, while the officers were arrogant and rude. They'd dismissed Hugo more than once and were less than helpful when he told them he wanted to report a crime. One or two of the officers had straight-out laughed at him. At least the officers were clean, though. The crew and civilians seemed to take no notice of their hygiene as they ran about completing their tasks. Their clothing was soiled and their hair was lank and greasy. It appeared that running a frigate was endless, sweaty work. I am fortunate to have my own yacht. The rules of hygiene still very much apply on the éternuer.

Hugo's hair and face were drenched, but he could not tell if it was from the light rain or the spray brought up by the Kirkland's imposing prow. He was beginning to shiver. An officer strolled by and Hugo reached out to grab him. "I need to see Mr Raymeady."

The man curled his lip up at Hugo and said, "The captain is busy. If you would like to have a message sent to him, then you can write a note and give it to one of the stewards when they do their rounds. He may then summon you if he wishes."

Hugo sniffed at that. The stewards were meant to meet with the boats of the fleet once a day, but it was lucky if you saw them once a month. Their little Kodiak speedboat was more often filled with giggling women than messages from the fleet. Young men are as irresponsible today as they ever were.

The officer shrugged free of Hugo's grasp and marched away. Hugo was so frustrated that he was close to tears. A terrible crime had been committed, yet nobody wished to hear about it. It made him worry for his daughters; it was not good to raise them in a world where crime was not taken seriously. The fleet had always made him feel safe, but today that feeling of security was ebbing away, one rude dismissal at a time.

There was some hustle and bustle up ahead and Hugo looked across at the ship's big equipment hanger. There was a man coming out, stomping about angrily, while other men hurriedly moved aside. Hugo knew at once who the angry man was. The Roman.

Hugo had heard many tales about the man named Roman. The other sailors said he had received the nickname because of the spear and sword he carried; while others said that he was an Italian known for his cruelty and arrogance. Some people even said he'd survived a zombie bite by cutting off his infected hand. One thing that Hugo knew for sure was that the man spoke directly with the captain. I could give my report to the Roman. He will see that it reaches the captain's ears.

So long as he doesn't just swat me aside like a fly. I hear he is a very unfriendly man.

Hugo swallowed and set off towards Roman. The man had headed starboard and was leant over the edge, staring out towards the distant pier.

"Erm...excuse me, monsieur." Damn it. Hugo's French crept back in when he was nervous. Roman didn't acknowledge him, just kept his gaze on the distant pier. "I-I am sorry to interrupt your thinking, but I need a man who will listen to me."

"That's not me," Roman said. He spoke in a tone that should have been enough to frighten Hugo away, but Hugo wanted to get back to his daughters, and he could not do that until someone heeded his words.

"I must report a crime. You are the mighty Roman, yes? You are the captain's good man, no?"

Roman turned and snarled at Hugo. The sword on his belt suddenly looked very heavy. And sharp! "I am nobody's man," he growled. "I do as I wish and the captain does as he wishes. Do not combine my actions with his."

Hugo took a step back, but did not retreat. "My apologies, monsieur." Damn it. "I must report a crime."

"Tell it to somebody else."

"A murder. A body dumped in the sea."

At last the man seemed interested. He turned around and gave his full attention. Hugo had been right to seek out him out. Roman was one of the captain's men, and despite his rude demeanour, he was obligated to heed reports of serious crimes. "What are you talking about?" he said. "What body?"

"Out at sea, this dawn passed. I saw a yacht returning from the pier. There were two men, but one went overboard, I believe already dead."

Roman shrugged as if he was unconvinced. *But at least he is listening.* "How do you know it was a body being dumped?"

Hugo couldn't help but laugh. "We live in a world seized by the dead, and you ask me how I know a body when I see one. I know death well, as do we all. The man on the yacht was sinking a body beneath the ocean, this I saw."

Roman glanced back out at the pier and dropped his head so that his chin hung against his chest. When he spoke again, he spoke sadly. "If you know death so well, then you should understand it has no meaning anymore. One corpse is literally a drop in the ocean. It's not worth noticing, let alone reporting. I suggest you go back to your boat, old man, and concentrate on not joining the dead yourself. Count yourself lucky to be alive."

Was that a threat?

"Monsieur, if we start ignoring murder then this was all for nothing. Even those of us lucky enough to be alive are in fact truly dead. We are human beings and we must care about each other if we have any chance of truly being alive. We must be as one."

Roman laughed. For a moment he almost seemed to drop his defences. A slim smile appeared on his face, but it quickly faded away, replaced by a hard, impassive stare. "Go back to your boat, and stop telling tales. It's likely to get you killed."

A threat indeed.

Hugo nodded. He had told the closest person he could find to the captain, and still his words were disregarded. I have done all I can. Now I must return to my daughters and think on this. Things are not as I believed them to be. There is no law and order here. The men and women here are empty.

"Thank you for your time, monsieur." Hugo left Roman at the gunwale and headed back towards the rigging, which would lead him back down to his yacht. His daughters had been alone far too long already. He felt naked without them by his side. I even miss my little Houdini. I hope he's been looking after them and not leaving foul messes everywhere.

"Excuse me."

Hugo turned around to see a tall blonde officer striding towards him. He smiled wearily at the man. "Yes, can I help you?"

"Perhaps. I am Petty Officer Dunn. I've noticed you came aboard some hours ago. Was there something you needed help with? I saw you talking to Roman."

Hugo nodded. "Yes, a most unhelpful man, I am afraid."

The officer laughed. "You're not wrong. What was it you were looking for help with?"

"I wanted to report a crime, a murder. Although Roman told me not to speak of such things any longer."

Dunn shook his head and pouted. "How very wrong of him. Come, would you like a cup of tea? You can give your report to me. It sounds very serious and I would most like to hear it. A murder, you say? Heaven's above."

Hugo smiled and sighed a breath of relief. Finally, someone was willing to take him seriously. "I would love a cup of tea," he said. "Please, lead the way."

Officer Dunn gave Hugo a warm smile and did just that. They sat and drank hot tea while the officer took careful notes of everything Hugo was saying.

POPPY

OPPY WISHED GARFIELD was home more than ever. She felt guilty over what had happened. It was all her fault. She shouldn't have gone with Birch in the night. She should've known better. Garfield had given her magazines to teach her how to be a grown-up woman, but it was obvious now that she was still just a kid – and part of her was glad about it. She didn't understand grown-ups yet. Their constant fighting and shouting scared her. If that was what adults did, she would stay a child for as long as possible.

"We're going to have dinner in an hour," Anna called up to her. Poppy had been sitting on the roof of the Sea Grill restaurant for the last few hours, once again watching the horizon for Garfield's return. It would probably be several more days, but Poppy intended to sit on the rooftops until she spotted him upon the edge of the village. He might not love me, but I love him. I need to tell him how sorry I am for all the trouble I caused. She was passing the time by drawing. She could often get lost amidst her pencils and crayons, stroking and shading the images in her mind until they came to life on the page.

"Did you hear me?" Anna shouted up again. Alistair was beside her. His face was bloated and purple where bad Mr Birch had beaten him up. Both of them were wearing thick winter coats, but Poppy had not noticed how cold it had gotten.

"I heard you," said Poppy. "Can I stay here for a little while longer?"

Anna sighed. "It's getting dark and I don't want you hanging around on your own. We need to stick together after what happened last night. First thing tomorrow morning we're all going to make a plan, but right now we need to look after each other."

Poppy nodded. She didn't want to be alone, and neither did she want to disobey Anna after what had happened. She and Alistair had fought to protect her and both were battered and bruised as a result. Poppy felt an awful feeling in her tummy when she thought about how she was responsible. "I...I just want to wait for Garfield, but...I'll come."

"No," said Alistair. "You stay there, Poppy. I'll come and sit with you while dinner cooks."

Anna looked at Alistair. "You sure? How on Earth do you plan on getting up there?"

"I'll find a way. You go get yourself in the warm, Anna, I'll bring the urchin along later."

Anna patted Alistair on the back and smiled. "Okay, I have to check on Tim first, anyway. His bandages need changing. Don't be too long." She looked up at Poppy on the roof. "And you behave up there, Poppy."

Poppy nodded.

After Anna had left, Alistair put his hands on his hips and stared up at the roof, clucking his tongue. "Now, how the hell do I get my fat arse up there, huh?"

Poppy giggled. "There's a big metal bin around the back. I climb up on there."

Alistair nodded. "Right-o. I'll be up in a jiffy."

Poppy sat and waited while Alistair disappeared behind the Sea Grill. A few moments passed and then she could hear his huffs and puffs as he climbed up on top of the bin.

"Do you need help?" she called out.

There was another huff and a puff and Alistair's head appeared above the roof. His cheeks had gone bright red. Poppy went over and offered him her hand. Together they managed to get his bulk up onto the roof. The wooden timbers creaked, but they held.

"Getting down is harder," she said.

Alistair keeled over. "Christ. I may just have to live up here, then."

"Thanks for keeping me company."

Alistair ruffled her hair and sat down on the rooftop. "You're very welcome. Can't leave you to mope around up here on your own."

Poppy sat down beside him and began gathering up her pencils and crayons. "I'm sorry I caused trouble."

"Don't you go apologising for what those men did. You did nothing wrong."

"Doesn't feel that way."

Alistair smiled at her. "That's because good people feel guilty about bad men's sins. It's good that you're sorry about the things that happened, but don't you go blaming yourself. We're a family here and we look after each other. I don't think we really realised it until last night. I guess I was so wrapped up in surviving, that I forgot to take a step back and realise how lucky we all are to have each other."

"You're usually so mean to me."

Alistair sighed and shrugged at her. "Tell you the truth, I'm not very good with kids. I suppose I always saw them as useless. What happened last night made me realise how precious you are, though. There's nothing wrong with being a kid. I'm sorry I didn't realise it sooner."

"You and Anna stuck up for me."

"We stuck up for our little girl, and we'd do it again. Don't you worry about ever being alone, because you have us and we have you."

"I miss Garfield."

Alistair nodded and stared out at the horizon. "I know you do, lass. I miss him, too."

Poppy was surprised. "You miss Garfield?"

"You're not the only one who gets on with him, you know. He's as much a part of the group as anyone else. I play cards with Garfield most nights when he's back, while you're sleeping."

"I...I didn't know."

Alistair chuckled and slapped her on the back. It hurt her a little bit. "That's because you think Garfield belongs to you. He doesn't. He wants you to grow up and be your own person. You're a part of this entire group. We all love you in our own way."

Poppy nodded. "I don't think I want to grow up anymore."

"None of us do. You have some time yet, though. What's that you have?"

Poppy looked down to see what he was talking about. When she saw her drawing spread out on the roof, she quickly snatched it up and blushed. "It's not finished."

Alistair grinned. "Don't be shy, lass. We all know you're handy with a pencil. Let me see what you've drawn."

Poppy rumpled the drawing in her hands, but slowly straightened it out and showed Alistair. He smiled as he examined it. "It's-"

"I can see what it is," he said. "It's beautiful. You really do have quite the talent, young lady. One day you'll be famous."

Poppy blushed and folded the picture away in the breast pocket of her cardigan. The she shuffled around to face the other way, towards the sea. It was growing dark, but the big grey boat illuminated the horizon with a hundred blinking lights. Lots of smaller ships twinkled all around it. "Do you think they're going to come back?"

"I'd say so. We still have their man."

"Why don't we just hand Tim over to them? We only just met him and he's making people come after us."

"That's not how we do things, Poppy. Anna and Rene want to ask Tim some more questions about the man in the big ship first."

"He's a bad man?"

"Might just be the worst."

"Even more reason to give him what he wants."

"We do that, sweetheart, and we might as well walk into the sea. We can't give in to threats and violence. Garfield has gone away to find guns so that we don't have to. We're not going to give Tim up, it would be wrong, but he's decided to go on his own. It was his choice. He wants to do what's right. We will do what is right, too, because that's what's...right."

"Garfield told me that people used to be bad a lot in the old days. I remember my old house used to have an alarm that my dad would set every night because of bad people."

Alistair rubbed a hand over his thigh and nodded. "There have always been bad people, Poppy. That's why we need to look after each other, and why we won't bend to people who threaten us. We do it once and we'll forever be in danger. Bullies prey on the weak. We will never be weak."

"Those men last night scared me. I don't want to see any more of them. I want Garfield and the others to come back."

Alistair wrapped his arm around her. "Garfield will come back soon. That man loves you too much to be gone for long."

Poppy glanced at Alistair. "He loves me?"

"Of course he does. He'd die for you, you silly thing."

Poppy smiled. "He's never told me that he loves me."

"People find it hard to say what they feel. Take me, for instance, I shouted and raved at Garfield when he was taking half the camp with him on his foraging expedition, but my real concern was that I just didn't want them all to leave. They'll be back soon. Then Garfield will give you a great big hug and give you presents."

Poppy grinned. "I hope so. That would be nice." She peered out at the sea. The big boat was moving. "Hey...look."

Alistair placed a hand over his eyes and squinted. "What?"

"Something's moving. See?"

On the side of the big grey boat, a big piece of metal started to move. It was like a big long pipe pointing at the sky. Slowly it lowered so that it was pointed directly towards the pier. What's it doing?

There was a sudden explosion and several little puffs of fire burst out the end of the big long pipe. Bam bam bam bam bam....

Poppy grinned wide. It looks like fireworks.

GARFIELD

A GATHERING OF CROWS took flight. The carcass on the road looked like it had belonged to a fox, but it was difficult to tell for sure in the glaring headlights. Animals didn't concern the dead, and as a result there were more foxes, badgers, and rats than ever before. They made good eating if you could catch them, but they'd become increasingly brave in the new world and quite often carried disease. A light scratch from a feral cat could fester and rot. It was easier to forage than to hunt.

Garfield studied the picture Poppy had drawn for him. It was impressively realistic; every time he looked at it he noticed additional details. In addition to the family of moorhens in the foreground, there were fireflies hovering above the pond and a stalk wading in the background. Just like Poppy had hoped, it cheered him up looking at it. *She's such a sweet thing. I really hate being away from her so long. I wonder what she's up to.*

Garfield missed Poppy and the pier. It was the longest he'd ever been away since they'd first come upon it. The further away he got from it, the worse things seem to get.

Things amongst the foragers were tense after two-and-a-half days on the road. They had stuck to the fields and farmland, which meant the scenery was bland and samey. The many hours of travelling had left them weary, depressed, and irritable. Danny and Squirrel dying three hours ago had just made things worse. *Those careless fools.*

Danny and Squirrel had been at the pier since the beginning, having originally discovered the place with Alistair, Anna, and a few others who'd stumbled upon each other on the south coast. The two young men were well liked and brave, an important part of the group. Garfield hated to say it, but they were also stupid.

Squirrel had been a dope smoking benefit-seeker in the old days, and his ambitions became no greater once the world had ended. Squirrel was happy to take orders when necessary, but would slack off the rest of the time. He barely even managed to wash without being told to. When Squirrel wasn't being directed, he was a liability. Danny had been much the same, a shop worker back in his old life. Now both of them were dead.

Kirk had been driving the minivan through another field when they'd come upon an old village pub. The Tudor-style building was on it's own, set off from two intersecting roads. Its name was The Jubilee and it was deserted. There were no cars parked outside, as if it'd been closed when the infection hit. Nightfall was only an hour away, so Garfield had agreed the pub would make a good campsite for the evening. Kirk pulled the minivan over and set it outside the front doors. Pubs often had a cellar full of soft drinks and long-life snacks such as crisps and pork scratchings, but Garfield knew what the other men were truly excited about.

I should have had Kirk turn around right then.

Garfield had no problem with alcohol. It was something he avoided on the road, but it was nice to have a swig back at the pier when the opportunity presented itself. It was an undeniable luxury to get rat-arsed nowadays, one of the only things unanimously missed. But drinking in the field was dangerous. They'd lost a man named Barry because of it. He'd been legless on Brandy when he stumbled down the long escalators of an abandoned supermarket. His leg broke and he screamed like a trapped piglet. The dead had come quickly, attracted to the noise. With his broken leg, the other foragers had no choice but to leave Barry to his fate. There had been little sympathy for drunkenness in the field ever since. Still hasn't stopped us losing people, though. Maybe I'm not cut out for this.

The Australian, Sally, seemed to take a different view on alcohol. As soon as they entered the pub they found optics full of spirits and fridges full of wine and beer. Immediately the Australian grabbed a bottle of German Larger and bit the top off. "It ain't Ozzy beer," he had said. "But it'll do."

Garfield told the men that they would take the alcohol back to camp and drink it in safety, but Sally laughed and grabbed another beer from the fridge. "Sod that, squire."

"We're not allowed to d-d-drink in the field," Lemon told him, but his eyes were wide with wonder. The alcohol was calling to him.

"Not allowed? Are you a man or a possum?" Sally grabbed a third bottle of beer and lobbed it Lemon's way. "You pommes are too serious. Lighten up and enjoy a beer. Life doesn't have a lot of moments like this. Snatch at 'em while yer can."

Lemon looked at Garfield uncertainly. Garfield stared back at him with a stern expression on his face.

"I'll have a brewski," said Kirk. "It's been a long day."

"That's a bad idea," said Garfield.

"Probably," said Kirk. "But it'll sure feel good." He uncapped a beer with his teeth and took a long pull from the bottle. He gasped and wiped at his mouth with the back of his hand. "God, that's good."

It hadn't taken long before every one of them was drinking; everyone except for Garfield. He chose to sit on a corner bench and rest up for a while. He snagged himself a bottle of lemonade and was content enough with that. Hopefully, come morning, the foragers would not be too hungover to get up off the floor. Can't blame them. Alcohol was a temptation even before everything that's happened. It feels even better to escape nowadays.

Garfield would have enjoyed nothing more than to have joined the drunken revelling of the others, but he made the decision that at least one of them should stay sober. Lemon was already staggering and Kirk was downing vodka shots like they were apple juice. There was no need of designated drivers anymore, but having someone alert and lucid was as important as ever. Still, Garfield winced every time someone raised their voice or smashed a glass. It had grown dark outside and he had frequent visions of zombies creeping up to the windows in their droves. What Garfield never considered was that the dead were already inside. I should have checked the building out thoroughly.

After having enjoyed themselves for nigh on two hours, Cat suggested that they should make bed spaces now, rather than later when they might be incapable. She had let out a mighty belch to punctuate her thoughts.

Sally jumped up on the bar and lay down, pouring whiskey down his throat and giggling. "You fellas don't mind me. I'll just keep drinking until I pass out right here. Reminds me of being back in Brisbane. I used to drink the whole weekend through back in my younger days, different bird on each arm. Some real beauts I used to get me."

"We should check out the upstairs," said Lemon. "We'll probably find beds up there. I'd like to sleep in a real bed."

"First dibs," shouted Danny and he and Squirrel rushed behind the bar. In their drunkenness they decided it was a good idea to karate kick the door that led to the backroom area.

As soon as the door flung open the dead piled into the cramped bar aisle and let out a chorus of hungry moans. In all of their raucous partying, no one had heard them scratching at the door.

A skeletal woman fell on Squirrel and tore out his windpipe with her teeth. He stumbled backwards against the bar, spraying blood all over the place. Sally, who'd been lying on the bar at the time, tumbled to the ground and shouted, "Crikey!" although he almost seemed amused by what he was seeing.

Danny went to drag Squirrel away, even though there was no point. Squirrel was already screwed. A dead man set upon Danny at once, grabbing him by the lapels of his jacket. He tried to turn on his heels, but the alcohol in his system made him clumsy and he fell down to his knees. The dead man seized him immediately and tore away the flesh at the back of his neck, biting down all the way to his spine. Half a dozen hungry corpses piled into the bar from the open doorway.

Garfield leapt up from the bench and thought fast. He picked up a stool and threw it behind the bar, slowing down the awkward strides of the dead trying to escape from the aisle. "Everyone get in the van, now," he shouted. "Move, move, move!"

Everyone piled out of the pub, shoving through the front entrance and towards the minivan. The dead were outside, too, attracted by the noise. Garfield had to take down the nearest with a wrench he kept strapped to his chest. Sally and Kirk fought, too, while everyone else leapt into the minivan or climbed into the horsebox attached to the back. Once everyone was onboard, Garfield headed for the front passenger seat, but was surprised when he found Sally sitting there. There was no time to argue, so he slid open the door at the side of the van and dove across the laps of the others.

Kirk gunned the engine and they took off. A dead man snatched at the horsebox and was dragged a few metres until his arm tore loose and he fell facedown on the tarmac. They managed to burn rubber just as a dozen zombies piled out of the building and started towards them.

That had been three hours ago.

They'd driven in silence since then. Kirk focused on the road with a frown on his face, and even the Australian was quiet. Why did he decide to head for the front seat? Was it just something he did in the heat of the moment, or was there an agenda? Those in the back with Garfield stared into space glumly. Cat sobbed quietly. Dawn was only an hour away and hangovers were beginning to take hold. Everyone needed sleep.

"I think we need to find somewhere," said Garfield. "Kirk, stop at the next safe place you can find."

Out of the blue, Kirk smashed both fists against the steering wheel. The horn went pip! "Safe? I think we just learned that no place is safe. What the hell happened back there?"

"I said not to drink," said Garfield. "We made too much noise."

"Why the hell did you let everyone drink, if you knew it was such a bad idea?"

Garfield shook his head in disbelief. "What would you have me do? I'm not your babysitter. You all knew that drinking was a bad idea, but you did it anyway."

"Seems to me," said Sally. "That a decent leader would keep his men in line. The troops don't always know what's best for themselves. Soldiers need a strong hand."

Garfield snorted. "Then maybe I should deal with your insubordination by dumping you on the side of the road. Is that a strong enough hand for you?"

"Don't have a go at Sally," said Kirk. "He has nothing to do with this, and he's right. You should have stopped everyone from drinking. Danny and Squirrel are dead because of you."

Garfield felt the same way, but he knew it was just his guilt. The truth was their own stupidity got them killed. They may call Garfield 'leader', but the truth was that every man was responsible for himself. "If you want to blame me, Kirk, then fine. But don't kid yourself, okay? You all knew you were taking a risk by getting drunk. If any of you think you can do a better job being in charge, then we'll discuss it when we're back at the pier. I'm more than happy to let someone else take the responsibility. Tell you the truth, I'm sick of it."

"The pier?" said Sally. "Is that where your camp is? That sounds bonza. Anyway, why should everyone discuss it at the pier? Why not now?"

There was silence in the minivan.

"Because now is not the time," Garfield said.

"Seems to me that now is the only time. Don't want anyone else dying because of bad leadership, do yer?"

That's it. This guy is out on his arse. Garfield was about to shout an order to eject the Australian when Kirk turned his head to look back at him. "We're almost there," he said excitedly. "We've found it."

Garfield shifted forward to look out the windscreen. There was a sign coming up on the left. It was lit by the minivan's high-beams. It read: DEFENCE TRAINING ESTATE, ROYAL SCHOOL OF ARTIL-LERY, LARKHILL. 12 MILES. PLEASE WATCH YOUR SPEED.

Garfield let out a sigh of relief. "We're here," he said. "Let's keep our fingers crossed."

"That there are weapons there?" asked Lemon.

"No," said Garfield, shaking his head. "Let's cross our fingers that no one else dies."

ANNA

ANNA OPENED HER eyes but could see only black. At first she thought she was blind, but then she saw the burning embers across the sand and the crackling fires up above on the pier. She coughed, spluttered, and sat up. The beach was unsafe. Sometimes the dead washed up on shore and began crawling around. No one ever set foot on the beach. So what am I doing down here?

She could only stare at the fire above her for a moment, marvelling at its beauty and enjoying the heat. It took her a few moments until she comprehended what it meant. The pier is burning. Something... something happened. A bomb, or an explosion...

Anna dragged herself up off the sand and staggered to her feet. Her head was swimming and she noticed fluid dripping from her fingertips. Her heart beat faster at the sight of her own blood, and she patted herself down frantically, looking for the source. A jab of pain on her right elbow alerted her to the fact that a long shard of wood had slid into her flesh and torn her open. She grabbed a hold of the giant splinter and cursed as she yanked it free. I...I don't understand what's happened.

But then she knew. She looked out across the moonlit sea and saw the bright lights of the frigate. 30MM guns, pointing right in our direction, she remembered someone saying. Roman had warned her, but she'd naively assumed he would return to negotiate. There had been nothing to gain by firing on the pier. But they did it anyway. Even now, after all the death and destruction we've seen, men will still kill to protect their vanity.

Anna spat at the ground and kicked sand into the air. She wanted to swim right up to the frigate and throttle whoever was in charge. Samuel Raymeady...

There were moans up above and suddenly Anna panicked that the dead had arrived. While she may have found herself stunned and disorientated on the beach, there was nobody else beneath the pier. The moaning could be coming from Alistair, old man Bob, or any of the others. *Where is everybody? Are they okay?*

Anna grabbed a hold of a twisted piece of the pier, which had collapsed from above. The large steel strut had twisted and bent inwards, making that whole section of pier list precariously to one side. The lowest part of the tilting deck was only ten feet above and almost within reach.

Anna placed a foot up onto the skewed piece of steel and hoisted herself higher. From there she was able to grab a hold of a plank jutting out from the deck. She winced as splinters bit into her palms, but she kept on climbing, pulling herself up, one handhold after another. By the time she pulled herself up onto the pier she was huffing and puffing, and her wounded elbow had split wide open. But none of that mattered.

The pier was on fire.

The amusement pavilion at the far end had collapsed into the sea. The top section of its tented roof was sticking above the waves like a coral reef. The decking that had led to it had splintered and snapped, bits of it now floating on the sea. The village side of the pier was still intact, along with the gate, but the middle section, where the diner and various gift shops were situated, was blackened and aflame. The deck fell away about eight feet behind where Anna was standing; only sea and sand existed where it had once been. *If I'd been somewhere further down the pier I would be dead. Where were the others when we were hit?*

As if to answer her question, old man Bob, Jim, and Samantha appeared from behind the toilet block. They were covered in ash and their eyes were wide and frightened. Even after surviving the apocalypse, they can still only take so much. Some of Samantha's jewellery had snapped and broken. The bracelets on her wrists rattled a little less than usual.

Anna stumbled towards them, tears in her eyes as the relief washed over her that she was not alone in surviving the attack, but then she saw that they carried a body between them and she suddenly felt sick.

It was Chris. The middle-aged man was burned so badly that Anna could only recognise him from the bright red wellies he wore. His face was a twisted mask of swollen, blistered flesh.

"We were hoping you could help him," said old man Bob.

"But he's already dead, isn't he?" said Samantha glumly.

Anna nodded and stayed silent for a moment. "What happened?" she eventually asked.

Old man Bob spat a mouthful of ash onto the deck. "We were bombed...shot...I don't know, whatever. That godless ship fired on us."

"All because of that man they wanted?" said Samantha. She was a mixture of sad and angry. "Just because of him? We didn't deserve this. We did nothing. Why did they do this to us?"

Anna couldn't answer the question, so she asked one of her own. "Where's everybody else? Poppy, Rene, Alistair, Tim?"

Bob shrugged. The older man looked like he was about to die where he stood. "Just us, lass. I haven't seen the others."

"Then we need to find them now." Anna stared at the fires that illuminated the middle of the pier. The roof of the Sea Grill restaurant had collapsed in on itself and was slowly succumbing to the flames. The toilet block was all brick and hadn't caught alight. Neither had the ice cream shop where Garfield and Poppy stayed. Further down, the last section of the pier was completely untouched by flames, but the only buildings it contained were a small cashpoint vestibule and a tourist helpdesk. And the gate. Thank God the gate still stands. "Everybody, get searching," she ordered. "There'll be time to cry later." And time to figure out how to make someone pay for this.

They found Rene inside the diner. They spotted him staggering out of the burning building with Tim slumped over his shoulder, like some action hero in a movie. Tim was still conscious and swinging his crutches left and right, batting away the burning debris as Rene carried him out onto the deck and placed him back on his feet.

Anna threw her arms around Rene when she saw him. "You're alive," she said, stating the obvious, but glad to be able to say it.

"But injured," Rene grunted, easing her back and wincing. Along his neck, from his chest to his chin, a deep burn glistened. The flesh was bright pink amongst his normal healthy dark skin."

Anna winced. "Jesus Christ."

Rene nodded. "May he guide me back to health. I am okay for now, Anna. What needs to be done?"

Anna answered immediately. "We need to find Poppy. Alistair, too."

"I'm sorry," said Tim. "This is all my fault."

Anna marched up to the cripple and snarled. "No, its half your fault. That son of a bitch on his little toy boat is responsible for the other half." She walked away and began her search for Poppy. She would deal with Tim later.

Poppy and Alistair were on the rooftop. I remember because I left them to head for the diner. I was outside on the deck when the pier was hit. I must have been thrown onto the beach. If the sand wasn't so wet I might have died when I landed.

Anna angled her run and headed for the Sea Grill. The rooftop had gone, fallen-in from the fire, but where were Alistair and Poppy? Had they been hit? Or thrown free like Anna had been? Damn it! Where are you two?

Flames had not yet consumed the interior of the restaurant. It smouldered and smoked in some places, but the fire was yet to fully take hold. Anna pushed open the door and stepped inside. The smoke made her choke immediately. She shoved a sleeve over her mouth and swallowed hard. The stars shone down from the centre of the room through a large gap where the ceiling had split open. The far side of the diner was completely devastated by the heavy, burning lintels of the roof, which had snapped like twigs and fallen to the ground. At the back of the room was the open-plan kitchen, currently unharmed.

Alistair lay on the ground ten feet from Anna. He was bleeding heavily. A pool of blood surrounded him on the cracked tiles, congealing quickly in the heat of the nearby fires. Anna leapt down beside him and placed a hand against his cheek. "Al, it's okay, I'm here. It's Anna. I'm going to help you."

Alistair spluttered and a mouthful of blood ended up on his chin. "Y-you can't help me, lass. I've been violated, huh."

Anna frowned and wondered what he meant, but then she saw. A steel shard had violated his groin in the space between his bellybutton and his genitals. Whether the thick shard had come from the shell that hit the pier or from something else, she did not know, but it had torn Alistair's insides apart. Shit, this is bad.

Anna felt herself cry. For a long time she'd not wanted to love or trust anyone besides Rene, but she knew now that she'd come to love the people on the pier like family. Alistair was an obstinate asshole, but he was like a brother. She wished she'd realised it earlier.

Alistair forced a smile onto his face and struggled to speak again. "I'm g-glad you're okay, Anna. I was w-w...worried."

Anna laughed. "Don't you worry about me, you silly sod. You should..."

Alistair eyes had gone still. His chest had stopped moving.

Anna never even had the chance to say goodbye. Death didn't wait for pleasantries, she knew that, but she'd hoped for another minute or two. She leant forward and kissed Alistair's cheek, then stood up and walked towards the kitchen. Rene tried to enter the restaurant behind her, but she shouted at him to leave. Nobody else needs to see this.

Anna took a deep breath and held it for a minute. The smoke inside the restaurant was thickening and burning her eyes, but she couldn't leave yet. Poppy had been with Alistair when the shells hit. Anna had to find her. She'd promised Garfield she would look after the girl. I need to find her. I need to find her.

Poppy lay beneath a table by the kitchen. Her blonde plaits were blackened and half her face was missing. Despite that, she seemed peaceful. Her body was lying comfortably and her mouth was pursed into a smile. The intense heat of the blast had taken her instantly, but that didn't make Anna's sadness any less. The little girl didn't even seem real anymore. She looked more like an old porcelain dolly with a broken face.

There was something poking out of the breast pocket of Poppy's cardigan. It looked like a charred piece of paper. Anna removed it carefully and unfolded it. She couldn't help but smile as she looked at the drawing.

The picture was unfinished and the top half was burned, but Anna could clearly see the pier sketched in pencil. Atop its deck, brought to life by dozens of colours were all of the people of the pier. Anna spotted Garfield, bigger and stronger than everybody else, with bright red hair. Standing beside him was Alistair with a bright big grin and huge muscles. Then Anna spotted herself. Poppy had drawn her in a long white dress with a golden tiara upon her head. She stood next to Rene who was holding the train of her dress. She thinks I'm a princess? At the bottom of the picture, below the two-dozen people drawn on the pier were two words written in wiggly capitals: MY FAMILY.

Anna felt a fire burning. At first she thought it was coming from her gut, but then she started to feel it against her skin. The delicate flesh of her cheek started to tingle and burn, but she did not care. She breathed in the pain like it was power. The more it hurt her, the more conviction that filled her heart, until she could stand it no more and stumbled away. She headed back outside and ignored the desperate queries of her campmates – her family. Instead, she stared out across the moonlit sea at the frigate all lit up like a beacon of hope. It mocked her.

Anna thought about the man onboard, Samuel Raymeady, and how she was going to kill him.

DAMIEN

DAMIEN STARED OUT at the fires on the shore and fought the urge to throw up over the side. If he'd eaten recently, he probably would have. What he'd just witnessed was beyond belief. Even though he'd known it was coming, Samuel's actions itched at his soul. Damien had naively hoped that Frank would persuade his son to stay his hand, but it appeared that the captain was without mercy. He destroyed the pier and killed everyone. Just to kill one man!

It's my fault. If I'd just brought back that goddamn cripple.... Now people are dead because of me. A child is dead because of me.

Damien gripped the gunwale and squeezed so hard that the bones in his hand creaked. His body shuddered and he was unable to blink. The fires shimmered on the water and lit up the night. The inferno held his gaze, unwilling to let him look away from what he'd done. What Samuel did. I need to stop blaming myself. I didn't have the power here, Samuel did.

But I could have done something. Anything....

"Do you still need convincing of what Samuel is?"

Damien didn't turn around. He knew Harry's voice well enough to recognise it. "I should have killed your friend the first chance I got. I should never have flinched."

Harry joined him at edge. "What do you mean?"

"I mean I had a clear shot at his head but I flinched at the last second. Now I wish I'd pulled the trigger without thinking about it."

"You're not a murderer," said Harry. "That's a good thing."

Damien snorted. "I killed two men less than twenty-four hours ago. Fox and Birch."

Harry said nothing.

"If Samuel finds out I killed both men he sent with me to the pier, he'll have me killed. He already knows I killed Birch, but at least then I had reason. He won't ignore me killing Fox."

"Why did you kill Fox? He seemed harmless enough the few times I spoke with him."

"To protect you, you bloody dickhead. Fox would have told Samuel everything that Tim had said, about how you two were involved together. He'll still find out one way or another, though. We're both screwed."

Harry nodded and looked serious. "All the more reason to listen to what I've told you. Samuel Raymeady is evil, a monster. He needs to be stopped before more things like this happen. Those people on the pier are burning alive because of the casual orders Samuel gives from the comfy chair in his chambers. He's craven, unwilling to bloody his own hands. He must be stopped. The people on this boat are already brainwashed, but it's not too late to do something. We can st-"

"Stop!" Damien hissed. "Just...stop. Samuel isn't evil. There is no good or evil. There's just people. And people are weak or they are strong, they are selfish or they are dead. I'm not interested in staging a coup just so some other bully can take control later on down the road. People like Samuel Raymeady have always controlled the human race, because the rest of us don't want to make the tough decisions. If he's willing to take on all of the lost souls of the fleet, then he's entitled to do as he pleases. Taking innocent lives is just part of the gig, survival of the fittest. Thousands of years of history have taught us that."

"There is no history," Harry said angrily. "The history books were erased when the dead rose to eat the living. Mankind has started anew and none of the old mistakes need be repeated. If the human race is resurrected on the back of a man like Samuel Raymeady, then we might as well have died. What are we even living for, if not to do things better this time around?"

Damien closed his eyes for a second and tried to ignore the stench of burning wafting from the shore. Even if he agreed with Harry and wanted to do something, there was nothing he could do. The people of the fleet were happy to follow Samuel. They had watched the pier burn and not one of the ships had broken away from the fleet. Not one single person had headed for the mainland to help those who may still be alive. Nobody cared. People only wanted what was best for them.

"You have to do something, Damien."

"Why do I? Why do I have to do anything? Why don't you go and plant a sodding bomb like your friend, Tim."

Harry looked away and sighed.

Damien shook his head. Please, don't tell me.... "You have, haven't you? Harry, if you've done something, un-do it now. I won't watch while they string you up and turn you into a figurehead for the Kirkland's bow."

"Then don't watch."

Anger took a hold of Damien and before he was able to stop himself he backhanded Harry across the face. A couple of civilians playing cards a few metres down the deck looked up to see the ruckus, but they quickly lowered their heads when they saw who was involved. Damien stared at his friend and saw the blood trickling from the corner of his mouth. "H-Harry, I'm sorry."

Harry wiped the blood away with his sleeve. "Don't apologise. Just do what's right. Show me that what I saw in you years ago was right. You're the man people should be following, not Samuel." He pointed at the burning pier. "If you're half the man I think you are, you won't let any more innocent people die. The world is what we make it, Damien, so don't tell me to just fucking live with it! If you won't do something, I will." Harry turned and walked away.

Damien went to hurry after him, but another man quickly blocked his path. It was petty officer Dunn. "I don't have time," Damien snapped at the weasel-faced man. My best friend might have set a bomb somewhere on this ship and right now he seems pissed off enough to trigger it.

"The captain wishes to speak with you."

Damien shoved Dunn out of his way. "Later."

"No, now!" Dunn placed a hand on Damien's shoulder, which was the man's first mistake. The second mistake was not ducking when Damien turned and head butted him. Dunn squealed as he hit the floor. Damien was about to grab him up off the ground and send him on his way when he realised he was surrounded. Four other crewmen pressed in on him in a semi-circle. Each of them glared at him like zoo wardens about to tackle a lion. Damien raised his spear and placed a hand on the hilt of his sword.

Dunn climbed up off the ground, cursing and spitting blood. He scowled at Damien. "The captain would see you now," he growled. "It is a matter of importance and he has demanded to see you immediately. If you won't come then he has authorised me to use force."

"Going to hit my head with your face again, are you?"

Dunn snarled. "There are five of us. As much as you may fancy yourself as some post-apocalyptic warrior, you're still just one man."

"Bruce Lee was one man."

"Bruce Lee isn't here."

Damien couldn't argue with the statement. "Fine, I give up. I'll come with you."

Dunn smiled like a well-fed cat. "Wonderful. You're not as stu-"

Damien head butted him again. Immediately the other crewmen grabbed Damien by the arms and restrained him. From on the floor, Dunn bawled, clutching at his ruined nose. "You said you'd come with me."

"I didn't say voluntarily."

"Take him to the captain," Dunn screamed at the other men. "The sooner he gets what's coming to him, the better."

FRANK

"ARE YOU OKAY, father? You seem aggravated."

Frank looked at his son and for a moment saw only a monster. He had to grit his teeth to picture the sweet boy he'd raised in the countryside of Gloucestershire. "I...I don't know why we fired on the pier."

Samuel seemed confused. "But it was you who gave the order."

No I did not. I told the gunnery sergeant to 'miss'. I told him to 'miss'. I don't understand what happened. "I...I...."

Samuel spoke over him. "I gave you the order to pass on to the gunnery sergeant, so why the surprise? If you did not agree with my orders, then perhaps you should have mentioned it at the time."

I thought I could handle it back then. My plan was to avoid this. How did it happen? Frank could say nothing. Words were failing him.

"I must admit," said Samuel, "I was concerned that the gunnery sergeant might refuse you. Not all men possess the steel to fire upon a defenceless enemy." Frank grimaced. Innocent people, not enemies. "So I sent for the man myself, to reconfirm my orders."

Frank's eyes widened. He looked at Samuel and tried to read his thoughts. It was as impossible as ever. He spoke to the gunnery sergeant? Did the man say anything about the orders I gave him? He must have.

Samuel picked up some papers from his desk and shuffled them carefully. "It's a good thing I did speak to him, father, because the man had his orders all wrong. He had it in his head to fire a warning shot. Imbecile."

Frank laughed and wished he didn't sound so guilty. "I-I'm sure he misunderstood me."

"Of course he did. I didn't think for one minute that you would undermine me, father. Not after having owned my trust for so many years."

"No, Samuel. Of course not."

"If you were to betray me, I would be so hurt that I would probably do something quite dreadful." He laughed heartily. "My, I would probably do something unbelievably bad. I dare not even imagine. I'm just glad that you would never do that to me. You're the only man in this world I trust. Nobody else do I listen to but the man who raised me after so much tragedy had befallen me as a boy. I owe you a great deal, Frank. I will repay my debt to you, one day. You will get what you deserve."

Frank swallowed and remained silent. *I'm sure we all get what we deserve in the end.*

There was a buzz at the door. Samuel pressed a button on his desk and the hatch door released. Petty officer Dunn stepped through, backed by four crewmen and a struggling Roman. Samuel stood up from behind his desk and for once moved around in front of it. His lanky legs and long arms were like iron pipes either side of him as he waited to hear from his men.

Dunn was bleeding from the nose and sported a black eye. He sounded in pain as he spoke. "He resisted arrest, but I got him here, sir."

Samuel disregarded Dunn and kept his dark eyes fixed on Roman. His lips parted and his upper teeth showed through like a hungry wolf.

Roman stared right back at him.

Frank shifted uncomfortably. Whatever was happening, Samuel hadn't informed him about it. It was unusual for him to keep things from him and it made Frank worry. *He doesn't trust me?* What made him worry even more was that the two guns that Samuel kept mounted on the wall behind his desk were gone. *Why has he taken them down? Does he feel in danger, or is he planning on shooting someone.*

Samuel told the four crewmen to leave, but allowed Dunn, Roman, and Frank to stay. He, himself, remained standing in front of his desk, clutching his hands together. "Roman," he eventually said, speaking the word softly, almost pityingly. "Roman, Roman, Roman, ROMAN, RO-MAN...ROMAN!" In his fury, Samuel seemed to have grown by a foot. He towered over Roman so much that the usually implacable man took a step backwards. Even Frank edged towards the wall. *I've never seen Samuel this angry. He's losing control of himself.*

Roman went to speak but was unable to. Samuel backhanded him across the face so hard that blood appeared on the man's cheek. Despite the force of the blow, Roman remained standing in place. Petty officer Dunn smirked from the back of the room. Frank winced. *A leader should not strike his followers. Justice needs a calm hand.*

Samuel took a breath and suddenly seemed calm again. "I apologise," he said. "But treachery puts me in the foulest of moods."

Roman said nothing. The blood on his cheek dribbled down onto his jawbone.

"Do you have nothing to say?" Samuel asked.

Roman shrugged. "Do you have any beer?"

Samuel struck Roman again. Again Roman remained standing in place. "You insolent wretch. You stood before me and told me Fox and Birch died in unavoidable circumstances. You lied to my face after all I have given you. After all I have done for you cockroaches and I am still defied at every turn."

Frank kept quiet in the corner, yet hung on every word with interest. He was unaware what information Samuel was acting on. *I knew Roman was lying, but I never said anything about it to anyone. Who's been speaking to Samuel?*

"Dunno what you're talking about, mate," Roman said. Frank had noticed that the man's speech patterns would change whenever he lost his cool. *He tries to hide the fact he's an uneducated thug.*

Samuel shook his head and laughed resignedly. "You killed Birch, you admitted it, but you lied about killing Fox, didn't you? A member of the fleet saw you dump the body."

A look of understanding came over Roman, almost as if he had known about the witness. Frank sighed. The revelation didn't shock him, but he knew that what happened next would not be pretty.

"You do not seem surprised," said Samuel. "You knew there was a witness?"

"The witness spoke with Roman on the aft deck," said Dunn. "I noticed the exchange and investigated. The man's name is Hugo Alban. He told me that he reported seeing a body dumped at sea, from a yacht he saw leaving the pier."

"Well," said Samuel. "That could only be the yacht I sent you ashore in. Quite condemning. That this lawful citizen gave his story to the very culprit of the crime is ironic, don't you think? Good thing petty officer Dunn was there to see justice prevail."

"I am honoured to serve the fleet," said Dunn like a trained parrot. Frank did not like the man. He was a sycophant with an agenda, always ready to clutch a man's hand in friendship, but let go of it over a cliff. Roman turned and glared at Dunn with a baleful grin on his face. Dunn stepped back towards the hatch door, all of his swagger suddenly melting.

Samuel folded his long, bony arms across his chest and let out a breath. The room filled with a pungent odour. "I am disappointed in you, Roman. I thought you were a man of worth, but you're nothing but a Judas. You are a murderer and a traitor."

"You're the murderer," Roman spat. "You killed all those people on the pier, and for what? To keep Tim quiet? To stop him telling everyone that it was you who released the infection which killed billions of people."

Frank balked. Of all the things he'd heard said of his adopted son, that was the most audacious. Many theories existed about the rise of the dead, from meteorites to God's wrath, but to place the blame on a single man was absurd. Samuel is just an easy target for blame.

Samuel cackled so hard that his pale cheeks went red. "You believe such nonsense? Officer Dunn, do you think I have the power to raise the dead?"

Dunn was in hysterics. Between belly laughs he shook his head and said "no."

"You had the money and power to raise the dead," said Roman. "If anyone could be responsible for the plague that ended the world, it's a man like you; a man with endless resources and no conscience. There was a little girl living on that pier, I told you, and you fired at them anyway. You're a monster."

"They were enemies of the fleet."

"They were innocent. You're the only enemy of the fleet."

Frank swallowed. As much as he dismissed claims that Samuel caused the end of the world, he thought his actions toward the pier were unnecessarily cruel. He wanted to speak in Samuel's defence but found himself unable to. Perhaps when things blew over he could find time to explain to his son the error of his ways. He's just young. Where are those guns he took from the wall? Why does he need them?

"The captain was doing what he had to for the good of the fleet," said Dunn, but nobody paid any attention to the man. Roman and Samuel were focused only on each other.

"The people on that pier got what they deserved," said Samuel. "They were given the option of friendship, but they chose defiance. They left me with no option. The same way you, Roman, have left me no option but to sentence you for the murders of Birch and Fox. You will be put to death at noon tomorrow. I hope you serve as an example to all others who find murder acceptable. To think I had such high hopes for you."

Frank sighed. He hated to see any man put to death, but murder was murder. Roman had always concerned him and it appeared that it was with good reason. The man was a loose cannon and murder demanded the harshest sentence. Samuel's judgement was fair.

Roman stood silently in front of Samuel. The news of his pending execution seemed not to bother him in the slightest.

"Did you hear me?" said Samuel. He took a step towards Roman so that the two men were almost nose-to-nose.

Roman brought his spear arm up and drove it towards Samuel's thin waist. Frank was too slow to react and too far away. Oh, Jesus, God, no.

The shaft of metal moved quickly.

Samuel twisted to one side.

The spear missed its target and stabbed thin air.

Samuel grabbed the wooden shaft and shoved the metal tip down on his desk. Then he snapped it in two with his other hand. The spear tip skittered across the desk and Roman lost his balance. Frank rushed forward and grabbed him in an arm lock, while Dunn hurried forward to help him.

As Roman struggled, Samuel shook his head pityingly. "Stupid, stupid, stupid. I was going to give you a quick death, a beheading, but now I might just tie you up from the stern and leave you to starve to death."

"Do whatever the fuck you want," spat Roman. "You're a dead man. I promise you."

Samuel grinned. "I'll die when I'm ready, not when you decide. That's the difference between you and I, Roman. I have the power over life and death. Frank, take him to the brig."

Frank yanked Roman by his arm and swung him around. As he did so, Roman head butted petty officer Dunn right in the face. The man fell to the floor bellowing. Frank stepped over the crying officer and led Roman away. In his gut he had the horrible feeling that everything was beginning to fall apart.

HUGO

HUGO HELD HIS daughters close as they watched the fires burning on the shore. The frigate had fired several shots from a mighty cannon on its starboard side. The shells had looked like fireworks heading into the night sky, but when they returned to earth they brought no joy or mirth, just death and burning. *It is an atrocity. I do not understand why the captain would do this.*

"What happened, Daddy?" asked Sophie. "Why is there fire?"

Hugo shook his head. "I do not know, my sweet. Something very bad has happened, but I do not know why."

"Weren't there people on that pier?" asked Daphne. "Are they dead?"

Hugo thought about lying, but couldn't. "Probably."

Daphne started to cry. "It was the big boat that blew them up. Was it protecting us? Were the people on the pier, bad, papa?"

"I don't know. We should go inside and think of other things. Would you like to play Canasta?"

Both girls shook their heads, but they at least went into the cabin. Hugo did not want them looking at the fires and thinking about death any longer. *What on earth happened? What did the people on the pier do? Were they behind the murder I witnessed?*

Hugo glanced about in the darkness at the other boats all around him. Some of them were filled with gawping spectators, mumbling amongst themselves and pointing at the shore. Hugo did not want to be a gawper himself, so he went inside the cabin.

Houdini had been frightened by the explosions and had scarpered inside already. He was curled up on the armchair, shaking. Hugo swatted him down to the floor and took his seat. "Sorry, mon ami. My legs are older than yours." Houdini went and curled up under the coffee table.

Daphne and Sophie curled up under the duvet on the sofa and held each other. They were so delicate and frail. The yacht had been their shelter for almost an entire year now. They'd spoken little with anyone besides Hugo. *Am I doing the right thing for them? The world has ended, the dead walk, and I am keeping them cooped up on this yacht and acting like all is well. The fleet has made us all feel safe, but are we really? In the last few days I have witnessed murder all around me. The Kirkland is not the centre of civilisation I thought it was. There are other people out there in the world. People like those on the pier. Why are we destroying them? Are we making enemies? Will we remain at sea forever, fighting anyone we find on land? Is that what I want for my daughters?*

Hugo rubbed at his forehead and blinked slowly. He looked at Sophie and Daphne. "Girls, are you happy?"

Daphne and Sophie looked at him, puzzled. "Papa?"

"Do you feel happy and safe aboard the éternuer?"

Sophie shrugged. Daphne looked like she wanted to speak, but couldn't.

"Tell me, Daphne. What do you think about our lives?"

"I hate it, papa. It is... ennuyeuxe."

Hugo sighed. "You find it boring?"

Daphne nodded.

"What else?" asked Hugo.

"I find it sad," Sophie added. "I miss things, lots of things. There are no toys or games, no fleurs or grass. It is just boats and grey sea. There is no point to any of it."

"Would you rather be somewhere else?"

Both girls nodded.

"Where?"

"On the land," said both of them together.

"You want to go on the land? It's dangerous out there."

Sophie nodded. "We could still stay on the boat, but we could stay close to the shore. We could find a quiet beach and go play. We might find other people like the ones that were on the pier. It's better than floating around in the middle of the sea."

Hugo thought about the people on the pier and what had just happened to them. Yet, what his daughters were saying made sense, they could hug the shore and stick to the beaches, maybe even move inland via a river. If there were people on the pier, there could be people other places, too. Suddenly, he didn't want to be part of the fleet anymore. The thought of leaving had overtaken him.

"What would we do for food?" he asked.

"Poisson," said Sophie. "If we stick close to the shore we can live off the sea, same as now. We have rods."

Hugo sighed. Even if they caught fish, they would still be at the mercy of thirst. If they couldn't find fresh water to last them days at a time they would all die. Once again, Hugo thought about the people at the pier. While they may have been obliterated by the Kirkland's gunfire, the area in which they lived must have been somewhat safe. They may have cleared away all of the dead. They could have stockpiled supplies. Maybe it would be safe to land on the beach and check it out.

What if they're still alive?

Then I offer them my help. What the frigate did to them was terrible. I am not their enemy. I do not condone the actions of the fleet.

But what if they're dangerous?

Then we die a quick death instead of a slow, weary one at sea. I want to keep my daughters safe, but I also want them to live. I need to give them more than saltwater and petrol fumes.

"It is almost light," he said. "Lie down and get a little more sleep. At dawn we will head ashore to look for survivors at the pier. If there are, maybe we can think about joining them."

Daphne and Sophie both cheered. Hugo felt sick to his stomach. He stepped out of the cabin and looked out at the distant fires. The flames were beginning to die down; the rain and sea spray helping the situation. While it was too dark to see if anyone still lived, Hugo could see that not all of the pier was damaged. The structure had been vast and long and the barrage had not covered the entire area. There was a chance that people had survived. They must have been surviving on the pier since this whole thing began. The sea is not the only safe place. But if they live, are they friendly? Why did Mr Raymeady fire on them? I need to find out before I can know what to do.

Despite knowing nothing of the community on the pier, Hugo hoped the best for them. But after what the Kirkland had done, Hugo was worried that the people on the pier would see him as their enemy. He was about to take his daughters into peril, after so long protecting them, but they were lucky to have survived this long. Hugo had faith that people were still good and that the people on the pier must be better than those on the Kirkland. If I am wrong then I am about to make a mistake. A huge, terrible mistake.

The sun began to rise and Hugo prepared to set sail.

GARFIELD

REMARKABLY, AS THEY'D cut through the fields and woodland, Garfield and the foragers had come upon Stonehenge. Despite its myth and allure, Garfield had never visited the national monument before and found it ironic that it'd taken the end of the world to get him there.

There was a building erected nearby that contained a small museum and gift shop, as well as a moderate café. They'd all been pleased to find it well stocked with snack food and bottled pop. They covered up the broken window through which they'd entered with a large tablecloth, then settled down in their sleeping bags for a few hours. The Army base was nearby, but Garfield had wanted to wait until daylight to catch up on the sleep they'd never got last night. No one complained and within minutes everyone was snoring loudly. It was cold, Garfield pulled his long woollen coat over the top of his sleeping bag. The coat was two sizes too big, but it was warm. Poppy had lugged it over to him from where she'd found it in an old Laundromat on the outskirts of Western-Super-Mare. Garfield had hated it at the time and felt weighed down by its bulk, but he could tell the gift meant a lot to Poppy. It was one of the first signs of affection she had shown after the horror she had gone through at her home. Eventually the coat had grown on him. The pockets were deep and the wool thick. The thick cuffs had even protected him from a zombie bite once. He'd been sure he was done for until he rolled the coat up his arm and saw that his skin was untouched. He hardly ever took the coat off since then. It reminded him of Poppy, and to keep his guard up.

Garfield had lain awake for a while, going over his past mistakes and the ones he hoped to avoid in the future. He thought about Poppy and how she was doing, but inevitably, sleep had yanked at his eyelids and pulled him down into its well of darkness.

When he awoke, he was startled to see Sally standing over him. The man held a large knife in his hand, which made Garfield immediately reach for the one he had hidden inside his sleeping bag.

"Settle down there, fella," said Sally, turning the knife in his hand. "It's made of stone not steel. I found it in the museum. It's a relic or something."

Garfield looked at the brittle stone blade and sniffed his sinuses clear. "It's useless. Put it back."

Sally shrugged. "What's it to you?"

"It's part of our history. It was here thousands of years before we were. There might not be many people left, but those who survive will be grateful one day for the history left to them. That knife is more important now than ever."

"Looks like a bit of old stone to me, mate."

Garfield huffed. "It's proof that mankind endures. People made that thousands of years ago and here we are looking at it today. It shows that we can make it through this."

Sally laughed. He examined the knife with newfound interest. "You always so profound in the mornings?"

"Only when I wake up at the most ancient site in Europe. It tends to put things in perspective."

"Yer, it does, I suppose." Sally dropped the knife on the tiled floor where it quickly broke into pieces.

Garfield balked. He wriggled out of his sleeping bag, leapt up, and got in the Australian's face. "What the hell are you doing?"

"Just proving a point."

"What point, you idiot?"

"That mankind is fragile and that holding onto history is a waste of time. Sentimentality will only get you killed. As much as you try to hold on to the past, some fella will come along and smash it, so why bother?"

Garfield swung at Sally, but the man was too quick and ducked. Before Garfield had the chance to swing again, Kirk ran over and grabbed him. "What the hell are you doing, Garf?"

"He's a piece of shit," Garfield shouted at Kirk. "He needs to go. We're done with him."

Sally stepped back, looking wounded. His hands were out in front of him as if he meant no harm. Kirk shoved Garfield back a step while Lemon took Sally by the arm and ushered him away.

"The guy is trouble," Garfield told Kirk.

"No, he's not. He's just been surviving on his own too long. He lacks manners, but he'll fall in line."

"I want him gone. He can't be trusted."

"No one can be trusted," said Kirk. "Sally stays. No one has a problem with him but you."

Garfield felt his cheeks reddening. "I am in charge here, Kirk."

"Maybe, but when it comes to taking in new survivors we're a committee. We're not going to kick a guy out on his arse, just because you don't like him."

"Fine. On your heads be it," said Garfield, shrugging away.

Sally walked towards him. There was an amiable smile on his face and he was laughing. "Sorry about that, cobber. That old lump of stone just fell right out of my mitts. I didn't realise old junk meant so much to yer. What is it they used to say? Those who can't make history, study it."

Garfield threw another punch. This time it connected, almost as if Sally had decided not to try and avoid it this time. The man stumbled backwards and flopped to the floor dramatically. Kirk grabbed Garfield in a chokehold.

Lemon rushed to help Sally back to his feet. The Australian brushed himself off. "Now, is that anyway to treat a mate? Crikey, what's your bloody problem?"

"You're my problem. I don't know what your game is, but I'm on to you." Sally shook his head and walked away. "Bloody mad pomme bastard."

Kirk let go of Garfield and shoved him hard in the chest. "You've lost the plot, Garf. We don't fight each other in the field, ever. That's rule one."

"That only applies to family."

Kirk sighed. "Sally became our family the moment we took him with us. That was your decision if you remember. You need to cool it. I'm taking over until we make it home."

Garfield snarled. "Like hell you are. I lead this group."

"You're not leading anything. What happened at the Jubilee was a complete balls-up, and now you're throwing punches. We'll discuss things when we get home, but for now you're a liability."

"Sod you, Kirk. Nobody wants you as leader. They follow me."

Kirk looked at Garfield like he was a lost child. The man was arrogant and foolish, but it didn't seem like he was acting out of spite so much as pity. "Are you so sure of that, Garf? They blame you for Squirrel and Danny, and they all like Sally. If you want to play the popularity vote, you'll lose. We can put it to a vote right now, if you want, but I would rather you avoid the humiliation and just accept that I'm in charge until we get back. Then we can vote for a more permanent solution, when things have settled down. It's for the best."

Garfield had to fight the urge to punch Kirk in the mouth, but he was right. The foragers had lost faith in him when Squirrel and Danny died. He'd let them down, and out here in the wild, people couldn't afford to be let down. They would forgive him in time, right now emotions were high. If there was a vote, the group would put Kirk in charge out of anger for the brothers they had lost.

"Fine, you take charge," Garfield said. "But if I find out that Sally is planning anything shady, I'm going to kill him."

Kirk's expression darkened. "You kill anybody, it will be because I say so."

Garfield slumped in utter confusion as the others gathered up their stuff around him and got ready to move out. *What the hell just happened? I've only been awake ten minutes....*

Everyone headed out through the broken window and marched across the tarmac to where the minivan waited. As he followed after them, Garfield glanced at the great circular outcropping of standing boulders that made up Stonehenge. He felt an ominous doubt in his gut. Stonehenge was a ruin, many of its stones broken or missing. Nothing survived forever, not even hard stone. It made him realise how fragile life was, and both how little and how much it mattered. Nothing Garfield did would matter in a thousand years, but it mattered more than anything right now, this minute and the next. He would make it home safely to Poppy, no matter what, and if anyone tried to jeopardise that, he would leave them broke and abandoned like the great boulders of Stonehenge. *This trip has been bad from the start. Sooner it's over the better.*

When Garfield went to get in the minivan, he found it full. With Danny and Squirrel gone, everyone managed to fit inside now, but there was no room for one more. Garfield sighed and hopped up into the horsebox. There was barely any room amongst the forager's tools and backpacks, in addition to all of the supplies they'd scrounged from the museum, gift shop, and café, so he was forced to squat awkwardly. *This is insane. I went from the front seat to this in less than a day.*

A wooden tenderiser mallet lay amongst a pile of things Lemon had scrounged from the café's kitchen. Garfield managed to shove it down inside his trouser pocket for safekeeping. *Can never have too many weapons*, he thought. *Especially now, with Sally poisoning everyone against me. We used to be a tight unit until he arrived. Now I'm sat in this horsebox like an unwanted guest.*

Kirk started the engine and got the minivan moving. Garfield rocked backwards onto his butt and fell amongst a pile of magazines. He settled back against the sidewall and plucked a couple of them up.

He thought about the magazines he'd given Poppy several days ago, and how she'd disliked them. Maybe she would like these ones more. They were British History books from the gift shop. I'm sure Poppy told me once that History had been her favourite subject at school. Garfield leafed through the magazines with a smile on his face. Poppy would enjoy looking at the pictures of druids, Saxons, and knights. These are perfect. He couldn't wait to take them back to her.

As the minivan made its way across the fields in the direction of the Army base, Garfield started collecting up the magazines that he thought Poppy would like most. They bent and flexed in his hands as he leafed through them and something suddenly occurred to him that got him thinking. A man can never have too many weapons, but there are other things he needs too. Things that will make a difference if things continue getting worse.

Garfield got to work.

ANNA

ANNA HAD SOME ointment in her medical bag, but her medical bag was inside the diner. Right now, it would have been of great use to ease Rene's pain, but it would be too dangerous to retrieve it from the ruined building. The skin of his neck had sloughed off in thin, wet sheets and every time he moved it hurt him. *He'll get an infection for sure,* Anna thought glumly.

The fires started to peter out. The pier had been constructed after an older, smaller pier burnt down. It'd been erected with fire-safety in mind. The gaps between the buildings were sufficient enough that they didn't fall like dominos and the decked walkway was lined with strips of galvanised steel. The rain, which dawn had brought, only helped to stymy the flames further. The pier was destroyed, but half of it, at least, still stood. Most importantly, the gate still remained in place.

The dead were drawn to fire like bumbling moths. The sound of the initial explosion had drawn them from miles around. Now they lined up at the gate in their dozens. Anna knew that, given time, they would assemble in their hundreds. The gate would fall. *It's all lost. Once the dead get through that gate, they'll be nothing but blood and guts come the time when Garfield gets back. There already is....* Losing Poppy is going to break him.

Anna studied herself, examining the blood that caked her from head to toe and the soot that clung to every inch of her clothing. Then she looked at the three bodies laid out in a row on the decked walkway: Chris, Alistair...Poppy. A child.

Anna had seen hundreds of dead children in the past year, but this was the first to truly matter on a personal level. The sight of Poppy's ruined face burned down right to Anna's bones, as if the fires themselves had consumed her. *Samuel Raymeady will pay for this.*

Rene placed an arm around her. It was the first time he'd ever done so. When she looked at his face, she could see that the pain from his wounds was nothing compared to the agony going through his mind.

"This is so messed up," said Jimmy, limping over to the railing. "What are we going to do? We've got the dead on one side and those boats on the other. What do we do?"

"We should all head down to the beach," said Samantha. She walked down the deck towards the sea and the others followed after her. "We'll have to go along the shore."

"That's probably our only option," said Anna. "We can't go into the village. Not with all of the zombies arriving. We'll have to trek down the beach and try to find somewhere safe."

"What about Garfield?" said old man Bob. "He'll be back soon. If we're all gone...."

"He'll have to look for us," said Anna. "Better that than he finds us all dead. We can't wait for him. For all we know, he might never make it back. Who knows what the foragers ran into out there?"

The thought made everyone drop their heads in sadness. One day ago, they'd been a family, safe and sound. Their only danger each day had been irritation at each other. Now it had all gone to pieces in a heartbeat. Their home, their family, had been torn to shreds. Surviving long enough to find the pier in the first place had been a miracle. None of them could hold out much hope of finding another sanctuary. They would probably all be dead soon.

Anna stared out at the frigate. Now that morning had arrived, it looked like the queen bee at the centre of a hive. A hundred smaller boats surrounded it and Anna had no vessel of her own. The only way to get to the frigate was to sail to it, but any of the boats in the fleet would likely just finish their captain's job and kill her. *Please, God,* don't let me die without taking that tyrant with me. He can't get away with all he's done. If what Tim said is true....

Something caught Anna's eye as she stared out at the fleet. One of the boats was coming closer. It was a small yacht, piloted by a man. Rene went to speak but she nodded before he had chance. "I see it. Probably someone come to finish us off."

"What should we do, Anna?" old man Bob asked.

"Arm up and get ready. We didn't make it this long to go down without a fight."

Tim was sitting on the deck with his legs dangling over the collapsed edge of the walkway and his crutches lay across his lap. He said it was easier on his back to sit down. Now he was pointing to the small yacht coming their way. "I don't think it's coming to hunt us," he said. "Look."

Anna did as Tim asked and looked harder. As she squinted, she made out a man piloting the boat. He looked harmless enough: shaggy brown hair atop a benign face. It was the two people standing either side of him that made him seem completely unthreatening. "He has two children with him."

"And a dog," said Tim. "And it's way too small to be an attack dog."

Anna nodded. The little dog was more like a longhaired rat than a Rottweiler. The two young girls standing beside the man were about Poppy's age and both were waving their hands. Anna frowned in confusion. "Get weapons," she said. "I don't trust anyone at this point."

Everybody nodded and went and fetched whatever they could find. Luckily, most of the pier's weapon stockpiles were close to the gate, which was at the untouched front end of the pier. Once they all returned they looked like a huddle of gladiators.

The yacht came closer and Anna saw that its passengers looked even warier than those on the pier. The man at the wheel kept his daughters close to him and seemed to be speaking words of caution, if the grave expression on their faces was anything to go by. Anna knew her own face was unfriendly, her expression hostile, but she couldn't help it. She wasn't about to trust anybody on a boat.

The unknown man waved a hand. "A-ahoy! Is...is anybody hurt?"

Anna snorted. The man had a French accent, which made him sound cultured and intellectual, but the words out of his mouth were stupid. "What do you think?" she said. "Your captain just bombed us."

The man looked embarrassed. "I apologise. That was stupid of me, yes? I...I do not know what has happened to you, or why the Kirkland fired at you, but I am here to help if I am able. Is there anything I can do?"

"Yeah," said Anna. "Piss off!" Rene grabbed her wrist and gave her a chiding look. Anna sighed and rethought her approach. "I'm sorry. Your captain has ruined us. Some of our people are dead because of him. That makes you our enemy."

"I am no one's enemy," said the man. "My name is Hugo, and I am worrying that my great captain is a bad man, no?"

"He is evil," said Tim. "I used to be on that frigate, but when I left he sent a man to kill me and bombed this pier when he found out I was here."

Hugo puttered the boat the last few feet so that he was directly underneath them. His young daughters looked hardened by life at sea, but they also had that naïve innocence that only young girls possessed. Poppy had had it too.

"I do not know who you are," Hugo told Tim, "but if these people are guilty only of knowing you, then the captain's actions are most wicked. My boat is too small to take you all aboard, but I can spare supplies, maybe pass on a message to the captain for you. Perhaps he will accept surrender."

"Sod the captain," spat Anna. "And sod surrender."

Hugo winced. "Please, madam, my girls..."

"Sorry," said Anna.

"It is okay. I understand. I wish only to see you safe. Ask of me what you will and I will do what I can."

"Give us your boat," said Tim.

Anna looked at him and frowned. Hugo frowned, too. "This I cannot do for you, sir. It may not be much, but the éternuer is my home. My daughter's home."

"We only wish to meet with the captain and discuss terms of safe surrender," Tim explained. "You will have your boat back within the day."

"No, I am sorry."

Tim went to argue, but Anna put a hand up. She was beginning to form ideas of her own. "We don't need your boat, Hugo. We'll give you terms of surrender to deliver to the Kirkland for us. No one else has to die today."

Hugo nodded. "I am glad to help in this."

"We need to sit down and discuss it first," she said. "Our home is a little battered right now, but we have plenty to drink and some fresh fish. It might be a bit overdone after the fires, but we will gladly welcome you as a guest while we decide the content of our message to the captain."

Hugo's face fell and suspicion washed over him. "I...I do not think that would be a good idea."

Anna smiled. "I understand you don't trust us, but we are not the bad guys here. How long have you been at sea?"

Hugo sighed. "Many many months."

"Then come aboard for an hour and feel the ground beneath your feet. Let your daughters stretch their legs and your little dog sniff something new. It'll do you all good. I promise we'll do nothing to harm you and we cannot take your boat without your keys, anyway."

Hugo's daughters both muttered to him. From the look on the man's face, he was obviously being nagged. He looked up at the pier anxiously. "We will come aboard, but please, I beg you, do not show yourselves to be bad people. My faith in men has been badly damaged these last few days, and I cannot cope with more badness. My daughters..."

"Are beautiful," said Anna. "And we would never dream of treating them as anything other than friends. Climb up, Hugo. We would usually drop down a rope, but with the struts in the mess that they are, it's pretty easy to get up without."

Hugo nodded. "Oui."

The Frenchman's hands were shaking as he helped his daughters climb up from the yacht. *He's afraid of us. Afraid for his daughters. But he's desperate enough to take the risk.* Anna and old man Bob helped them up, while Hugo attached the yacht to the pier. Once he finished tying a large mooring knot, he hoisted up the little dog, which wriggled and yipped! "Be careful with my little Houdini," he said. "He has not made new friends in quite a while."

Yip!

Anna managed to hang down and grab the little dog under the flanks. Old man Bob held her from behind and yanked her back with the animal in her arms. She set the dog down and watched in amusement as it spun in a circle of disbelieving excitement. Within seconds, the small hound was sniffing the ground and peeing up the railings. *Make yourself at home, champ.*

Hugo switched off the yacht's engine and pocketed the keys. He grabbed a hold of the pier's twisted struts and pushed himself upwards. Anna grabbed him by the hand and yanked him up over the edge. As soon as his feet hit the deck he smiled.

"Feel good to be on solid ground again?" Anna asked him. *Don't get too used to it.*

Hugo bounced a little. "I can feel it in my knees. It...it has been too long. Thank you for allowing me into your home."

"What's left of it," said Anna, waving a hand over the burning debris of the more unfortunate buildings. "We're going to have to move on soon."

"I am sorry for your pain. These are my daughters, Daphne and Sophie. This little man is Houdini."

Anna patted the friendly dog on the head and smiled at each of the girls. That was when Hugo leapt backwards and almost fell into the sea. Anna grabbed him just in time. "What is it?"

Hugo pointed down the pier at the gate. "The...the dead."

Anna chuckled. "They can't hurt us. The gate will hold them for now. Don't worry, you get used to them. I suppose you haven't seen the dead much from the sea."

Hugo shook his head. His bottom lip quivered. "Are they everywhere? Is nowhere safe?"

"This place was safe," said old man Bob. "Until your boss destroyed it."

Anna sighed. It was not Hugo's fault. She could tell that the man's concern for them was genuine. There was nothing to be gained by giving him a hard time. But I don't have a choice. "There are some safe places, but they're hard to find, Hugo. We'll move on from here soon and look for someplace new. Somewhere with thick doors and a way of finding food. You can come with us if you want." Would he want that? Is the fleet really so great?

When she made the offer, both of Hugo's daughters looked at him expectantly. Hugo stammered for a second, but declined the offer. "A bad idea, I think. I must keep my daughter's out of harm's way."

"I understand," said Anna. "Worst thing in the world is seeing a child hurt, wouldn't you agree?" We'll see what you truly think of it in a moment.

Hugo nodded emphatically. "Absolutely. I cannot let anything happen to my young ladies."

Anna patted the man on the back and started him moving. "Let's go and decide what we're going to give the captain. Here, this way. We can rest a little."

Anna led Hugo and his family down the deck and past the burnt-out diner. Hugo looked worried as they moved closer to the zombies at the gate, but his anxiety turned to abject horror when he spotted the three bodies lying in a row. A hand went to his mouth and he looked like he was going to be sick. Both his daughters started to cry, while Houdini sniffed at the bodies and backed away.

Anna cleared her throat. She felt bad for what she was inflicting on the French family. "You're a guest, Hugo, so you should meet all the family. Allow me to introduce you to Alistair, Chris..." she stepped forward and pointed down at Poppy's partially-burned body. "And this little angel is Poppy. She's nine. How old are your girls, Hugo?"

Hugo swallowed and spoke in a voice thick with saliva. "E-eight and nine."

Anna pursed her lips. "Same age. What a coincidence. I'm sure Poppy and your daughters would've gotten on really well. Pity she's dead. Your captain burnt her to death."

Sophie and Daphne sobbed and buried their heads in their father's chest. Houdini barked. "Why are you doing this?" Hugo asked. "You... you promised not to harm us."

"We're not going to harm you, Hugo. You have my word. All I'm trying to do is show you why we need your boat."

From the look on Hugo's face, he didn't understand. "My boat?"

Anna nodded. "You need to give us your boat, Hugo. We won't take it from you, but you need to give it to us."

"Why?"

"So we can sail to the Kirkland and give ourselves up," said Tim, obviously understanding the plan that Anna had already formed in her head. "Samuel wants me," he continued to explain, "so Anna will take me aboard and hand me over. She'll be brought aboard to speak with the captain. He'll want to thank her – and gloat about the fact he's battered her into submission."

"Then I'll kill him," said Anna, "and make sure that no more little girls have to die. You're a father, Hugo. What would you do if this were your girls lying here? What if Samuel decides one day that your daughters belong to the fleet? Samuel needs to be stopped. Give us your boat and I will give him what he deserves, and believe me it goes much further than this. He's responsible for much much worse."

"But that's a story for a different day," said Tim. "Please help us."

Hugo was shaking his head. "I cannot give up my boat. It is my home. My daughters need a home."

"Then stay here with us," said old man Bob. "There's another dozen of us due back soon. We'll all set out together and find somewhere safe. Somewhere without a captain making all the decisions about who lives and dies."

Hugo's mouth opened and closed like a fish. He was faltering.

"Give them the boat, papa," said the older girl, Sophie. "I don't want to go back out to sea, ever. Just look how happy Houdini is?"

They all looked at the little dog, which was happily squeezing out a turd at the side of the deck. When he saw them all looking, a strange expression of pride seemed to come over him.

Hugo sighed. He'd gone white as a sheet. When he reached into the pocket of his jeans, his hand was shaking like a leaf in the wind. He pulled out his keys and handed them over to Anna. "I pray I do not regret this."

Anna shrugged. "No more than you would staying with the fleet and witnessing senseless slaughter whenever it takes the captain's fancy." She turned to Tim. "We'll leave in a few hours, so get some rest and make your peace. We're not going to make it back again." She nodded to Hugo. "Thank you."

Hugo nodded back, but the uncertainty was written all over his face. "You are welcome. Good luck to you."

"I am coming, too," said Rene. "We started this journey together, Anna. I would like to end it that way."

Anna gave Rene a hug. "You're always welcome by my side. Just make sure I kill that son-of-a-bitch before he kills me, then I can die happy."

"I promise," said Rene.

"I would like a cup of tea if you have one," said Hugo, wobbling on his feet and growing pale. "And perhaps something to eat for my girls."

"I'll see what I can find you folks," said Old man Bob. "Come on, follow me. We need to gather together what we can, ready for the journey." Everyone agreed that was a good idea. They all headed over to the Sea Grill to spend their last few hours together as a family.

GARFIELD

KIRK STOPPED THE minivan next to the chain-link fence and everybody got out. There was an entrance to the Army base ahead, but the small guardhouse had been reinforced with planks of wood, a huge engine block, an antique cannon, and endless bundles of razor wire – the entire compound was ringed with razor wire. Garfield grimaced when he spotted decaying dead men ensnared in the barbs every hundred feet or so. It was clear that at some point a last stand had been made, but now the place seemed deserted.

The foragers stood in a group outside the chain-link fence, and peered in at the place they'd been searching for. "Didn't think we'd make it for a minute there," said Kirk. "She's quite a place, though, ain't she?"

Garfield stared through the metal links and found himself agreeing. The base was huge. A wide main road with multiple side roads branching off from it gave the appearance of a small town centre. There must have been close to a hundred buildings, as well as several large open spaces, some of them paved, others just overgrown fields. An Army ambulance lay abandoned ahead and a row of 4-tonne trucks lined up in front of a nearby building. There was also a bright green fire engine poking out of an open shed.

"I'll get the cutters," said Lemon. Everyone waited while he headed to the back of the horsebox and began rooting around inside his baggage. Kirk and Sally stood side by side, discussing something quietly. Cat, David, and the others leaned up against the fence, pushing their faces against the mesh to see better. Garfield patted himself down and made sure all of his weapons were in place.

Lemon returned with his wire cutters and quickly got to work snipping the metal links. Garfield glanced around nervously while they waited. So far the journey had been damaging, and now that they were finally at their destination, he could not shake the feeling that something even worse was going to go wrong.

"We're in," said Lemon. He stepped back proudly to reveal a large hole in the fence wide enough for each of them to duck under. Kirk went first, with Sally close behind. The others quickly followed with Garfield going last. As he stepped through he made sure to make a note of his bearings. If they had to retreat there would be no time to cut a new hole. They would need to remember where this one was.

"Wonder where the goodies are," Sally said, glancing around with his hands on his hips. "We're looking for guns and ammo, right?"

"Primarily," said Kirk. "But keep your eyes peeled for anything worth taking back."

"Back to this pier of yours, yer? How many mouths you got to feed back there?"

"About another ten."

Sally blew air into his cheeks and then said, "But it's you guys that have to go out and risk your necks all the time, yer?"

Kirk shrugged. "The people back at the pier fish and look after the place."

"Screw fishing. Anyone can do that. They should be out here risking their necks with you."

"Poppy's just a kid and old man Bob is...well, old. Not everyone can make it out here."

Sally flapped his hands and slapped them against his thighs. "Then they die. Who made them your burden? Are you telling me that if we find heaps of treasure here, you're gunna trek it all the way back to the coast and divvy it up?"

Kirk looked embarrassed, but Garfield was angry. "We look after each other, Sally. You might have been alone this last year, but some of us are still human."

Sally put his hands up. "Hey, don't hit me again, big man. Was just making an observation. Still allowed to do that, ain't I?"

Kirk stared at Garfield. "No playing up, okay? Let's just do this and get ourselves heading back for home."

Garfield snarled, but didn't push the issue. He was glad Kirk made the statement of heading back home. It sounded like Sally was in favour of banding together and becoming a group of marauding nomads.

"Where do we start?" asked Lemon. "This place is h-h-huge."

"We start there," said Garfield. "At that building. There're guns inside."

Kirk frowned. "How do you know?"

Garfield pointed. "Look there, can you see that narrow sandpit that runs all down one side?"

"You want to build a sandcastle?" asked Sally. "Somebody get this man a spade."

Garfield ignored him "When soldiers return their rifles, they dry fire them to make sure the chambers are clear. They aim at the sand-bank in case a round fires off accidentally. Also, that building is small with no windows and a big steel door. No easy way to break in. If you're asking me, that's where the guns are."

"This place is huge," said Sally. "That building isn't big enough to hold all the guns for this place."

Garfield shook his head and snorted. "How much of a good idea is it to put all the weapons together? If some gang of criminals with brass balls tried to rob an armoury, why make it easy for them? The guns will be placed in separate caches. Probably one per regiment."

Kirk nodded. "Makes sense to me. Okay, people. We need to find a way inside that building."

"What about that fire engine?" said Sally. "If we can get that sweetheart running, we could just ram into the side of the building."

Garfield whistled. "Just ram the side of a building full of explosives. Smart."

"Do you have a better idea?" asked Kirk. "That door don't look like it's gunna come loose with Lemon's skeleton key."

Garfield thought for a few seconds but was forced to shrug his shoulders. "I guess not."

"Okay," said Sally, clapping his hands together. "Let's go jack us a fire truck. Reminds me of this time in high school when...actually, never mind."

Kirk put down his backpack and started giving orders. "Okay, Cat, David, go check out those trucks parked over there, but be careful. Lemon, do you think you can hotwire that fire engine, or whatever it is you do?"

"Looks, pretty old. I'm sure it won't be difficult."

Kirk nodded. "Do it."

Lemon tottered off towards the shed containing the fire engine, carrying his bag of tricks over his shoulder. The man was never happier than when he had something to break into.

"What about the rest of us, mate?" asked Sally. "You want us to go explore?"

"That would be a bad idea," said Garfield. "We need to stay close in case we get cut off."

"I was asking the boss, fella," said Sally, turning and smiling at Kirk.

Kirk chuckled. "Stop trying to wind Garf up, will you? Anyway, he's right. I think it's better if we take things slow and stick close. The rest of us can set up a cache here for everything we find."

Garfield agreed with the plan. It wasn't the quickest, but it was the smartest. Maybe Kirk wasn't as impetuous as he thought. "We need to be ready if Lemon gets that truck moving. The noise of the engine alone will bring any dead in the area to come running."

Kirk nodded. "I know. I'll have someone go back to the minivan, make sure it's ready to go the second we beat a retreat."

"Or we could stay and fight," said Sally. "There're enough of us to handle a few moaners. Are we men or possums?"

Garfield sighed. The Australian was really beginning to get on his nerves. "Perhaps, but what if we lose someone. Is losing a person worth it? We don't fight the dead. We avoid the dead."

"What's one life if it means getting this place locked down? This place is a goldmine. We could set up a camp here and defend it till the end of time."

"Then why is it empty?" asked Garfield. "The entrance is barricaded up, so people were here once. They're not no more, though. Why?"

Sally kicked a stone across the floor with the toe of his boot like a surly teenager. "I dunno, mate. Old age?"

Garfield rolled his eyes. "The infection hit less than a year ago. I don't think anyone died of old age."

Sally shrugged. "Aliens, then?"

"Aliens? Genius."

Kirk waved a hand. "Shut the hell up, you two. You're giving me a headache."

Garfield flushed with anger, but then remembered that he wasn't in charge anymore, Kirk was. "Fine. I'm going to go see if Lemon needs help with anything. That okay, boss?"

Kirk nodded.

Garfield spun around and marched to go find Lemon. On his way he passed the three trucks that Cat and David had been told to check out. Neither of them were anywhere to be seen. They must have jumped up inside the truck beds for some rumpy pumpy. It wouldn't be the first time the two of them had snuck off for some alone time. Who could really blame them?

Garfield wondered if he would ever have a woman in his life again. It would be nice to have another heartbeat beside him while he slept, but it just wasn't something he could imagine right now. His priority was Poppy. There would be time for his own needs later, when she was grown.

The fire engine was up ahead, it's nose poking beneath the shutter of the open shed. Garfield eyed the front passenger seat but couldn't see if Lemon was inside. Knowing Lemon, he would probably be rummaging in his rucksack somewhere inside the shed, trying to find the perfect tool for the job at hand.

Garfield reached the shed and stepped inside. It stunk of engine oil and petrol. Lemon's rucksack was laid out on the floor, just as he had suspected, but Lemon wasn't beside it. "Hey, Lem, he shouted. "You need a hand?"

No answer.

Garfield turned and walked further into the shed, towards the back of the fire engine. There were tools lined up on the back wall above a workbench. He went to get a closer look and couldn't help but smile at the pristine tools and blades. "Hey, Lemon," he shouted again. "There's some grade-A stuff here. You should take a look when you're done."

No answer.

"Hey, Lemon. You deaf?" Garfield turned around, frustrated. He walked around the back of the engine and headed for the driver's side door. He placed a foot up on the running boards and felt the air shift behind him. He spun back around, yanking free the carving tongs he had strapped to his triceps at the farmhouse.

There was no one there.

Garfield frowned. After so many days surviving on the road, sensing danger had become like a sixth sense. He couldn't say why, but something was unsettling him.

Something was wrong.

"Lemon," he shouted a third time. "Say something, man." He crept back up onto the running boards and peered through the driver's window. There was the shadow of a man inside that could have been Lemon – it had the same stumpy shape – but if it was Lemon, he was making no effort to answer Garfield's calls. What's wrong with him?

Garfield placed his hand around the door release and took a breath.

When he opened the door he found Lemon inside as he'd hoped, but had not expected to find him gagged and bound. Before he had chance to try to process the situation, a gloved hand covered his mouth and dragged him backwards off the running board. He tried to strike out with the carving tongs, but his arm was quickly yanked behind his back and he dropped them. He pulled out his wooden tenderising mallet with his other hand but that was quickly taken from him too.

Violently, he was yanked around, smashed in the temple with a fist, and then tripped head over heels. Before he even knew what was happening he was on his back with a boot at his throat. Who...what?

The man glaring down at him was like death: two white eyes gleaming out from behind a black mask. Garfield tried to plead with him, but a gag went in his mouth and his arms were suddenly zip-tied behind him. The whole thing had taken about five seconds. I'm dead. Whoever has me is meaner and badder than anyone I've ever met.

When Garfield realised that there were three men wearing black balaclavas, he knew once and for all that he was done for. Cat and David had also been bound and gagged and were lying at the rear of the shed by a side door. There were tears in David's eyes, but Cat wore an expression of steely determination. Garfield knew the woman would never give into a man easily. She had survived the early days of the infection all by herself, fighting off a half dozen rape attempts of desperate men. She would not allow her female sensibilities to weaken her.

The three men produced assault rifles and Cat's eyes went wide, but still she did not weep. Garfield eyed the assault rifles anxiously and imagined how quickly they could tear him apart. Their muzzles were polished metal with thick plastic grips positioned beneath. The scopes on top of each rifle were like menacing eyeballs staring at him. We're so screwed.

Garfield struggled against his bonds and tried to shout a warning through his gag, but one of the soldiers gave him a tap with his boot and then placed a finger over his lips to shush him. Kirk and the others are outside. They won't know what hit them. He started to shimmy along the concrete floor like a worm, trying to reach the edge of the shed where the others would see him. Before he even got half way, he was yanked to his feet by the soldiers and frogmarched forward. They took him to exactly where he had wanted to go: out into the road where Kirk would see him.

Lemon, Cat, and David were marched along behind him, their unsteady legs wobbling. Kirk spotted them immediately, but just stood there confused. Sally was crouched down on the floor, swigging from a bottle of water. When he saw the armed men marching Garfield and the others along, he smiled and shook his head. He thinks this is funny.

"Nobody move," said the lead soldier. He grabbed a hold of Garfield's hair and shoved him to the ground. The other two soldiers did the same with Cat, David, and Lemon. All four of them sat bound and gagged in a line.

"Who are you people?" Kirk asked.

"That's a question you need to answer first," said the soldier, "and if you say Jehovah's Witnesses, you're dead."

Kirk had gone pale, likely from the sight of the soldier's assault rifles. He stuttered as he spoke. "W-we're just people. We wanted to find some guns."

The soldier pointed his rifle. "Well, you found some, mate. I'll show you the bullets, too, if you want?"

"No, please," said Kirk. "We're not here to cause trouble. We didn't know anyone was here."

The solider pointed with his rifle. "You people make that hole in our fence?"

Garfield shuffled on to his side to get a better look at Kirk. The lad was clearly scared, but he was dealing with things in the best way possible: by being polite. "I'm sorry," he said. "We thought this place was abandoned so we cut through. We can barricade it back up if you'd like."

"Good as new," said Sally. "You won't even know we were here, mate."

"We're not your mates and we'll deal with the fence. You people are leaving."

"Come on," said Sally. "You three fellas don't need all this stuff to yourself. Surely you can spare a few rifles and one of those trucks."

"Yes," said the soldier. "We could. We could spare a lot. But what's to say you people won't take our rifles and use them to kill innocent people? That's the problem, you see? Most men get their hands on a gun and they start misbehaving. Even the men at this base headed off on the road to become kings of their own fiefdoms. I don't know what happened to them, but I know it wouldn't have been good for anyone who got in their way. There's been enough death, without us letting a bunch of weaponry fall into the wrong hands."

Garfield frowned. They're good guys. But, despite the fact that the three soldiers seemed to endorse non-violence, they'd still taken Garfield and the others captive. There was no telling what could still happen, so he reached down into the shin pocket of his cargo pants and pulled out the can opener Anna had given him. Then he got to work, sawing at the zip-tie around his wrists.

"You need to leave," said the soldier. "Once you're back in your van, we'll send our prisoners after you. You can pick them up at the end of the road."

"Screw that," said Sally. "We came a long way to get here. We have a pier full of people on the south coast that need protecting."

The soldier shuffled and readjusted his rifle. It was obviously getting heavy in his hands. "You have a camp? Huh, I thought all that was left was a handful of bandits."

"Yeah," said Sally. "We have a little girl there and an old man. We're a community." Garfield gritted his teeth as Sally spoke about his home; the home the Australian had never even visited.

Kirk took a step forward. "Actually, Sally here has never been to the pier. We picked him up en route here. That's what we do; we help those in need. We only wanted weapons to protect our people. Nothing more."

Garfield nodded. Kirk was handling the situation well. The soldier started to relax a little. Even so, Garfield continued sawing at the zips around his wrists. The can opener was blunt but it was slowly biting through the plastic. Nearly there.

The soldier took a step forward and shook his head. He raised his rifle and pointed it right at Kirk. "Leave. I won't ask you again. You're not taking our guns. Just be glad you're leaving in one piece."

Kirk took another step forward and went to speak, but a loud clack of gunfire cut him off. The noise was followed by absolute silence. Garfield stared in horror as he waited for Kirk to fall. Damn it. He pushed too far. That step forward had been a mistake. But he was taken by surprise when the soldier in front of him tumbled backwards, clutching his gut. Garfield couldn't see the blood, but he could smell it, along with a foul smell that must have been coming from the man's pierced bowel. What the hell just happened.

The two other soldiers opened fire. Kirk threw himself through the air and to the ground, which was when Garfield spotted Sally holding a smoking pistol in his hand. Where the hell did that come from? Instead of trying to work out the answer, Garfield slit the last shred of plastic zip-tie and sprung his wrists free. He leapt up to his feet and barrelled into the nearest soldier, yanking a metal pole from his inside pocket and clonking it against the man's head. The soldier fell to the floor unconscious. Garfield grabbed his rifle just as Cat leapt up and charged the remaining soldier. Her hands were still bound but that didn't stop her from knocking him off-balance. By the time the soldier recovered, Garfield had the rifle aimed squarely at his face. "I have no idea how to use this thing," he said, "but if I pull the trigger you die, right?"

The soldier snickered. "Way you're holding it, it'll take your shoulder off."

"But you'll still die, right?" The man scowled and then nodded his head, defeated. "Then drop your weapon and I'll keep my finger of the trigger."

The soldier did as he was told and Kirk and the others came rushing over to secure him and the other soldier that Garfield had bludgeoned. They tied the men up with their own zip-ties.

"They killed Tom and Gavin," said Kirk, shaking his head.

"You fired first," said the uninjured soldier. He pointed down at his dying comrade. "You shot Haltek in the stomach."

Kirk looked down at the man. "I'm sorry about that."

Garfield wasn't sorry, he was angry. "What the hell were you doing, Sally?" He shoved the man backwards and fought the urge to open fire on him with the rifle. "Where the hell did you even get that gun from?"

Sally shrugged. "Farmer had it back at that farmhouse. Figured he wasn't going to use it wandering around the kitchen."

Garfield hissed and swore, but then went very silent as a thought occurred to him. He put a few things together in his head before he spoke again. "You...you told us you never went inside that farmhouse. Trespassing you called it."

Sally shrugged. "I lied. So what? I wasn't sure what you fellas were like, so I kept a few things to myself. Truth is I saw you lot coming and went out the back. Came round the side with my hands above my head."

Kirk shook his head. "Who cares? "What difference does it make?"

"It makes a lot of difference," said Garfield. "He said he took the gun off the old man in the kitchen, but I was in the kitchen and nobody was there. The only old man we found was hanging by his neck, along with his wife and child."

Kirk's pupil's flickered as the memory came back to him. He had been deeply affected at the time and had needed Garfield to deal with the situation. He turned to Sally. "You...you hung them up by their necks? Why?"

Sally shrugged. "Dunno, really. It gets boring being on yer own. Mind does all sorts of thing. Look, mate, I'm sorry. It was a bit of a sick thing to do, but I didn't harm anyone. They were already dead."

"This man wasn't, though," said Garfield, pointing down at the soldier who had finally died whilst they were talking. "He didn't need to die. He didn't want to shoot anyone. Kirk could have talked him around."

"No way, mate," said Sally. "We were about to leave with our tail between our legs. After coming all this way, we were about to leave with nothing. I got you all this place, so stop having a pop at me. Just chill out, mate."

"I'm not your mate."

"No, you're a bleeding whinger. Best we just leave your moany arse behind." He turned his attention to the soldier. "Do you have the keys to those trucks over there? And the Armoury?"

The soldier said nothing, so Sally yanked off his balaclava and got in his face. The man had a shaved head and high, angular cheekbones. His chin looked like it could dent iron.

Sally stood nose to nose with the man before saying, "We can either get the keys from your corpse or you can hand them over."

The soldier sighed and reached into the pockets of his utility belt. His hand came out with a large bundle of keys. "Everything I have is on there. Haltek has the rest of the keys. You can get them from his corpse."

Sally snatched the keys and then went to retrieve the other set from the dead soldier. During that time, Garfield asked the soldier a simple question. "What's your name?"

The soldier grunted. "Sergeant Price, 2684573. First Battalion, Parachute Regiment."

So that's why these guys are such badasses, thought Garfield. Garfield had briefly considered joining the Army when he was a teenager. He had consumed every war movie and magazine he could find. One thing quickly became obvious; you don't fuck with the Paras. When Garfield's father had died, leaving his mother all alone, he had put all thoughts of travelling the world in a uniform aside. But how different might his life have been if he had taken the same path as Price? The two of them were of a similar age. "Was Haltek a para as well?" Garfield asked.

"All three of us are. When the other soldiers stationed here set out on the road, we chose to remain here and protect the base from people like you."

Garfield sighed. Although he hated it, he was pretty sure he was one of the bad guys in this situation. "Look, what Sally did, killing your man, was nothing to do with the rest of us. We picked him up on our travels. I didn't even know he had a gun."

"If you don't support his actions, punish him. If you do nothing then you are condoning his actions."

"That's not true. I...I'm not in charge here. It's not my responsibility."

"Yes, it is. Haltek would never have fired on your people. You could have all left safely if the dingo hadn't fired that cap gun at us."

"Might have been a cap gun," said Sally, overhearing them. "But it took care of your mate alright, didn't it?"

Sergeant Price made a move towards Sally, but Garfield raised the rifle in his hands and shook his head. "Let's make sure no one else gets shot, okay?"

The soldier glared at him. "This burk is going to get you people killed. I've seen men like him plenty of times before. Most of them ended up dead or in the Glasshouse."

"Nah, mate. You ain't. I'm one of a kind. A real beaut."

"Alright," said Kirk. "Let's just get what we came for and we can leave these men in peace."

Sally scoffed. "Are you kidding? Soon as we try to set off, GI Joe and Private Pyle here are going to grab themselves a weapon and become unpleasant. Can't leave them alive."

"What should we do?" Garfield spat. "Hang them by their necks?"

"Good a method as any."

Kirk grabbed Sally by the arm. "Just get to work. I'll decide what to do with the soldiers when the time comes."

Sally shrugged his shoulders and snapped off a salute. "Yessir. Right away, sir." Then he swaggered off towards the armoury."

Kirk strode over to sergeant Price. "Get down on the floor beside your buddy. Sit on your hands and don't try anything. We'll be out of your hair before you know it."

When Price didn't respond, Kirk kicked the man's legs out from under him and dragged him over to the other soldier who Garfield had struck with his metal pipe.

Somehow Garfield couldn't help but feel like a brutish Viking sacking a defenceless village. It left a bad taste in his mouth. *We're the bad guys here.*

PRICE

PRICE COULDN'T BELIEVE how hard he'd failed. People always expected him to feel proud of being a member of the illustrious Parachute Regiment, but they didn't realise that there was nothing to be proud of. 1 Para wasn't the pinnacle of the British Army Special Forces. The maroon beret was second to one other: the beige beret. The sand-coloured beret his father owned. Who Dares Wins.

Price had twice attempted to pass the brutal trials of the SAS, but both times he had failed. The forced marches over the Brecon Hills left him hospitalised on each occasion. Being a Para just reminded him that he would always be second best to a select few who had more ability than he did – men who were made of sterner stuff. His father had always said he was too weak to make it in the elite of the elite, and it had turned out he was right. Even now that the world had ended, Price knew that the SAS would be holed up somewhere, surviving the apocalypse with ease and turning the air blue with their foulmouthed jokes. His father might even be with them; the SAS looked after their own. They were a family. A family that Price had always longed to join but never would. *Not like I ever belonged to my own family.* The Special Air Service was trained for any situation and the dead would be little more than a minor obstacle to the SAS.

They would never have let an entire Army barracks fall to a man with an antique pistol. *I'm a fuck-up. The Sarge is dead because I didn't get my gun up fast enough. My father will be rolling in his grave.*

Fuck him.

Price wasn't done yet. The carrot-top in the long black coat might have taken his SA80, but he still had his 9mm tucked in a holster hidden at his back, beneath his vest. It always helped to have a weapon or two hidden. *Soon as I get chance, that dingo bastard is taking a dirt nap.*

Price knew his life was already forfeit. The least a soldier could do before the bodysnatchers came for him was take as many of the enemy with him as he could. For the last hour, he had sat on his hands as required and watched silently as the group of bandits raided the Colonel Gadaffi and snatched at the boxes of military rations. The eight-hundred-and-fourteen Operational Ration Packs contained enough food to feed a man for 24 hours, or a starved survivor for 48. They also contained water purifying tablets, matches, tissues, tea bags, and chicken stock. The bandits had just hit the mother lode. The thought of them surviving happily for the next year on those rations made Price feel sick to his stomach.

Now the bandits had turned their focus to the armoury. There were six caches and all had been opened. The Australian and his buddies were currently in the process of loading up the 4-tonne trucks with dozens of SA80 battle rifles, Browning 9mm handguns, a couple of L7A2 General-Purpose-Machine-Guns, and a batch of recreational hunting rifles. The dingo was strutting around with an L128A1 semi-auto shotgun on his hip like he knew how to use it – he didn't. The bandits even took a crate full of L109A1 HE grenades. *They use one of those and the dead will come running from a hundred miles around.*

Corporal Barker had recovered from the blow to his head and was sat upright beside Price. The carrot-top kept a watch on them both, with Price's SA80 held loosely to his shoulder. *He'll break his collarbone if he pulls the trigger on that thing.*

During the last ten minutes, the two of them had been sawing away at the zip-ties around their wrists. They rubbed the plastic against the sharp edges of their belt buckles. It was slow work, but working.

"You got a plan, Price?" Barker asked him in a whisper.

Price nodded. "Yeah, go down fighting."

"Sounds good to me."

"You got your 9mm tucked away?"

Barker chuckled. "Yeah, the stupid bastards didn't bother to check me. They're almost begging to die."

"Well, lets not disappoint them."

"Let's do this for Haltek."

"For Haltek."

Price was just about to leap up and snap his zip-ties when the bandits formed-up a few feet away. If it were not for the fact that the dingo pointed a shotgun in their directions, Price would have followed through with his plan of grabbing for his 9mm and going down in a bullet storm. But the plan was to take the bandits by surprise to maximise their casualties. Price wouldn't even get a shot off if that shotgun went off in his face. He grabbed a hold of Barker and shook his head. "Wait."

The carrot-top moved around behind Price and Barker and pointed the rifle at the back of their heads. The ginger guy wasn't so bad as the others. It seemed like he would have handled the situation differently. The problem was the dingo and the guy in charge. The kid who'd but Price on his arse with a judo sweep. He'll pay for that.

"The trucks are all stuffed full. All three of them," said the stumpy guy Price had tied up in the fire engine. 'Lemon' the other men called him. The leader of the bandits nodded. "Good work. We're ready to go then?"

Lemon nodded.

"Great, lets load up and get going then."

"What about the squaddies?" the dingo asked. He was pointing the barrel of the shotgun right in Price's mug. If he kills me now I won't even have a chance to reach for my gun. Fuck!

"Leave them," said the carrot-top. "We've done enough already."

The dingo laughed. "They're the enemy. We don't let the enemy go. They killed Tom and Gavin."

"Because you fired at them, you fool. You didn't even know Tom and Gavin."

Both men looked to the leader of the group, but the younger man just stood there looking increasingly stressed. It was clear that the guy wasn't cut out for leadership. He was too indecisive – an obvious people pleaser. He couldn't make a decision unless it suited everyone, and that was never possible. If anyone should be in charge, thought Price, it should be the carrot-top. He was the only one who spoke up rationally and thought things through. The dingo was a blagger with an ego. Men like him never lasted long on the field, but sometimes they managed to fuck things up before they went.

The carrot-top shrugged at the leader. "Kirk, will you tell Sally to chill out. We don't kill innocent people. We've got what we came for, so let's just leave."

Kirk nodded. "Okay, you're right. Everyone get in the trucks. We're leaving."

"No, we're not," said Sally. "You're not the boss of me, mate. I'm taking those trucks for myself along with anyone else who wants to join me."

Kirk's mouth dropped open. "N-no you're not. We all stick together."

"I'm not asking for your permission. Your men are coming with me. They're tired of risking their necks and having to share. They want what's theirs and I'm going to give it to them. Life is better out on the road."

Kirk said nothing, and in fact he seemed to shrink. He was holding no weapon, while the dingo held one of the most intimidating weapons a man could face. The carrot-top raised his rifle away from Price's skull and aimed it at the arguing members of his group.

Price made eye contact with Barker and nodded subtly. They're distracted. It's almost time. Price began to slide his hand around to the 9mm at his back.

"Who the hell do you think you are, Sally?" demanded the carrot-top. "We picked you up when you were all alone and now you're pulling this shit."

"I don't owe you people anything. None of you have done anything other than let me tag along. When I did some asking around, it turned out that this happy little group ain't so happy. They want to break out on their own. With the trucks and the guns, we can take whatever we want."

The carrot-top shook his head. He looked utterly gobsmacked. Price felt sorry for him, he seemed like a decent guy. The man glanced around at the assembled group and waved his arms. "Who is a part of this? Who wants to leave with this piece of shit? Come on, if you have the balls to turn your back on the pier, then have the balls to stand up for your convictions? Who wants to go with Sally?"

The man almost seemed to fall down in pain when the hands of nearly the entire group went up. The stumpy guy called Lemon didn't put his hand up, nor the man and woman Barker had captured by the trucks. Everyone else's did, though. It was almost unanimous.

The carrot-top looked at Kirk and shrugged. "You're in charge, Kirk. You wanted this. You handle it. Are you with Sally, or are you going to grow some balls?"

Kirk wobbled on his feet and grew pale. He spluttered and glanced around nervously. "I...I...If everyone is going with Sally, then we should, too. We shouldn't separate after so long together. We need each other."

"And what about the others at the pier? Anna, Rene...Poppy?"

Kirk shrugged. "You do what you want Garfield. The guys at the pier are safe. If you want Poppy then go back for her. Nobody is stopping you."

"You fucking coward," said the only woman of the group.

Kirk's face bunched up in anger. "Screw you, Cat. I'm just trying to survive. Nobody ever said we had to stick together at the pier forever. I joined you all much later, anyway. None of you treat me the same as the others. I should have been in charge of this group months ago."

Garfield huffed. "I think you're showing the reason why we didn't put you in charge. You can't handle it."

"Screw you, Garf."

Garfield didn't answer back. He just sighed at the other man and seemed genuinely sad. "Fine, Kirk. You do what you want. I'm going back to the pier with anyone who wants to come with me. I'll take the minivan."

"Me and David are with you," said the woman.

"Me t-t-too," said Lemon.

"Okay," said Sally. "Then we've all made our decision. We go our separate ways. All that's left to do is kill the squaddies."

Price balked. He had grasped his 9mm in his hand but had gotten so wrapped up in the bitter exchange between the bandits that he hadn't yet brought it around. By the time he did, it would already be too late. The dingo had his shotgun pressed up against his forehead

Price closed his eyes. I've failed again. My father was right. That grumpy old git.

Just when Price expected his head to explode, there was a loud thud! He opened his eyes to see that Garfield had struck the dingo in his head with the butt of the SA80. The Australian went reeling to the ground. The shotgun he had been holding skittered away across the pavement. Blood oozed from a gash on his hairline.

Garfield glanced down at Price and Barker. "You two, get up. You're not our prisoners."

Price clutched his 9mm and thought about yanking it free and firing off a few rounds, but his instincts told him to hold off and see what transpired. As much as he should have, he didn't want to shoot the carrot-top.

Garfield stood over Sally and growled. "You're done."

The dingo laughed. Blood covered his face but he didn't seem to care. The men and women who had sought to take off with the man had faltered. They glanced at one another nervously and then shuffled their feet. A mutiny only lasts as long as its leader, thought Price.

"Okay," said Sally. "You got me. I beg for mercy."

Garfield shook his head and sighed. "More than you deserve, but unlike you I don't kill people if I don't have to. Take the minivan and get the hell out of here. If I see you again I'll take your goddamn head off."

Garfield lowered his rifle and started to turn away, but the dingo sat up suddenly and let off two quick bangs! Garfield reeled backwards. His finger squeezed around the trigger of his SA80. It bucked violently in his hands and wrenched his shoulder in his socket just like Price had warned him. The bullet spread went wide, clanging off a group of empty oil barrels. Clunk clunk clunk! The rifle fell to the ground with a clatter! Another shot rang out and Garfield fell to the ground beside it.

When Price saw the antique pistol that had killed Haltek he brought around his 9mm and fired off a tight grouping right into the dingo's chest. The man was dead before he even knew he'd been shot. The smell of gunpowder hung thick in the air and the sound of the shots seemed to echo for miles around. That's not good.

Immediately, a standoff ensued. Price and Barker held 9mms, but were being faced down by an assortment of assault rifles and other 9mms. The leader, Kirk, shook his head and did nothing. The guy was a wet blanket.

Price sighed and took pity on the younger man. He glanced down at the carrot-top, lying on the floor where three bullets had struck his chest. "Barker, lower your weapon," he said. "Nobody else has to die today."

Barker did as he was told and Price lowered his weapon too. He re-holstered the 9mm behind his back and knelt down beside Garfield. The guy they called Lemon did the same. "Is he going to be okay, sir?"

Price sighed. Sir? This guy likes to obey. "No, he's not going to be okay. He just took two slugs in the chest. And don't call me 'sir', I work for a living." He cleared his throat. "I'm sorry for your loss. He seemed like the only one of you with any sense."

There was silence amongst the group and Price crossed the dead man's arms across his chest and repositioned his head. It was the least he could do.

It scared the shit out of him when the man started to cough and splutter. "Jesus Christ, you're alive."

The man was out of breath, gasping and struggling, but he had the strength of an ox and Price could do nothing as he forced himself into a sitting position. He continued coughing for a good few minutes, but when he was done, he grasped at the buttons on his shirt and tore them loose. His shirt fluttered open and Price was surprised to see that neither slug had managed to enter the man's chest. Three hunks of lead were lodged into a thick barrier of what looked like history magazines. The man had wrapped them around his torso like armour. It was a novel idea, but probably wouldn't have worked against a modern calibre bullet. Luckily, the dingo had fired two ancient lead rounds from an antique pistol. The magazines had been enough to save his life.

Price helped the man to his feet. "You okay, buddy? It's Garfield, right?"

The man nodded, clutching his chest. Even though the bullets hadn't penetrated, the force of the blow would still have been like standing in the way of a bull. "I...yeah, I'm fine. I'm...I'm sorry all this happened."

Price sighed. "Well, if anything, it showed me that not everyone is out to murder and rape. If I thought you were the one in charge, I would let you leave here with everything you ask for."

"He is in charge," said Lemon. "He's always been in charge."

Price looked at Kirk. The younger man was trembling. "That true, lad? I thought you were the head honcho of this outfit?"

Kirk shook his head. "N-no. Garfield has always been in charge. I only took over yesterday because..."

"Because you all got charmed by the dingo and stopped following orders. You know what happens to deserters in the Army, lad?"

Kirk looked ashamed. He turned around and walked away.

In the distance there was moaning. "The dead are coming," said Price, sighing. "The gunfire has attracted them."

"We need to get that hole in the fence filled in," said Garfield.

Price waved his hand. "You people need to get out of here or else you'll never get the chance. The dead will surround the entire base before long. We've only survived this long by keeping quiet."

Garfield opened his mouth and closed it again. "I...I'm sorry. This was your home and we've endangered it."

"Just get out of here," said Price. There was no point making apologies that fixed nothing.

There was a rumbling of an engine. Price looked over to see that Kirk had jumped up into one of the trucks and started the engine. Two other men had run off after him and jumped into the rear bed of the truck.

Garfield shouted. "Kirk, what the hell are you doing? Lenny, Luke.... Stop right now." Kirk disobeyed him and ground the gears into first. The truck began to move. It headed for the chain link fence, picking up speed. Price ripped a grenade from his utility vest and went to pull out the pin. Garfield grabbed his wrist. "Please, don't. He's a stupid kid, more scared than I realised. This is my fault. I lost control of the group. People panic when there's no leader. He's a good person, and so are Lenny and Luke. Let them go, please."

Price stared at the other man and shrugged. He placed the grenade back in his belt. "Your call. Would only attract more dead anyway."

Kirk sped up and the truck roared. It's huge weight rushed forward. The front of the vehicle smashed into the chain link fence and dragged it along. It folded beneath the truck's giant wheels and slapped into the dirt. As the truck took off at full speed, a length of fence twenty metres long went with it.

The dead moaned in the distance, but were already closer.

Price grunted. "There goes the neighbourhood. Get out of here before the dead give you no choice."

"Come with us," said Garfield. "We took away your safety, but we have a camp at a pier on the south coast. It's safe there and we all look after one another."

It felt like charity, but Price knew that staying at the barracks was a death wish. He had to move on; the only question was whether or not to go with Garfield and his men. He glanced at Barker. Barker shrugged. "Fine. Let's just get the fuck out of here and quick. What's the quickest way to your camp?"

"The motorway would take less than a day," said Garfield, "But it's choc-a-block with cars and zombies."

Price scratched his jutting chin and smiled. "I may have just the thing."

When he showed Garfield what he had hidden at the back of the camp beneath a large green tarp, the man began to bellow with laughter. "I guess we're taking the motorway, then," he said. "Anna is never going to believe this."

FRANK

FRANK WAS OUTSIDE taking a breath when he saw the small yacht approaching from the distance. Night had fallen but an interior lamp lit up the small vessel. The lamp's glow was puny compared to the fires of the night before.

The Kirkland's aft deck was bustling, as it usually was in the evenings. Men played cards and flirted with the handful of women on board, sharing their alcohol rations like their was no tomorrow. The fireworks show at the pier had made everyone rowdy.

The supply of booze to the crewmen of the Kirkland had been lowered recently after a rash of drunken behaviour that stretched all the way from bad language to rape. The men and women aboard the frigate were tired, weary, and had left their souls back on land. There was a constant air of aggression and fear that made people paranoid and selfish after a while. Frank often wondered where the future would take them all. Could they go on like this perpetually? Or was something bound to give? The grey, salt-stained decks of the frigate could not sustain them forever, he thought.

The little yacht got closer and Frank saw that they were waving a white flag. Frank saw a dark-skinned man and a stout woman. He recognised neither, but when he saw the third man his eyes went wide. Leaning over the bow on a pair of crutches was Tim Golding – the man Samuel referred to as the 'cripple' and the man who had tried to obliterate the fleet's flagship.

Frank hurried over to the rigging set up along the Kirkland's starboard side and removed the guard stationed there. He would receive these guests himself.

The woman attached the yacht to the rigging and secured the vessel. She then took Tim by the arm and helped him up on to the thick rope latticework. The cripple climbed up the centre with the man and woman helping him on either side. The progress was slow, laborious, but they gradually made their way towards the deck above. Frank waited to seize them the moment they stepped foot aboard.

The woman reached the gunwale first and shoved a pair of crutches into Frank's unsuspecting arms. "Here, mate, hold these, will you?"

Frank spluttered but did as he was asked. The three visitors managed to tumble over the gunwale and onto the deck. Tim asked for his crutches back and Frank handed them over begrudgingly. "Excuse me," he eventually said. "Might you state your business?"

The woman looked at him. "My name is Anna. This is my colleague, Rene. And this man, I'm sure you know, is Tim."

Frank snorted. "Yes, I know a terrorist when I see one."

"Actually," said Tim. "I'm more of an attempted terrorist. I never actually got to blow anything up. More's the pity."

"Why have you come here? You're a wanted man."

"That's why I'm here. I'm giving myself up before any more innocent people are hurt."

"Your captain killed a nine-year-old girl," said Anna. "So we surrender, okay? You're all big men with great big dicks and we're afraid of you. We're here to bend our knee to your king."

"Samuel is not our king," said Frank firmly, but he couldn't help but think about the nine-year-old girl. "He is our captain."

"Some might say that a captain is a king aboard his own boat. Certainly seems like he has the power to do whatever he wants."

Frank said nothing. Samuel would be pleased that the cripple had given himself up. He hoped his son would show kindness to the surviving members of the pier and leave them alone. They were no longer defying him, so perhaps they could be forgiven.

People on the aft deck spotted the newcomers and started to point and mutter. "Come with me," said Frank. He turned to Tim. "People want your head, so best we don't dawdle. I'll take you to Samuel immediately."

As Frank ushered the three guests into the ship's interior, he ignored the many angry glares of the crewmen. If Samuel did anything other than execute Tim, there would be outright mutiny. The men and women on the Kirkland were bored and lost. When they were given a villain to collectively hate, they did so with gusto. Tim could have been guilty of no more than killing a spider and the inhabitants of the frigate would still want his blood. Frank couldn't help but sigh with relief when they reached the captain's chambers. He was less happy to find petty officer Dunn standing guard at the door.

"Wow, Frank, where did you find these three? The very man that Samuel is looking for and you bring him right to his chambers. Not bad."

Frank nodded. "They have come to surrender, and you would do well to refer to Samuel as 'captain.'"

"Of course. Shall I tell him you're here?"

Frank shoved the man aside. "I don't need you to announce me. Samuel is my son." He took the guests inside and was aggravated when Dunn followed.

Samuel stood up immediately when he saw Tim. "You!" he said in a tone that could have crumbled concrete.

Tim hobbled forward on his crutches. "I heard you were looking for me. What seems to be the trouble?"

Samuel smashed his fist down on the table. "You know the trouble. You tried to kill me."

"Oh, that. Yeah. I don't suppose you'd be willing to let bygones be bygones, would you? I did fail after all."

Samuel snarled.

Frank introduced the man and woman. "Samuel, this is Anna and Rene from the pier. They have surrendered Tim in order to secure a truce."

"Nice to be here," said Tim. "I've missed your smile captain."

Samuel turned his frown into a predatory smirk and examined the woman standing before him. "She'd like to secure a truce, would she?"

"Yes, she would," said the woman irritably.

Samuel laughed. "You seem bitter, miss. Does friendship not taste sweet to you? Would you prefer enmity?"

"I would prefer that you hadn't killed a bunch of innocent people, but that's the past now. I'm only hoping to protect those of us still left. We want no part in your quarrel with this man. You wanted him, you got him. Now leave the pier in peace."

"I won't fight you," said Tim. "I'll admit to what I did. Just leave these people alone. They've done nothing."

Frank caught Samuel's eye and nodded. There was no reason to take issue with the people on the pier. They had suffered enough for helping the cripple. Now that they had handed him over there was no harm done.

"I disagree," said Samuel. He looked down at his desk and shook his head slowly. His hands clenched into fists. "What would my people think of me if I allowed our enemies mercy? They would become frightened and weak. They must know that I will protect them from any threat. The people on this pier harboured a terrorist, a man who sought to end me. What is to say they will not hatch some future plot against us?"

"We will not," said Rene. The man had a Nigerian accent and a peculiar way of talking, almost like his words were precious and he used them only sparingly. "We want only peace."

Samuel eyeballed the man like he was some strange species. "You're a long way from home. Nigerian?"

The man blinked. "The pier is my home."

"I understand. The Kirkland is my home. The man standing beside you tried to blow it up. Should I just ignore that?"

"Yes. As we will ignore that you blew up our home. You are guilty of a crime this man only tried to commit. You are a bad man, which is why we are here to beg for peace. Take your boats and go."

"Do not demand anything of me," shouted Samuel. He glanced at Dunn. "Lieutenant Dunn, these people are now prisoners of the fleet. Lock them up until I decide sentencing."

Dunn smiled and nodded. "Yes, Captain."

Frank balked. Not only had Samuel promoted a wretch like Dunn to Lieutenant, he had also imprisoned two people seeking mercy. "Samuel, I would plead you to think about this. A show of mercy can be as powerful as a punishment. We hit the pier and caused them heavy casualties. There is nothing to be gained by further action."

"Please, sir," said Rene. "We are just ordinary people. We do not wish to fight you."

"You'll have no choice," said Dunn. "You're going to be in a cell."

"Are you so afraid of rumours and stories that you would punish innocent people?" Anna, spat.

Samuel glared at her. "I have no idea what you mean. You are my enemy. That is all."

Anna smirked. "No, it's more than that. You don't want the men and women of your precious fleet to find out that you caused the apocalypse. You're the devil."

Samuel growled like a wolf. He marched around the side of his desk and backhanded her. She fell backwards but Dunn caught her in his arms, making to sure to get a good grope of her breasts as he did so.

Like the jaws of a snapping alligator, Rene grabbed Samuel around the neck and got behind him. The chokehold was so tight that Samuel's pale face immediately went purple. He reached out to Frank and pleaded. Frank took a step forward to help, but Dunn beat him to it. The officer leapt forward and smashed Rene in the back of his skull with the grip of a rigging knife he pulled from his belt. Samuel broke free of the chokehold, gasping, and Rene fell to his knees in a daze.

Samuel caught his breath and pointed to the man who had just tried to kill him. "Kill him!"

"No," screamed Anna. Suddenly she produced a screwdriver that had been tucked up her sleeve. Frank cursed himself for not having patted her down. He dove in front of Samuel and managed to get his arm in the way. The tip of the screwdriver buried itself in his forearm and made him yell out, but it didn't stop him from using his elbow to smash the woman in the eye socket. She slumped to the floor, the fight taken completely out of her. The cripple raised one of his crutches as if to join the melee, but a stern look from Frank was enough to put that idea to bed.

Samuel leant back against his desk, panting. He pointed at Rene again. "I said kill him. Kill him now!"

Anna crawled along the floor and let out a scream as Dunn stood over the man and quickly slit his neck open from ear to ear.

Samuel was grinning. "Now take the other two away. I'll deal with them later."

Anna screamed all the way as Dunn dragged her out of the room and towards the brig. Frank stood there in shock, wondering how much longer he could convince himself that Samuel was a good man. Rene's blood spread out beneath him in a bright red puddle.

"Oh, and Frank?" said Samuel.

"Yes, Samuel?"

"If you ever disobey my orders again, it will be you bleeding on the floors of my chambers. And I would have you call me 'captain' or 'sir' from now on. Do you understand?"

Frank nodded. "Yes...sir."

"I didn't come this far just to be undermined by the man who raised me. Years of planning have gone into this and I cannot afford to let anything in my way."

Frank cleared his throat, but found a lump stuck there. "Years of planning? What do you mean?"

Samuel smirked and shook his head. "I think you know what I mean, Frank. Now, leave my sight."

Frank slunk away with tears in his eyes, trying to process what he had just heard. Years of planning...

My son is a monster.

But he is still my son. Although now I must call him 'sir'.

HUGO

ETTING THE STRANGERS take his boat had been a grave mistake. At first, being at the pier was a wonderful experience. Hugo had leant besides the railing and watched as his daughters played chase with an excitable Houdini. It was just the way things were meant to be, and for a while it felt like the right decision, but during that time the dead had continued lining up at the gate. Now there were dozens and dozens of them, moaning and rattling at the bars. I can already see the gate weakening. Every hour its hinges loosen more.

The people still at the pier – Bob, Samantha, and Jim – were worried also; he could see it in their faces. When night had arrived, the dead seemed to become even more menacing. They became a shifting, moaning shadow – a single entity rather than a collection of individual bodies.

"We can't wait for the others," said Samantha. "We're going to have to gather whatever supplies we can and climb down the side of the pier to the beach."

"The dead are on the beach, too," said old man Bob. "A dozen of them appeared a couple hours ago."

"We can deal with them," Samantha said. "But we have no hope against the hundreds in the village. We have to go soon."

Hugo glanced at his daughters, playing at the side of the pier. Both of them fussed at Houdini and acted as though all was fine, but he knew better – he was their father. The girls were frightened, but it was they who insisted coming aboard the pier. They would not voice their discontent now. My girls are proud and brave.

"We're screwed," Jimmy fretted. "We're like hamsters up a butthole."

"We'll be fine," said Samantha. "We just have to be careful."

"We go down to the beach in pitch blackness, the dead will be on us before we take two steps," moaned Bob.

"The moon is full. We have enough light to see by."

Hugo looked down at the beach and saw the shadows moving beneath him. Just ten feet below his feet was a death pit, full of clawing hands and biting teeth. The only thing protecting them all from death was a single iron gate. They were mice trapped in a maze, with hungry predators at every exit.

"The tide is in, the beach is too narrow to make it through the dead," Jimmy complained. "We'll be like a turd in a u-bend."

Samantha groaned. She was becoming frustrated. "Another couple hours and the tide will go out again. We need to gather our things and be ready to go then. We can't stay here. You can all see that."

The gate seemed to creak then as a reminder. The dead weighed down on it like a tide of sand. Hugo listened to their moans and screeches and wondered how much longer until the gate toppled completely.

"Wait!" Jimmy said. He tilted his head. "What's that noise?"

Everyone was quiet.

The moaning and screeching continued.

Hugo frowned. *Do the dead make screeching sounds? I thought they just moaned.*

Samantha's hand went to her mouth. "Oh God! I hear screeching. There's an infected person in the village."

The screeching got louder. It was coming in their direction. Hugo had heard tales of the infected, had even seen a few on his panicked retreat out of France, but he'd been at sea so long that they'd faded into imaginary monsters. "What are the infected?" he asked, almost not wanting to know.

Old man Bob looked positively sick. He shook his head as he spoke and didn't blink at all. "A person gets infected when they get bitten by a dead man or another infected. They get sick – real sick – before slipping into a sort of coma. Once they get back up, though, they're like wild animals – unstoppable killing machines. We call them sprinters. They come at you like something straight out of Hell. We haven't seen any for almost a year now. They all died off and turned into zombies – the infection kills them after a while, you see. We can handle the dead, Hugo, but the sprinters are a whole different type of badger."

Hugo looked at his daughters. He hoped they were not listening. "What do we do now? About the...badger?"

"We arm up," said Samantha, already marching away. "And we pray."

Hugo huffed. The last thing he would do was pray, but arming up he could do. Too long had he floated around in the sea, relying on the protection of others to keep his daughters safe. Now it was time to prove he could look after them on his own. If something bad was coming, then it was going to have to get though him. *And over my dead body.*

The screeching continued endlessly, getting closer and closer. Hugo thanked Samantha for a carbon steel shovel and gave it a few practise swings. It cut through the air nicely. The garden tool was light but strong, sufficient to smash in a skull or two.

"What is going on, papa?" Sophie asked. "I hear someone out there screaming."

Hugo gave her a quick hug. Daphne came over and got one too. "It is not a person," he told them. "It is a monster and your papa is going to take care of it. The world that has been left to you is a dangerous place, my darlings, but if I have any hope of seeing you grow up I must stop hiding it from you. We must fight and protect one another. The times ahead will be hard and sometimes you will want to cry, but we will face it together and we will be okay."

"I'm afraid," said Daphne, hugging her older sister. "But I will be brave. I won't let you down, dad."

Hugo smiled at the English word. Letting go of papa was a sign that his daughter was finally leaving her old life behind.

"I won't let you down either," said Sophie. "I will do whatever I have to do to look after you and Daphne."

Hugo patted her on the head. "We are glad to have you watching over us, Sophie. Now, both of you go get something to protect yourselves with and find someplace to hide."

His two girls did as they were told, obedient, as he'd raised them to be. A twinge of pride took a hold of Hugo and for a moment the anxious butterflies in his belly flapped away. They soon flew back, though, because the screeching was coming from right up at the gate.

Hugo hurried after the others to the front of the pier. The twisted gate that met him there was almost enough to make him turn the other way. Hundreds of dead men and women filled the village and all of them were trying to get inside the pier. At the front of the mob, ramming his entire body against the metal bars was an infected person – a sprinter.

The young man had a thick black beard and shaggy hair – the look of a long-term survivor. Under the moonlight, his bulging eyes seemed to glow red and his gnashing teeth gleaned silver. The bulbous winter jacket he wore made him look twice as big as his skinny body likely was underneath. For some reason he smelt of rotten fish. It was so overpowering that even the stench of death could not overcome it.

Samantha charged forward and jabbed through the railings of the gate with what looked like a steel litter spike. She missed the infected man's head but ended up burying the tip in his shoulder. She yanked it back and stabbed again. This time, the infected man seized the litter spike and tore it out of her hands. The sudden yank made Samantha stumbled forward against the gate. Immediately the dead men and women set upon her, clawing at her through the bars. She fought hard and desperately, trying to drag herself away from the gate, but a dead postman had a hold of her bracelets. She was hooked like a duck at the fair. An old lady took a big hungry bite out of her wrist.

Samantha screamed and managed to yank her arm back through the bars, but it was too late. She fell to deck, clutching her wrist and sobbing. Blood poured down her arm and glistened.

The sprinter threw himself against the gate harder, impassioned by the blood.

Bob and Jimmy went and dragged Samantha to her feet. They shook her by her shoulders and tried to get her to focus, but she would not. Great, wracking sobs seized her and would not let go. Eventually, between breaths she managed to say, "I'm screwed. I'm...I'm fucking screwed."

"You can die like a sobbing wench," said old man Bob. "Or you can snap out of it, duc, and help those of us who still have a chance."

Samantha fought to control herself, but eventually nodded. Her sobbing petered out and stopped. "Okay...I...I'm okay. I'm okay."

The hinges of the gate whined and creaked. Then the entire thing moved by almost a metre. The bars slanted towards them.

"The gate is falling," said Jimmy. "We have to get out of here right now. Hugo, get your girls. We're heading for the beach."

Hugo got going immediately, but before he even made it halfway down the deck, Samantha yelled out a warning. He span around. The infected man had leapt the slanting gate and made it over onto the deck. The animal was inside the cage and sprinting toward Hugo. Merde!

Hugo raised his shovel and prepared to meet his attacker, but was horrified when the sprinter stopped halfway and turned sideways. Sophie and Daphne huddled in the nearby doorway of an ice cream shop. The infected man had seen them.

"Hey, Mr Beard, over here." Hugo waved his arms and rushed towards the infected man, shouting and whistling, trying to draw attention away from his daughters. But it was no good. His daughters cowered and cried in the doorway and the infected man was transfixed on them. Please God, no. Do not let him eat my daughters.

Houdini appeared out of nowhere. The little dog puffed up in front of the infected man and started barking in a tone Hugo had not heard before. The infected man looked down at Houdini with interest. Hugo's heart skipped a beat. Good job, Houdini. You are protecting your girls, just like we used to talk about.

But the sprinter was quickly losing interest in the dog. It was Sophie and Daphne he was interested in. As he turned his attention back towards Hugo's daughters, Houdini took it to the next level. The tiny papillon clamped his jaws down on the sprinter's ankle and began tugging on it like a rawhide bone. It was enough of a distraction to keep Daphne and Sophie safe for another ten seconds.

Hugo charged at the sprinter and swung for the cheap seats. The sharp edge of his shovel connected with the infected man's temple and sent him tumbling sideways, but, somehow, the blow did not fell the man. He snarled and spat, then lunged through the air at Hugo like a hissing adder.

There was no time for Hugo to bring the spade around again, so the sprinter barrelled into him and sent him sprawling onto his back. Hugo spluttered as the wind escaped him. The spade went rolling across the deck. *I am done for.* He grabbed at the infected man's chin, yanking his bushy black beard and trying to keep the snapping jaws away, but it was like wrestling an alligator. Houdini snapped and barked, but was no longer able to cause a distraction. The dead man was unwaveringly focused on ripping Hugo apart. *I can't fight him much longer. He is too strong...too wild.*

But then the sprinter tumbled away from Hugo.

Hugo rolled onto his chest and thrust himself back up onto his feet as quickly as his weary bones would let him. Samantha had grabbed the infected man from behind and was wrestling him to the ground. He bit and tore at her arms and wrists as she fought to keep him restrained. "Get the spade," she screamed. The pain was obvious in her voice. "Get the spade and end this."

Hugo scurried over to where the spade had fallen and snatched it up. He took a run-up and swung the tool like a golf club. The blade struck the infected man in the centre of the face. Fresh blood – infected blood – exploded onto the deck and made Hugo shy away. The infected man continued to thrash and writhe in Samantha's arms, not yet beaten. Hugo lifted the shovel again and let out the scream of a caveman. He thrust the blade down at the sick man's neck, opening up his throat and lifting his chin. Blood gargled from the ragged gash. Hugo placed his foot on the back of the shovel and pushed with all his might.

The sprinter's head sprang from his shoulders and rolled across the decking. Hugo threw the shovel down onto the deck and tried not to vomit.

Samantha collapsed onto her back, panting. She stared up at the stars and blinked. "Now me," she said calmly.

Hugo frowned. "What?"

Samantha kept her head flat against the deck, exposing the pale flesh of her neck. "I'm infected," she said, "and I don't have long left. You need to make sure I don't get back up."

Hugo shook his head. "No. I cannot."

"Do it. If you have any hope of keeping those daughters of yours safe you will do what needs to be done. Put the shovel against my throat and take my fucking head off. I'm going to be just like that guy in a few minutes. You need to deal with me now."

"I'll do it," said old man Bob, marching up beside Hugo and reaching down to pick up the shovel.

Hugo reached down and grabbed the shovel first. "No. I'll do it." Time to start doing what needs to be done. The days of floating around aimlessly are behind me. He strolled up to Samantha and carefully placed the shovel's blade against her throat. Then he leapt up with both feet and brought his full weight down on her neck. It still wasn't enough.

Samantha's neck split open and her head lolled sideways, but she still lived. She gargled and coughed as blood filled her airways.

"Shit," said Jimmy. "Do it again."

Hugo jumped back up onto the spade and completed the job. Samantha's spinal cord snapped and her head came away from her body. Hugo strangely felt nothing. The woman had been dead when she was bitten, not when he removed her head. It would have been nice to know her better, but the world held little regard for friendships anymore.

Before anyone had time to mourn Samantha, the gate fell inwards with a resounding crash! Immediately the dead fell forward in a clumsy heap of bodies, falling to the deck and rolling around, but slowly they clambered back to their feet, one by one. Before long there were dozens of them making their way down the deck.

Hugo went and grabbed his daughters and held them close. Houdini yipped by their feet. There was no time to make it down to the beach now, and even if there was, the dead waited down there too. They were done for. En toute chose il faut considérer la fin.

Old man Bob and Jim closed-in beside Hugo with their weapons held high. "Looks like the end of the road, me ducks," said Bob. "I'm sorry you didn't all get to live as long as me."

"That's a blessing," said Jimmy. "Your nutsack is like a dried-out teabag."

Both men laughed, but Hugo did not join them. He kissed the top of his daughter's heads and held them close. "I am sorry, my darlings. Je vous aime tous les deux."

"We love you too, daddy."

The dead got closer and Hugo fought not to close his eyes. He needed to be strong for his daughters. "Don't be afraid, girls. It will be over soon. I am with you."

Yip!

"Houdini too."

The rotten, pus-filled faces bore down on them, broken ankles and twisted knees carrying them forward. Rotten teeth chomped the air, seeking living flesh. Soon they would have it.

When the dead were only a dozen feet away, the entire pier rumbled and shook. A monstrous sound filled the air and suddenly the dead began to part and fall beneath a wondrous beast. When the sound of gunfire began, Hugo could barely trust his eyes. "I don't believe it," he said to his girls with disbelief and excitement in his voice. "We are saved."

GARFIELD

THE CHALLENGER 2 Battle Tank had made short work of the motorway, clearing a steady path for the pursuing 4-tonne trucks. Lemon drove one while Cat and David commanded the other. The two paratroopers, Price and Barker, piloted the tank, while Garfield sat in the open hatch ring, manning a heavy machine gun on top of the turret. It was fixed in place and hopefully wouldn't tear his shoulder to pieces like the SA80 assault rifle had. His deltoid muscle still cried out every time he moved.

The motorway was littered with wrecks and dead men, just as Garfield had expected, but the heavy tank shunted the puny vehicles aside as if the road was a bowling alley and the Challenger was a 14lb ball. Garfield made light work of any dead standing in the way, ripping them apart with the GMPG he manned on the turret. Any that came too close fell under the front of the tank and came out the back as bloody paste.

Their small convoy arrived at the pier a few hours before dawn. What Garfield found there made him cry out.

The first thing he saw was smouldering flame, lighting up the dark like a litter of bonfires. The first thing he heard was the moaning of the dead everywhere. Oh God, he had thought. The pier is gone.

But it had not been gone, not completely. Half the pier was missing, while the other half smouldered from dying fires. The dead swarmed everywhere like ants over an ice cream cone. Their collective moaning was so loud that it almost drowned out the roar of the Challenger's monstrous engine. Something had happened while they were gone. The pier was gone. Where are they all? Where's Poppy?

The tank flew forward up the deck, flattening hordes of the dead and leaping up over the fallen gate. Garfield fired the machine gun madly, shearing off heads and arms by the dozen. He didn't realise it at first, because of the racket, but he was screaming at the top of his lungs. Empty bullet casings filled the air like angry wasps. His finger ached on the trigger.

Movement at the end of the broken pier made Garfield swivel the machine gun around, ready to fire at a new target. He was just about to pull the trigger again when he saw old man Bob standing there. The dead were closing in on him. Garfield swivelled left and right, taking down as many dead as he could find. When nothing else moved, he climbed out of the turret and leapt down to the deck. Barker had given him a 9mm browning and shown him how to use it, so he pulled it from his waistband and popped a shot off into a dead man's skull that had reached for him from the floor. He glanced around, searching for any more danger, but Lemon had angled one of the trucks across the gate and blocked any more of the dead from getting inside. Can always rely on Lemon. Where's Poppy?

Up ahead, old man Bob was hunched over, grabbing his knees and taking great big breaths. There were people beside him who were all sobbing. It was clear the cavalry had arrived just in time. "What happened?" he yelled. "Where's Poppy?"

Old man Bob remained crouched over. Standing with him was Jimmy, and a middle-aged man he didn't recognise. There were also two young girls and a dog. Who the hell are they?

Jimmy couldn't look at Garfield as he spoke. Instead he turned away and pointed at the gaping hole where the other end of the pier used to be. "Things are bad, man. You got here just in time. Everyone's gone."

Garfield hurried across the deck towards him. Bodies lay everywhere and he had to hop over them with each step. "What do you mean, gone? What happened, Jimmy? Tell me!"

Jimmy pointed out at the sea. In the darkness, Garfield could see several ships lit up and two dozen more lurking in shadow. A huge Navy frigate floated amongst them, lit like a beacon. "Some boats came. A shit-tonne of 'em. They were looking for that guy you found in that lorry container. Tim, his name was. Some douchebag with a spear for a hand came aboard and started throwing his weight around, but Alistair and Anna were having none of it. One of the men who came aboard tried to..." Jimmy cleared his throat. "Tried to hurt Poppy. Things got screwed up and that battleship out there fired at us."

Garfield felt like he was going to throw up. He had to take three deep breaths just to stay standing. "Okay...let's take this slowly. You're telling me that someone came and did this? Because of the man I found?"

Jimmy nodded. "His name is Tim."

Garfield didn't care what the man's name was. "Where's Poppy?"

Jimmy looked away.

"Where is she?" Garfield yelled.

A man he did not recognise came forward to answer his question. The way the two young girls were clinging to him, they must have been his daughters. He had a French accent. "I am sorry for what has happened, my friend. I think the little girl you are talking about is the one just behind you."

Garfield turned around slowly. There was no one behind him other than Lemon, Chris, Cat, and the two soldiers – certainly no Poppy. Barker and Price were doing clean up, taking out any dead that still wriggled and crawled along the deck. "What are you talking about?" asked Garfield. "Where is she?"

"The little girl, Poppy. She is lying just there behind you." The Frenchman pointed. "I am sorry."

Garfield looked where the man was pointing and felt as if his stomach was about to explode. Acid rose up his gullet and burned his throat. His breath came out in wounded gasps. There were bodies all around, which was why he'd missed her the first time.

Poppy was laying in a row of bodies, with Alistair and Chris either side of her. Her face was ruined, blackened and torn, but she was still his beautiful little girl. One of her plaits had come unravelled but the other lay over her shoulder. She looked peaceful. Garfield fell to his knees beside her and cradled her in his arms. She felt so light that he wondered how she didn't just float away. It was a child's body in his arms.

I was so scared of her becoming a woman. Now she'll never be one. Garfield knew it was his fault. He brought the injured man to camp, then set off and abandoned everyone. He was so fixated on getting guns to protect the pier that he ended up leaving it defenceless. The irony disgusted him.

He leapt back to his feet. "Who did this? WHO FUCKING DID THIS?"

The Frenchman staggered backwards and clutched his daughters. The little dog at his feet barked at Garfield, but he didn't care. He would happily beat them all bloody if they didn't tell him, right now, who was responsible for everything that had happened.

Old man Bob had managed to catch his breath and straightened up. Tears streaked his face. They glistened like silver slug trails in the moonlight. "The captain of that fleet is Samuel Raymeady. He is responsible."

Garfield showed no reaction. He just wanted the facts. "The richest man in the world?"

Old man Bob nodded. "Yeah, he was the head honcho of Black Remedy, that company which seemed to own just about everything back before the infection hit. The man you found, Tim, tried to blow Samuel up by planting a bomb on the ship."

"Why?"

"Because he knew Samuel was responsible for everything that happened one year ago. Black Remedy engineered the virus that killed everybody. Samuel planned to start a new kingdom or something, I dunno. It's all a bunch of bloody drama and fairy tales, but one thing is true: that son-of-a-bitch fired his cannon at the pier and now Poppy, Alistair, Samantha, and Chris are all dead. That ain't no fairy tale."

Garfield clenched his fists, but needed to hear more before he acted. There were names missing from old man Bob's story. "Where are Anna and Rene?"

"With Tim," said Jimmy. "The three of them took Hugo's boat and headed for the frigate. Anna's plan is to surrender and then try to take Samuel Raymeady down. They won't be coming back. It was a suicide mission."

Garfield stood stiff and swallowed the lump in his throat. Every fibre of his body wanted to turn around, pick Poppy up and take her away from all this, but he was sure that if he did he would shatter completely and never recover. For now, he had to put Poppy out of his mind. There was a situation that needed to be dealt with. Without word, he left the others and walked down the pier.

He found sergeant Price standing next to the Challenger. He was stamping his thick army boot onto the heads of any dead men still moving. The deck had become thick with bloody slurry.

"This the camp you were telling me about?" Price asked.

Garfield nodded.

"Shit luck. You know what happened?"

"Yes, and I know who is responsible. Will you help me?"

Price narrowed his eyes. "You wreck my home, kill my commanding officer, and then drag me along to a burning ruin." He laughed. "Yeah, I'll help you."

The man had a point. Garfield had brought him nothing but disaster. "Why will you help me, after everything that's happened?"

"Because when that bloody dingo was trying to take my head off with a shotgun, you intervened. You even got shot for it – good thinking with the magazines by the way. You're one of the good guys – or at least whatever counts for one these days – and whoever caused all this is definitely not. The world is on a knife-edge. It could go either way. Personally, I want to see the good guys win and the bad guys get their arses kicked. You want my help, you got it."

Garfield nodded. He wanted to hug the man, but he doubted it would be appreciated. Instead he turned to the Challenger tank. "Will this thing still fire?"

Price smirked. "Old Betsy? Oh, she'll do more than just fire. She will rain the wrath of the God's down upon her enemies. She will shock and she will awe, scorch the earth dry until nothing remains but crust and sand. She can kick some bloody arse, is what I'm telling you."

"Good," said Garfield. "I want you to fire on that Navy frigate out there, the one all lit up like a floating village. The man who did this to the pier is the captain of that boat."

Price smiled wider. "You mean I get to shove it to a bunch of Marines? Bleedin' marvellous. Barker! Load up Betsy."

Corporal Barker nodded and got to work.

DAMIEN

WHEN DAMIEN AWOKE, he was surprised to find that the adjacent cell had been filled. He was even further surprised when he saw that it was the woman from the pier and the cripple. *Should stop calling him that. I think he had the right idea trying to blow up the Kirkland. Jesus, what am I saying?*

Anna looked broken. The bags under her eyes could have carried bricks and the determined glint in her eye had faded away to a weary sullenness. Despite that, she still managed to make a joke when she saw he was awake. "I hear the room service makes up for the beds."

Damien sat up and stared at her through the gloom between the cells. "How the hell did you two get here?"

"I changed my mind," said Tim. "I gave myself up, hoping Samuel would show mercy to those who survived at the pier. I feel quite naive now."

Damien glanced down at his stump, where the broken shard of his spear lay and felt much the same. He had tried to eliminate Samuel but been found wanting. The captain was far stronger than he looked. "Samuel doesn't have mercy," said Damien. "I learned that lesson the hard way, too, so I guess we're all fools."

"I thought you were one of Samuel's men," said Anna.

"I was my own man. Only reason I stayed on this goddamn ship was to keep my friend, Harry, safe. When the infection first hit, Harry and me were close to death. We were floating out I the middle of the sea on a cramped dinghy. Samuel rescued us, so I guess I felt like I owed him. Loyalty only goes so far, though."

"You saw what he did to the pier?"

Damien nodded. "I'm sorry. I...huh, it doesn't matter."

Anna looked at him. There was no defiance in her anymore, not like there had been back at the pier. "Tell me," she said.

Damien sighed. "I tried to defend you people when Samuel said he was going to fire at you. I told him you were all innocent, but he gave the order anyway. I didn't do a thing to stop it."

"Thank you," said Anna. "I don't think there's anything you could have done. I should have handed Tim over at the beginning when you came to the pier."

"No," said Damien. "There's never a good reason to give into bullies. You were right to keep Tim from me. Samuel is the bad guy here. Looks like the bad guy's going to win, though. We'll all be dead by the afternoon. Samuel will want to make our deaths part of the morning festivities."

"Oh, don't be so sure," said Dunn, suddenly appearing. He was swaggering through the brig towards their cells. "I think Samuel may just string your deaths out for a few days, perhaps even a week. The people want blood."

Damien stood up and went over to the bars of his cell. "Petty officer Dunn. How's the nose?"

Dunn's nose was purple and bent to one side, both his eyes were blackened, but he managed a great beaming smile anyway. "Nothing that won't heal, Roman, and it's 'Lieutenant' Dunn now. Samuel rewards those who are of use to him. Those who are not end up like you - expired."

Damien smirked. "It's a wonder you can get your nose so far up Samuel's arsehole after I broke it so many times." Dunn smashed at the bars with the blade of a bloodstained knife. Damien hopped back from the bars and noticed that Anna was crying. "You okay?" he asked her.

"That's the knife he killed Rene with. He doesn't even have the decency to clean the blood off it."

Dunn laughed and held the knife up in front of her like a prize.

Damien kicked at his bars. "Hey, show some goddamn respect and put that away. You think killing people is a joke? You're a moron."

"And you're a dead man, so I would spend your last words more wisely."

"Go fuck a goat."

Dunn hissed and grabbed for the keys on his belt. He pulled the bundle loose and levelled one of the keys towards the lock on Damien's cell. That's it. Come inside and I'll break your nose a fourth time. I just wish I had my sword to chop your goddamn dick off.

Suddenly Dunn stopped. He started laughing. "You think I'm an idiot? You won't fool me into opening your cell, so just be quiet."

Damien snarled. I'll get you before I'm through. I promise you.

Dunn called for two crewmen to appear. Both men were big and burly.

"Evening up the odds, are you?" said Damien. "You're gunna need more."

Dunn shook his head and sighed. "Roman, you do amuse me. I'm here for the cripple, not you. He'll be put to death soon, although it may take several hours – maybe even a week. I'm sure you'll get your turn as well before long. Samuel really does hate a traitor."

Anna did nothing while the two crewmen took Tim away. She was a pale shadow of the woman he'd met at the pier. That women would have bitten and clawed until someone knocked her unconscious. She'd put Birch's lights out without a twinge of doubt.

Once Dunn and the crewman departed with Tim, Damien turned to Anna and reached through the bars with his one hand. "Hey, you okay? Snap out of it."

"Just waiting to die," she said. "Kind of looking forward to it actually."

"Hey, stop thinking like that. You were a proper little badass at the pier. You even made me think twice, so why are you letting a slug like Dunn bother you. They may kill us, but do you want to make it easy for them?"

Anna huffed and shook her head. She stared down at her shoes. "Samuel Raymeady killed billions of people and got away with it. He's still killing people now, so what's the point in fighting? I know you don't believe me, Roman, but Samuel is evil. He released the virus that destroyed the world. He can't be stopped. Rene and I tried..."

"My name isn't Roman, it's Damien, and, yes, I do believe you. I've seen Samuel taking control for almost the last year. I've seen him do terrible things a hundred times over, but I didn't do anything. I was the same as you: I thought, 'what's the point?' But when he bombed the pier he went too far. A man evil enough to do something like that is evil enough to do anything. I believe he could easily have been the one who released a plague upon the earth. Samuel Raymeady had more money than some countries. If any man could have been behind the virus, it's him. In fact, I believe that now with my whole heart."

"Finally," came another voice. "You listened to me."

Damien span around. "Harry? What are you doing here?"

"I've come to rescue you? Still against staging a coup?"

Damien leant against the bars and smiled at his friend. "I'm still not interested in becoming the new Grand Supreme Leader, but I'm more than happy to kill the current one."

Harry grinned. "Then let's get you out of that cell." He produced a set of keys from his jeans and jangled them in front of Damien's face.

"How did you get those?"

Harry lifted up a heavy wrench with his other hand. "Took it off the guard in the corridor. I'm pretty handy with tools, remember?"

Damien stepped back from the bars and waited while Harry fiddled with the ring of keys. "Hurry up, man. I've got a lunch appointment."

"I'm trying, I'm trying. There's like a hundred bloody keys here."

Damien turned to Anna. He reached through the bars to her but she was still staring at the floor. "We're getting out of here, okay?"

"And go where? We can't exactly sneak off the ship. Even if we could, the pier is gone. There's no point. You're just making it harder on yourself."

"Yikes," said Harry. "Where did you pick up Miss Sunshine?"

"Leave her alone," said Damien. "Samuel murdered half her family. We're taking her with us and she's going to snap out of it."

Anna huffed. "Whatever."

Harry was still fiddling with the keys when the two guards who had left with Dunn returned. They saw Harry and immediately started running.

"Shit!" said Damien. "Get this pissing thing open?"

"Okay, okay." Harry fiddled with another key...and then another....
Clink!

Damien burst out of his cell and tackled the first guard around the thighs, taking him to the ground and mounting him. He let fly with rights followed by rights followed by rights. His left stump hung uselessly in the air, missing its spear. Eventually the stunned guard managed to fight back. He punched Damien in the windpipe, sending him backwards, spluttering.

Harry swung his wrench at the other guard's head but missed and was quickly taken down with a headlock.

Damien lay on his back, gasping. His throat seized and his breath would not come to him. The guard he'd been battling rose up and stood over him. "I'm gunna mess you up," he said, spitting out a mouthful of blood. Then he booted Damien in the ribs and knocked out what little air he had left in his lungs. The guard reared back to aim another kick at Damien's head, but was knocked to the ground when something hard struck his skull.

Harry dropped his wrench on the floor when the other guard had taken him down. He'd also dropped the keys. Anna picked them up and let herself out of her cell. She grabbed the fallen wrench and flung it at the standing guard's temple so hard that it had killed him instantly. Now the remaining guard was outnumbered. He let go of Harry's throat and stood up. He was worried, but still willing to fight. Harry lay unconscious, but Anna joined Damien and put her fists up.

Damien was just about to lunge at the remaining guard, when he heard shouting.

Three more guards entered the brig.

Bollocks.

"Time to go," shouted Anna. She threw a haymaker and caught the distracted guard in the chin. His lights went out and he fell to the ground.

Damien stared at her in awe. "Damn!"

Anna grabbed him. "Come on!"

Damien allowed himself to be dragged and the two of them started running. "We need to get Harry," he said.

"There's no time. He's out. We have to go."

Damien glanced back at Harry. The three guards were coming in fast. There was no way to get Harry and carry him out of there. *I can't just leave him. But there was no choice.* The three guards gave chase. Damien cursed and sprinted forward, catching up with Anna as she made her way into the next passageway. They ran as fast as they could. Damien knew the ship, so he took the lead, heading for the surface. Several crewmen got in their way en route, but the men were confused and did not try to stop them. Eventually, Damien made it onto the promenade deck at the portside of the ship. "This way," he shouted at Anna. "If we can get to the aft deck we might be able to steal a lifeboat."

Anna nodded. Her steely determination had returned to her and she was once again ready to kick ass. All it'd taken was seeing an ally in danger. *The woman could not stand by while the guards kicked the shit out of Damien and Harry. If we don't die, I should take her out to dinner someplace. A nice, run-down restaurant in the wasteland. It'll be nice.*

Damien and Anna took off down the promenade deck and made it out onto the wide-open space of the aft deck. Lieutenant Dunn and a dozen guards were standing there, waiting to receive them. Dunn still clutched the bloodstained rigging knife, but two of his men clutched iron bars as thick as Damien's arm.

Anna skidded on her heels and stumbled into Damien's back. "What is it?" she asked, but then saw the group of men coming towards them. "Oh, shit."

Damien smiled at her. "My advice, go for the balls!"

"Please! I've been kicking men in the balls for as long as I can remember. My advice to you is not to get in my way."

Damien sniggered. "Nice meeting you, Anna."

"You too, Damien."

They turned to face the approaching mob, unarmed yet ready – ready to die fighting.

Then something struck the ship and all hell broke loose.

ANNA

Anna woke up on her back, surrounded by fire and debris. For a moment she thought she was lying on the beach again beneath the burning pier, but then she blinked the dust from her eyes and saw that she was still on the Kirkland. The vast grey ship was listing to one side and as Anna lay on her back she saw the sun rising on the horizon. Dawn had arrived and brought yet more chaos.

Anna sat up and looked around. Many men were bleeding, some were burned, and lots were dead. Anguished screams filled the air, joined by the wrenching and shifting groans of folding steel. The large open area at the back of the ship was blackened and scorched as if some great meteorite had stuck it. Part of the gunwale was missing and a gaping hole had opened up on one side of the ship. *Why do people keep blowing me up?*

Hands grabbed Anna beneath her arms and yanked her to her feet. Her legs were weak and she nearly fell right back down again, but the man kept a tight hold of her. It was the man with the broken nose. Damien had called him Dunn.

"Are you responsible for this, bitch?" he demanded of her.

Anna shook her head. Nothing made any sense to her right then. "Responsible for what?"

"One of your people just fired on us with a goddamn tank."

"T-tank? What are you talking about?"

Dunn slapped her to the ground. "Fine, have it your way. You and your people are finished."

Up ahead, members of the Kirkland's crew were starting to get a hold of themselves. Those uninjured, or at least able-bodied enough to stand, were regrouping at the centre of the aft deck. Anna watched glumly as two guards wrestled Damien to his knees. Tim had been shoved down beside him.

Lieutenant Dunn dragged her across the deck by her hair and left her to fall face-first next to Damien. Damien reached out his arm and helped her up onto her knees. He was all bloodied and she saw a tooth missing when he spoke. "I think your friends at the pier fought back," he said. "Did you know about this?"

Anna shook her head in confusion. "I have no idea what's going on. They said it was a tank. The pier doesn't have a tank."

"Someone out there does," said Damien. "Something hit the ship hard."

"How long have I been out?"

"Half-hour. I tried to put up a fight when the ship first got hit, but there was a dozen on me before I could blink. You were out the whole time."

"Sorry I wasn't there to back you up. I-" A sudden prod in the small of Anna's back sent her sprawling forward onto her front. Tim and Damien fell facedown either side of her, the three of them now on their bellies. The guards stood on their backs and pinned them to the deck. Suddenly the hustle and bustle on deck stopped and a hush descended. Footsteps rang out against steel and got louder. Anna tried to crane her neck but could not make out whom it was.

Then Lieutenant Dunn made it easy for her. "Attention! Captain on deck."

Anna gritted her teeth as a pair of highly polished boots stepped in front of her. "Let them up, Lieutenant."

"Yessir. Guards, let the prisoners up."

A guard grabbed Anna's shirt and yanked her to her knees. She cursed at him and lashed out with her elbow, caught him in the shin but probably hurt herself more. She was surrounded by sailors and civilians on all sides. All of them glared at her and shouted for her blood.

Samuel Raymeady looked down at her. He was wearing full Navy Officer whites. "You're quite the cockroach, aren't you?" he said. "You come aboard my ship asking for peace, and this is how you expect to find it?"

Anna sniffed. The smoke in the air was stinging her eyes and clogging her sinuses. "I came aboard your ship asking for peace, and you threw me in a cell. Do you really expect people to just sit back and fold their arms while you murder and kill anyone you please?"

Samuel's eyes were so full of malice when he looked at her, that she was sure he would strike her. Instead he just laughed. "I do what is best for the fleet. All I do I do for the good of us all."

Now it was Anna's turn to laugh. "Do you honestly believe that, or is it just for the benefit of those listening?"

"He likes his speeches," said Tim. "I think he's trying to make up for other...insecurities." He covered his mouth and coughed. "Small penis!"

Samuel smiled like a cat and turned away. He raised his hands in the air, imploring the men and women around him. "Members of the fleet. We are of a lucky few. We are what's left of mankind. We are the hope and the courage that will see humanity through to a new day, a new dawn. Together we have beaten extinction and turned away our deaths. Each and every man and woman aboard this ship is a testament to the strength and will of the human spirit. What is left of the world is ours to rebuild. We will do so with love and honour and strength. The fleet is life itself and we must protect it at all costs, even if that means taken the roads less savoury. H. G. Wells once said 'If we don't end war, war will end us.' We must extinguish our enemies now lest we lose our own in battle later. My recent actions are not acts of war, they are acts of mercy, to the fleet. The bridge is already training our sights on the shore. We have our attackers in sight and soon we will unleash hell on them, but first we must deal with the enemy on our decks."

The men and women of the fleet cheered Samuel's name, louder and louder. It made Anna feel sick. Humanity was backing the wrong horse. The horse Samuel rode in on was pestilence and now he's riding off on the back of war.

"There are those who wish to destroy us," Samuel continued. "To take what we have and reduce it to ashes. They are our opposites; they are evil and self-consumed, and if we have any chance of forging ahead and creating a new world, we must extinguish evil in all its forms."

Samuel! Samuel! Samuel!

"They drank the cool aid," said Tim. "Now do you see why I had to blow the entire ship? No point taking out the Ringleader if the Circus keeps on travelling."

Anna tried to stand up, to scream at the stupid men and women that they were deluded, but Dunn kicked her in the ribs and sent her back down to her knees. She wheezed and spluttered.

"You're all monsters," said Damien. He raised his voice. "How can you people follow a man who attacks innocent people?"

"The people at the pier were harbouring a terrorist," shouted Dunn. "Terrorists must be dealt with."

Another cheer from the crowd.

"One man's terrorist is another man's freedom fighter," said Tim.

"A terrorist is a terrorist," Dunn snarled.

Samuel turned around and nodded enthusiastically. "Exactly. A terrorist is an enemy of society and order. The fleet deals with its enemies with a firm hand. Who would like to see the first example?"

The crowd roared, a baying mob. Anna managed to catch her breath and glanced around as the crowd parted behind her. Someone was being dragged, half-conscious, towards the centre of the deck. It didn't take long to realise that it was the man who had come to rescue Damien from his cell. Harry.

Harry was bloody and bruised. His toecaps dragged along the deck as two crewmen carried him to Samuel. When Damien saw his friend his eyes went wide and suddenly he seemed terrified. "Leave him alone," he shouted. "He hasn't done anything."

Samuel laughed. "He attacked the Kirkland's jailer and released the fleet's prisoners. This he did as part of an on-going collusion with known terrorist, Tim Golding – the cripple. Harry Jobson is an enemy of all of us."

Kill the traitor! String him up? Terrorist!

"They're a bunch of animals," Tim muttered under his breath.

Samuel smiled and seemed to breath in the chants and cries for blood like they were sweet-smelling perfume. "I think the people have spoken," he said, sighing euphorically. "Guards! String him up. Let him dangle above our broken tail as an example to what happens to our enemies. Let those onshore see that our spirit will never be broken. We will never succumb to evil."

Damien leapt up. He swung his arms wildly and struck guards left and right. "Harry!" he screamed as he head-butted a crewman standing in his way. "Harry, fight. Get out of here." Harry hung weakly between his guards and blinked slowly. There was a smile on his face that was more sadness than mirth. Damien kicked a guard in the knee and threw him aside, cutting himself a little closer to his friend. "Harry, I won't let them kill you. I won't."

A man flew in from the side and pummelled Damien in the stomach with a baseball bat. A second man raced up behind him and wrapped his arm around his neck. Damien struggled but another blow to his ribs dropped him onto one knee. Still he tried to fight, but it was useless. Harry looked at him and shook his head sadly. "It's over, Damien. We had a good run while it lasted. I'll be glad to finally be free of the headaches. I'm tired of holding on to all the things I know. It's gotten too hard."

Damien struggled to try and make it the last three feet to Harry but the two guards held him back. Anna considered leaping up and helping him, but there were men and woman everywhere ready to beat her down at the first sign of resistance. She had no choice but to watch Damien and Harry's final exchange from her knees.

"I won't let these fuckers kill you," Damien said.

Harry laughed. "They can't kill me. I got places to be. You might think I'm crazy, with all my talk of Heaven and Hell, but trust me we all get what we deserve in the end. Just make sure your final minutes count. Sometimes our last minute counts more than all the other minutes that came before combined. Redemption can take but a single second, Damien. Remember that."

Damien struggled to get closer. He managed to gain a foot, but couldn't get any further. He reached out, only two-steps away from his friend. The anguish on his face was unbridled and clear for all to see; but nobody cared.

Harry took his guards by surprise and lunged forward. He threw his arms around Damien and squeezed him tightly. "I'm glad I took a chance on you, Damien. You're the one thing in my life I did right."

Anna realised she was crying. She didn't know either man well, but she felt their love for one another, and knew she was going to see them both die. What was worse was that the men and women in the crowd thought it was justice.

As the guards tried to force the two men apart, Anna noticed Harry's hand bury itself into the back of Damien's jeans. At first she found it odd, but then she realised.... He just shoved something under Damien's waistband.

Harry stood up straight and pushed Damien aside. He stared right at Tim. "It was me that told about your plan, Tim. I'm sorry. I thought it was wrong to destroy the whole ship. I was worried I wasn't thinking straight and I told on you."

Tim's eyes went wide. "You? I..."

"Don't worry," said Harry. "I've made it right. I fixed it."

"I don't know what you mean," said Tim.

"If you live long enough, you will."

Damien reached out for Harry, but the guards stepped in and forced the two men apart, delivering a quick beat down to them both. Damien fell onto his back and shuffled away. Harry tumbled to his knees and was dragged towards the Kirkland's stern.

Tears streamed from Damien's eyes as he lay, incapacitated, on the deck. He didn't make a sound, but his eyes never left Harry as he was led through the crowd at the back of the ship. He kept his eyes open as they threw a rope over the side of the rear gunwale, looping it through a rigging hook and folding it into a knot. He kept his eyes open as they tied Harry's hands behind his back and fastened a noose around his neck. He was given no chance to look away as Lieutenant Dunn shoved Harry hard in the back and sent him overboard.

Anna wanted to close her eyes, but couldn't. She heard Damien moan behind her and wished she could spare him from what he was seeing.

Harry's body disappeared over the gunwale and the rope went taut. The snapping sound rang out like a gunshot. Damien's moans turned to a growl. Anna glanced back to see him and the animalistic look on his face made her flinch. His humanity had deserted him with the snap of his friend's neck. Anna reached out her arm to him, but he shrugged it away. He's gone to a dark place.

Lieutenant Dunn walked away from the gunwale and back towards the centre of the deck. The man was laughing. "I thought his head was going to come off. Did you hear that snap?" It was obvious the man was trying to get a reaction out of Damien, but it didn't work. Damien just stared into space, unblinking and faraway.

Samuel was grinning, too. Once again he raised his arms to implore his people. "Who is next? Who would you see face justice?"

The crowd shouted out riotously, bickering amongst themselves until a cohesion fell upon them and a single word became a chant. Cripple! Cripple! Cripple!

"Quiet," said Samuel. "Quiet. The people have spoken and I have listened." He turned and pointed at Tim. "Lieutenant Dunn, take his eyes."

Dunn swallowed and seemed confused. The thought of the act obviously didn't appeal to him. While he was all for playing executioner, he didn't seem to have the stomach so visceral. Nonetheless, he got moving gingerly. Clearly the thought of disobeying Samuel appealed to him less than taking out a man's eyes.

Tim went pale when he heard his sentence. He began to blink rapidly as he anticipated the horror about to be bestowed upon him.

He pleaded nervously with Dunn. "Come one, dude. I'll just take the plunge like Harry did. No need to go all Red Dragon on me."

Dunn gritted his teeth and hissed. "Shut up."

"You don't have to do this," Tim pleaded. "You never signed your life away to Samuel, but once you do this you're nothing but his slave. Come on, dude. Don't do this."

Dunn pulled his bloodstained knife from his belt and held it out towards Tim's face. "Hold him," he snarled at the nearest guard.

Two guards grabbed Tim and held him down by his shoulders. The man began to cry out for mercy and screamed at the top of his lungs when Dunn approached him with the blade.

Samuel grinned the whole time. The mob hollered excitedly. Damien stared into space and gritted his teeth. Anna felt sick.

Tim struggled to free himself, thrashing left and right against his guards. His eyelids fluttered as the blade wiggled in front of his face. "Come on, man. Please! Please, don't. Plea- Argh!"

Dunn sank his blade into Tim's left eye and twisted. He yanked back and pulled the popped eyeball from its socket. Strands of flesh, nerves, and blood spewed from Tim's empty orbital bone and his entire body shuddered violently. When Dunn shanked his other eyeball, he lay on his back gibbering and vomiting on himself.

"Throw him overboard," said Samuel dismissively. "Let him swim around blindly like the fishes."

Two guards dragged a gibbering Tim away and discarded him over the gunwale like a bag of rubbish. Anna stared down at one of the man's eyeballs lying on the deck and almost vomited. Despite her fear, she was not worried about her own approaching demise. After all she'd seen, death no longer held its ominous veil over the world. The Reaper's dignity had been walked over by seven billion agonising deaths. She did fear pain, though. Pain was not death, it was life. And life scared her.

Samuel glared at Anna and then at Damien. "Now, what to do with the two of you? I think you see now what happens to those who act against me. It is much better to fall in line than to defy me. Harry and Tim were terrorists. Do you accept that?"

Damien said nothing. That steaming animosity was still on his face, but his mind was far away – he had gone to a place of demons and nightmares. Anna wanted to beg, to plead for a quick death, but she would not allow herself to show weakness in her final minutes. Her enemies would not be given the satisfaction of seeing her weep. Instead of hoping for mercy, her mind instead turned to who had fired at the Kirkland. They said it was a tank. That's crazy. Could it be the foragers?

Garfield had left days ago, seeking an army base. Had he actually found one? Did he discover a tank and bring it home? The thought gave Anna a small flicker of warmth in her belly. Someone ashore was still alive to fight Samuel. Someone was still alive to avenge her. And Poppy. Anna knew that if it was Garfield on the shore and that he'd discovered what had become of Poppy, he wouldn't rest until Samuel was dead. Anna just hoped he came up with a better plan than she had. I didn't even get close to taking out Samuel. Hopefully Garfield will fire again and take this whole ship down.

"It's time to make a decision," said Samuel. He was looking at Damien. "You have been confused and conflicted by an old friendship, but I believe there may still be hope for you, Roman. You have served me faithfully for many months and have never acted against me before. I would see you have one final opportunity for redemption. Do you wish to hear my offer?"

Damien said nothing. He gritted his teeth and breathed in and out heavily.

Samuel sighed. "I will take that as a 'yes'. Frank, if you would?" Samuel always called him 'Frank' in front of company.

The grey-haired man from Samuel's office appeared from the crowd and stood before his captain. The look on his face was almost a grimace and his eyes were moist from recent tears. The man didn't look like a crier – too grizzled and stoic – but obviously something had upset him.

Unlike the other members of the fleet, the grey-haired man did not seem to relish the on-going spectacle that counted for Samuel's 'justice'.

Frank held something in his hands: it was the sword that Damien used to carry on his belt.

Samuel nodded to the grey-haired man. "You have been a disappointment to me as well, father, but I would also see you given opportunity to prove your loyalty to the fleet. Hand Roman his sword. If he tries to use it on me, kill him."

Frank offered the sword to Damien, hilt first. The look on his face was pained, yet, despite the man's obvious dislike of what was happening, his hands were stone stiff as he handed the sword over.

Damien didn't acknowledge Frank, but his eyes quickly focused on his old sword. A rush of emotion seemed to return to him as he eyed up the sharp shaft of metal. He reached out his hand and took the blade, flipping it around and catching it by the hilt in one smooth motion. He leapt to his feet, but made no move to strike. Everyone aboard the Kirkland was silent. The air was so tense it was like breathing in oil fumes.

Anna waited on her knees, unsure of what to do. If Damien tried to fight, would she fight too? Of course I will. Better to die fighting.

Frank yanked a combat knife from his own belt and held it out in front of him. His stance made it obvious he knew how to use it. He and Damien faced off, grizzled knife-wielder against one-handed swordsman, but neither man made move to attack.

Samuel raised a hand for calm. He studied Damien and managed to make eye contact. "Roman," he said calmly. "Use your sword to take off this woman's head and all will be forgiven. Show me that your heart belongs to the fleet and you will be welcomed with open arms."

Damien examined the sword in his hands, eyes moving up and down the sharp shaft. He seemed possessed. The vacant expression had returned to him and he seemed more animal than human. He turned to face Anna.

Anna wouldn't beg like Tim had, she had already decided that. She was going to die, one way or another, sooner it just be over with. One thing she did do, however, was stare Damien in the eye. She wanted him to look at him as he killed her. *I hope my face haunts his dreams.*

Damien lifted the sword in the air and let it hover above her neck. There was utter silence from the crowd.

"Frank, be ready," said Samuel. "Cut him down the moment it looks like he might make a bad decision. We'll torture the woman for the next year while he watches."

Anna saw a brief flicker in Damien's eyes and a quivering lump in his throat. *He still has a conscience,* she thought. *This isn't easy for him, but he has no choice. Can I even blame him?* Now that she knew he felt guilty for what he was about to do, Anna did Damien the kindness of closing her eyes and looking away.

"That's it Roman," said Samuel. "Do it, and all will be forgiven."

"My...name...is...Damien."

Anna opened her eyes and saw Damien spin around and kick Frank in the guts. Two crewmen immediately went to accost him, but he sliced both of them down with a vicious slash from his sword. Blood splattered his rage-filled face and made him look like some ancient berserker. Anna wanted to get up and flee, but there was nowhere to go. She was frozen on her knees as the chaos erupted all around her. *I need to do something.*

Samuel pulled a pistol from inside his officer's coat and pointed it in Damien's face, ending his rampage before it even got truly started. Frank recovered from being winded and seized Damien by the shoulder. "Big mistake," Samuel said. "You think I wasn't ready for that? You fool."

Damien smirked, blood covering his face. He threw his bloody sword down on the ground at Samuel's feet. "No, captain," he said. "But were you ready for this?" He dove down to the floor and flopped on top of Anna, pancaking her to the deck. Anna struggled and squirmed beneath Damien, but was confused as he yanked something from the back of his jeans. It's whatever Harry handed to him.

Samuel pointed his pistol and hissed in anger.

Damien pressed a button in his hand and all hell broke loose. Again.

DAMIEN

DAMIEN HAD KNOWN right away what Harry had slipped into his waistband. It was a detonator. Working in the Kirkland's workshop meant Harry was no stranger to a bit of chemistry and he had inferred earlier that he had rigged something up to do what Tim had failed to. There were many industrial chemicals in the workshop, from cleaning fluids for the machinery and tools, to gasoline and fuel for the welding rigs and acetylene torches. If anyone could rig a bomb aboard the Kirkland, it was Harry. What Damien had not known was where the bomb was or how big it was. When he pushed the button he was finding out the answer along with everybody else.

The answer turned out to be: very big.

The explosion started as a deep rumbling beneath their feet but quickly travelled throughout the ship until it shook the deck like an earthquake and bucked the entire frigate forward. Bodies flew everywhere and water travelled upwards like rain in reverse, exploding from the sea. Damien lay on top of Anna and clung to the deck to keep them from going overboard. Dozens were less lucky and plummeted into the sea like flailing ragdolls. Blood and screams filled the air like a whirlwind. Holy shit, Harry. What the hell did you put in that bomb?

The Kirkland's bow raised up at a 45-degree angle as the aft deck began to sink beneath the water. The entire rear of the ship sloped towards a maelstrom of flaming saltwater, which waited to consume the flesh of anyone unlucky enough to fall into its boiling waters.

Anna moaned beneath Damien. "Why do people keep blowing me up? This is like the third time this week."

"I don't know," said Damien. "You must be a real arsehole."

Anna laughed and Damien suddenly felt better. He was certain he would die in the next five minutes, but at least his final actions had brought a smile to a woman's face. Harry's talk of redemption was not lost on Damien; he wanted to make his final minutes count.

He leapt up and looked around for his sword, but it was gone. No doubt it had skittered down the sloping deck and into the sea. He was sorry to see it gone. *I have a man to kill but no weapon. Guess my bare hands will have to do.*

Anna got up from the tilting deck and staggered towards him. He caught her in his arms and set her right on her feet. "Thanks," she said to him. "What's the plan, Rambo?"

Damien shrugged. "We could go to the bow and cuddle. I could shout 'I'm the King of the world'?"

Anna frowned. "I'm more of a Terminator 2 kind of gal."

Damien held his hand out to her. "Then come with me if you want to live."

Anna took Damien's hand and they raced through the chaos on deck. People wept and bled everywhere, but Damien held no compassion for them. They were happy enough to execute Harry and Tim. They got what they deserved.

"Where are we going?" Anna asked breathlessly as they ran. It was hard keeping balance on the uneven deck. He wondered if her shins were crying out as much as his were.

"We're going after Samuel," he told her. "If he's still alive, there's only one place he'll be."

"His chambers?"

"No. He'll be on the bridge, readying the guns. He won't take this lying down."

"Shit!" said Anna. "He'll fire on the pier again?"

"Yes, only this time he won't be using the cannons. He'll fire missiles."

"We have to stop him. There are another eleven of us at the pier. They were away when everything started, but they must have come back. We have to save them."

"We will," said Damien. "Samuel Raymeady is going to go down with this ship, I promise you."

They entered a hatch door at the side of the ship and entered the passageway inside. It was cramped, narrow, and at an angle, but the walls made it easier to balance. Damien turned a corner up ahead but skidded on his heels. Anna bumped into the back of him. She has to stop doing that. I'm going to end up with a bruised arsehole.

Lieutenant Dunn was blocking the passageway with another man standing beside him. The man had a hand missing just like Damien did, but his stump was bloody and bandaged. It was the American, Wade Cannon. The guy I dismembered. Wonderful. In Wade's good hand was Damien's sword. Guess it didn't fall into the sea after all.

Dunn smirked. "End of the line, Roman. You're about to die by your own sword. How deliciously ironic." He turned to Wade and gave an order. "Civilian, kill these two terrorists and you'll have the thanks of the captain and the entire fleet. You'll be a hero."

Wade grinned and raised Damien's sword. "You took my hand, Roman," he growled, but then he turned to face Dunn beside him. "But it wasn't so long ago that you were going to execute me as a criminal, Lieutenant Dunn."

Dunn suddenly looked unsure of himself. He eyed the sword wavering in the air between them. "Now...look. That was just my job. I was doing wha-"

The American shoved Damien's sword into Dunn's guts and left it there. Blood exploded from the officer's mouth and splatted the walls of the passageway.

Dunn staggered towards Damien with his blood-soaked hands out, pleading. Damien head butted him in the face and let him fall to the floor. He yanked his sword free from the man's guts and left him to die in pain.

Damien strolled up to the American and cleared his throat. "So did you want to take a shot at getting your revenge on me? Because now's the time, Wade. I'll be dead later."

The American smiled and shook his head. "You saved my life. A missing hand was a small price to pay."

Damien nodded. "Plus the chicks dig the stump. You'll see."

The American laughed.

"Get out of here, Wade. If you're lucky, you'll get picked up by one of the boats of the fleet. The Kirkland is going down."

Wade nodded and fled through the passageway towards the deck.

"I'm not going to even ask about the history between you two," Anna said. "The stumpy twins."

"Best you don't ask," he said, and then led her down the passageway to a ladder leading upwards. "The bridge is up there. You ready?"

Anna nodded.

They climbed the ladder quickly. With the ship canting the way it was, it was more like crawling forward than climbing upwards.

Damien entered the bridge ahead of Anna and was taken by surprise when someone tackled him before he had chance to straighten up.

Anna called out to him.

Frank glared at him.

Damien raised his stumped arm and tried to bring his elbow across the man's chin, but Frank kneed him in the thigh and sent searing pain throughout his entire body. Damien tried to bring his sword up, but Frank swatted it away and judo-threw him to the floor. Damien lay on his side and winced. This old sod's tougher than he looks.

Samuel stood at a wide console across the room, fingering buttons and pulling levers. Anna emerged from the hatch and froze when she saw what was happening. Frank booted Damien in the ribs to keep him down, but it didn't stop him from calling out to Anna. "Samuel," he wheezed. "Get...Samuel."

Frank snarled. He yanked Damien up off the floor like a ragdoll and looked him in the eye. "You try to kill my son? You try to kill my little boy. You don't understand anything. You're an idiot. AN IDIOT!" He head butted Damien in the nose and broke it. Damien fell to the floor, clutching his face in agony. I probably deserved that.

Anna sprinted towards Samuel but was knocked to her knees by a vicious backhand. Samuel followed it up by booting her in the stomach and sending her into heaving spasms. He took off his captain's jacket and threw it to the floor angrily. "Do you people never learn? You are like mosquitoes on my hide. I am a lion and you are worthless bugs. The fleet is the future of humanity. I will lead mankind to a new dawn, for I am its new god."

"You're insane," said Anna. "No man is a god. You're no different to any other deluded lunatic from history who thought power equals greatness. But look around you, Sammie; Rome is burning. Your empire is crumbling."

Samuel chuckled. "An apt metaphor, considering the company. Frank, stop playing with Roman – or whatever his name is – and bring him here. I would have these two watch while I show them what strength my crumbling empire still possesses."

Frank shoved Damien forward and held him against the console in front of the window. Samuel picked up Anna and shoved her up beside him. Through the bridge's wide glass window, Damien saw a hundred ships scattered across the sea. Some headed towards the Kirkland, collecting men-overboard, but many others sailed away into the distance. They're fleeing. The Kirkland's charade of safety has been shattered and they're scurrying away like cockroaches found beneath a fridge.

In the distance, Damien spotted the ruined pier. It was too far away to see anyone, but he imagined a tank hidden on the shoreline, ready to sink them with one last shell from its mighty turret.

Samuel lifted up a Perspex lid, which covered a large red button beneath. The fact that the button was big and red was almost comical, but there was no cause to laugh when Samuel began to prep the frigate's missile bay. Two hatch doors opened on the foredeck, revealing the two Tomahawk X triple-launchers hidden there. Damien knew that each missile carried a 1,200lb warhead – Harry had told him about them after having been put in charge of their maintenance one time. If Samuel fired the entire barrage at the pier, there would be nothing left for a square mile.

"Would anybody like to do the honours?" asked Samuel. "No? I thought not."

He was about to press the button, when Frank spoke out. "Samuel, enough people have died today. The Kirkland is lost. We must leave while we have chance. Vengeance has no use."

Samuel turned on his father with a vengeance. "I will not tolerate any more disobedience from you, Frank. Vengeance is all we have left. The Kirkland was what gave me power and I must make use of it if I have any hope of regaining control."

"You don't need to be in charge," said Frank. "You've already saved enough lives that people will forever respect you."

"I was born to be in charge. I was born a leader."

Frank looked at Samuel pityingly. "You were born a babe like anyone else. Circumstances made you who you were. The things that happened to you as a child hardened you, but now you have a chance to step back and be the man you want to be, instead of the man you were born to be. There's no reason to fire those missiles, son. Let's just get out of here." He reached out his hand.

For the first time Damien had seen, Samuel's face softened and a sliver of doubt appeared. For a brief moment, he sounded remorseful. "You have served me well, father. You raised me when everybody else had died or abandoned me. I had dreams of you growing old by my side and watching me achieve greatness."

"You have achieved greatness, Samuel."

"I haven't, but there is still time." Samuel pulled his pistol from a holster beneath his armpit and fired it into Frank's forehead. The old man fell backwards like a domino and hit the floor. Damien blinked. Jesus Christ. Anna shook her head silently.

Samuel turned the pistol on the two of them, preventing them from capitalising on the distraction. There were tears in his black eyes as he spoke. "I always knew Frank was weak. He fought it as much as he could, and I naively hoped he would overcome it, but he was never cut out for the new world. I'll miss him."

Damien snarled. "You just killed your own father, you psycho. Now you say you'll miss him like it was some kind of tragedy."

Samuel sighed. "He was no one's father. My own father died many years ago. I barely knew the man."

"So you have daddy-issues," said Anna. "Figures."

Samuel snarled. He pointed the gun at Anna, apparently done with idle chitchat and reminiscing. "Press the button," he told her. "I want you to say goodbye to your precious pier."

Anna shook her head. "I won't. You want them to die, you do it."

"Oh, but where is the fun in that? I like to see people take responsibility for their actions. Press the button or I'll take out both your knees." He lowered the pistol and aimed it at her legs.

That was all the chance Damien needed. He smashed Samuel in the face as hard as he could with his fist, but the blow was weak. His body was tired and broken. His strength had departed him. Samuel staggered backwards, more from surprise than pain.

His pistol went off.

Damien had to follow up the attack before Samuel recovered. He threw his arms out and shoved the captain back against the command console. He tried to get his fist up, to throw another punch, but his arm would not rise. It remained limp at his side.

Samuel growled, clamped his teeth around Damien's ear and tore away a chunk of lobe. Then he smashed him in the side of the head with his elbow. Damien slumped to the floor and spotted the reason his arm had not responded: the bullet from Samuel's pistol had shattered his elbow. Fuck, that hurts.

Samuel aimed the pistol down at him and fired again.

Damien's vision went white, then black, then every colour in between. Stars speckled his vision and a deep sickness washed over him. He glanced down at himself and saw blood spilling from his stomach like water from a leaky pipe. He tried to move but couldn't. He tried to shout but couldn't. His mouth filled with a thick liquid that tasted like old pennies.

Samuel chuckled. "You lose again, Roman. How many times must I beat you? Oh well, if you want something done right, best you do it yourself." Samuel reached out for the big red button on the console, ready to launch the missiles.

Damien tried to get up, but the whole world spun before him.

Samuel's fingertips settled on the top of the button and he grinned at Damien. "Here come the fireworks," he said, grinning even wider.

Then the smile turned to a grimace and the tip of a sword appeared through his chest.

Samuel's black eyes bulged like swollen inner tubes. His mouth opened to speak, but only thick, dark blood came out. He clutched at the sword jutting from his chest and stumbled around to face the other way. Anna stood before him, panting and wincing, but unflinchingly defiant. Samuel reached out for her neck, perhaps to try and throttle her, but he fell to his knees before he was able to get her. Anna grabbed the top of his head and pushed him sideways, where he promptly toppled and bled out on the floor. "Hasta la vista, bitch," she said.

Damien wanted to cheer, but his lungs felt like two blocks of ice and he couldn't find his breath.

Anna stared down at him with concern. "Shit, are you okay? You're shot."

Damien tried to smile, but could not feel his lips. The only thing he felt was cold. His vision was curling inwards at the edges like a piece of rolled-up parchment.

Anna dropped down beside him and looked into his eyes. "I can help you," she said. "I used to be a vet."

Damien managed to swallow whatever liquid had filled his mouth and caught a shallow breath. His words were frothy and wet as his spoke. "D-don't be a dickhead. The ship is...sinking. I'm done."

Anna shook her head. "I'll get you out of here. We're leaving together."

Damien blinked. Sadness and happiness combined to overwhelm him. His life did not flash before him like the movies said. Instead he saw only the present; it was a place without guilt or regret, a place where he had done what was right. That was all that mattered in the end: not how things started or even progressed, but how things were finally left. He couldn't help but feel peaceful as he felt his life slipping away. The battles of his life were coming to a finish and he was satisfied with how they had ended. The last few minutes of his life almost made the errors of his past meaningless. Violence had consumed his entire life, from his childhood to now, but he was thankful that his final act of rage had served a purpose. The people on the pier would live. Anna would live. Most importantly of all, Samuel would not. Damien was happy with how the scales of his life had balanced. He was ready to let go. And so he did.

Anna seemed to understand that too. Her look of concern changed to a soft smile. She ran her hand against his cheek, but he could not feel it. "Good knowing you, Roman."

He smiled. "My name is Damien."

Then he closed his eyes and never opened them again.

ANNA

NNA SAT AND watched Damien for a while. He was dead, but he seemed so peaceful, just like Poppy had, that she, too, felt calm simply by looking at him. There was a time when death used to freak people out, but now its almost beautiful. Beautiful to see someone truly dead, instead of walking around as a zombie.

Samuel had been dealt with, but Anna's life was still in peril. When the ship lurched again and the floor tilted at an even harsher angle, she made the decision that her time was up. She had to leave now, or sink beneath the ocean with the Kirkland. How the hell do I get off this ship, though? Are there life rafts? Damien said there was.

Anna crouched inside the ladder hatch and climbed back into the passageway below. As she headed back the way that Damien had brought her from, she was running as much on the walls as she was on the floor. The ship had turned almost sideways. It's like a maze in here. I don't know if I'm heading up, down, left, or right.

When she finally made it out to the aft deck, she had to grab a hold of the hatch doorway before she plummeted into the sea. The deck had become a steep ramp, leading down to the sea. A dozen men and women nearby clung to whatever was bolted down, while another handful battled to stay afloat in the frothing waters below. A smattering of boats had dared get close enough to offer rescue, but it was a dangerous task as the sinking frigate created a vortex and pulled down anything caught inside it.

I'm screwed, she told herself. Even if I survive the fall, I'll end up drowning. If a boat picks me up, they might just turn on me for being a 'terrorist'.

She glanced off into the distance. It was a nice day. There was no rain for once and the sky was clear. The sun shone. The pier sat peacefully beyond the shore and almost seemed to call to her. All of the fires there had now gone out and it once again looked like home. But she would never get to return. I knew this was a one-way journey. I came here to kill Samuel and I have. I won.

So why do I feel like I've lost?

Anna wondered if Garfield was at the pier, watching the ship as she watched the shore. Would he have Poppy's body in his arms, or would it hurt him too much to even look at her? Anna wished she could be there to tell him 'sorry'. She could have done things differently, and would have given the chance. Poppy might still live if she'd made different choices. At least I killed the son-of-a-bitch responsible.

"Whore!"

Anna spun around, balancing precariously in the open hatchway. She was startled to find Samuel standing behind her. The sword was still poking through his chest, but he didn't seem to care. Blood stained his teeth and made him look demonic. He snarled like a demon, too. How the hell is he still alive?

Anna was defenceless. She had no weapon and both her hands clutched the open hatchway and kept her from falling. So when Samuel charged her like a bull and struck her in the stomach, she had no way to shield herself.

Her breath escaped her body and she plummeted backwards through the hatch. Samuel stayed right with her, his arms and legs entangled with hers. They fell fifty feet before they hit the hard surface of the water.

The ice-cold sea took her breath away. Her lungs seized up and she felt like she would never take a single breath again. She sunk beneath the surface, her eyes stinging and blind with salt. The swirling water almost rocked her to sleep. The weariness seemed to ebb from her bones and turn her to jelly. It was peaceful beneath the sea. Part of her wanted to stay there.

But a bigger part wanted to live.

Anna kicked her legs and clawed with her hands. She didn't know which way was up but she prayed it was the direction in which she was heading. Her lungs ached and she felt like her chest was going to implode. The surface of the water seemed forever away and light and darkness mixed together and disorientated her. I'm not going to make it.

The pressure in her chest was unbearable now. She wanted more than anything to take a breath, but the moment she did the sea would take her. I'm going to drown. My body will sink into darkness and never be found.

Anna's lungs could take no more. She opened her mouth to take the breath that she knew would end her.

Something grabbed her from above, snatching at her as if she were a fish on the end of a hook. She took a gasping breath and her lungs filled with blessed oxygen instead of the suffocating flood of seawater she'd expected. She found herself being dragged upwards. Two men were yanking her into a small fishing boat. She gasped at the air and pawed at her saviours – I'm still alive – but something else pulled her in the opposite direction.

Samuel leapt up from the water like a shark and seized her around the throat. Anna slipped from her rescuers hands and clung to the side of the boat. Suddenly her air was cut off again as Samuel squeezed the life out of her. His black eyes swirled with malice and bloody spittle flew from his mouth. The sword still jutted from his chest, but he had lost none of his strength as he kneaded her windpipe with a vice-like hand.

The men aboard the ship reached down and tried to free her from his grasp, but it was no good. They tried to drag her upwards, and almost got her over the railing, but Samuel seized the side of the boat with one hand while he continued to choke her with his other. She slipped back down again. Samuel would not let go. Anna gritted her teeth as she felt the blood collecting in her head and the oxygen in her lungs dry up. *He's going to kill me. I stabbed him but he didn't die. It isn't fair.*

Yip!

Anna was taken by surprise as she saw Houdini leap from atop the fishing boat's railing and clamp his tiny jaws around Samuel's supporting hand. The little dog balanced half on, half off the side of the boat and tore and twisted at the fingers in his mouth. If Samuel moved his hand away, he would slip into the sea. The only free hand he had was the one around Anna's neck. He cursed and let go of Anna in order to swat the small dog aside, but Houdini dodged the blow and clambered back aboard the boat.

Anna seized on her chance and grabbed the tip of the sword jutting out of Samuel's chest. The sharp blade opened her palms like a knife through butter, but she hissed through the pain and yanked it upwards, twisting it.

Samuel's mouth exploded with more blood. Anna twisted the sword harder. The blade shifted inside his chest and cut a furrow through whatever organs lay in its path. His body shuddered. He glared at Anna and snarled, but then he coughed and choked on his own blood. The swirling of his black eyes ceased and his body slumped against the side of the boat. He hung limply from the railing by one hand. He looked at Anna and spluttered. "You...you...whore!"

Yip!

Houdini bit Samuel's hand again and he finally let go. The two men on the fishing boat hoisted Anna upwards and Samuel sank beneath the water. He stared up at her as he descended, but seemed more confused than angry.

Anna collapsed onto the deck of the fishing boat, panting, wheezing, bleeding, and crying. Each time death had tried to snatch, she'd escaped, but she was tired and upset and broken. *I can't take any more.*

Hugo peered down at her and smiled kindly. "I am glad to see you again, Anna. I think your mission was a success, no?"

The American man, Wade, was standing beside Hugo, peering down at her with the same kindness. "You told me to find a boat, so I did. Didn't want to leave without the two of you, though. I take it Roman..."

"He didn't make it, and his name was Damien." Anna sat up and caught her breath. "Hugo what...how?"

"Garfield is back," he said. "He has a tank. He fired at the Kirkland and tried to sink it. He was about to fire again, but saw you were on-board. Then a fishing boat came ashore to greet us. Three fishermen wished to flee the fighting and try to make it on land – they had been planning to set off for Spain a few weeks ago, they told me, but Samuel had made one of their friends disappear for even discussing it. They do not love the fleet.

"They were not using their boat, so I took it to come and rescue whomever I could find. I found Wade and he told me you were still alive. I am glad to have found you, Anna. My girls and your campmates are waiting for us back at the pier. Are you ready to go?"

Anna nodded emphatically. "Yes," she said. "I want to go home. Get me the hell away from this goddamn ship."

Hugo nodded behind her and made her turn around. "Anna, my friend, there is no more ship."

Anna couldn't help but laugh. The Kirkland was gone, sank beneath the sea. Good riddance.

GARFIELD

ARFIELD HAD FIRED at the Kirkland as retribution and had been intending to do so again, but when Price allowed him to look through the Challenger's targeting optics he'd been surprised by the magnification. The damage to the large grey vessel had been mostly cosmetic, but had wiped out a great many members of the crew. Garfield was shocked to see Anna standing amidst the chaos. He couldn't fire on the ship again with her still alive onboard, so he told Barker to hold off. He had to think of a way to get Anna back.

When a group of fishermen came ashore, wishing to escape the fighting, the opportunity presented itself.

When another explosion rocked the frigate, some sort of combustion from within its bowels, the timing seemed perfect. Garfield wasted no time in sending Hugo out to the sinking frigate; to rescue Anna on the off chance she'd been lucky enough to survive the explosion. The chances were slim, but she at least deserved a chance.

Garfield peered through the Challenger's powerful optics again an hour late and could barely believe it when he saw Hugo start the journey back to shore with Anna safely onboard. The chances of her having survived all of the fireworks and bloodshed had been astronomical. Despite the sorrow in his heart for Poppy, he couldn't help but smile as he greeted Anna at the shore.

Garfield had gotten the whole story of the past few days from old man Bob – about the men who had come ashore and how one of them had abducted Poppy. He didn't blame Anna. It was a harsh world and all anyone could do was his or her best. Anna would never have let Poppy come to harm if she could've helped it. He would rather mourn with her as a friend than hate her as an enemy. The man responsible for Poppy's death was dead. Maybe that would be enough in the end.

I don't think anything will ever be enough.

There was no place to lay Poppy's body so Garfield decided to carry her out onto the beach. She had wanted so much to explore, that it felt right to let the waves take her small body into the Channel and carry it away. Who knows where she would end up? Her body could circle the globe with time. Poppy would have liked that.

Price and Barker secured the area with automatic rifle fire, while the survivors of the pier said their goodbyes to those they'd lost. In the background, ships scattered into the distance and left them alone with their grief.

Old man Bob went first. "Alistair liked his food and not a fat lot else. He cared about everyone, though, even if he didn't always show it. Sometimes he would get drunk and tell me about how he was bullied as a kid. I think that had a lot to do with how he was as a man. I'm glad he was part of our family, though. I think, before he died, he truly felt like he belonged."

Everyone nodded and Jimmy had his say. "Chris was always walking around in those stupid red wellies. He used to say the salty air gave him athlete's foot, but I think he just liked them. They made him look like a clown at the beach."

That was all Jimmy had to say, so they moved onto Samantha. Old man Bob spoke again. "Samantha was a fox. If I'd been twenty years younger...well, all I can say is that she was a sweetheart and things won't be the same without her. Her pretty face and friendly smile used to brighten up my day."

"Me too," said Jimmy.

They all stared at Garfield. It was his turn and they all knew whom he would choose to speak about. "Poppy was..." He sighed and stared out to sea. Her body had almost disappeared beneath the waves, but the golden white of her remaining braid still floated on the surface of the water. For a moment he wanted to dive in and bring her back, but he knew he had to let her go. He pulled out the crumpled drawing from his pocket and examined it. The peaceful pond with the moorhens was as beautiful as ever. If there was a Heaven, he hoped Poppy could go back there and be with her parents. The thought made him smile. "Poppy was the best thing that ever happened to me," he said. "Not just in the last year, but in my entire life. She's the reason I'm alive. Before I found her I was slowly losing part of myself, but she made me keep a hold on who I was, and then she helped me become someone even better. Having her around the pier was good for all of us. Her innocence reminded us what we were all living for. She reminded us of the good things we'd lost and why we had to get them back. She was our only child and she's gone, but we have to keep going, so that one day there will be more little girls like her. Keeping her safe was my biggest failure, and it probably won't be my last, but I swear that I will never let another person I love be taken from me. We're going to make it through this, and when we do, we will remember those lost to us. We can use their memories to give us strength, so that we never give up, no matter who turns up on our doorstep and tries to hurt us. We're a family and as long as we have that, the world will never be over. We didn't ask for this, but it's what we've got, so let's make the best of it – together."

Everybody nodded, Barker, Price, and the newcomers included. Garfield walked up the beach towards a rocky outcropping where Anna was sitting. The two French girls sat in the sand with their dog and smiled when they saw him coming. He smiled back at them, but it was Anna he wanted to talk to.

During the funeral, she had stayed back, tears in her eyes and blood on her face. She had been through something terrible, something she probably would not speak about for a while, if not ever. The thing that was truly hurting her, though, was the people they had just cast out to sea. She feels responsible. Perhaps she is. Perhaps we all are.

He sat on the rock next to her and placed an arm around her. She stiffened up at his touch, but did not fight him as he pulled her into a cuddle. The two of them had never been intimate as friends or otherwise, but Garfield was tired of being so guarded. The time of low self-esteem and personal barriers seemed petty now. Anna was family and right now she was hurting. So was he.

He reached into his coat pocket and handed her something.

"What is it?" she asked.

"It's a Army ration pack," he explained. "It has a multivitamin in there. You wanted vitamins, right?"

Anna laughed and nodded, but then her expression creased and she fought not to cry. "I'm sorry," she said.

"Don't be. Looking back at the way things might have gone is no different from imagining how the future might be. It's out of our control. You couldn't have known what was going to happen."

"But I didn't have to start a fight. I could have played ball with the men on the boats."

Garfield huffed. "And then what? Get treated like slaves or intimidated into giving away whatever we had. They tried to hurt Poppy, I heard all about it. If I'd been here, I wouldn't have done anything different. You were protecting Poppy. I wouldn't have had you do anything more."

"I got her killed."

Garfield shook his head. "We're all on borrowed time. You kept her safe for the last year, we all did. We should be thankful we had her while we did. There'll be time to blame ourselves later. Right now we need to stick together and get out of this alive. We still need to leave."

Anna nodded.

"I won't leave you again, Anna. From now on, we stick together no matter what. I abandoned you and I'm sorry."

Anna wiped snot from her nose and chuckled. "You're saying sorry to me?"

"I am. I'm sorry for a lot of things. I'm sorry I've never given you a cuddle before. I'm sorry I brought Poppy a bunch of magazines she didn't want. I'm sorry I wasn't here to help you when you needed me."

Anna leaned into him. "I forgive you. You did bring a tank back for me, after all."

"Yeah, I did do that, didn't I? And here was you saying that a tank would be useless." He kissed the top of her head. "I'll let you ride in the turret if you want."

Anna giggled. "Tell you the truth, I would rather just sleep in the back of the truck and have you wake me up in a year. I don't think I could take any more excitement."

"So I hear."

"Thanks for rescuing me."

"You're welcome," he said, then looked out to sea and saw that Poppy was finally gone for good. The only thing that made him feel better was the Kirkland was too.

Garfield had fired at the Kirkland as retribution and had been intending to do so again, but when Price allowed him to look through the Challenger's targeting optics he'd been surprised by the magnification. The damage to the large grey vessel had been mostly cosmetic, but had wiped out a great many members of the crew. Garfield was shocked to see Anna standing amidst the chaos. He couldn't fire on the ship again with her still aboard, so he had told Barker to hold off for the moment. He had to think of a way to get Anna back.

When a group of fishermen came ashore, wishing to escape the fighting, that opportunity presented itself. When another explosion rocked the frigate, some sort of combustion from within its bowels, the timing seemed perfect. Garfield wasted no time in sending Hugo out to the sinking frigate; to rescue Anna on the off chance she'd been lucky enough to survive the explosion. The chances were slim, but she at least deserved a chance.

Garfield peered through the Challenger's powerful optics and had barely believed it when Hugo started the journey back to shore with Anna safely onboard. The chances of her having survived all of the fireworks and bloodshed had been astronomical. Despite the sorrow in his heart for Poppy, he couldn't help but smile as he greeted Anna at the shore.

Garfield had gotten the whole story of the past few days from old man Bob – about the men who had come ashore and how one of them had abducted Poppy. He didn't blame Anna. It was a harsh world and all anyone could do was his or her best. Anna would never have let Poppy come to harm if she could've helped it. He would rather mourn with her as a friend than hate her as an enemy. The man responsible for Poppy's death was dead, thanks to her, and maybe that would be enough in the end.

The remaining members of the pier – old man Bob, Lemon, David, Cat, and Jimmy – made their way from the beach back up to the pier. With them went the new members of their family – Hugo and his girls, the soldiers, Barker and Price, an American named Wade, and the three fishermen who had surrendered their boat to Hugo. Garfield decided to stay with Anna on the rocks for a while longer, watching out for sounds of dead approaching down the beach. They seemed to have a bit of time for now. It felt good to just sit there and enjoy the warmth of another body. As long as there was time to do that, perhaps all was not lost. They had a good chance of making it.

The group's numbers were not inconsiderable and their bond was already strong. They had a large stockpile of guns and rations, along with two very heavy trucks, and a tank. What they needed now was a home.

But for now, they all stood on the pier, gathering up supplies and preparing for the future. Samuel may have killed the pier the same way he had killed so many men, but he would never take away what it had meant: that mankind could survive and pull together as one. Now that Samuel was gone, perhaps the remaining members of the fleet would pull together too. The time for leaders had passed. Community was the only thing that would get them through now. They were brothers and sisters, members of the same struggling species. They must all live and fight as one. Or die alone and apart.

Garfield gave Anna one final squeeze. "Time to go," he said, but neither of them moved. Instead, they held one another and wept until the sun died and the moon arose.

HUGO

BEING ON THE road with his new companions had been unbelievably dangerous. The dead were everywhere as they trekked northwards. With no particular location in mind they hoped only to find someplace safe to set up a new camp. That didn't mean they were willing to stop at the first place they found, though. They were more than a dozen in number and wanted to find a place where they could be safe, but also have the opportunity to build a life for themselves. They had passed up various supermarkets, sports stadiums, and farms in favour of continuing the search. They all hoped that when they found what they were looking for they would know it.

One thing they agreed on, however, was that the pier had kept them prisoner. If they found a chance to rebuild, they wanted to live as people again. They would plant seed and round up whatever animals they could find. They would build fences and cull the dead. The soldiers would show them how. It would be a dangerous existence, for sure, but so far no one had been hurt on the journey and their confidence of survival was growing. They had faced the dead many times, in numbers great and small, but they had remained earnest and acted without risk. They watched out for one another and made decisions via committee. Each member of the group was equally important – even Hugo's daughters – and for that every man and woman was faultlessly loyal to their new family. There were no leaders and no dissent. There was no power and no egos. The only danger was the dead, and they faced that threat together, as one. It had kept them safe for a long time.

With each passing day, Hugo began to feel more and more hopeful. Three months had passed since they'd left the pier and his daughters had now begun to smile much more than they ever had at sea. They were in constant danger, but they were alive and free. They had friends, family, and a future. Hugo was no longer their sole protector and guardian, he was just their father again, there to love them. A dozen others were there to help keep Daphne and Sophie safe; Hugo could finally relax and find a little peace, even amongst the ruins of Great Britain. I wonder whatever became of France? Will I ever see it again? Somehow he didn't care. He had his family and that was all that mattered.

The group had made it all the way past Stoke now. They had done so in convoy, kept safe by the big Army trucks, and the tank, which led their way. Each man and woman had been trained to use a rifle or a handgun and they hung out of the truck beds and the tank's turret whenever the dead came too near. By keeping up their speed and making their shots count, they had remained safe and made good time. The dead fell before them like cardboard cut outs in the wind. They were no longer the hazard they once were – being organised and well armed made them a manageable threat. Life was still a struggle, but it was doable. Once they found a place to settle, things would hopefully get easier still. Cat was six weeks pregnant – a supermarket urine test had told her so. David was constantly filled with glee, but his attempts to mollycoddle the mother of his child were always met with an elbow to the ribs. Cat was a tough cookie and wouldn't be looked after, but it was clear that the pregnancy filled her with a poorly guarded glee. Hugo couldn't wait to see the baby brought forth into the world. Sophie and Daphne had already volunteered to be aunties, which Cat had graciously accepted.

Hugo smiled. We truly are a family now.

Humanity would come back from the brink of extinction, one baby at a time. Hugo now dreamt about his daughters finding love and giving him granddaughters. It would have been absurd to think about only three months ago, but now...

Hugo chuckled and threw the tennis ball across the abandoned football pitch. Houdini raced off after it, racing all the way. A group of pigeons took flight as the little dog zoomed towards them, and Hugo laughed even harder. The group had spent the last night camped out at an old leisure centre and were getting ready to move on soon. Hugo felt alive and well. Last night he had closed his eyes and slept like a baby for the first time in over a year. Somehow the world didn't seem quite as horrible on land as it had done on the sea. A man's feet should be on the earth. It is where we belong. As long as mankind keeps on walking, we'll make it to tomorrow.

END

ABOUT THE AUTHOR

Iain Rob Wright is from the English town of Redditch, where he worked for many years as a mobile telephone salesman. After publishing his debut novel, THE FINAL WINTER, in 2011 to great success, he quit his job and became a full time writer. He now has over a dozen novels, and in 2013 he co-wrote a book with bestselling author, J.A.Konrath.

WWW.IAINROBWRIGHT.COM